108課綱、各類英檢考試適用

最新版

Key Idioms & Phrases 800

關鍵片語 *800*

郭慧敏/編著

三民書局

國家圖書館出版品預行編目資料

Key Idioms & Phrases 800：關鍵片語800／郭慧敏編
著.——修訂二版十一刷.——臺北市：三民，2021
面；　公分.——（英語Make Me High系列）

ISBN 978-957-14-4368-3　（平裝）
1. 英國語言－成語,熟語

805.123　　　　　　　　　　　　　　　　94016073

英語 *Make Me High* 系列

Key Idioms & Phrases 800——關鍵片語 800

編 著 者	郭慧敏
發 行 人	劉振強
出 版 者	三民書局股份有限公司
地　　址	臺北市復興北路 386 號 (復北門市) 臺北市重慶南路一段 61 號 (重南門市)
電　　話	(02)25006600
網　　址	三民網路書店 https://www.sanmin.com.tw
出版日期	初版一刷 2004 年 3 月 修訂二版一刷 2005 年 10 月 修訂二版十一刷 2021 年 9 月
書籍編號	S804720
I S B N	978-957-14-4368-3

三民書局

序

英語 Make Me High 系列的理想在於超越，在於創新。

這是時代的精神，也是我們出版的動力；

這是教育的目的，也是我們進步的執著。

針對英語的全球化與未來的升學趨勢，

我們設計了一系列適合普高、技高學生的英語學習書籍。

面對英語，不會徬徨不再迷惘，學習的心徹底沸騰，

心情好 High！

實戰模擬，掌握先機知己知彼，百戰不殆決勝未來，

分數更 High！

選擇優質的英語學習書籍，才能激發學習的強烈動機；

興趣盎然便不會畏懼艱難，自信心要自己大聲說出來。

本書如良師指引循循善誘，如益友相互鼓勵攜手成長。

展書輕閱，你將發現……

學習英語原來也可以這麼 High！

給讀者的話

每當學生一升上高三，面臨模擬考時，都會問英文老師一個相同的問題：我要怎麼準備？畢竟英文不同於數學、物理、化學、地理、歷史等科目，有一定的範圍，固定的章節，學生很容易逐章逐節複習，老師也容易自編教材或選定坊間書籍從旁輔助。反之，英文可說毫無範圍可言，變化之大，讓許多英文學習者無所適從。

事實上，學習英文永不改變的法則：單字、片語、文法。花了一個月時間看遍坊間書店所有的片語書後，我問自己：我該如何為學生整理出一本方便、有效的片語學習書？將近二個月的思考，終於有了這本書的架構。其後歷時六個月的整理，期間讓我自己的學生試用，直到學生喜歡使用它，我決定出版這本書，以幫助更多學生有系統地學習高中生必備關鍵片語。

800 個關鍵片語是過濾近年大考的試題，整理出所有出現過的片語。此書分為二個部分，第一部分有 20 回，每回 29-30 個高頻率片語，第二部分有 9 回，每回 24-25 個超高頻片語。片語依字母序 (a-z) 呈現，針對片語不同的意思均有例句說明，例句儘量簡短，以方便讀者記憶，花較少的時間達到有效的學習；同時標示出該片語的用法提示、同義片語、及觸類旁通等附加單元，希望讀者在統整的過程中，學會「一槍打數鳥」的功夫。每回之後的 Exercise 絕大部分都是曾經出現過的聯考試題，希望讀者經由「學習→演練」的歷程，進一步了解片語在考題中的呈現方式，從中掌握一些技巧，提昇自我的超高戰鬥力。

總而言之，學習是一段辛苦的歷程，希望我的努力能在你學習中成為你信心的支持力。祝福每一位使用這本書的人都能心想事成。

郭慧敏

Table of Contents

Section Two 超高頻片語

Acknowledgment

The Close Test articles in this book are written by Montoneri Bernard and Carol Lauderdale. The author and publisher would like to thank them for their kind effort and help. All rights reserved.

Key Idioms & Phrases 800

Section One

Unit 1 ～ 20

高頻率片語

❶ a bit of 小量的

I want to spend a bit of time with him before he leaves.　我想在他離去之前花點時間陪他。

It was a bit of a strange decision.　這是個有點奇怪的決定。

 a small amount of、a little of

 1. not a bit

= not at all

= not in the least　一點也不

2. not a little

= not a few　相當多；不算少

❷ a burst of 爆發

The van gave a sudden burst of speed when the light turned green.　那輛小旅行車在燈變綠時突然一股勁猛衝。

There is often a burst of applause coming out of his classroom.　他的教室常常傳出陣陣掌聲。

❸ a flock of 一群 (sheep, goats, birds)

A flock of sheep ran towards us when we were walking in the countryside.　當我們走在鄉間時，一群羊衝向我們。

 a crowd of

 1. a school of (whales, fish)　鯨魚、魚

2. a herd of (cattle, elephants)　牛、大象

3. a group of (people, trees)　人、樹

4. a swarm of (bees, ants, crickets)　蜜蜂、螞蟻、蟋蟀

5. a pack of (dogs, hounds, wolves)　狗、獵犬、狼

❹ a great/good deal of 大量的；很多的

It takes a great deal of time and effort to succeed.　成功需要許多的時間與努力。

His work has attracted a great deal of attention.　他的工作已經引起很大的注意。

 much

❺ a great/good many　大量的；好多好多的

A great many students decided to join the rally.　好多好多學生決定參加集會。

　many

　上面的片語後面都接複數可數名詞

　many a + 單數名詞 + 單數動詞
　　　　　　　＝ many + 複數名詞 + 複數動詞

❻ a herd of　一群

There are herds of cattle running in the fields.　一群群的牛奔馳在草原上。

❼ a large quantity/amount of　大量的

He consumed a large quantity of alcohol when he was young.　他年輕時喝了大量的酒。

❽ a large sum of　大筆的

Peter owes me a large sum of money.　Peter 欠我一大筆錢。

　a great deal of

❾ a sense of duty/responsibility　責任感

I like Jessica—she has a strong sense of duty.　我喜歡 Jessica，她是個有強烈責任感的人。

　a sense of humor/safety/direction　幽默感、安全感、方向感

❿ a series of　一連串的

The police are investigating a series of attacks in this area.　警方正在調查這個地區一連串的攻擊事件。

A whole series of accidents happened on this road.　這條路上發生一連串的車禍。

⓫ a shortage of　缺乏

Luckily, there is no shortage of water this summer.　很幸運的，今年夏天不缺水。

　a lack of

⓬ a solution to the problem　問題的解決方法

His idea is the perfect solution to all of our problems.　他的點子是解決我們所有問題的完美方法。

　a key to the door/success　門的鑰匙、成功的關鍵

⓭ above all 最重要的是；尤其是

Mandy is hardworking, optimistic, and above all honest.

Mandy 努力、樂觀，最重要的是誠實。

 most important of all

⓮ acquaint A with B (A) 使 A 熟悉 B；(B) 認識

A. You need to acquaint the police with the facts.

你必須讓警方知悉這些事實。

B. Are you acquainted with my boss Rose Hunter?

你認識我的老闆 Rose Hunter 嗎?

 認識：A be acquainted with B

⓯ afford to 負擔得起做…

We can't afford to go on vacation this summer.

今年夏天我們付不起渡假的錢了。

I couldn't afford the rent on my own.

我無法靠自己負擔租金。

 can afford + to V/N （常與 can, can't 連用）

⓰ aim at 針對；瞄準

The criticism was not aimed at you.

這項批評不是針對你。

He aimed his gun at the target but missed it.

他把槍瞄準箭靶但卻沒有擊中。

觸類旁通 be aimed at + V-ing 旨在；目的就是要…

This website *is aimed at* providing teachers with important teaching resources.
這個網站旨在提供老師重要教學資源。

⓱ all walks of life 各行各業

Our volunteers include people from all walks of life.

我們的志工包含了各行各業的人。

⓲ and so on 等等

Most neighborhoods have parks, restaurants, bookstores, schools, and so on.

大部分鄰區會有公園、餐廳、書店、學校等等。

The things you can do for your health are going on a diet, taking exercise, quitting smoking and so on.

為了健康，你可以做的事有節食、運動、不抽煙等等。

 and so forth、and the like、and what not、etc.

用法 使用以上片語時，必須用在連接對等的名詞，且最後一個名詞前不可用 and。

⓳ apart from 除了…之外

Apart from the ending, it's a really good film.

除了結局外，它是部不錯的電影。

Apart from the cost, we need to think about how much time the job will take.

除了成本，我們必須考慮這份工作所需花的時間。

 同義 　aside from、except

⑳ arm oneself/sb with...　以…武裝自己；提供…給某人

The local farmers armed themselves with rifles and pistols.

當地的農夫以來福槍及手槍來武裝自己。

The guidebook arms the readers with a mass of useful information.

這本教戰手冊提供大量有用的資訊給讀者。

㉑ around the clock　日夜不停地

We have been working around the clock to finish the task in time.

我們日夜不停地要把工作及時完成。

 同義 　round the clock、all day and all night without stopping

㉒ as long as　只要

You have nothing to worry about as long as I'm with you.

只要我和你在一起，你就沒有什麼好擔心的。

As long as we keep practicing, we'll win the game.

只要我們繼續練習，就能贏得比賽。

㉓ as many as　多達

There are as many as 1,000 residents coming down with SARS.

多達一千個居民感染 SARS。

㉔ as scheduled　如預定的

We are sure to take a vacation as scheduled.

我們一定會如期去渡假。

㉕ at all　到底；究竟；全然

Has the situation improved at all?

情勢到底改善了沒有？

"Do you mind if I stay longer?" "Not at all."

「你介意我待久一點嗎?」「一點也不介意!」

 用法 　這個片語常與否定與疑問句連用

㉖ at birth　出生時

He only weighed 2,000 grams at birth.

他出生時體重只有兩千公克。

❷❼ at dawn 黎明；破曉

The first flight takes off at dawn.　　　　　第一班飛機黎明起飛。

 at daybreak

 at dusk　黃昏

❷❽ at first glance 第一眼

At first glance, this village seemed deserted.　　　這個村莊第一眼看起來似乎很荒涼。

　1. at a glance　一眼

　　　　　I recognized him *at a glance*.

　　　　　我一眼就認出他。

　　　2. at first sight　初見時；一見

　　　　　Romeo fell in love with Juliet *at first sight*.

　　　　　Romeo 對 Juliet 一見鍾情。

❷❾ at (the very) most 至多

My English teacher is at most 30 years old.　　我的英文老師最多不過三十歲。

The boy looks nine at the very most.　　　這男孩看起來最多九歲。

I. 片語選填

| a large sum of | can't afford to | at most | arm oneself with | a series of |
| a flock of | as many as | shortage of | above all | |

1. _____ migrant birds flew to our island yesterday. (84)

2. I am curious about how John came by such _____ money. (85)

3. In fact, my life can be described as consisting of _____ "ups" and "downs." (92)

4. Mom and Dad _____ hire a tutor for me. (87)

5. _____, remember to hand in your application form. (86)

6. _____ 60 pilot whales swam ashore. (84)

7. I could lend you 500 dollars _____. (86)

8. The blueness to the patient's face was caused by _____ oxygen in the blood. (84)

9. Living in a highly competitive society, you definitely have to _____ as much knowledge as possible. (92)

10. 選擇機器人作為大學畢業典禮的演講者引起相當的爭議。(87)

    There was quite _____ _____ of controversy over the choice of a robot as a commencement speaker.

11. 電子郵件的作者享受隨時與世界上任何角落的人溝通的莫大自由。(88)

    An e-mail writer enjoys _____ _____ _____ of freedom in communicating with anyone in any place of the world at any time.

12. 有些獵人把一群野獸，如馬、野牛等，從陡峭的崖壁上趕下去，而其他的獵人就在山腳下等著，然後將他們一網打盡。(84)

    Some hunters drove a _____ _____ animals like horses or buffaloes over the steep cliffs, and the others waited at the bottom of the cliffs to finish the kill.

13. 他帶著許多貨物同行，包括大量的帆布。(85)

    He took many goods with him, including a _____ _____ of canvas.

14. 她有很強的責任感，對所有工作都全力以赴。(91)

    She had a _____ _____ of _____ and worked very hard at all her tasks.

15. 他所想到的是解決問題的好方法。(86)

    What he thought was a good _____ to the _____.

16. 這名教授盡力讓學生熟悉新觀念。(84)

    The professor did his best to _____ the students _____ the new ideas.

17. 其中一些措施是針對惡靈的，因鬼無法抬腳跨過障礙，也不能 90 度轉彎。(84)

    Some of these measures _____ _____ evil spirits, because ghosts cannot lift their feet over barriers, nor can they make 90-degree turns.

18. Jack 的客人來自各行各業。(86)

    Jack's clients are from all _____ of _____.

19. 我們能夠做許多高科技的手術等等，但一旦談到心靈和身體如何合作時，我們真的就不太清楚了。(86)

    We can do many high-tech operations and _____ _____, but when it comes to how the mind and body work together, we are really not very well-informed.

20. 除了稍微自私些，她是迷人的女孩。(88)

    _____ from being kind of selfish, she is a charming girl.

21. 因整座城市都陷入黑暗，所以電力工人必須日夜不停地工作去修理電線。(92)

    The power workers had to work around _____ _____ to repair the power lines since the whole city was in the dark.

22. 只要語言不死，其細胞就會繼續改變，形成新字，並淘汰那些不再使用的字。(89)

    _____ _____ _____ a language is alive, its cells will continue to change, forming new words and getting rid of the ones that no longer have any use.

Unit 1

23. 那時就決定 Alan Shephard 應該在太空套房中解大小便，並繼續原定計劃中的任務。

It was then decided that Alan Shephard should relieve himself in his space suite, and continue with the mission as _____ .

24. 我一點都不同意你。(86)

I don't agree with you _____ _____ .

25. 培養兒童對閱讀的愛好，最好的方法就是唸給他聽，從呱呱落地開始，持續地唸給他聽。(87)

The best way to cultivate children's tastes in reading is to read to them, starting at _____ and keeping on and on.

26. 因為是鋼的建築，所以大樓可以有許多樓層。(90)

With steel construction, buildings could then have a _____ _____ stories.

III. 克漏字選擇

Afternoon Tea

Afternoon Tea sounds like a typical British tradition. __27__ , the tea plant comes from Southeast Asia. The Chinese were already drinking tea for __28__ of years when the English began to drink tea in the 17th century. Anna, Duchess of Bedford (1783-1857), introduced the custom of afternoon tea in 1840. Dinner was served very late and people were feeling hungry during the afternoon. Anna found __29__ the problem: she asked to be served some tea and a snack in her room. She enjoyed it __30__ much that she decided to drink tea every afternoon. People followed her and invited guests between 3 and 5 pm. This habit slowly became a complex ceremony. Rich women replaced the snack by __31__ expensive goods. They bought the most expensive leaves of tea. They used the most beautiful cups. They ate cakes, lobster, smoked salmon __32__ . There was a competition among Ladies. It was an opportunity to display their most beautiful silverware. Afternoon tea was a social event. Gentlemen were smoking cigars, drinking a lot of alcohol and __33__ tea in coffee houses. Women were talking at home with friends and sharing gossips. They were playing cards and __34__ music. But afternoon tea was not only reserved to the rich and famous. The women who __35__ to spend a lot of money invited each other at home. The snack, the furniture and the ceremony were just simpler. A "low" tea was served during the early afternoon, while a "high" tea, less fashionable, was a real meal, served late in the afternoon. Nowadays, afternoon tea is just a biscuit or small cake and a cup of tea. And most of the British use tea bags!

(　　) 27. (A) In fact　　　　(B) As actual　　　　(C) In a matter of fact(D) In advance

(　　) 28. (A) much thousand of　　　　(B) thousand of
　　　　(C) thousands of　　　　(D) many thousand of

(　　) 29. (A) a way of　　(B) an error in　　(C) an excuse for　　(D) a solution to

(　　) 30. (A) too　　　　(B) such　　　　(C) even　　　　(D) so

(　　) 31. (A) a good size of　　　　　　　　(B) a large quantity of

(C) a great many of　　　　　　　(D) a great deal of

(　　) 32. (A) or so　　　(B) and so on　　(C) and alike　　(D) as such

(　　) 33. (A) a bit of　　(B) a sense of　　(C) a series of　　(D) a herd of

(　　) 34. (A) hearing about　(B) hearing of　(C) hearing from　(D) listening to

(　　) 35. (A) couldn't help　(B) couldn't afford　(C) couldn't but　(D) couldn't stand

Unit 1

Unit 2

❶ at one time 曾經有一度

At one time she wanted to be a nurse, but the thought of working at night put her off.

她曾經有一度想當護士，但是想到要夜間工作就令她打退堂鼓。

 one/two/...at a time 一次一個／兩個／…

Only *one* interviewee can come in *at a time*.

一次只能進來一位受試人。

❷ at the beginning of 一開始

There is a short poem at the beginning of every chapter.

每一章節的開始都有一首短詩。

A

❸ at the bottom of 在底部

He was standing at the bottom of the stairs waiting for his girlfriend.

他站在樓梯下等女友。

❹ at the end of **(A)** 在…的最後；**(B)** 在…的盡頭；**(C)** 到達…的極限

A. At the end of the day, he finally uttered a word.

一日將盡，他終於吐出一句話。

B. The library is at the end of the road.

圖書館在馬路的盡頭。

C. I'm at the end of my ability.

這是我能力的極限。

❺ at the first/last moment 在第一時間／最後一刻

The flight was cancelled at the first moment.

這班飛機在第一時間取消了。

The operation was cancelled at the last moment.

手術在最後一刻取消了。

 at the moment

= currently 此刻；目前

At the moment, I have no plans to take a trip abroad.

目前我沒有計劃出國旅行。

❻ at/from the outset 在開始時

It's best to have a positive attitude at the outset.

在開始時就能有正面積極的態度是最好的。

A person with many qualifications can get a better paid job at the outset of their career.

擁有許多條件的人在剛入職場時能找到待遇較好的工作。

❼ at the same time　**(A)** 同時；**(B)** 但是

A. Jimmy and I immigrated to Brazil at the same time.

Jimmy 和我同時移民到巴西去。

B. I know she is tricky, but at the same time, I must admit she is a person of ability.

我知道她會耍把戲，但不得不承認她是個有能力的人。

❽ at will　隨意地；任意地

The police cannot arrest people at will.

警察不能任意逮捕人。

He can't just fire people at will, can he?

他就是不能任意開除他人，不是嗎？

❾ attend to　**(A)** 料理、處理；**(B)** 照顧；**(C)** 專注

A. I still have one or two things to attend to.

我還有一兩件事要處理。

B. He has to attend to his father in hospital after work.

下班後他必須照顧住院的父親。

C. Larry decides to quit working and attend to his studies.

Larry 下定決心停止工作，專心於課業。

 照顧：take care of、look after、care for

用法　attend to + N

❿ away from　遠離；避開

Stay away from the fire. It's too dangerous.

離火遠一點，太危險了。

She sat ten feet away from the microphone.

她坐在距麥克風十呎遠之處。

⓫ back and forth　來來回回地

The security guard walked back and forth in front of the bank.

那警衛在銀行前面走來走去。

We travel back and forth all the time between Taipei and Kaohsiung.

我們一直往返於台北高雄之間。

同義　to and fro

⓬ back out of　打退堂鼓

The government is trying to back out of the commitment to reduce pollution.

政府正設法打退堂鼓，想不兌現減少污染的承諾。

⓭ be about to　　即將

Work was about to start on a new factory building.

新的工廠大樓即將開工。

We were about to leave when he entered the room.

他進房間時，我們正要離開。

 be going to、be on the point of

 1. be about to + V 是「迫在眉睫的將來」，一般不與表示將來的副詞片語共用。

2. 但 be going to 可以表達「較遠的將來」，此時就可以接表示將來的副詞片語。

⓮ be alive with　　**(A)** 充滿了（生氣、活力）；**(B)**（場所等）熱鬧的，擁擠的

A. Her face was alive with excitement.

她的臉上洋溢著興奮。

B. The shrub is alive with bees.

矮樹上蜜蜂滿佈。

⓯ be all for　　完全贊同

I'm all for giving people more freedom.

我完全贊成給人們更多自由。

⓰ be associated with　　**(A)** 與⋯有關聯；**(B)** 與⋯交往

A. He was not associated with the democratic movement.

他與民主運動無關。

B. I don't like these layabouts you're associated with.

我不喜歡你交往的這些遊手好閒之徒。

 1. S + associate + N + with + N （原動詞用法）

2. associate oneself with　　贊同

We actually *associate ourselves with* your idea.

事實上，我們贊同你的點子。

⓱ be attached to　　**(A)** 被貼在⋯上面；**(B)** 纏著某人不放；**(C)** 喜歡

A. Several labels are attached to the trunk.

行李箱上貼著幾張標籤。

B. The little baby is deeply attached to his mother.

那個小嬰孩緊粘著媽媽不放。

C. He is very attached to this antique car.

他對這輛古董車非常喜愛。

1. attach A to B　　將 A 黏在 B 上；使 A 屬於 B

He *attached* a label *to* his luggage.

他將一張標籤貼在他的行李箱上。

The company *attached* him *to* the management division.

公司分派他到管理部門。

2. attach oneself to　　參加

Linda *attached herself to* the Republican Party.

Linda 加入共和黨。

⓲ be attributable to   起因於

His death was attributable to gunshot wounds.　　　　他的死因是槍傷。

⓳ be bound to   (A) 勢必；(B) 有義務要…、不得不

A. Such a hardworking student is bound to succeed.　　這樣用功的學生一定會成功。

B. Students are bound to obey the school regulations.　學生有義務遵守校規。

 勢必：be certain to、be destined to

有義務要、不得不：be obliged to、be obligated to

 be bound for + (place)   開往（地方）

The train *is bound for* Hualien.

這班火車是開往花蓮的。

⓴ be capable of   (A) 能夠做；(B) 有…可能的

A. The manager is not capable of handling such a tough deal.　　這位經理沒有能力處理這麼棘手的交易。

B. Your English is capable of improvement.　　你的英文還有改進的空間。

 be capable of + V-ing/N。應為動名詞或表示動作的抽象名詞，不可以是具體的東西。

 be incapable of + V-ing/N

= be unable to + V   沒有能力做…；不能勝任…

㉑ be compared to   比喻為

Life is often compared to a voyage.　　　　　人生常被喻為海上航行。

㉒ be concerned about   關心；擔心

Your parents are concerned about your health.　　你父母很關心你的健康。

Mother is often concerned about how little food I eat.　媽媽常擔心我吃得太少。

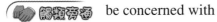 be concerned with

= concern oneself with

= be connected with

= connect oneself with   和…有關

More than one person has *been concerned with* this scandal.

不只一個人與這件醜聞有關。

He *concerns himself with* CIA.

他與美國中央情報局有關係。

❷❸ **be confronted with** 面對

After graduating from college, we are confronted with a bewildering amount of choices.

大學畢業之後，我們面臨許多令人困惑的選擇。

 be faced with

❷❹ **be connected to** 與⋯連接

The printer is connected to the computer with a USB cable.

印表機透過 USB 纜線與電腦相連接。

 connect A with B　把 A 與 B 聯想；由 A 想到 B

We often *connect* Texas *with* cowboys.

我們常把德州與牛仔一起聯想。

B

❷❺ **be curious about** 對⋯好奇

I was quite curious about the motive of the murderer.

我對這兇手的動機很好奇。

She was curious about how he would react.

她很好奇他會如何反應。

❷❻ **be decorated with** 以⋯裝飾

The walls of the classroom were decorated with children's pictures.

教室的牆壁都以學生的圖畫做裝飾。

❷❼ **be dedicated to** 奉獻於⋯；致力於⋯；對⋯很執著

My father is dedicated to doing research.

我父親對做研究很執著。

Many volunteers are dedicated to preserving our native woodland.

許多志工致力保護我們的國家林地。

 be devoted to、dedicate oneself to、devote oneself to

 be dedicated to + N/V-ing

❷❽ **be deficient in** 缺乏

This vegetable is deficient in iron and vitamin B.

這種蔬菜缺乏鐵及維生素 B。

Patients who are deficient in vitamin C tend to catch cold.

缺乏維生素 C 的病人容易感冒。

 be lack of

❷❾ **be disappointed at/about/with** 對⋯（事）失望

I was totally disappointed at the fact that he refused to take my advice.

他拒絕接受我的建議，這點讓我失望透了。

Local residents were disappointed at the decision.

當地居民對該決定失望。

be disappointed at/about/with + sth

be disappointed in sb　對…（人）失望

They *were* deeply *disappointed* in their daughter because of what she said to them.

他們因女兒所說的話而對她感到非常失望。

㉚ be envious of　羨慕；忌妒

Many classmates were envious of her success when she got the scholarship.

當她拿到獎學金時，許多同學都羨慕她的成功。

 be jealous of

 out of envy　出於嫉妒；出於羨慕

His furious criticism about your performance is merely *out of envy*.

他對你的表演所做的猛烈批評不過是出於嫉妒罷了。

I. 片語選填

be attributable	be curious about	be capable of
be deficient in	back and forth	

1. Walking _____ in the living room, the father seemed worried. (89)

2. Those unnecessary deaths _____ in part to the woman's choice of a large automobile. (84)

3. These cleaners don't look too revolutionary, but you'd be surprised at what they _____. (90)

4. I _____ how John came by such a large sum of money. (85)

5. If your diet lacks variety, you are bound to _____ nutrition. (87)

II. 引導翻譯

6. Victor 的同學非常羨慕他，因為他剛剛收到一份生日禮物：一支新手機。(92)

Victor's classmates are very _____ _____ him because he has just received a new cell phone for his birthday.

7. 這棟房子曾經屬於一個非常重要的人物。(90)

This house at _____ _____ belonged to a VIP.

8. 在這個新階段的開始，我要給你一些勸告。(86)

At _____ _____ _____ this new stage, I have some advice for you.

9. 有些獵人把一群野獸，像馬、野牛等，從陡峭崖壁上趕下去，而其他的獵人就在山腳下等著，然後將他們一網打盡。(84)

Some hunters drove a herd of animals like horses or buffaloes over the steep cliffs, and the others waited at _____ _____ _____ the cliffs to finish the kill.

10. 在第一時間，警方抓住扒手的手臂。(88)

At _____ _____ _____, the police grabbed the pickpocket by the arm.

11. 由於許多大型動物，像是獅子、老虎、大象等，正在快速地大量減少，它們不能再被人們任意的獵殺。(84)

Because many big animals like lions, tigers and elephants are decreasing in number rapidly, they can no longer be hunted _____ _____.

12. 你最好先處理病患，是緊急事件。(88)

You'd better _____ _____ the patient first. It's an emergency.

13. Soapy 總是想盡辦法待在室內，避免在戶外受凍，也能不花分文地飽食三餐。(91)

Soapy always found the way to stay indoors, away _____ the cold and had three meals a day without paying one cent.

14. 蜘蛛人明星 Tobey Maguire 可能會因為他的背傷被迫退出續集。(92)

Spider-Man star Tobey Maguire may be forced to _____ _____ of the sequel because of his back injury.

15. 我正要問自己相同的問題。(92)

I was _____ _____ ask myself the same question.

16. 我完全贊同你對這個案子的看法。(85)

I am _____ _____ your idea upon this case.

17. 還有另一種造新字的方法，就是使用與字意有密切關聯的人名或地名。(89)

Still another way in which new words are formed is to use the name of a person or a place closely _____ _____ that word's meaning.

18. 即使朋友嘲笑她裝在擋風玻璃上的怪異發明，Mary 並未屈服於同儕壓力。(91)

Even though her friends teased her about her awkward invention _____ to the windshield, Mary didn't give in to peer pressure.

19. 這位西方遊客為何將台灣的寺廟比喻成銀行？(84)

Why is a Taiwanese temple _____ _____ a bank by this Western visitor?

20. 許多大企業和二十多所主要大學都很關心人們傾聽習慣不佳的問題。(86)

A number of major industries and more than twenty leading colleges have become _____ _____ our bad listening habits.

21. 既然我的電腦已連上網路，我就能看電子報、收發電子郵件和下載軟體。(91)

Now that my computer is _____ _____ the Internet, I can browse e-paper, send and receive e-mail, and download software.

22. 柱子和屋簷經常都是以龍來裝飾。(84)

The pillars and the roof-line are frequently _____ _____ dragons.

23. 至於購物，知道店舖何時有營業是很重要的，否則你可能會看到所有的店都關著，而感到失望。(87)

With regard to shopping, it is important that you know when shops are open, or you may be _____ _____ seeing all the shops closed.

24. 每一個人都必須試著竭盡全力做到最好，同時在獲得部分成果或遭遇部分失敗之際，必須對自己說：「我已盡了全力。」(87)

One must try to do one's best and at the same time, one must, when rewarded by partial success or _____ with partial failure, say to oneself, "I have done my best."

Unit 3

❶ be equal to (A) 能勝任…、有…的能力；(B) 和…匹敵

A. I'm not sure if he is equal to the task.　　　　我不確定他是否能勝任那份差事。

　　Are you equal to this challenge?　　　　　　你能勝任這個挑戰嗎？

B. Nobody is equal to him in the field of bio-tech.　在生物科技的領域中沒人可以比得上他。

 用　法　be equal to + N

　　　　　　　be equal to the occasion　能應付局勢；能隨機應變

❷ be equipped with 配備有

All the rooms here are equipped with air-conditioners and personal computers.　　　　此地所有的房間都配備有冷氣和個人電腦。

Our students are all equipped with skills they need for applying for a job.　　　　我們的學生都具備申請工作所需的技能。

❸ be essential to 不可或缺的

Window locks are fairly cheap and absolutely essential to your safety.　　　　窗鎖相當便宜，而且對你的安全是絕對必要的。

❹ be excused from 被免於…；獲准離開

Can I be excused from swimming today? I have a cold.　我今天可以不游泳嗎？我感冒了。

　　　　　　　excuse oneself from　免除某人（作某事）

❺ be exposed to 暴露於…；接觸到…

Some people are never exposed to computer in their lives.　有些人一生都沒有接觸過電腦。

The report revealed that those workers had been exposed to high levels of radiation.　報導揭露那些工人們曾暴露在高度的輻射中。

　　　　　　　expose oneself to　暴露於…

❻ be faced with 面對

I was faced with the awful job of breaking the news to the girl's family.　我面對一份討人厭的工作，要第一個把壞消息告訴那女孩的家人。

　　　　　　　face up to　勇敢的面對；承擔（不愉快的事）
　　　　　　　He *faced up to* the problem with a strong will.
　　　　　　　他以堅強的意志去面對那個問題。

❼ be famous for   以…而聞名

Kenting is famous for its natural beauty.

墾丁因其自然風光而出名。

France is famous for its wine.

法國以葡萄酒而聞名。

 be noted for、be renowned for、be well-known for

1. be famous as + 身分   以…身分而聞名
   Mr. Smith *is famous as* an artist.
   Smith 先生以藝術家的身分而聞名。

2. be notorious for   因…而惡名昭彰的
   This district *is notorious for* smog.
   這個地區以煙霧聞名。

❽ be fascinated by/with   對…著迷

It's amazing that ancient Greeks and Romans were also fascinated by the idea of magic.

令人驚訝的是，古希臘人和羅馬人都對魔術的想法著迷。

I was fascinated with the singer's voice, so I bought her CD.

我對這位歌手的聲音著迷，所以買了她的 CD。

❾ be full of   充滿了

The kitchen is full of smoke.

廚房充滿了煙。

 be filled with

❿ be gone   消失；不見了

I turned around for my bag, but it was gone.

我轉身找我的包包，但它不見了。

His wife has been gone for years.

他的妻子已經去世多年。

 disappear

⓫ be good at   擅長於

Alice is very good at languages.

Alice 非常擅長語言。

He is poor at math but quite good at English.

他數學很差，但英文卻很好。

 master

 be poor at   不精通…

⓬ be good for   對…有益

Fresh air and vegetables are good for your health.

新鮮的空氣和蔬菜對你的健康有好處。

 be good for nothing　一無是處

She thinks her husband *is good for nothing* just because he cannot make much money.

她認為她丈夫一無是處，只因為他賺的錢不多。

❸ be grateful for　感激

I am so grateful for your help.　　　　　　　　我非常感激你的幫忙。

❹ be harmful to　對…有害

Burning the midnight oil is harmful to one's health.　　熬夜有害健康。

Chemicals are harmful to our environment.　　化學物品對我們的環境有害。

　do harm to...

　be beneficial to + N　對…有益

❺ be inclined to　易於…；有…的傾向

People who lack confidence are inclined to take failure for granted.

缺乏自信的人容易視失敗為理所當然。

He is inclined to self-pity.　　　　　　　　他容易自憐。

　be prone to、be apt to、be likely to、tend to、have a tendency to

❻ be inferior to　劣於

His achievement in studies is inferior to mine.　　他的學業成就比我差。

Their performance was inferior to that of other teams.　　他們的表現比其他隊伍差。

　be worse than

 　1. be superior to = be better than　比…優秀

　　　　　2. be junior to = be younger than　比…年輕

　　　　　3. be senior to = be older than　比…年長

❼ be interested in　對…有興趣

I've always been interested in classical music.　　我一向對古典音樂有興趣。

　take (an) interest in

　be interested in + N/V-ing

　have (an) interest in　和…有利害關係

She *has an interest in* this investment.

她和這項投資有利害關係。

❶⓼ be intimate with 和⋯親密

He is very intimate with his parents. 　　　　　他與他父母親非常親密。

❶⓽ be involved with 與⋯有瓜葛；與⋯結緣

The manager denied that he was romantically involved with his secretary. 　　經理否認和他的秘書有瓜葛。

Fathers are encouraged to be more involved with their family. 　　　　　　父親受鼓勵多與家人相處。

❷⓿ be known as 因（身分）⋯而眾所週知

Bill Gates is known as a successful businessman in the world. 　　Bill Gates 是世界知名的成功商人。

 1. be known for
　　　= be famous for
　　　= be noted for
　　　= be celebrated for　因（特質）⋯而聞名
　　　The town *is known for* its buildings.
　　　那個城鎮以其建築而聞名。

　　2. be known by　由⋯可知，表示判斷的基準
　　　One *is known by* the company he keeps.
　　　近墨者黑。

❷❶ be known to 被⋯所認識／知道

The pop music legend is known to everyone of us in Taiwan. 　　在台灣我們每個人都認識這位流行音樂傳奇人物。

 be unknown to　不為⋯所知
　　　The causes of many cancers *are unknown to* human beings.
　　　人類對許多癌症的起因一無所知。

❷❷ be late for 遲到

Hurry up, or you'll be late for the train. 　　快點，否則你會趕不上火車。

❷❸ be likely to + V 可能會；有可能⋯

He is likely to come any time. 　　　　　他隨時有可能會來。

The votes are likely to have to be counted again. 　　選票可能必須再計算一次。

 (as) likely as not　大概；可能

He knows nothing about it *(as) likely as not*.

他大概對此一無所知。

❷❹ **be limited to**　受限於

The damage is limited to the roof.

損壞僅限於屋頂。

❷❺ **be linked to**　與…有關聯

Some birth defects are linked to mothers' drinking during pregnancy.

有些出生時的缺陷與母親懷孕期間酗酒有關。

❷❻ **be linked with**　與…有關聯

Economy in Asia is closely linked with America's.

亞洲的經濟與美國經濟關係密切。

❷❼ **be made from**　由…製造而成

Paper is made from wood.

紙是由木材製成的。

 成品無法從外觀上判斷原料的成分或特質時用 be made from。

 1. 成品能夠從外觀上判斷原料的成分或性質時用 be made of。

This ring *is made of* gold.

這只戒指是用黃金做的。

2. 強調「製造過程」時，用 make A out of B。

We *make* chopsticks *out of* bamboo.

我們用竹子做筷子。

3. 僅談到材料的其中一樣時，用 make A with B。

I *made* the soup *with* a lot of garlic.

我做這個湯的時候加了很多大蒜。

❷❽ **make A into B**　將 A 變成 B

My parents made my room into a study.

我父母把我房間改成書房。

❷❾ **be nervous about**　對…緊張／焦慮

He is very nervous about his admission to college.

他非常擔憂大學入學一事。

He was so nervous about his math test that he couldn't sleep.

他對數學考試感到緊張得睡不著覺。

 be anxious about

I. 片語選填

be grateful for	be interested in	be known as	be late for	be famous for
be limited to	be made from	be harmful to	be faced with	be equal to

1. This museum _____ its collection of modern paintings. (84)

2. Whenever I open my eyes, I have to _____ a variety of problems. (85)

3. We _____ his generosity in giving a large contribution to our educational foundation. (87)

4. But new studies have found that smoke from cigarettes can _____ non-smokers. (83)

5. Most young men _____ pop music. (86)

6. Even before Prince Albert died, Victoria _____ a very serious woman.

7. He _____ the meeting as a result of the heavy rain. (88)

8. Some people think the damage of smoking _____ smokers. (83)

9. In this method of printing, individual letters _____ separate pieces of metal. (83)

10. I may not _____ the task, but I'll try as hard as I can. (87)

II. 引導翻譯

11. 現代的獵人們配備著強而有力的武器，但對他們多數人而言，打獵為了娛樂要多過於為了覓食。(84)

Modern hunters are _____ _____ powerful weapons, but for most of them, hunting is more for pleasure than for food.

12. Neumann 小姐的學生有時會被准許從學校離開，是因為他們需要去工作。(90)

Miss Neumann's students are sometimes _____ _____ school because they need to go to work.

13. 一個人接觸到說英語的環境越多，他就會將該語文學得更好。(89)

The more one is (e)_____ _____ the English-speaking environment, the better he or she will learn the language.

14. 各地的小孩都為超人著迷，也買了無數本有關超人英雄事蹟的漫畫。(89)

Children everywhere were _____ _____ Superman and bought hundreds of thousands of comic books with stories of his heroic acts.

15. 電腦產業充滿了自認為和傳統西裝畢挺的生意人不一樣的年輕人。(91)

The computer industry is _____ _____ young people who think of themselves as very different from traditional business people in suits.

16. 我所有的錢都不見了，而我所謂的「朋友」甚至已拿走了我的手錶和鞋子。(88)

All my money _____ _____, and my "friend" had even taken my watch and my shoes!

17. 他特別擅長的杯子與球的戲法仍然由全球各地的魔術師表演。(92)

The "Cups and Balls" trick which he was particularly _____ _____ is still performed by magicians all over the world.

18. 此外，好的聽者易於接受或容忍，而非評鑑和批判。(88)

In addition, good listeners are _____ _____ accept or tolerate rather than to judge and criticize.

19. 處理家庭瑣事的機器人仍然比傳統的電器品差一些，因為他們既不便宜也沒有效率。

Household-chore robots are still _____ to conventional appliances, because they are neither cheap nor efficient.

20. 我們和很多人沒有性關係仍可以很親密。(86)

We can be _____ _____ many people without sexuality.

21. 他可能對目前所從事的某種或某些嗜好感到興致盎然。(88)

He may get quite excited about a hobby or some hobbies he is currently _____ _____.

22. 吉他是人類所知道最古老的樂器之一。(92)

The guitar is one of the oldest instruments _____ to man.

23. 定期運動的人看起來可能更年輕。(92)

A person who exercises regularly is more _____ to look young.

24. 我們個人的慶祝會也與飲酒關係密切。(84)

Our personal celebrations are closely _____ with drinking.

25. 大仲馬 1848 年的小說「鐵面人」最近被製成電影。(90)

A. Dumas' 1848 novel, *The Man in the Iron Mask*, was recently _____ into a movie.

26. 或者你對新科技感到緊張，是所謂的「科技焦慮者」? (91)

Or are you _____ _____ new technology, a so-called technophobe?

III. 克漏字選擇

Something About Tom Hanks

Tom Hanks was born in 1956 in California. His parents __27__ when he was five. He spent his childhood with his father, a cook, and his two brothers. Tom certainly __28__ changing schools and stepmothers __29__. His family finally settled in Oakland. Later, in 1978, he went to New York and married his first wife Samantha Lewes. At that time, he __30__ a TV actor. He __31__ minor roles and his choices of projects were not very wise. American director Ron Howard decided to cast him in *Splash* (1984). The movie was an unexpected success, and made Tom Hanks worldwide famous. He divorced in 1985 and remarried in 1988 with Rita Wilson. Tom Hanks began to choose wisely his roles as an actor. As a very sensitive and emotional man, Tom ___32___ playing conflicted regular men. As an actor, he can play comedies ___33___ drama. He won his first Best Actor Oscar in 1993 with *Philadelphia*, the story of a lawyer ___34___ AIDS. One year later, he won a second Oscar for his role *Forrest Gump*. The blockbusters *Apollo 13* and *Saving Private Ryan* made Tom Hanks one of the top Hollywood stars. In 2000, he played in *Cast Away*. His great performance ___35___ the success of the movie. It is the story of a man, who is isolated from ___36___ on an island after a plane crash, learning how to survive. He was certainly proud and ___37___ joy when, in 2002, he received from the hands of Steven Spielberg, the American Film Institute's Life Achievement Award.

(   ) 27. (A) fell in love   (B) fell asleep   (C) broke out   (D) broke up

(   ) 28. (A) stopped from   (B) suffered from   (C) came near   (D) gave rise to

(   ) 29. (A) all the time   (B) at time   (C) at the same time (D) at all

(   ) 30. (A) was known to   (B) was known by   (C) was known as   (D) was known for

(   ) 31. (A) was limited to   (B) was linked to

        (C) was likely to   (D) was involved with

(   ) 32. (A) is inferior to   (B) is intimate with (C) is grateful for   (D) is interested in

(   ) 33. (A) as soon as   (B) as well as   (C) as good as   (D) as long as

(   ) 34. (A) approved of   (B) spoken for   (C) afflicted with   (D) died away

(   ) 35. (A) is responsible for   (B) takes the place of

        (C) makes a fool of   (D) is equipped with

(   ) 36. (A) the other part of the country   (B) another role of the film

        (C) the rest of the world   (D) the remaining of the area

(   ) 37. (A) full of   (B) filled of   (C) bursting into   (D) crowding with

Unit 4

B

❶ be obliged to 感激

I am much obliged to you for helping me pay the college 　我非常感激你幫助我付大學學費。
tuition.

> 用法　be obliged to sb + for sth

> 觸類旁通　be obliged to + V　使某人非做…不可；迫使某人做某事
> The salesman *was obliged to* report at least once a week.
> 銷售人員被要求一星期至少報告一次。

❷ be of great/little importance to　對…（非常／一點都不）重要

What he said is of great importance to me. 　他所說的話對我非常重要。

The news is of little importance to the citizens. 　這則新聞對市民一點都不重要。

> 觸類旁通　be + of + 抽象名詞 = be + 該名詞衍生之形容詞
> of great value = valuable　有價值的
> of great use = useful　有用的
> of no use = useless　沒用的
> It *is of no use* to ask him to help us.
> 要求他幫我們的忙是沒有用的。

❸ be open to　(A) 對…開放；(B) 易受…的

A. The speech contest is open to all the residents in this 　這次的演講比賽開放給本區所有
area. 　的居民。

B. His careless words are open to misunderstanding. 　他的無心之言很容易受到誤解。

❹ be pleased with　對…感到高興、滿意的

Most fans are much pleased with the ending of the film. 　大多數影迷對該片結局感到滿意。

> 用法　be pleased with/about + N/V-ing

> 觸類旁通　be pleased to + V　很高興做…
> I *am* very *pleased to be* your friend.
> 我很高興成為你的朋友。

❺ be senior to　比…年長／資深

She is also an experienced actress, but senior to me. 　她也是一位有經驗的演員，但比我
　資深。

凡字尾有 -ior 的皆是源自於拉丁文字，意指「比較」，其後須接 to 而非 than。

senior to = older than　比…年長

junior to = younger than　比…年輕

superior to = better than　比…優秀

inferior to = worse than　比…差

prior to = earlier than　比…早

posterior to = later than　比…晚

❻ be sent to jail　被送入監牢

He was sent to jail for a few days because of drunken driving.

他因為酒醉駕車而坐牢數日。

 be put/thrown in jail = be sent to jail

He was *put in jail* due to his corruption.

他由於貪污而被送入監牢。

❼ be serious about　對…認真、真的要…

Are you serious about giving up the chance for further study?

你是真的要放棄深造的機會嗎?

❽ be shaped like　形狀像…

The cake he made is shaped like a boot.

他做的蛋糕形狀像靴子。

❾ be stereotyped as　被定型為…

Homeless people are commonly stereotyped as alcoholics or drug addicts.

遊民一般被定型為酗酒者或有毒癮者。

❿ be struck by　受到攻擊；受創

The ship was struck by a torpedo!

船被魚雷擊中了!

 sb be struck by...　…打動某人的心；…給某人留下印象

We *were* all *struck by* her warm hospitality.

我們都因她的熱情好客而深受感動。

⓫ be suitable for　適合於

I don't think she is suitable for the position.

我不認為她適合這個職位。

　be fit for、be appropriate for/to sth

 Unit 4

B

27

⑫ be sure of   確信

He was so sure of his promotion that he bought a new house.

他對升遷很有把握，所以買了一棟新房子。

 同　義   be certain of

 觸類旁通   Be sure that S + V = Make sure that S + V 之後加子句，子句中的時態應使用現在簡單式或現在完成式。中文譯為「務必要」。

Be sure that you close all the windows and doors before you leave.

你務必要在離開前將所有的門窗關好。

⑬ be topped with   以⋯為頂

The pie can be topped with fresh fruit.

派的上方可放上新鮮的水果。

⑭ be torn into shreds   被撕為碎片

The letter was torn into shreds during their argument.

信件在他們爭執時被撕為碎片。

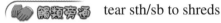 觸類旁通   tear sth/sb to shreds

= tear sth/sb to pieces

嚴厲地批評某事或某人

Mary's boyfriend *tore* her behavior *to shreds*.

Mary 的男友嚴厲地批評她的行為。

⑮ be unique to   對⋯而言是獨特的

The kiwi bird is unique to New Zealand.

奇異鳥是紐西蘭特有的。

⑯ be up to   忙於（打著不好的主意；圖謀不軌）

The children are very quiet. I wonder what they are up to?

小孩子們真安靜。我懷疑他們在打什麼鬼主意？

 觸類旁通   1. be up to (doing) sth   擅長做某事 （通常用於疑問句或否定句）

It seems that David *is not up to* the job.

David 似乎不擅長於這份工作。

2. be up to sb   由某人決定

You can come over on Friday or Sunday. It'*s up to you*.

你可以自己決定星期五或星期日過來。

⑰ be worth sth/V-ing   值得

The antique vase must be worth quite a lot of money now.

這個古董花瓶現在一定價值連城。

A lot of temples in Taipei are definitely worth visiting.

台北許多寺廟肯定值得一遊。

 同　義   be worthy of

⓲ beat around/about the bush 拐彎抹角

Don't beat around the bush. Just tell us what you really want! | 別拐彎抹角的，就告訴我們你真的想要什麼吧!

⓳ become/be accustomed to 習慣於；適應於

My eyes quickly became accustomed to the dark. | 我的眼睛很快就適應了黑暗。

 accustom oneself to、be used to

 become/be accustomed to + N/V-ing

 be adapted to
= be adjusted to
= adapt (oneself) to
= adjust (oneself) to + N/V-ing　適應

You should *adapt yourself to* the new environment as soon as possible.
你應該儘快適應新環境。

⓴ become/be suspicious of 懷疑、猜忌

Some of her colleagues at work became suspicious of her recent behavior. | 她的一些同事對她最近的行為感到懷疑。

㉑ begin...all over again 一切從頭開始

I have to begin my report all over again. | 我的報告得一切從頭開始。

㉒ believe in 相信…的存在；確信…的價值

Do you believe in ghosts? | 你相信鬼的存在嗎?

 believe 與 believe in 的區別:

a. believe sb/sth 是指「相信這件事是真的」或「這個人說了實話」;

b. believe in 是指「相信某事物存在」、「某件事很棒」、或「相信某人會成功」。
Nobody *believed* what he said.
沒人相信他所言。
My parents always *believe in* me.
我父母一向信任我。
I do *believe in* private education.
我真的相信私校教育很不錯。

㉓ believe it or not 信不信由你

I won the lottery, believe it or not! | 信不信由你，我中了樂透!

㉔ belong to　屬於；為⋯的一份子

Everything you see belongs to you now.

現在你看到的東西都是屬於你的。

 be attached to

 被擁有者 + belong to + 擁有者，沒有被動語態，不可用進行式。

㉕ big deal　說定了；大事

It's no big deal. Everyone forgets things sometimes.

沒啥大不了的。每個人都偶而會忘記事情。

1. (a) big deal　重要且令人興奮的事
   This interview is *a big deal* for Alice.
   這次的面試對 Alice 很重要。

2. 口語中的 big deal 還有另外一個意思，表達「不認為某件事情很好或令人印象深刻」，也就是有點酸溜溜的說「沒什麼了不起」的意思。
   So she's got the leading role in the school play? *Big deal*!
   所以她在學校的戲劇演出中擔任主角了？沒什麼了不起的!

3. make a big deal (of)　把某事看得很重要
   You are just *making a big deal* out of nothing. Things are not as bad as you think.
   你真是把事情看得太嚴重了。事情沒有你想得那麼糟。

㉖ blend with　與⋯融合

The pink walls blend perfectly with the bedroom.

粉紅色的牆與臥室調和得十分完美。

㉗ break even　收支平衡、不賺不賠

I hope we'll at least break even, and perhaps make a small profit.

我希望我們至少能收支平衡，也許小賺一點。

㉘ break one's neck　(A) 竭盡心力；(B) 致人於死（用在假意的威脅）

A. I'll break my neck to fight for our rights.

我會竭盡心力地為我們的權益而奮鬥。

B. If you come near this place again, I'll break your neck!

你要是膽敢再靠近這個地方一步，我就要你的命!

 竭盡心力：do one's best

 save one's neck/skin/bacon　逃出危險

He ran over 50 miles and *saved his neck* from the kidnapper.

他跑了五十英哩後才得以從綁架者的手中脫困。

Unit 4

B

❷❾ **break up**　　(A) 驅散、解散；(B) 拆散；(C) 使人捧腹大笑

A. The police were needed to break up the fight.　　靠著警察才驅散了這場架。

B. It seemed that the plane just broke up in the air.　　那架飛機似乎剛就在空中解體了。

C. His behavior really breaks me up!　　他的行為真是令我忍不住要大笑。

❸⓿ **break up into**　　分散成

The plane exploded in the air and broke up into four pieces.　　飛機在空中爆炸，解體成四塊。

❸❶ **break with**　　與…決裂、與…斷絕關係

He has broken with his family for years.　　他和家人決裂多年了。

 觸類旁通　　get/be even with sb
= take revenge on sb　　報復
He promised to *get even with* you one day.
他保證有一天一定向你報復。

 Unit 4 **Exercise**

I. 片語選填

be topped with	be unique to	break one's neck	of great importance
belong to	serious about	break with	be pleased with
beat around the bush		become suspicious of	

1. I found it ＿＿＿＿＿＿＿＿＿＿ to cope with the SARS in no time. (86)

2. Everybody in the commencement ＿＿＿＿＿＿＿＿＿＿ the arrangement. (87)

3. I am not quite ＿＿＿＿＿＿＿＿＿＿ getting married. (85)

4. The tower will ＿＿＿＿＿＿＿＿＿＿ a flower of five petals of 700 square meters each.

5. The ability to shed tears ＿＿＿＿＿＿＿＿＿＿ humans. (89)

6. He didn't ask her directly; on the contrary, he just ＿＿＿＿＿＿＿＿＿＿. (88)

7. If you give them expensive gifts, they may ＿＿＿＿＿＿＿＿＿＿ your intentions. (86)

8. Who this car ＿＿＿＿＿＿＿＿＿＿ or why it was left there is not known. (90)

9. The couple ＿＿＿＿＿＿＿＿＿＿ each other without saying anything rude. (91)

10. I'll ＿＿＿＿＿＿＿＿＿＿ to fight for our rights. (92)

II. 引導翻譯

11. 我十分感激您在我初進這部門時的指導。

　　I'm much＿＿＿＿＿＿ ＿＿＿＿＿＿ you for your instruction when I first entered the department.

12. 藉寫小說賺了一大筆財富之後，他在巴黎郊外建了一座大廈，開放給飢餓的藝術家、朋友、甚至是陌生人。(90)

    After making a fortune by writing novels, he built a mansion outside Paris and kept it _____ _____ starving artists, friends, and even strangers.

13. 我哥哥比我大三歲。(84)

    My elder brother _____ _____ to me by three years.

14. Willing 坐牢一年。(83)

    Willing was _____ to _____ for a year.

15. 貝殼可能圓如月亮，長如蝴蝶刀，或是形狀像盒子、扇子或蓋子。(88)

    The seashells can be round like the moon, long like a jackknife, or _____ _____ boxes, fans, or tops.

16. 在許多小說和電影中，繼母常被定型為邪惡的女性。(89)

    In many novels and films, step-mothers are often_____ _____ wicked women.

17. 多年以前，一位天才型的年輕指揮家 Clive Wearing 受創於一種幾乎會摧毀他記憶力的腦部疾病。(88)

    A few years ago a gifted young conductor, Clive Wearing, was _____ _____ a strange brain disease that virtually destroyed his memory.

18. 她對自己很有信心。(91)

    She was also very _____ _____ herself.

19. 尾帆被撕裂為碎片。(86)

    The rear sail was _____ _____ (s)_____ .

20. 我已經好多年沒有看到你。你一直都在忙什麼? (89)

    I haven't seen you for years. What have you _____ _____ to?

21. 建立社區大學是一個令人欽佩的計劃，而且值得在你的家鄉看看是否有類似的計劃在進行。(86)

    Establishing the community college is an admirable project, and it is _____ finding out if a similar one operates in your hometown.

22. 只有數個人與鯨魚一塊，以便讓鯨魚不會習慣與人類在一起。(84)

    Only a few people worked with the whales, so that they would not become _____ _____ human beings.

23. 他決定放棄財富，一切從頭開始。(87)

    He decided to give up his fortune and began _____ _____ _____ .

24. 信不信由你，美國最喜愛的零食是洋芋片。(90)

    _____ _____ _____ _____ , America's favorite snack is potato chips.

25. A: 我給你十塊錢，你借我數學筆記。B: 一言為定。(89)

    A: I give you ten dollars and you lend me your math lesson. B: Big _____ !

26. 蜥蜴會改變皮膚的顏色，與他們週遭的樹或葉子融為一體。(85)

Lizards can change the color of their skin and _____ with the trees and leaves around them.

27. 那對夫妻一了解彼此不再相愛，就分手了。(92)

As soon as the couple realized that they didn't love each other anymore, they _____ _____.

28. 大約兩億年前，這個超級大陸分散成兩個洲：Laurasia 和 Gondwana。(92)

About 200 million years ago this super-continent _____ _____ into two continents: Laurasia and Gondwana.

29. 無論 Nasreddin 說什麼，他都相信。(89)

He _____ _____ whatever Nasreddin said.

30. 我認為她不適合留學。(86)

I don't think she is _____ _____ overseas study.

❶ **breathe in** 吸入

Relax and breathe in more fresh air, and you will feel better.

放輕鬆，多呼吸點新鮮空氣，你就會覺得好些。

 breathe out 吐氣

The doctor asked me to breathe in deeply and *breathe out* slowly.

醫生要我深呼吸，然後慢慢吐氣。

❷ **bring about** 造成；導致

A huge amount of damage has been brought about by the destruction of the environment.

環境的破壞已經造成大量的傷害。

 result in、lead to、give rise to、cause

bring about + N/V-ing

❸ **bring around/round** （A）拿過來；（B）說服某人支持／相信…；（C）使甦醒

A. I'll bring the food around later.

我待會兒會把食物拿過來。

B. I am sure I can bring her around to my point of view.

我確信能說服她相信我的觀點。

C. The doctor patted the patient's face several times to try to bring him round.

醫生輕拍了病人的臉幾下，企圖使他甦醒。

說服：bring over
使甦醒：bring to

❹ **bring down** （A）使降落；（B）擊（射）落；（C）使下降

A. The pilot managed to bring the plane down safely.

駕駛員設法將飛機安全降落。

B. Joe brought down an eagle with one shot.

Joe 一槍射落一隻老鷹。

C. The government took measures to bring down inflation.

政府採取措施使通貨膨脹下降。

❺ **bring in** （A）提出；（B）吸引（顧客）；（C）獲利、賺進

A. He brought in an anti-copy law in the meeting.

他在會中提出一項反盜錄的法規。

B. We have to bring in more customers if we want the department store to survive.

如果希望百貨公司生存下去，我們必須吸引更多顧客。

C. The business brings in $1,000 per day.

這個生意每天獲利一千美元。

❻ bring sth with sb　隨身攜帶

Jane had to bring a laptop with her for the meeting.

為了開會，Jane 必須隨身帶著她的筆記型電腦。

❼ bring/put...to an end/a close/a halt　使⋯結束

His disloyalty brought their marriage to an end.

他的不忠實使這場婚姻走到盡頭。

　put/bring an end to sth

❽ browse through　瀏覽

The man is browsing through the pictures on the wall.

那個人正在瀏覽牆上的畫。

❾ build up　(A) 增加、擴大；(B) 捧紅、讚揚；(C) 建立

A. Taking exercise will build up your strength.

運動能增強體力。

B. The coach has been building the players up before the game.

教練在比賽前一直誇獎選手。

C. He has built up a good reputation for honesty.

他因誠實而建立好名聲。

　建立：set up

❿ burst into (tears/laughter)　突然⋯起來

Cindy looked as if she were about to burst into tears.

Cindy 看起來彷彿要哭出來了。

　burst out crying/laughing

　burst into flames　突然起火

The truck hit the safety island and *burst into flames*.

卡車撞上安全島後突然起火。

⓫ by accident　意外地；偶然地

I bumped into my teacher by accident last night in a video game store.

昨晚，我在一家電動玩具店內意外碰到我的老師。

He overheard your conversation by accident.

他偶然聽到了你們的對話。

　by chance、accidentally、unexpectedly

⓬ by and by　不久；很快

It will get warmer by and by.

天氣不久後會漸漸的變暖。

　soon、before long

❸ by contrast 相比之下

In this opera recording, the orchestra plays beautifully but, by contrast, the singers sing awfully bad.

在這部歌劇錄音中，樂團的演奏很優美，但相比之下，歌手們的演唱實在差勁。

❹ by no means 絕不

He is by no means a mischievous boy.

他絕不是個頑皮的男孩。

By no means do you cheat your parents.

絕不可欺騙父母。

 not by any means、in no way、under no circumstances

以上這幾個片語放在句首，務必使用倒裝句，請注意下面例句。
In no way should you be late for the interview.
面試不應遲到。
Under no circumstances must you leave early.
你絕不可以提早離開。

❺ by post 郵寄

Did you send the document by post?

文件你用郵寄的嗎?

 by mail

❻ by the name of 名叫…的

I met a guy by the name of Michael Baxter on the trip to Spain.

我在去西班牙的旅途中遇到一個叫 Michael Baxter 的人。

 called、named

 in the name of 以…的名義
I booked a table at Friday's *in the name of* the company.
我以公司的名義在星期五餐廳訂了一桌。

❼ by then 直到那時

The fire had been burning for 5 minutes, and by then most people had run out of the building.

大火已經燒了五分鐘，那個時候大部分的人都已經逃出了大樓。

 until then、by that time

❽ call back 回電話

Can you ask Sue to call me back when she gets in?

Sue 進來時，你能不能請她給我回個電話?

⓳ call for　(A) 需要；(B) 要求

A. Success calls for hard work.

成功需要努力。

B. Human rights groups are calling for the release of political prisoners.

人權團體要求釋放政治犯。

　需要：demand

⓴ call off　(A) 取消；(B) 叫…走開

A. The meeting was called off because of the 911 Attacks.

這次的會議因九一一攻擊事件而取消。

B. Call your dog off! I'm scared.

叫你的狗走開，我很害怕。

　取消：cancel

㉑ call out　(A) 召喚、使出動；(B) 大聲叫喊

A. The army was called out to help fight fires.

軍隊被召集出動協助救火。

B. The group called out, "Hi, we are here!"

那群人大叫：「喂，我們在這裡!」

㉒ call sb up　(A) 打電話；(B) 召喚

A. I'm going to call up and cancel my flight.

我打算打電話去取消我的機位。

I called him up the other day and broke the news to him.

我前幾天打電話給他，並把這消息透露給他。

B. Local people believe the witch can call up the spirits of the dead.

當地的人相信，這名女巫能召喚死者的靈魂。

　打電話：give sb a call、give sb a ring、give sb a buzz

㉓ call sth into question/doubt　對某事提出疑問

The mistaken decision called the leader's ability into question .

這個錯誤的決定讓人懷疑這位領導人的能力。

　bring/throw sth into question

㉔ carry on　(A) 繼續做、堅持 (+ with)；(B) 經營；(C) 吵鬧

A. Stop fooling around. You should carry on with your work.

別再混了。你應該繼續你的工作。

B. Rising costs made it difficult to carry on the business.

成本不斷上升，使事業經營困難。

C. The machine has been carrying on a bit.

那台機器一直有點吵。

㉕ catch on (A) 流行；(B) 了解到

A. The idea of glasses being a fashionable item has been slow to catch on.

「眼鏡是時髦商品」的想法，很慢才流行起來。

B. It is usually a long time before the parents catch on to what their children are really doing.

父母親真正了解孩子在做什麼時，通常已經過了很長一段時間了。

㉖ catch one's breath 喘口氣

Take a rest here—let me catch my breath.

在此休息，讓我喘口氣。

㉗ catch one's eye 吸引某人的注意力

The guy's strange behavior really caught my eye.

那傢伙奇怪的舉止確實引起我的注意。

On the way to school, a huge billboard caught my eye.

上學途中，一幅巨幅廣告看板吸引了我。

> 同義 catch one's attention
> 用法 eye 一定要用單數。

㉘ catch up with 迎頭趕上；追上

Fast as I ran, I still couldn't catch up with the thief.

雖然我跑得很快，仍然追不上那個小偷。

㉙ (change) for the better 為了更好而（改變）

The room has been changed for the better, so my grandmother could feel comfortable in there.

這房間已被改得更好，如此一來，我奶奶在裡面就能感到很舒適。

> 觸類旁通 change for the worse 變得更糟
> In the afternoon, the weather *changed for the worse*.
> 下午天氣變得更糟了。

Unit 5 Exercise

I. 片語選填

browse through	by post	burst into tears	catch up with	call off
bring in	bring about	by contrast	catch on	call for

1. It was his carelessness that _____ the tragic accident. (90)

2. The sale of the company's new product is overwhelmingly good. It had _____ two million dollars so far. (89)

3. For those who prefer to stay in town, tourists can _____ a number of interesting shops. (84)

4. Kevin _____ on the spot because his teacher punished him in front of the whole class. (92)

5. You are kind and sincere, but _____ she is superior. (88)

6. Disks are usually sent to the Disk Doctor _____. (86)

7. We should leave; please _____ the bill now. (87)

8. It is a popular style in Taiwan, but it never _____ in America. (89)

9. You go first, and I'll _____ you in a few minutes. (89)

10. The game was _____ because of the heavy rain. (85)

II. 引導翻譯

11. 不抽煙的人，可能會因為吸入他人的煙，而有染上肺癌的風險。(83)
Non-smokers could risk getting lung cancer from _____ _____ other people's cigarette smoke.

12. 在八〇年代手提箱炸彈擊落泛美航空 103 班機事件之後，行李與人相符的檢查在歐洲與亞洲變成一種標準作業。(92)
Bag-matching became standard practice in Europe and Asia after the suitcase bombs _____ _____ Pan Am Flight 103 in the 1980s.

13. 當節目結束時，我關掉收音機，並把飲料拿過來。
When the program was over, I turned off the radio and _____ _____ the drinks.

14. 只要有英文課，就要記得隨身帶字典。(90)
Remember to _____ the dictionary _____ you whenever you have English class.

15. 年齡和金錢的話題，很快會終止你們的對話。(88)
The subjects of age and money may rapidly _____ your conversation to an _____.

16. 有可能是那位女士在爬用冰雕刻的樓梯時，意外掉落的嗎? (87)
Was it perhaps dropped by _____ as the woman climbed up the stairs carved out of ice?

17. 你很快就會忘記他。(83)
You will forget him _____ and _____.

18. Kennedy 被暗殺的真相完全難以肯定。(88)
The truth of Kennedy's being assassinated is by _____ _____ certain.

19. Carnegie 聽說，一個叫 William Hunter 的年輕人，在救其他兩個快滅頂的男孩時喪生。
Carnegie heard about a young man _____ _____ _____ of William Hunter who lost his life trying to save two other boys from drowning.

20. 我希望，到時候你已經把工作完成。(87)

I hope you will have finished your task _____ _____.

21. 反之，你應該提議，在雙方都方便的時間裡再回電話。(86)

Instead, you should offer to _____ _____ at a mutually convenient time.

22. 恐怕這項醜聞會叫人懷疑他是否適合這個職位。(90)

I'm afraid that this scandal _____ into _____ his suitability for the post.

23. 我一到目的地就會打電話給你。(88)

I'll _____ you _____ upon arriving at the destination.

24. 喝完咖啡之後，我們可以繼續討論。(89)

We can (c)_____ _____ our discussion after a coffee break.

25. 一張有多種漂亮顏色的大型海報吸引了許多人。(84)

A large poster in beautiful colors _____ the _____ of many people.

26. 這是強迫休假，但至少讓我可以喘口氣。(92)

It was an enforced absence from work, but at least it gave me a little time to

_____ _____ _____.

27. 果菜市場似乎為求更好而漸漸地改變。(90)

The vegetable market appears to be _____ for the _____.

III. 克漏字選擇

Welcome to Barcelona

Barcelona is the capital of the Spanish province of Catalonia. This international and rich city is one of the most beautiful places in Europe. As a seaport on the Mediterranean Sea, Barcelona __28__ nice weather and attracts a lot of foreign tourists. Transportation is very convenient in Barcelona: you can __29__ a taxi, take the metro or the bus. There is also a *Bus Turistic* if you want to visit __30__ attractions in one day. If you prefer to walk, take the great boulevard known __31__ *La Rambla*. All kinds of people can be found on this typical street situated between the Place of Catalonia and the port. Street actors, such as a woman dressed like the Egyptian Queen Cleopatra and an old man and his cute dog playing music, __32__ each other to attract the tourists. Tourists also come to Barcelona to admire its beautiful architecture. Among the city's landmarks, three constructions particularly __33__ people's attention: the Güell Park with its colorful dragon, *La Pedrera* and *La Sagrada Familia*. The great Spanish architect Antoni Gaudi (1852-1926) was asked in 1883 to __34__ *il Templo de la Sagrada Familia* (the Church of the Sacred Family). Unfortunately, Gaudi died in an accident in 1926. After his death, the project was __35__ and the church was left unfinished. The construction continued in 1979. Nowadays, Spain's most famous landmark is still __36__.

(   ) 28. (A) benefits from   (B) results from   (C) brings in   (D) differs from

(   ) 29. (A) burst into   (B) pay for   (C) call for   (D) call off

(   ) 30. (A) a good deal of   (B) a plenty of   (C) a great many of   (D) a minimum of

(   ) 31. (A) in the name of   (B) by the name of   (C) by the way of   (D) in the way of

(   ) 32. (A) compete with   (B) come up with   (C) catch up with   (D) chat with

(   ) 33. (A) catch   (B) pay   (C) drew   (D) attracted

(   ) 34. (A) bring about   (B) burst into   (C) build up   (D) break even

(   ) 35. (A) brought down   (B) called out   (C) carried on   (D) called off

(   ) 36. (A) under control   (B) under construction

              (C) beyond description   (D) at will

Unit 5

❶ change...into...   **(A)** 變成；**(B)** 換穿

A. A witch changed the prince into a frog.　女巫把王子變成青蛙。

B. Just let me change into something casual.　等我換穿輕便一點。

> 同義　變成：turn into

❷ charge sb with sth　控告；指控

The prosecutor charged him with robbery.　檢察官指控他搶劫。

> 同義　accuse sb of sth

❸ chat with　與…閒聊

I chatted with my parents for a long time last night.　昨晚我與父母長談。

> 同義　have a chat with

❹ cheer up　使振奮起來

Here's a good news that will cheer us up.　這是個令我們振奮的好消息。

❺ clean up　徹底清除

I don't mind you using the kitchen as long as you clean it up afterwards.　只要你使用後能打掃乾淨，我不介意你使用廚房。

> 觸類旁通　clear up　講清楚；整理
> There are a couple of points we need to *clear up* before the interview.
> 在面試之前，我們有幾個重點要先講清楚。
> I had a lot of tasks to *clear up*.
> 我有很多工作必須處理。

❻ climb up　爬上去

They climbed up into the attic.　他們往上爬進小閣樓。

❼ (a) cloud on the horizon　地平線上的烏雲，指不祥的陰影

The only cloud on the horizon is his wife's illness.　唯一不愉快的事，就是他太太生病了。

❽ come across   **(A)** 巧遇、偶然發現；**(B)** 被理解、予人…印象；**(C)** 突然浮現

A. I came across an old diary in the basement.　我偶然在地下室發現這老舊日記。

B. I don't think I came across well in the interview.　我認為我面試時的表現不好。

C. A good idea came across my mind upon seeing you.
一看到你，我腦中突然浮現一個好點子。

 巧遇：run across、run into、bump into、meet...by chance

❾ **come around/round** (A) 恢復知覺、甦醒過來；(B) 改變立場；(C) 消氣；(D) 重新到來

A. After receiving first aid, the man came around.
經過急救之後，那個人甦醒過來。

B. He'll soon come around to our opinions.
他很快就會同意我們的觀點。

C. Leave her alone and she'll soon come around.
別煩她，她一下就會消氣了。

D. Summer vacation will soon be coming around.
暑假很快就會到了。

 甦醒過來：come to (oneself)

 改變立場：come around to

❿ **come back to life** 重獲生命

Thanks to the help of the medical team, the man came back to life.
幸虧有醫療團隊的幫忙，那個人重獲了生命。

 come back to 被回憶起、想起；回到早先處理過的問題或情形

The movie "Blue Gate Crossing" made my life in senior high school *come back to* me.
「藍色大門」這部影片讓我回想起我的高中生活。

Can we *come back to* my proposal?
我們能回到我的提案上嗎？

⓫ **come by** (A) 偶然得到、獲得；(B) 順道短暫拜訪

A. Jobs are hard to come by these days.
最近工作難求。

B. He said he would come by after work.
他說下班後會順道過來。

 獲得：obtain

順道短暫拜訪：drop in on

⓬ **come down with** 感染

The doctor said that I came down with the flu.
醫生說我感染了流行性感冒。

 這個片語的「感染」是指感染到「不算嚴重的病」，如感冒發燒等。

⓭ **come into being** 形成；存在

When did the first cell phone come into being?
第一支手機是在何時問世的？

 come into existence

 1. come into　繼承

He will *come into* a large fortune after his father dies.

他父親過世後，他將會繼承一大筆財產。

2. 與 come into 連接的常用片語如下：

come into action	開始行動	come into sb's favor	合某人的意
come into fashion	開始流行	come into effect	付諸實施；生效
come into leaf	長出葉子	come into sb's own	發揮特長
come into play	開始運轉	come into power	掌權
come into season	進入旺季	come into service	開始使用
come into view	映入眼簾	come into the open	顯露出來

❹ **come on** 　(A) 算了吧；(B) 加油；(C) 來臨；(D) 現身（螢光幕、廣播或舞台）

B. Come on, you can do it! 　　　　　　　　　加油！你辦得到的。

C. There is a typhoon coming on. 　　　　　　颱風要來了。

D. Mr. President came on and gave his speech. 　總統先生在電視上發表演講。

 辨 析　解釋為「來臨」時，「來到」的通常不是什麼好事，如危機迫近、天氣轉壞，或者是潛伏在體內的病發作。

 come on for sb　替代某人

Derek Fisher *came on for* Kobe Bryant with only two minutes left in the fourth quarter on Wednesday's game.

週三的比賽，第四節剩最後兩分鐘，Fisher 出場，換下 Bryant。

❺ **come on in** 　請進

Come on in—I've made some fruit tea. 　　　　請進，我泡了一些水果茶。

❻ **come over** 　(A) 從遠方來；(B) 短暫拜訪；(C)（疾病、感情）襲擊

A. The ancestors of most Americans came over the sea from Europe. 　　大部分美國人的祖先，都是遠從歐洲渡海而來的。

B. Why don't you come over and join us tonight? 　你今晚何不順便過來加入我們呢？

C. A wave of anger came over him when he realized that he had been misjudged. 　當他知道自己被誤判時，他心中升起了一股憤怒。

 come over to　叛變而轉向…方

Some of their salesmen *came over to* us because they couldn't resist the temptation of money.

他們的一些業務員因禁不起金錢誘惑，轉而投靠我們。

❶⃠ come to 　　**(A)** 恢復知覺；**(B)** 總計為；**(C)** 想到

A. Angela didn't know what had happened when she came to (herself).

Angela 醒過來時，不知道曾經發生過什麼事情。

B. The charge for the trip came to $5,000.

所有旅行費用總計五千美元。

C. The melody came to John when he took a trip in Italy.

John 在義大利旅行時，想到了這段旋律。

come to + N（come to 還有一個接動詞的用法，請參照 Unit 23）

1. when it comes to sth...　　提到某件事時…

   When it comes to singing, we should ask some advice from Ms. Nora.

   提到唱歌，我們應該要請教 Nora 小姐。

2. 與 come to 連接的常見片語：

come to an agreement	達成協議	come to an end	結束
come to a conclusion	獲得結論	come to a head	到緊要關頭
come to sb's notice	被某人留意到	come to blows	開始打架
come to grief	遭到不幸	come to grips with	面對、處理
come to hand	到手	come to life	甦醒過來
come to light	被揭露、顯露	come to mind	想起
come to pieces	粉碎	come to rest	停止、安頓

❶⃣ come up to 　　**(A)** 及得上、不亞於；**(B)** 接近

A. The resort didn't come up to our expectations.

這個渡假地不及我們預期的好。

B. Strangers could not come up to him because he had two bodyguards.

他因為有兩名貼身保鑣，所以陌生人無法接近他。

come up to + N

1. come up　　提起、走近、浮出、發芽、上升、（事情）發生

   This question *came up* several times at the meeting.

   這個問題在會議中被提出討論多次。

   A stranger *came up* and asked me the time.

   一位陌生人上前來問我時間。

   The sun always *comes up* from the east.

   太陽總是由東方升起。

   After the typhoon struck, the price of vegetables *came up*.

   颱風侵襲後，菜價上揚。

   Please inform our service center if any accident *comes up*.

   如果有任何意外發生，請告知服務中心。

Unit 6

C

2. come up against   碰到、遭遇（困難、反對等）並處理之

We *came up against* the heavy rain and low temperature on the first day of our camping.

露營活動的第一天，我們就面對了大雨與低溫的考驗。

⑲ compare to/with   與…比較

Compared to his success, I'm just a small potato.

與他的成功相較，我只是小人物。

Comparing American English with British English, you'll find many differences.

若你比較美式英語與英式英語，你會發現兩者間有許多不同。

⑳ compete for   為…而競爭

The teams compete for the championship.

這些隊伍為爭奪冠軍而競爭。

㉑ congratulations on   恭喜

Give my congratulations on his admission to Harvard University.

替我恭喜他獲准入學到哈佛。

 congratulate sb on sth   恭喜某人某事

I heartily *congratulate* you *on* winning the gold medal in the race.

我衷心恭喜你在比賽中拿到金牌。

㉒ consist in   在於

Happiness does not consist in how much money you own.

幸福不在於你擁有多少錢。

Success consists in hard work.

成功在於努力。

 lie in

Happiness *lies in* contentment.   知足常樂。

 consist of

= be made up of

= be composed of   由…組成

The snack chiefly *consists of* flour, sugar, milk and butter.

這個點心主要是由麵粉、糖、牛奶和奶油所組成。

㉓ contribute to   **(A)** 造成；**(B)** 對…有貢獻；**(C)** 捐贈

A. Alcohol contributes to many deaths on the road every year.

每年因喝酒造成馬路上許多人的死亡。

B. Building a small library in every village contributes a lot to society.

每個村莊建一座小圖書館，對社會有很大的貢獻。

C. She contributed a lot of money to the charity.

她捐贈鉅款給那個慈善團體。

造成: lead to、bring about、result in、give rise to、cause

對…有貢獻: make a contribution to

 contribute + N + to + N

❷ **cost nothing　不值一文；不花一毛錢**

She likes to do activities that cost nothing, such as window-shopping.

她喜歡做些不花錢的活動,如櫥窗瀏覽。

❷ **count on/upon　(A) 信賴；(B) 依賴；(C) 期待**

A. We can count on Dean to keep his word.

我們可以相信 Dean 會遵守承諾。

B. The Superman thought, "These people's safety count on me. I can't give up!"

超人心想:「這些人的安危都靠我,我不能放棄!」

C. We count on twenty thousand people taking part in this parade.

我們希望有兩萬人參與這次的遊行。

 信賴: trust

依賴: depend on/upon、rely on/upon

期待: expect

❷ **couple A with B　(A) A 加 B 造成…；(B) A 與 B 結合聯想**

A. Lack of rain coupled with high temperatures caused the drought in this area.

雨水缺乏,加上高溫,造成此地的乾旱。

B. I couple this song with his name.

我一聽這歌,就聯想到他的名字。

❷ **cross out　劃掉**

I crossed out the name of Tim and wrote Peter.

我劃掉 Tim 的名字然後寫上 Peter。

❷ **cut in on　(A) 插嘴；(B) 超車**

A. Sorry to cut in on you, but I have one question to ask you.

對不起打斷你,我有一個問題想請教。

B. He cut in on a yellow March, forcing the driver to brake heavily.

他超車到一輛黃色 March 車的前面,迫使司機緊急煞車。

❷⑨ **cut off**　　(A) 剪斷；(B) 切斷；(C) 使…沈默；(D) 使孤立

A. Telephone service around the island was cut off for days because of the typhoon.　　因為颱風，全島電話中斷了數日。

B. One of his arms was cut off in the accident.　　他的一隻手臂在意外中被切斷了。

C. Father cut me off before I tried to say something.　　在我說話之前，爸爸就叫我閉嘴。

D. The city is cut off from the rest of the country due to the broken bridges.　　這個城市因為橋樑全部中斷，而被孤立於全國之外。

 使孤立：cut off + from + sth

 cut out　剪下、開闢（道路）

I *cut out* this article of the newspaper.
我從報上剪下這篇文章。
They *cut out* a path through the forest.
他們在森林中開了一條路。

❸⓪ **dash off**　　(A) 匆忙地跑開；(B) 一口氣做完

A. Paul dashed off before they had a chance to talk to him.　　Paul 在他們有機會跟他說話之前就匆忙地離開。

B. He dashed off the resignation letter.　　他一口氣寫完辭職信。

Unit 6 Exercise

I. 片語選填

consist in	come over	come around	change into
come up to	cut off	a cloud on the horizon	contribute to
cut in	come down with		

1. Belle is the person who _____ him _____ a gentleman. (92)

2. He won the lottery, but I'm afraid there's _____; his sons may ask him for money. (88)

3. He _____ and found himself lying on the floor. (87)

4. Mr. and Mrs. Wang were worried about their baby girl because she _____ the flu again. (92)

5. When did you first _____ to Taiwan? (87)

6. His latest novel hasn't _____ his usual high standards. (88)

7. Great wisdom _____ not demanding too much of human nature. (87)

8. No doubt his ability to listen _____ his capacity to write. (88)

9. You will cause a crash by _____ like that. (92)

10. He had his phone _____ because he didn't pay the bill. (85)

II. 引導翻譯

11. 然後，他們送他坐牢，並指控他沒有許可證，違法攀爬大樓。(83)

    Then they put him in jail and _____ him _____ the violation of law for climbing the building without a permit.

12. 當你家中有客人時，如果你接到電話，你不該與對方閒聊太久，而忽略客人。(86)

    If you receive a phone call while you have guests at home, you should not _____ _____ the caller too long and neglect your guests.

13. 為了使太太高興起來，他帶她去聽音樂會。(86)

    He took his wife to the concert to (c)_____ her _____.

14. 你把東西弄得亂七八糟之後，應該學會清理乾淨。(86)

    After you have messed up something, you should learn to _____ it _____.

15. 他們把週末花在逛一個個的拍賣會上，希望能碰上真正的寶物。(89)

    They spent their weekends going from sale to sale, hoping to _____ _____ a real treasure.

16. 他們請求大家幫忙，尋找能讓他們的兒子再一次活過來的藥物。(89)

    They asked everyone to help them find the medicine that would make their son _____ _____ to _____ again.

17. 關於這個片語如何形成，有兩種以上的解釋。(85)

    There are two more explanations as to how this idiom _____ into _____.

18. 沒關係，請進來。(89)

    It's OK. _____ _____ _____.

19. Mike 在烈日下昏倒在稻田裡。當他甦醒時，看到一位陌生人在身邊。(86)

    Mike fainted under the hot sun in his rice field. When he _____ to, he saw a stranger beside him.

20. 與另外一組含三十九位病情類似，並只服用一般止痛藥的病人比較起來，此試驗組的病人較能有效地控制疼痛。(90)

    _____ _____ another group of 39 similar patients, who had only the usual painkillers, the trial group was much more likely to have good control of their pain.

21. 首先恭喜你畢業了！(86)

    First of all, _____ _____ your graduation!

22. 參與不必花捐贈者一文錢，卻能對別人的生活造成如此重大的影響。(86)

    Participation _____ the donor _____ and can make such a difference to others.

23. 你可以信賴我。(90)

You can (c)_____ _____ me.

24. 這些火災，是由於乾旱，加上放火燒山以開闢森林的方法所引起，至今已經毀了超過 200 萬英畝的森林。(87)

The fires, caused by drought and _____ _____ fire-setting methods to clear forests, have destroyed more than two million acres of forests.

25. 劃掉他的名字，並打電話叫他不要再來了。(89)

_____ his name _____ and call him not to come again.

26. 這兩個城市競爭「國之冰箱」的頭銜。(85)

The two cities _____ _____ the title "the Nation's Icebox."

27. 我很好奇 John 如何得到這麼一大筆錢。(85)

I am curious about how John _____ _____ such a large sum of money.

❶ decide on （仔細考慮後）決定

Have you decided on the date for the party? 你決定了宴會的日期嗎?

❷ depend on/upon **(A)** 依賴、信賴; **(B)** 取決於

A. That country heavily depends on its oil exports. 那個國家大量依賴石油輸出。

B. It all depends on whether you support me or not. 那完全取決於你是否支持我。

 依賴: rely on、count on、be dependent on

 It depends.
視情況而定。

❸ derive from 來自; 起源於

The enzyme is derived from human blood. 酵素源自於人的血液。

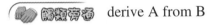 derive A from B 從 B 得到 A
You can *derive* much pleasure *from* reading.
從閱讀中可以得到很多樂趣。

❹ devote oneself to 致力於

He devoted himself full-time to his research in viruses. 他把全部時間投注在病毒研究上。

 be devoted to = dedicate oneself to = be dedicated to
Most of his time *was devoted to* helping the poor.
他把多數的時間投注於幫助窮人。

 devote oneself to + N/V-ing = be devoted to + N/V-ing

❺ differ from 與…不同

Even though Jim and Dave are twins, they differ greatly from each other in personality. 即使 Jim 和 Dave 是雙胞胎,他們在個性上卻大不相同。

 be different from
 differ from + N + in + N/V-ing

❻ differ from N to N 因（人、時、地）而異

The value of money differs from person to person. 金錢的價值會因人而異。

 1. from time to time
= sometimes 有時; 偶而

2. from country to country
= from one country to another 因國家不同而不同

❼ **do research on** 做…的研究

He's still doing his research on the liver cancer. 　　　　他仍在從事肝癌的研究。

 　　undertake research on、carry out research on/into、conduct research on/into

❽ **do without** 將就；沒有…也行

I can do without money, but I cannot do without your love. 　我沒有錢還可以，但沒有你的愛就不行。

 　　本片語常與助動詞 can 連用。

觸類旁通　can do with　有…就夠了
　　A: What would you like to drink?
　　B: I *could do with* a cup of coffee.
　　A: 你想喝什麼？
　　B: 我只要有杯咖啡就行了。

❾ **don't mention it** 不用謝；不必客氣

A: "Thank you for the ride home." 　　　「多謝你開車送我回家。」
B: "Don't mention it!" 　　　　　　　　「不用客氣。」

❿ **do's and don'ts** 須知；注意事項

The booklet lists the do's and don'ts of looking after your pet dog. 　這本手冊列有照顧寵物狗的須知。

⓫ **dress in (color)** 穿…（顏色）的衣服

Sue likes to dress in pink best. 　　　　　Sue 最喜歡穿粉紅色的衣服。

觸類旁通　dress sb in sth　幫某人穿上（衣服）
　　My mother *dresses* my father *in* his best suit every day.
　　我媽媽每天幫爸爸穿上最棒的西裝。

⓬ **drop in on sb** 順道拜訪某人

We'll drop in on you when we're in town next time. 　下次我們到城裡時，會順道來看你。

 　　drop in on + 人，指「順道拜訪某人」; drop in at + 家，指「順道造訪誰家」

⓭ **earn a reputation as...** 贏得…的名聲

His achievement has earned him a reputation as a tough guy. 　他的成就，為他贏得悍角色的名聲。

 　　gain/establish/acquire a reputation as...

⑭ enough to 足以

No one would be foolish enough to believe what he said.　沒有人會蠢到去相信他的話。

⑮ escape from **(A)** 從⋯逃脫；**(B)** 從⋯漏出

A. He failed in his attempt to escape from prison.　他越獄的企圖失敗了。

B. Oil is escaping from the mouth.　油從瓶口漏了出來。

⑯ even so 即使如此；儘管這樣

It seems a bit late now, but even so we can't give up the hope.　現在似乎有點遲了，但儘管如此，我們也不能放棄希望。

⑰ ever since 自從

His legs have been in poor condition ever since he fell and got hurt two years ago.　自從他兩年前跌倒受傷，雙腿就一直不好。

⑱ every now and then 偶而；有時

After graduation, I still see her every now and then.　畢業之後，我偶而還會看到她。

 now and then、every now and again、every so often、once in a while、from time to time、at times、occasionally、sometimes

⑲ except for 除了⋯之外

I felt fine except for a little headache.　除了有一點頭痛，我覺得還好。

⑳ excuse for ⋯的藉口

Lucy is always making excuses for her son's misbehavior.　Lucy 一直替他兒子的不當行為找藉口。

㉑ exposure to 暴露於；接觸到

Prolonged exposure to the sun may cause skin cancer.　長期暴露於陽光下可能會導致皮膚癌。

 1. exposure of　揭露不法情事

This reporter is famous for *exposure of* bribery in the government.

這位記者因為揭發政府裡的受賄行為而出名。

2. expose sb to sth　使某人接觸到⋯；使某人暴露在⋯

The report revealed that those workers had been *exposed to* high levels of radiation.

報導揭露那些工人們曾暴露在高度的輻射之中。

㉒ face up to   **(A)** 勇敢地接受；**(B)** 面對

A. You have to face up to the fact that your father has died.　你必須勇敢地接受父親去世的事實。

B. If he is found guilty, he faces up to 16 years in jail.　如果他有罪，將面臨十六年刑期。

 辨 析　這個片語的兩個意思，所「接受」或「面對」的，都不是好事情。

㉓ fail in   **(A)** 失敗；**(B)** 欠缺

A. He failed in his attempt to propose to Linda.　他試圖向 Linda 求婚，但失敗了。

B. She is an able worker, but fails in carefulness.　她是個有能力的員工，但欠缺細心。

㉔ fail to   不能

I fail to see why you cannot take advantage of the new technology.　我不明白你為何不能運用新科技。

 同 義　can't

 用 法　fail to + V

 觸類旁通　not/never fail to　一定做

He *never fails to* write to his girlfriend once a week.
他每星期必定寫信給女友。

㉕ fall apart   **(A)** 變成碎塊；**(B)** 狀況不佳；**(C)** 關係破裂

A. The glass fell apart when I accidentally dropped it on the floor.　玻璃杯在我意外的將它摔到地上時碎了。

B. Tony's old bike was rusty and falling apart.　Tony 的舊腳踏車生鏽而且還快散了。

C. Their friendship fell apart after that serious conflict.　他們的友情，在那場嚴重衝突後告吹了。

㉖ fall down   **(A)**（橋樑、建築物）倒塌；**(B)** 摔倒；**(C)** 失敗

A. The library is falling down and it will cost one million dollars to repair it.　圖書館快倒了，需要一百萬美元來修復。

B. The naughty child fell down and hit his head.　這調皮的小孩摔倒，還撞到頭。

C. Your plan is bound to fall down.　你的計劃勢必會失敗。

Unit 7

F

❷❼ **fall in love with** 愛上…

I think Jack and Jane have fallen in love with each other. 我認為 Jack 和 Jane 已經愛上對方了。

❷❽ **fall into** **(A)** 陷入…之中；快速進入某種狀態；**(B)** 分成

A. We fell into bed, exhausted. 我們非常疲憊而栽進床裡。

B. The novel falls into three parts. 這本小說分成三個部分。

觸類旁通 1. fall into conversation 與剛碰到的人開始聊天

2. fall into one's hands 被抓、落入…的控制之中

In World War II, most of the north China *fell into Japan's hands.*

二次世界大戰時，華北的大部分都落入日軍手中。

Unit 7 Exercise

I. 片語選填

differ from	enough to	face up to	fall into	except for
decide on	fail to	even so	do without	escape from

1. After several trips to pet shops, we ____________ a Dalmatian and named him Derek. (92)
2. How come your opinions often ____________ mine? (85)
3. He has no money to buy a car, so he'll just have to ____________. (86)
4. They are brave ____________ help in an emergency while others may stand by.
5. This passage is a story about a man who has ____________ the jail. (83)
6. Many people don't eat breakfast at all ____________ a cup of coffee. (87)
7. A grown-up must learn to ____________ his or her responsibility. (90)
8. This is why women can see many things which men ____________ notice. (85)
9. Most people ____________ one of these types. (85)
10. It was raining heavily, but ____________ I still had to leave. (83)

II. 引導翻譯

11. 到了 1997 年，這家依賴私人捐款的孤兒院已經收容了超過百位的嬰兒。(90)
As of 1997, the orphanage, which ________ ________ private contributions, has saved more than 100 infants.

12. 他的力量，主要來自他深受南方人民的歡迎。(84)
His power ________ mainly ________ his great popularity with the people in the south.

13. 歌手們將多數的時間致力於使音樂完美。(91)

    Singers _____ most of their time _____ making their music perfect.

14. 這些關於家庭的觀念也會因時間或因國家不同而有異。(89)

    These ideas about families also _____ _____ _____ _____

    _____ , or from country to country.

15. 他們正在從事因飲酒引起肝臟受損所造成影響的研究。(86)

    They are doing some _____ _____ the effects of liver damage caused by drinking.

16. 我們應該先了解語言教室的注意事項。(87)

    We should know the _____ _____ _____ in the language lab in advance.

17. A:「多謝!」B:「不用客氣。」(86)

    A: "Thank you very much." B: "Don't _____ _____ !"

18. 但是 Victoria 女皇穿黑色衣服穿了四十年。(91)

    But Queen Victoria _____ _____ black for forty years.

19. 它們逐漸風行全球,自從那時就一直流行到現在。(90)

    They gradually spread all over the world, and have remained popular _____

    _____ .

20. 有時他們會一塊去看電影。(85)

    _____ _____ _____ they go to a movie together.

21. 今天遲到的藉口為何?(84)

    What's your _____ _____ being late today?

22. 很多淘金客對這樣危險的旅行並沒有做好準備,而死於飢餓或暴露於嚴寒的氣候之中。(90)

    Unprepared for such a dangerous journey, many gold seekers died of starvation and _____ _____ the cold weather.

23. Soapy 的第二個計劃也失敗了。(91)

    Soapy also _____ _____ his second scheme.

24. 當我倉促地站起來時,玻璃杯摔碎了。(92)

    The glass _____ _____ when I stood up hastily.

25. Jack 打網球時摔倒,並嚴重地扭傷了他的腳踝。(84)

    Jack _____ _____ while playing tennis and twisted his ankle very badly.

26. 一般相信,Valentine 在坐牢時愛上一位年輕女孩。(90)

    While in prison, it is believed that Valentine _____ _____ _____

    _____ a young girl.

Saint-Exupéry, pilot and writer

Antoine de Saint-Exupéry was born in Lyon, France, in 1900. He became a commercial pilot in 1926. During a travel to Buenos Aires in 1930, he met Consuelo Suncin. She was smart and pretty. He immediately __27__ her. By April 1931, they were married. But Antoine was always __28__, accomplishing dangerous missions. His flights inspired him and he wrote many books about his experiences as a pioneer pilot. Before World War II, with books like *Southern Mail and Wind*, *Sand and Stars*, Antoine had already __29__ a great writer. *Night Flight* was adapted into screen in 1933, starring American actor Clarke Gable. After the German invasion of France in 1940, he went to America. He __30__ convince the Americans to enter the war. When they finally did, after the Japanese attack on Pearl Harbor in December 1941, Antoine was still in the United States. While he was __31__ an opportunity to go back to Europe and continue the fight, he began to write a masterpiece of world literature: *The Little Prince*. It is the story of a blond hair boy __32__ green and red, who travels through the universe and learns the meaning of love and friendship __33__. In 1943, Antoine finally got a chance to fight and went to North Africa. Unfortunately, his plane __34__ during a mission over the Mediterranean and disappeared in July 1944. His plane and his body were never found.

(   ) 27. (A) fell into debt for (B) broke up with   (C) broke down for   (D) fell in love with

(   ) 28. (A) on the move   (B) on the alert   (C) off work   (D) off duty

(   ) 29. (A) been notorious for   (B) was regarded as

        (C) earned a reputation as   (D) made a living as

(   ) 30. (A) was forced to   (B) determined to

        (C) failed to   (D) couldn't afford to

(   ) 31. (A) impelled to grasp   (B) making use of

        (C) pushed to improve   (D) waiting for

(   ) 32. (A) covered with   (B) dressed in   (C) put on   (D) worn in

(   ) 33. (A) on the world   (B) in the earth   (C) over the world   (D) on earth

(   ) 34. (A) fell down   (B) dropped in   (C) did research   (D) took off

Unit 7

❶ fall off **(A)**（質量、數量）下降、減少；**(B)** 摔下

   A. Audience figures fell off since the weather was worse than expected.

因為天氣比預期的更糟，所以觀眾人數減少了。

   B. The boy fell off the tree and broke his legs.

小男孩從樹上摔下，摔斷雙腿。

❷ feed on 以⋯為食

Snakes feed on chicken and other small animals.

蛇以雞或其他小動物為食。

❸ feel...about sth 對某事有⋯的感覺

After talking to the coach, I felt good about my recent performance.

和教練談過之後，我對自己近來的表現感到滿意。

John felt ashamed about cheating in the exam.

John 對考試作弊感到很羞愧。

用法   feel + adj + about sth

❹ fight for 為⋯而戰；為⋯而奮鬥

It stands to reason that you should fight for your wages.

你為自己的薪資奮鬥是合理的。

觸類旁通   1. fight against　對抗

They *fought* bravely *against* the enemy.
他們勇敢的與敵人戰鬥。

2. fight with　對抗（同 fight against）；與⋯合力戰鬥

The Soviets *fought with* the Americans against the Germans during World War II.
第二次世界大戰期間，蘇聯聯合美國對抗德國。

3. fight off　擊退

All the baseball fans hope our national team can *fight off* other opponents and win the world championship.
所有的棒球迷都希望國家代表隊能擊退所有對手，贏得世界冠軍。

❺ food for thought （思考的）資料

The teacher's advice gave me some food for thought in composition.

老師的建議，提供了我一些在作文方面思考的資料。

❻ fool around/about 虛度光陰；遊手好閒

We spent the afternoon just fooling around on our bikes. 　　我們整個下午騎腳踏車四處亂混。

 goof around、monkey around、mess around

 fool around with

= fool with 玩弄、擺弄

My younger brother *fooled around with* the knife and cut his own finger.

我弟弟亂玩刀子，結果割到自己的手指。

❼ for days 好幾天

He hasn't closed his eyes for days to take care of his sick wife. 　　他多日未眠去照顧生病的妻子。

❽ for pleasure 為了消遣、娛樂

Like most people of her age, Sherry struck up a friendship just for pleasure. 　　Sherry 像多數跟她同齡的人一樣，開始交朋友都只是為了好玩。

 for fun

❾ for sure 確信

No one knows for sure how life begins. 　　沒有人確切知道生命的起源。

 for certain

❿ for the last time 最後一次

My teacher warned me for the last time that if I don't hand in my report tomorrow, he'll fail me. 　　我的老師最後一次警告我，如果我明天沒交報告，他就要把我當掉。

⓫ for the purpose of 為了

For the purpose of assisting the homeless, they held an outdoor concert. 　　為了協助無家可歸的人，他們舉辦了一場戶外音樂會。

For the purpose of achieving his goal, he did everything without complaint. 　　為了達到目的，他做什麼都沒有怨言。

= With an eye/a view to achieving his goal, he did everything without complaint.

= He did everything without complaint in order to/so as to achieve his goal.

 in order to、so as to、with an eye to、with a view to

 除了 so as to 與 in order to 接原形動詞外，其餘都接名詞或動名詞。

⓬ frighten away 嚇跑；嚇走

Terrorist activity in this country has frightened away 70% of tourists.

這個國家裡的恐怖份子活動嚇走了百分之七十的觀光客。

 同義 frighten off

⓭ from head to toe/foot 從頭到腳

His body was shaking from head to toe when he was out in the snow.

當他在外面雪地裡時，他全身上下都在顫抖。

 同義 from top to toe

⓮ from time to time 有時候

Tragic accidents happen here from time to time.

此地偶有悲劇性的意外發生。

 同義 once in a while、every now and then、at times、occasionally

⓯ from top to bottom 從上到下；完全

Doris really has changed from top to bottom.

Doris 真的已經完全的改變了。

 辨析 from top to toe 是指一個人的全身上下，但 from top to bottom 是指「地方」或「機構」的從上到下。

⓰ gaze at （指長時間無意識地）注視

Gazing at the sky, he reminded himself of his past.

他看著天空，想著過去。

⓱ generally speaking 大體而言

Generally speaking, the more expensive the laptop is, the better it is.

一般說來，手提電腦越貴品質就越好。

 同義 in general、by and large、on (the) average、in the main、on the whole

⓲ get drunk 喝醉酒

Every time David gets drunk, I have to take him home.

每次 David 喝醉，我都得送他回家。

⓳ get in touch with 與…聯絡

Get in touch with me once you arrive at the airport.

一到機場後就跟我聯絡。

 1. keep/stay in touch with = keep/stay in contact with 與…保持聯絡

2. get in touch with sth 了解（感受）

The first stage is to *get in touch with* your perceptions and accept yourself.
第一階段是了解自己的感受並接納自己。

⑳ get/run into difficulty　遭受困難

The man soon get into difficulty with debt.　不久，那個人就遭受債務困擾。

㉑ get into trouble　惹上麻煩

Tim started to get into trouble at school because of his dishonesty.　Tim 因不誠實而在學校惹上麻煩。

 get sb into trouble　讓…有麻煩；把…一起拖下水

If John really breaks the windows, he'll certainly *get all of us into trouble*!
要是 John 真的把窗子都打破了，他絕對會把我們大家都拖下水!

㉒ get married　結婚

Nicole's brother got married last year.　Nicole 的哥哥去年結婚了。

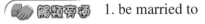 1. be married to　與某人結婚

My son is going to *be married to* Ms. Chang this summer.
我的兒子今年夏天要與張小姐結婚。

2. get divorced　離婚

Not being able to tolerate the great differences between each other, this couple decided to *get divorced*.
因為不能容忍彼此間的巨大差異，這對夫妻決定離婚。

㉓ get on　**(A)** 上（車、船、飛機）；**(B)** 進行、順利進展；**(C)**（年齡）接近

A. Crowds of students get on and off the bus every morning.　每天早上，成群的學生上下公車。

B. How is your business getting on?　你生意近況如何？

C. My grandfather is getting on 90.　我祖父年近九十。

 get off　下（車、船、飛機）

We're going to *get off* at the next stop.
我們將在下一站下車。

㉔ get out　**(A)** 逃亡；**(B)** 出去

A. He was determined to get out of prison.　他下定決心逃獄。

B. You'd better get out before he gets angry.　你最好在他生氣之前趕快出去。

㉕ get sb nowhere 讓某人一事無成

Doping will get you nowhere.　　　　　　　　　吸毒只會讓你一事無成。

 get somewhere

= make progress　成功

I think we'll *get somewhere* at last.

我認為我們最後會成功。

He is *making* great *progress* in English.

他的英文大有進步。

㉖ get to　　**(A)** 逐漸做…、有機會做某事；**(B)** 抵達

A. It'll take a while for you to get to like him.　你需要一段時間漸漸地去喜歡他。

B. When you get to Taipei, don't forget to give me a buzz.　當你抵達台北時，別忘了打電話給我。

 抵達：arrive in/at、reach

 逐漸做：get to + V

抵達：get to + place

arrive in + 大地方，arrive at + 小地方

㉗ get well/sick　病癒／生病

I got sick last winter and was in bed for a month.　去年冬天，我臥病在床一個月。

㉘ give a talk　發表談話；演說

Dr. Chen will give a talk on herbal medicine in the library.　陳博士將在圖書館發表草藥醫學的演講。

 make a speech、deliver a speech、address a speech、do a talk

㉙ give birth to　　**(A)** 生（孩子）；**(B)** 產生；**(C)** 引起

A. The Lin family was celebrating last night after Mrs. Lin gave birth to twins.　林家昨晚慶祝林太太生下一對雙胞胎。

B. Kinmen gave birth to many celebrities.　金門出了很多名人。

C. The football match gave birth to a violent controversy.　這次的足球賽引起一場激烈的爭議。

 give birth to + N

I. 片語選填

give a talk	fool around	fall off	gaze at
fight for	get on	frighten away	
food for thought	get in touch with	from time to time	

1. The demand for new houses has _____ sharply these years. (92)

2. In a democratic society, everyone can _____ his or her human rights.

3. The speaker's lecture is quite stimulating. It has given us some _____ .

4. He just _____ all day long, having nothing to do at all. (83)

5. The lobster produces the sound in order to _____ its enemies. (90)

6. These ideas also differ _____ , and from country to country. (89)

7. She sat _____ the sea, thinking of her parents in the distance. (85)

8. In Taiwan, it is more convenient to _____ people by calling them. (86)

9. Excuse me. Where can I _____ the next train for Taichung? (84)

10. Although I got up early this morning, I was still late for _____ in this meeting. (88)

II. 引導翻譯

11. 水中生物已經演化出獨特的聲音製造方式,用以與同類溝通,並警告捕食他們的天敵。

    Underwater creatures have evolved remarkable ways of producing sound to communicate with each other, and to warn off predators that _____ _____ them.

12. 他們不需要別人不斷地讚美與鼓勵,就會對自己很滿意。(83)

    They do not need constant praise and encouragement from others to _____ _____ _____ _____ .

13. 這場雨斷斷續續地下了好幾天。(85)

    It has rained on and off _____ _____ .

14. 現代獵人們配備強而有力的武器,但對他們多數人而言,打獵為了娛樂多過於為了覓食。(84)

    Modern hunters are equipped with powerful weapons, but for most of them, hunting is more _____ _____ than for food.

15. 她最後一次問她先生,是否曾經愛過她。(85)

    She asked her husband _____ _____ _____ _____ if he had ever loved her.

16. 在醫療上，大自然的聲音和美景的運用，是為了轉移病人對疼痛的注意。(90)

The use of natural sounds and beautiful scenery in medical treatment is _____ _____ _____ of shifting patients' attention from pain.

17. 新娘從頭到腳一身白色打扮。(89)

The bride was dressed in white _____ _____ _____ _____ .

18. 該委員會需要徹底改造。(89)

The committee needs reforming _____ _____ _____ _____ .

19. 一般說來，所有來到台灣的外國人，應該透過中華民國大使館或領事館申請入境簽證。

_____ _____ , all foreigners coming to Taiwan should apply for entry visas through the embassies or consulates of the R.O.C.

20. 除夕夜，是個要大家徹夜狂歡，不醉不歸的夜晚。(84)

New Year's Eve is an entire night dedicated to the proposition that everyone must _____ _____ .

21. 由於龐大的預算，這位科學家建造現代化實驗室的計劃遭到困難。(90)

The scientist's project to build a modern laboratory _____ _____ _____ on account of its huge budget.

22. "Kawasaki" 號在航程中何時首度陷入困境？(86)

When did the "Kawasaki" first _____ _____ _____ during the voyage?

23. 這個奇怪的宗教禁止單身男子結婚。

This strange religion forbids single men to _____ _____ .

24. 昨晚，其中一隻老虎逃出動物園。(90)

One of the tigers _____ _____ of the zoo last night.

25. 根據這位父親的看法，抱怨讓你一事無成。(86)

In the opinion of the father, complaining _____ you _____ .

26. 初次養狗的人，可能在如何漸漸認識和訓練他們的寵物方面遭遇到許多問題。(88)

First-time dog owners may encounter many problems _____ _____ know and train their pets.

27. 哪一類型的人生病時最有可能較快復原？(86)

What type of people are most likely to _____ _____ soon when they _____ _____ ?

28. 許多婦女利用呼吸及想像的技巧，來分散分娩時的痛苦。(90)

Many women use breathing and visualization techniques to distract them from the pain while _____ _____ _____ babies.

❶ **give feedback to**　給…回饋

Try to give some feedback to each student on the task.

設法給參與這份工作的每位學生一些回饋。

❷ **give out**　(A) 分發；(B) 發出

A. He stood at the corner to give out leaflets to all the passers-by.

他站在轉角發傳單給所有的路人。

B. The gas lamp gives out a pale yellowish light.

煤氣燈散發出泛黃的光線。

 分發：send out，特指將同樣的文件拷貝後分發給一大群人

發出：emit，特指「發出」瓦斯、光、熱等。

❸ **give rise to**　導致；造成

His speech on the election gave rise to a bitter argument.

他關於選舉的演講引起嚴重爭辯。

 contribute to、bring about、result in、lead to、cause

It's hard work that *resulted in* his getting a scholarship.

是因為努力，讓他得到獎學金。

❹ **give sb a lift**　讓某人搭便車

Ted gave me a lift home yesterday.

Ted 昨天讓我搭便車回家。

 give sb a ride

❺ **give-and-take**　互相讓步；遷就妥協

In any relationship there has to be some give-and-take.

在任何人際關係裡，都必須有些許讓步。

❻ **glance at/over/toward**　一瞥；看一眼

Sarah glanced nervously at her watch at the bus stop.

Sarah 在公車站緊張地看了手錶一眼。

 cast/shoot/throw a glance at

❼ **go after**　追求某事；追逐某人

Jane's father went after her to make sure she was not hurt.

Jane 的爸爸尾隨她，以確信她未受傷害。

❽ **go around/round/about** 著手做

Kevin was assigned the task, but he didn't know how to go around it.

Kevin 被派到這項職務，但是他不知道該如何著手進行。

 tackle

 go around/round/about + N/V-ing

 go around sth　很多人知道並加以討論

There was a lot of gossip *going around* the department.
該部門有許多八卦傳來傳去。

❾ **go back on** 違背承諾；改變計畫

It is shameful of you to go back on your promise.

你違背諾言，真是可恥。

G

❿ **go bankrupt** 破產

The company went bankrupt before they were able to complete the bridge.

在橋樑完成之前，公司就破產了。

⓫ **go crazy** 發瘋；瘋狂

The crowd went crazy when he shwed up on stage.

當他出現在台上時，大家都為他瘋狂了。

 go mad、go bananas

⓬ **go Dutch** 各付各的

She decided to go Dutch with me in the restaurant last night.

她昨晚在餐廳決定我們各付各的。

⓭ **go for a walk** 散步

Let's go for a walk. I could use some fresh air.

咱們去散步吧！我需要點新鮮空氣。

⓮ **go into a rage** 生氣；發怒

Carl became quite frightening when he went into a rage.

Carl 生氣時十分嚇人。

 get angry

⓯ **go off** **(A)** 爆炸；**(B)**（機器）停止運作；**(C)** 發生；**(D)** 離去、出發

A. The time bomb went off on the crowded downtown street.

那顆定時炸彈，在鬧區擠滿人群的街上爆炸了。

B. All the lights suddenly went off.

所有的電燈突然都熄滅了。

C. The whole concert went off peacefully.　整場音樂會平和地開始。

D. He went off to Japan an hour ago.　他一個小時前出發前往日本。

 爆炸：explode

發生：happen

⓰ **go on with** 繼續

After a short pause, Eddie went on with his story in Africa.　短暫停頓一下之後，Eddie 繼續他在非洲的故事。

He went on with his work as he talked to me.　當他和我說話時，他一邊繼續做他的工作。

= He went on doing his work as he talked to me.

 go on、continue

 go on with/go on/continue + V-ing，均表「繼續」先前在做的動作。

 go on to + V 是指所做的動作和之前的不同，表「接著做」之意。

Let's *go on to* discuss the cast.

咱們接下來討論演員陣容。

⓱ **graduate from** 從…畢業

He graduated from Harvard University.　他從哈佛大學畢業。

⓲ **greed for** 對…貪婪

People usually have a strong greed for more money and power than they need.　人們通常對金錢與權力有強烈的欲求，而且超過他們所需。

⓳ **grind to a halt** 漸漸停止

Traffic ground to a halt as it approached the accident site.　接近車禍現場，交通漸漸停頓了。

 grind 的三態：grind, ground, ground

⓴ **grow into** (A) 發展成，成為；(B) 適應

A. Sandra grew into a lovely young lady.　Sandra 長大成為年輕可人的女性。

B. With the help of Jack, you'll soon grow into the new job.　在 Jack 的幫助下，你很快就會熟悉新工作。

 作「適應」解時，是指「因為已經有足夠的經驗，而知道如何處理一個情況或擔任某種職位」。

Unit 9

G

❷❶ hand in　繳交

You must hand in your application form if you want to apply for the job.

如果你要申請這份工作，就必須要繳交申請表。

 同義　　turn in

 觸類旁通　hand out　分發；分散

The teacher *handed out* the uniform to everyone in the class.
老師將制服發給班上的每一位同學。

❷❷ hang on　(A) 撐住；(B) 取決於；(C) 不掛掉電話

A. Though I'm a bit tired, I can hang on a little longer.

雖然我有點累，但我還能撐一下。

B. Everything hangs on the outcome of the meeting.

每一件事都取決於會議結果。

C. Hang on a moment, please.

請等一下，不要掛電話。

 同義　取決於：depend on

辨析　當「撐住」解時，比較接近「堅持下去」的意思。

 觸類旁通　hang on one's every word　密切注意某人說的話

We are watching the teacher's face, *hanging on his every word*.
我們看著老師，專注於他的每一句話。

❷❸ hang on to/onto　緊緊握住；堅持

For the sake of safety, be sure to hang on to the rope.

為了安全，請確定你已緊握繩子。

❷❹ hang out　將…掛出去；廝混

I have no idea who she hangs out with.

我不知道她都跟誰廝混。

 觸類旁通　hangout (n.) 聚集處，指「特定一群人喜歡聚集活動的地方」。

let it all hang out　完全放輕鬆；絕對坦白

❷❺ (sth) happen to sb　（某事）發生在某人身上

The serious bus crash happened to those students last night.

昨晚那些學生碰上嚴重的公車事故。

 用法　happen 作「發生」解時，一定是「某事 happen to 某人」，主詞為事，受詞為人，故也不可能有被動語態。

觸類旁通　sb happen to + V　恰巧

happen 作「恰巧」解時，就可以用人當主詞。

I *happened to* meet him this morning.
今天早上我恰巧遇到他。

Unit 9　H

❷⑥ have a greater/better chance of 有較大的機會或勝算

Try this way and you may have a greater chance of winning a free meal.

試試這種方法，也許你會有更大的機會獲得免費餐點。

❷⑦ have a lot to do with 與…很有關係

It is said that lung cancer has a lot to do with smoking.

據說肺癌與抽煙很有關係。

 同　義　have much to do with

 觸類旁通　have nothing to do with　與…毫無關係
have little to do with　與…沒什麼關係
have something to do with　與…有一些關係

❷⑧ have a passion for 對…狂熱

She has a strong passion for arts and crafts.

她對藝術和手工藝有強烈的狂熱。

❷⑨ have an inclination for 對…有意願

The police should have an inclination for investigating the crime.

警方應該有調查犯罪的意願。

❸⓪ have trouble (in) 做…有困難

I have no trouble learning a wide variety of languages.

學習多種語言對我來說毫無困難。

 同　義　have difficulty (in)
Our math teacher *has difficulty in* hearing.
我們數學老師聽力不好。

 用　法　have trouble/difficulty (in) + N/V-ing

 觸類旁通　have trouble with sth　對…有困難
They are *having* much *trouble with* the new computer system.
他們對新的電腦系統仍然感到很大的困難。

Unit 9 Exercise

I. 片語選填

give rise to	greed for	hand in	go around
hang on to	go on with	go back on	give-and-take
have a lot to do with	happen to		

1. John's reckless behavior _____ endless trouble for his parents. (86)

2. In radio and television call-in programs, there is a lot of _____ between the host and the audience. (87)

3. That's not the best way to _____ about quitting your job. (89)

4. He _____ his word and deserted his family. (87)

5. All of these families learned to _____ their lives after their loved ones' deaths. (89)

6. I won't be able to _____ my homework in time. (87)

7. Take heart and _____ your goal for as long as it takes. (87)

8. Novels can be so close to the truth that it seems as real as something that _____ _____ you this morning. (91)

9. We believed he _____ the robbery. (86)

10. His _____ power led him into a tragedy. (85)

II. 引導翻譯

11. 然而，唱片公司卻從未給歌迷任何回饋─降低 CD 的價格。(91)

    However, the recording industry never _____ its _____ to the fans─by lowering the prices of CDs.

12. 沒有植物釋放出的氧氣和它們提供的食物，生命就會停滯，且所有的動物會挨餓。(88)

    Without the oxygen that plants _____ _____, and without the food they supply, life would stop and all animals would starve.

13. 搭我的便車好嗎？(87)

    Can I _____ _____ a _____ ?

14. 他很努力尋找工作。(86)

    He tried very hard to _____ _____ a job.

15. 他因為投資過多而破產。(92)

    He _____ _____ because he invested too much.

16. 他們認為，那對年輕夫妻因為嬰兒的死亡而發瘋了。(89)

    They thought the young couple had _____ _____ over the death of the baby.

17. 在餐廳用完餐後，John 對 Paul 說：「咱們各付各的吧!」(86)

    "Let's _____ _____," John said to Paul after eating dinner at a restaurant.

18. 他們散步時，Johnny 必須跨大步才能追上爸爸。(91)

    When they _____ _____ _____ _____, Johnny has to take long steps to keep pace with his father.

19. 當偉大的 Beethoven 被要求為吉他作曲時，他生氣地拒絕，但最後，甚至是 Beethoven，也不能忽視這項挑戰。(92)

    When the great Beethoven was asked to compose music for the guitar, he _____ _____ a _____ and refused, but eventually even Beethoven could not ignore the challenge.

20. 槍枝走火，子彈從他頭上飛過。(92)

The gun _____ _____ and the bullet went flying over his head.

21. Robot Redford 自 Maryland 的一所大學畢業。(87)

Robot Redford _____ _____ a college in Maryland.

22. 沒有植物釋放出的氧氣和它們提供的食物，生命將會停滯，且所有的動物會挨餓。(88)

Without the oxygen that plants emit, and without the food they supply, life would _____ _____ a _____ and all animals would starve.

23. 真空吸塵機器人易於在繞著傢俱、貓和樓梯移動時有困難。(90)

Vacuum cleaner robots tend to _____ _____ moving around furniture, cats and stairways.

24. 新的人際關係就像胚胎，需要時間、關心和注意，才能發展成它可能會形成的任何形式結果。(86)

A new relationship is like an embryo that requires time, care and attention to _____ _____ whatever it may evolve.

25. 假如所有的廠商能在這一波財務危機中撐住，下一季的經濟可能會好轉。(88)

If all the manufacturers can _____ _____ during this financial crisis, the economy may get better next quarter.

26. 有一些年輕人每晚在酒吧打混。(92)

Some young people _____ _____ in the pub every night.

27. 這三隻小鯨魚獲救，是因為年紀較小的鯨魚，比其他的鯨魚生還機會大。(84)

The three little whales were rescued because they _____ a _____ _____ survival than the others.

28. 我對武器所知不多，可說是完全不關心，但是我知道在我的小鎮上有許多人對坦克車十分狂熱。(88)

I know little and care nothing about weapons, yet I know that in my town there are many people _____ a _____ _____ tanks.

29. 那些對科技產物有意願的人，不會難以取悅。(90)

Those who _____ an _____ _____ technological products aren't hard to please.

III. 克漏字選擇

Tulip Mania in Holland

Tulips were first introduced in Europe from Turkey in the 16th century. The tulip __30__ then __30__ rare and people were ready to sell their house or their company just to buy a single bulb of the flower. The Dutch wanted __31__ to make easy money, but between 1634 and 1637, they __32__. They couldn't think about anything else than making tulips grow in their garden. Many left their home or their work to __33__ tulips full time. It went too far and __34__ a major economic crisis. People thought that the value of the tulips would be high forever. But actually, tulips were not so rare anymore. Their value was estimated much too high. The economy of the country was __35__. By forbidding people to speculate on tulips at the Amsterdam Stock Exchange, the government made things worse. In April 1937, the tulip prices collapsed and lots of Dutchmen __36__. Some people even killed themselves. The tulip mania ruined the country which couldn't afford a navy and colonies anymore. __37__, England won the commercial competition with Holland. After the Anglo-Dutch wars, during the second part of the 17th century, Holland lost New Amsterdam, renamed New York by the English. Nowadays, the Dutch still __38__ tulips, but they have become wiser: they make profit by attracting millions of foreign tourists.

(   ) 30. (A) regarded/as   (B) was/considered   (C) thought/to be   (D) was referred/to

(   ) 31. (A) at most   (B) at least   (C) at last   (D) at first

(   ) 32. (A) are out of mind   (B) went crazy   (C) got madness   (D) went into mad

(   ) 33. (A) care about   (B) take advantage of

         (C) take care of   (D) pay a visit to

(   ) 34. (A) gave rise to   (B) gave feedback to (C) gave out with   (D) gave a lift to

(   ) 35. (A) in reality   (B) in use   (C) in detail   (D) in danger

(   ) 36. (A) went bankrupt   (B) lost their temper (C) ground to a halt (D) went Dutch

(   ) 37. (A) After all   (B) In a word   (C) As a result   (D) To sum up

(   ) 38. (A) had an inclination for   (B) have a passion for

         (C) had a lot of to do with   (D) have trouble

❶ hear about 聽說

Sophia heard about the decision later and burst into tears.

Sophia 稍後聽說了這項決定,而放聲大哭。

❷ hear of (A) 聽說…的事; (B) 同意、贊成

A. I've heard of a position in the sales department just right for you.

我聽說,在業務部有一個職缺,恰好適合你。

B. I won't hear of your investment in the car industry.

我不贊成你投資汽車業。

 用法　當「贊成」解時,通常用在否定句,與 will not/would not 連用。

觸類旁通　1. hear from　收到…的消息
I haven't *heard from* him for years.
我已多年沒有他的消息。

2. hear about　聽說,一般用於聽到比 hear of 更詳細的有關內容。
I want to *hear about* my illness.
我想聽聽我的病情。

❸ help sb with sth 幫助某人做某事

My parents said they're going to help me with the fees.

我父母說會幫我付這些費用。

❹ here and there 到處; 處處

The classroom needs a bit of paint here and there.

這間教室處處都需要油漆。

 同義　everywhere

❺ hold on (A) 緊抓住某物; (B) 等待、堅持

A. Hold on to the rope, or you may fall down the steep cliff.

緊抓住繩子,否則你可能會掉下陡峭的懸崖去。

B. Even though he was far behind other runners, he still held on until the last minute.

雖然他落後其他跑者,他仍然一直堅持到最後一刻。

同義　緊抓住某物: hold on to

❻ hold on to/onto 握緊; 抓住不放

This man held on to his girlfriend's hand, asking her to marry him.

這男子緊握住女友的手,請她嫁給他。

 同義　hold on

❼ **hold one's ground** 站穩立場

Edward vowed to hold his ground, even if it meant losing his job.

即使意味著要失去工作，Edward 發誓堅守立場。

 同義 stand one's ground

❽ **hold one's horses** 不要倉促行事做出決定

Before we have enough evidence to prove his guilt, we should hold our horses trying to catch him.

有足夠證據證明他有罪前，我們最好先別忙著逮捕他。

❾ **hold out against** 忍受，抵抗

I didn't know how long I could hold out against their relentless questioning.

我不知道能忍受他們殘酷的質詢多久。

 **觸類旁通** hold out 伸出（手）; 維持

She *held out* her arms to welcome the guest.

她伸出雙臂歡迎客人。

The government said the water supply would *hold out* through the entire summer.

政府說，整個夏天都能維持供水。

❿ **how come** 為什麼

How come Mike is at school? Didn't he get sick and stay at home?

Mike 怎麼會在學校？他不是生病在家嗎？

 用法 雖然 how come 有 why 的意思，但 how come 只能用在口語上。

⓫ **how on earth** 到底如何

How on earth did you handle that tough task?

你到底如何處理那艱苦的工作？

 辨析 why/what/how/where on earth 都用在口語上，是用來強調後面所問的問題。如果一定要給個中文解釋，就是「到底、究竟」之意。

What on earth did you do that for?

你究竟為什麼那麼做？

⓬ **in a good humor/mood** 心情好

It seems that you're in a good mood this morning.

今天早上你似乎心情很好。

 觸類旁通 in a bad humor/mood 心情不好

⓭ **in a minute** 稍後; 片刻

Mr. Gibson will be with you in a minute.

Gibson 先生馬上會接見你。

 同義 soon

❶ in a word　總而言之

He is, in a word, full of energy.　　　　　　總而言之，他精力充沛。

 in a nutshell、in consequence、as a consequence、to sum up、to summarize、summing up、to conclude

 後面四個片語，包括 to sum up、to summarize、summing up、to conclude，通常都是用在論文寫作上，較為正式。

❶ in abundance　充裕；豐富

One quality our school team possess in abundance is fighting spirit.　　　我們校隊所擁有最充裕的一項特質，就是戰鬥精神。

 in abundance 通常用在句尾

❶ in accordance with　依照；根據

We should operate the machine in accordance with the users' manual.　　　我們應該要依照使用手冊來操作這台機器。

 according to

❶ in action　在活動／運轉／工作

They tried to take some pictures of ski jumpers in action.　　　他們設法在拍一些正在雪地跳躍者的相片。

 in action 用在「進行某人很在行的活動」或「經過訓練而做的工作」上。

❶ in addition to　除…之外

In addition to his good voice, Eric is known as a dancer.　　　Eric 除了聲音好之外，也是個知名的舞者。

 besides、apart from

 in addition to、besides、apart from + N/V-ing

❶ in advance　事先；預先

You'd better ask him in advance how much it will cost.　　　你最好先問他這東西要花你多少錢。

 beforehand

❶ in ancient times　在古代

In ancient times, people produced their weapons by stone.　　　在古代，人們利用石頭製造武器。

 in olden times/days

 in modern times　在現代

Unit 10

㉑ in and out　進進出出

I don't understand why he has been in and out all day long.

我不明白他為什麼一整天進進出出的。

㉒ in appearance　在外表上

The twin sisters are alike in appearance, but very different in their personality.

這對孿生姊妹外表相像，但個性很不同。

 by/to all appearances　根據觀察推斷

㉓ in comparison with/to　與…比較

In comparison to other recent TV programs, this one is really popular.

與最近其他的電視節目相比較，這節目真的很受歡迎。

 compared to

㉔ in conflict with　與…衝突

His opinion about how to address this singing contest is in conflict with mine.

對於如何著手進行這次的歌唱比賽，他的意見與我相左。

㉕ in connection with　與…有關聯

Let me ask you some questions in connection with the book.

讓我來問你一些與這本書有關的問題。

㉖ in contrast to/with　對照；對比

In contrast with your achievement, mine is nothing at all.

與你的成就相比，我的一點也不算什麼。

He looked quite happy in contrast to those around him.

和他周圍的人相比，他看起來十分快活。

 in contrast with = by contrast with

 in contrast to + sb; in contrast with + sth

㉗ in control　控制

Anti-government forces are still not in control in this area.

此區尚未被反政府勢力控制。

 in command、in charge

 in charge 是「不只是接管控制，還要為其負責」的情形。

   1. under control　（危險之後）得到控制
Don't worry. All is *under control* now.
別擔心，一切都在掌控之中。

2. in/under the control of　在…的控制中

3. out of control　失控

❷⑧ in danger　在危險中

The captured soldiers believe that their lives are in danger.　被俘虜的軍人相信他們的生命危在旦夕。

❷⑨ in defeat　敗北；挫折

He lowered his head in defeat.　他挫敗的低下頭。

I. 片語選填

in advance	in a word	in comparison with	hear of
here and there	in danger	hold one's horses	in conflict with
in action	in a good humor		

1. I said I had never _____ such a rule at a theater before. (90)

2. There are always many tourists _____ in the Disneyland. (90)

3. _____! Don't rush too quickly into a decision. (88)

4. _____, we should take pains before success. (89)

5. The best time to see kangaroos _____ is the evening and early morning.

6. One can possibly know _____ when an earthquake will strike. (90, 89j)

7. _____ her twin sister, Sue is much more optimistic. (87)

8. Architecture and society are _____ each other. (87)

9. Bats are _____ because of certain chemicals used by farmers to fight destructive insects. (85)

10. Mary is _____, because today is her birthday. (86)

II. 引導翻譯

11. Carnegie 聽說，有位名叫 William Hunter 的年輕人，為了救兩位溺水的男孩而喪生。
Carnegie _____ _____ a young man by the name of William Hunter who lost his life trying to save two other boys from drowning.

12. 在你出國讀書之後，誰會幫助我做功課? (87)

Who will _____ _____ _____ my homework after you go abroad for studies?

13. 別掛斷，我去拿筆。(90)

_____ _____ a minute—I'll just get a pen.

14. 另外一項許多人會容忍寵物的惡習，就是容許牠們咬住衣物不放。(88)

Another bad habit that many people tolerate their pets is allowing them to bite and _____ _____ clothing.

15. 她沒有站穩立場，而且還提出一項新的反對意見。(88)

She didn't _____ _____ _____ and put forward a new objection.

16. 為何一個心理非常堅強又樂觀的人，能比非常緊張的人忍受更多的壓力? (86)

Why can someone who is mentally very strong and optimistic _____ _____ _____ more pressure than a person who is very nervous?

17. 為什麼你總是有相同的藉口? (84)

_____ _____ you always have the same excuse?

18. 你們究竟是如何到達那麼遠的地方? (86)

_____ _____ _____ did you get so far?

19. 只要等一下，我馬上就好。(86)

Just wait a moment. I'll be ready _____ _____ _____.

20. 1920 年代，發明了機器馬鈴薯剝皮器，很快的使得洋芋片產量大增。(90)

In the 1920s a mechanical potato peeler was invented and soon there were potato chips _____ _____.

21. 依照他們的決定，我們取消畢業典禮。(88)

_____ _____ _____ their decision, we cancelled the graduation ceremony.

22. 很明顯的，掉眼淚除了有情緒上的好處之外，也有特殊的生理功能。(89)

It is clear that, _____ _____ _____ the emotional benefits, the shedding of tears has a specific biological function as well.

23. 民俗醫藥早在科學醫學發展前就興盛了，而且在古代遠比醫生的醫藥更為成功。(92)

Folk medicine flourished long before the development of scientific medicine and was more successful _____ _____ _____ than doctor medicine.

24. 多年來，Martha 一直進出監獄。(90)

Martha has been _____ _____ _____ of prison for years.

25. 對這兩種植物特徵的研究顯示，他們只在外表上是一模一樣的。(90)

The study of the characteristics of these two plants shows that they are identical only _____ _____.

26. 他已做好一項有關行銷策略的好計劃。(87)

He has made a good plan _____ _____ _____ marketing strategies.

27. 相較於愛斯基摩人的居所，這個圓錐形帳篷並非密不通風。(91)

_____ _____ _____ the Eskimo's shelter, the tepee was far from airtight.

28. 將軍現在完全控制局勢。(88)

The general is _____ full _____ of the situation now.

29. 也許她得挫敗的回到她的家鄉。(90)

Perhaps she had to return to her hometown _____ _____.

❶ in detail 詳細地

He described the notice of the test in detail before we started out.

在我們開始考試前，他詳細地描述注意事項。

❷ in doubt 不確定（的狀態）

The result of the peace talks between South and North Korea is still in doubt.

南北韓之間和談的結果仍不確定。

 1. beyond doubt　毫無疑問

What is *beyond doubt* is that his effort should be praised.
毫無疑問的是他的努力應被讚美。

2. without (a) doubt　非常確定；毫無疑問

Mr. Lin is *without doubt* an outstanding young English teacher.
林先生毫無疑問的是一位傑出的年輕英文老師。

❸ in due time 適當的時候

Further details will be announced in due time.

進一步的詳情將在適當時機宣佈。

　in due course、at the proper time

❹ in earnest 認真地

Let's discuss the schedule for the next semester in earnest.

咱們認真地來討論下學期的計劃。

　earnestly、seriously

❺ in excess of 超出；多於

The truck traveled at a speed in excess of 180 kilometers per hour.

那輛卡車以每小時時速超過 180 公里的速度行駛。

　more than

❻ in exchange for 作為⋯的交換

I've offered to clean the kitchen in exchange for a week's free meals.

我提供清潔廚房的條件來交換免費用餐一星期。

　exchange for　換得⋯

She *exchanged* her coat *for* my skirt.　她拿外套和我交換裙子。

❼ in favor of **(A)** 贊成、支持；**(B)** 對⋯有利

A. More than 200 Congressmen are in favor of the ban of drunken driving.

兩百多位國會議員贊成禁止酒後駕駛。

B. The manager made a decision in favor of the customers.

經理做出對顧客有利的決定。

 1. in favor　在某一特定時期流行或受歡迎

The Carpenters were widely *in favor* in the 1970s.

木匠兄妹在一九七〇年代十分受到歡迎。

2. in one's favor　支持某人；對某人有利

The delay of the wedding feast might work *in our favor* because we can make better preparation.

婚宴延期對我們可能是個幫助，因為我們可以做更好的準備。

3. out of favor

= out of date　過時的

What? You're still listening to Air Supply? Aren't they *out of favor*?

什麼？你還在聽「空中補給」的音樂？他們不是過時了嗎？

❽ in jail　坐牢

Susan's husband has been in jail for five years already.

Susan 的先生已經坐牢五年。

　in prison

❾ in love　戀愛；愛上

Teresa is madly in love with Andy.

Teresa 瘋狂地愛上 Andy。

 fall in love with sb　愛上某人

They *fell in love with* each other at first sight.

他們彼此一見鍾情。

❿ in modern times　現代

They are the youngest scientists in modern times to win the Nobel Prize.

他們是當代獲得諾貝爾獎最年輕的科學家。

⓫ in need　在貧困中

The local government should care for those in need.

地方政府應該照顧窮苦的人。

⓬ in need of　需要

Eddie is homeless and in desperate need of help.

Eddie 無家可歸且急須幫助。

⓮ in no doubt 毫無疑問

Sally was in no doubt one of the richest women in town a decade ago.

Sally 十年前無疑是鎮上最有錢的女人之一。

 同義 without (a) doubt、undoubtedly

⓯ in number 在數量上

The condors have rapidly decreased to less than one hundred in number.

禿鷹在數量上已快速減少到少於 100 隻。

⓰ in one's care 受某人的照顧

Mrs. Lin left her children in the babysitter's care when she's out of town.

林太太出城時將小孩交給保母照顧。

⓱ in one's honor 對…表示敬意

We held a farewell party in Principal Lee's honor.

我們為李校長舉辦一個惜別宴會，向他致敬。

 同義 in honor of sb

⓲ in one's/a tone 以…的語調

You'd better call her back, since there was urgency in her tone.

你最好回電給她，因為她的聲音有點緊急。

⓳ in orbit 在軌道中

The telecommunications satellite will go in orbit at the end of this year.

通信衛星將在今年底升上軌道中。

⓴ in other words 換言之

He is a man of his word. In other words, you can trust him.

他是個言而有信的人。換言之，你可以信任他。

 同義 that is (to say)、to put it differently、namely

㉑ in place 就定位

The chairs for the ceremony were all in place.

典禮所需的椅子全都就定位。

All the actors have to be in place ten minutes before the performance begins.

所有演員必須在演出前十分鐘就定位。

 1. in place of sb/sth

    = take sb's/sth's place

    = take the place of sb/sth   代替；取代某人／某事

    Brian entered the game *in place of* the injured player.

    Brian 代替受傷的球員參加比賽。

2. in one's place   站在某人的立場

    What would you do *in my place* if you happened to meet a foreigner?

    如果你是我，碰見一個外國人，會怎麼做？

❷❶ **in possession of**   擁有

She was found in possession of the stolen jewelry.   她被發現擁有失竊的珠寶。

 1. sth in sb's possession   某物在某人的手上

    Since my wallet was found *in your possession*, I'm afraid you'll be assumed for having stolen it.

    既然在你身上發現我的皮夾，恐怕你會因此吃上官司。

2. take possession (of)   開始擁有某件東西

    I *took possession of* this CD player since I graduated from senior high school.

    這台 CD 收錄音機是我從高中剛畢業時就擁有的。

❷❷ **in praise of**   讚美

The poet wrote a poem in praise of his lovely lover.   詩人寫了首詩讚美他可愛的情人。

❷❸ **in prison**   坐牢

Cathy visits her husband in prison every week.   Cathy 每週去探望坐牢的丈夫。

   in jail

❷❹ **in progress**   進行中的；進展中的

The building of the new bridge is in progress.   新橋的建設工程正在進行。

❷❺ **in proportion to**   與…成比例

The employees receive their bonuses in proportion to the company's overall performance.   員工所得到的紅利與公司整體表現成比例。

❷❻ **in question**   **(A)** 討論中的；**(B)** 受質疑的

A. The novel in question is my favorite one: *Hard Times* by Charles Dickens.   正在討論的小說，Charles Dickens 的「艱苦時代」，是我最喜歡的。

B. I'm afraid that his honesty is now in question.   恐怕他的誠信現在遭到質疑了。

Unit 11

 1. out of the question

= impossible　不可能

You can't leave without permission—it's *out of the question*.

沒有許可你不能離開一那是不可以的。

2. beyond question　不容置疑

With so much evidence, your committing the crime is *beyond question*.

鐵證如山，你犯罪的事實不容置疑。

❷ **in return for**　作為…的回報；作為…的交換

I treated him to dinner in return for his help.

我請他吃晚餐以回報他的幫忙。

❷ **in the dark**　**(A)** 全然不知；**(B)** 在黑暗中

A. He was kept in the dark about the project.

他對於這個計劃完全不知情。

B. The little girl crouched in the dark crying, for she got lost.

那個小女孩因為迷路而蹲在黑暗中哭泣。

〔同義〕　在黑暗中：in the darkness

❷ **in the extreme**　非常地

This experiment seems interesting in the extreme.

這項實驗似乎非常地有趣。

❸ **in the hope that/of**　希望

He left for the Orchid Island in the hope that he could live a simple life.

他前往蘭嶼，希望能過簡樸的生活。

Mary works very hard in the hope of becoming a millionaire.

Mary 非常努力的工作，希望能成為百萬富翁。

〔同義〕　hoping that

〔用法〕　in the hope that + cl；in the hope of + N/V-ing

 Unit 11 Exercise

 I.片語選填

in return for	in other words	in exchange for	in due time
in possession of	in earnest	in need of	in the extreme
in proportion to	in love		

1. You can put forward your proposal _____. (84)

2. He told me _____ that he would do everything to help me. (85)

3. He gave the police a new evidence _____ his temporary freedom. (89)

4. Victoria and Albert were deeply _____ , and their marriage was extremely happy. (91)

5. After successive working, I am _____ a vacation. (90)

6. Health is above wealth; _____, the former is more important than the latter. (88)

7. He was found _____ illegal weapons. (87)

8. It is a well-known fact that one's success is _____ one's hard work.

9. He agreed to give evidence against the enemies _____ a guarantee for protection. (90)

10. The millionaire has been generous _____. (92)

II. 引導翻譯

11. 大門上畫的這些是兇猛的守護神靈，畫得非常仔細，生動而寫實。(84)

Those painted on the big doors are the fierce guardian spirits _____ bright and realistic _____ .

12. 今年的利潤會超出百分之二十。(88)

This year's profits will be _____ _____ _____ twenty percent.

13. 接著 Soapy 被帶到夜間法庭，而法官判他入獄服刑三個月。(91)

Soapy was then taken to the night court, where the judge sentenced him to three months _____ _____ .

14. 在現代，我們也必須負起責任以避免傳播疾病。(88)

_____ _____ _____ , we also need to take responsibility to avoid spreading illness.

15. 有時候這些神話英雄很窮或受傷。(83)

Sometimes these mythical heroes are _____ _____ or are hurt.

16. 由於許多大型動物，像是獅子、老虎、大象等，在數量上正在快速地減少，他們不能再被人們隨心所欲地獵殺。(84)

Because many big animals like lions, tigers and elephants are decreasing _____ _____ rapidly, they can no longer be hunted at will.

17. Neumann 被要求每天要花三小時在她所照顧的每個學生身上。(90)

Neumann is required to spend three hours per day with each student _____ _____ _____ .

18. 我最初的提議被委婉地拒絕。但當我以真誠的語調再試一次時，就被高興地接受了。

My initial offer was turned down politely, but when I tried again _____ my most sincere _____ , it was gladly accepted.

Unit 11

19. 數以百計的新安全措施已經準備好投入使用，使美國人更安全或至少感覺較安全。

Hundreds of new security measures have been put _____ _____ to make Americans safer, or at least feel safer.

20. 他們唱了一首歌讚美萬能的上帝。(90)

They sang a song _____ _____ _____ the Mighty God.

21. 一般認為 Valentine 在坐牢時，愛上一位年輕女孩。(90)

It is believed that Valentine fell in love with a young girl while _____ _____.

22. 上課時請勿接電話。(85)

Please do not answer the phone while a lesson is _____ _____.

23. 所討論的那所大學是我國最好的大學之一。你可以申請入學。(87)

The college _____ _____ is one of the best in our country. You may apply to it for admission.

24. 他們打開包裹，以期裡面有東西能顯示此包裹從何而來，或將寄往何處。(89)

They opened the package in _____ _____ that something inside would show where the package came from or was going to.

25. 因很多學生對演講一事完全不知情，所以參與人數比預期的少。(92)

Because many students were kept _____ _____ _____ about the lecture, the attendance was much smaller than expected.

III. 克漏字選擇

Secret to Success

Recently, the president of a major company gave a speech at a dinner held __26__. He said that he is often asked about the secret to his business success. Many people seem to think that there is some magic formula for success but they are __27__ about it. This CEO responds that there are some basic rules of thumb. For example, the success you experience is __28__ the effort you make. __29__, even if it does not seem likely at the moment, __30__ there will always be a reward __31__ your hard work. But beyond those simple rules, he explained, success really comes from making right decisions. To make right decisions, you are __32__ experience. And where does experience come from? It comes from making wrong decisions.

(　) 26. (A) in his honor   (B) in no doubt   (C) in his care   (D) in detail

(　) 27. (A) in number   (B) in jail   (C) in earnest   (D) in the dark

(　) 28. (A) in excess of   (B) in possession of   (C) in proportion to   (D) in addition to

(　) 29. (A) In no way   (B) In other words   (C) In reply   (D) In contrast

(　) 30. (A) in due time   (B) in his favor   (C) in modern times   (D) in the extreme

(　) 31. (A) instead of   (B) in exchange for   (C) in favor of   (D) in return for

(　) 32. (A) in need of   (B) in place of   (C) in praise of   (D) in terms of

❶ in (the) light of　按照，依據

She views life in (the) light of money.　　　　　　她以錢的觀點來看人生。

 在the light of 屬於英式用法，美語中直接說 in light of

❷ in the majority　多數

In Taiwan, Buddhists are in the majority.　　　　在台灣，佛教徒佔大多數。

❸ in the meantime　同時

You go check the stove; in the meantime, I'll go to the supermarket to buy some vegetables.　　你去檢查爐火，同時，我要到超市去買些蔬菜。

 meanwhile、at the same time

❹ in the name of　以…的名義

Those cruel experiments on animals were carried out in the name of science.　　那些殘酷的動物實驗都藉科學之名進行。

 in name only　徒具虛名

His declaration of being an alumnus of this famous university is merely *in name only*, because he flunked out in the second semester, not graduating from it.
他說他是這所知名大學的校友，根本只是徒具虛名罷了。他第二個學期就被退學，並沒有真正念到畢業。

❺ in the past　從前

The zoo was a forest in the past.　　　　　　　　這座動物園以前是森林。

 before

 all in the past　一切都過去了

Don't mention the failure again. It's all *in the past* now.
別再提起失敗的事了！現在一切都過去了。

❻ in the process of　在…的過程中

The factory is in the process of producing new products.　　工廠正在進行生產新產品的程序中。

 in the process　過程中同時有兩件事情，第二件事情的發生是做第一件事所造成的後果

The waiter spilt the hot tea, burning himself *in the process*.
服務生潑出熱茶，在過程中還燙到了自己。

❼ in the truest sense of the word　就此字的最真實的意義而言

He described the constancy in friendship in the truest sense of the word.

他以此字的最真實的意義描寫出友誼的持久。

 in every sense of the word
= in every way　每一方面
Paul is a tough guy *in every sense of the word*.
Paul 在每一方面都是個狠角色。

❽ in the vicinity of　**(A)** 在⋯附近；**(B)** 大約⋯左右

A. The stolen car was found in the vicinity of the shopping mall.

失竊汽車在大賣場附近被找到。

B. All vases are of the same age, in the vicinity of 470 years old.

所有花瓶都是同年代的，大約470年之久。

❾ in those days　那些日子裡

Life was simple in those days.

那個時候的生活相當純樸。

　at that time

❿ in trouble　有麻煩

I'll be in big trouble if Mom sees my transcript.

如果媽媽看到我的成績單，麻煩可就大了。

⓫ intend to　意圖；計劃要⋯

I intend to go home next week.

我計劃下星期回家。

　intend to + V；若表達「計畫讓某人做某事」，句型為 intend sb to do sth

be intended for　為了⋯設計
The magazine *is intended for* young women aged 20-35.
這本雜誌是為 20 歲到 35 歲年輕女性設計的。

⓬ intermix with　互相融合；互相混合

Pour 50 grams of fresh milk and intermix with 100 grams of sugar.

倒 50 公克的鮮奶，並與 100 公克的糖混合。

⓭ invest in　投資

Peter made a fortune by investing in coffee chain stores.

Peter 藉投資咖啡連鎖店賺了一筆。

He's going to get married. I think it's time for him to invest in a house.

他要結婚了。我想他也該投資買棟房子了。

invest in 在口語中也可以當作「買」的意思，不過是指「購買你所需要，而且會用得很久的東西」。

 1. invest with　給予某人或組織權力、影響力或獎賞（常用被動）

He is *invested with* a decoration by the Royalty.

皇室授與他一枚勳章。

2. invest sb/sth with sth　使某人或某物擁有一些特徵

The hard times in his childhood *invested him with* being strong and cold.

童年時代的艱苦生活，使他堅強而冷酷。

❹ **It seems**　似乎

It seems to become colder today.　　　　　　　　　今天似乎變得比較冷。

It seems that Jack will miss you soon.　　　　　　Jack 似乎很快就會思念你。

 It seems to + V；It seems that + cl

 1. It seems to sb that...　對某人而言似乎…；某人覺得…

It seems to him that this movie is quite boring.

這部電影對他來說，好像頗為無趣。

2. It seems like + cl...　看起來好像

It seems like the concert is over.

這場音樂會似乎已經結束了。

3. It seems + as if/as though + 假設語氣條件句　看起來似乎（但是與事實相反）

It seems as if/as though he understood the whole event.

看起來他好像對整件事瞭若指掌。（事實是他什麼都不知道）

→第二點與第三點最大的不同，在於 it seems like 是一種對事實的推測，用直說法即可；但 it seems as if/as though 卻是說話者故意說反話，後面接的子句是與事實相反的，因此需要用假設語氣條件句。

❺ **join in**　加入；參加

We laughed loudly, and then the teacher joined in.　　我們笑得很大聲，接著老師也一起笑。

 participate in、take part in

He refused to *take part in* any activity we held.

他拒絕參加任何我們辦的活動。

It was very wise of you not to *participate in* the party.

你沒有參加宴會，真是明智。

 join up　入伍；與某人見面或工作；合作完成一件工作

Every man above the age of 18 in Taiwan needs to *join up* for two years.

台灣滿十八歲的男子都必須入伍服役兩年。

Sally is going to *join up* Ray on the way to Europe.

Sally 在去歐洲的路上將與 Ray 碰頭。

Sam *joined up* this research with us, and he really did a good job.

Sam 與我們合力完成這個研究，而且他的表現真的很好。

❶⑥ **just as** 正如

I love my family just as you do.　　　　　　　　　　　我愛我的家人，正如你一樣。

❶⑦ **keep...from...** **(A)** 保護…使免於；**(B)** 對…隱瞞；**(C)** 抑制

A. Put the pizza in the middle of the oven to keep it from burning.

把披薩放在烤箱的中層，免得它烤焦。

B. Keep the bad news from grandmother temporarily.

暫時對祖母隱瞞這個壞消息。

C. Please keep from telling our secret to anyone else.

我們的秘密你一定要守口如瓶。

 keep + N + from + N/V-ing

 1. keep away from　遠離

Parents often warn their children to *keep away from* strangers.

父母親常警告子女要遠離陌生人。

2. keep back　另有隱情

Although he said he liked this job, I could feel that he *kept* something *back*.

雖然他嘴上說喜歡這份工作，我可以感覺出來他並未說出實情。

❶⑧ **keep off** 使遠離

They use a special device to keep the flies off the food.

他們使用一種特殊的裝置將蒼蠅趕離食物。

 1. keep out　使某人或某物不要進入一個地方

The motorcycles and scooters are *kept out* of freeways.

機車不能進入高速公路。

2. keep out of　不與某事扯上關係

If you had not fooled around with them, you might have been *kept out of* this murder case!

你若沒和他們混在一塊，或許就不會與這件謀殺案扯上關係了！

❶⑨ **keep one's temper** 忍住脾氣

I find it difficult to keep my temper when I see my girlfriend with other men.

當我看到女友與其他男人在一起時，我很難不發脾氣。

用法 若「控制不向某人發脾氣」，則 keep one's temper with sb

Even though David is a naughty boy, you still need to *keep your temper with* him.

就算 David 是個淘氣鬼，你對他也得忍忍性子。

 觸類旁通 lose one's temper (with sb)　發脾氣

I promise you, my boy, that if you keep watching TV like that instead of going inside studying, I will certainly *lose my temper*.

我可以向你保證，兒子，要是你還繼續看電視，而不進去唸書，我一定會罵人。

❷⓿ keep out　使不進入

In front of the gate there is a sign saying, "Danger: Keep out."

大門前有個標語寫著：「危險！勿入。」

❷① keep pace with　跟上；跟…並駕齊驅

To "keep pace with times", my grandmother is learning how to use the computer.

為了「跟上時代」，我祖母跑去學用電腦。

 同義　keep up with

❷② keep sb waiting　讓某人等候

Ted kept his girlfriend waiting downstairs for thirty minutes.

Ted 讓他的女友在樓下等了 30 分鐘。

❷③ keep track (of)　了解…的動態；掌握…的線索

It's very difficult to keep track of all the new development in biotech.

要掌握所有生物科技上的新發展是非常困難的。

 觸類旁通 lose track (of)　失去…的掌控

I just *lose* all *track of* time whenever I surf the Internet.

我一上網就忘了時間。

❷④ keep up with　並駕齊驅

I have to walk very fast to keep up with you.

我必須走很快才能趕上你。

 同義　keep pace with

 觸類旁通 keep up with the Joneses　與鄰居比闊氣

Alice always *keeps up with the Joneses*; upon seeing her neighbor buying a new TV, she bought one too.

Alice 喜歡與鄰居比闊氣；她一看到鄰居買新電視，她也買了一台。

㉕ kill time 打發時間；消磨時間

I often kill time by going to the movies.

我常藉著看電影消磨時間。

 kill two birds with one stone 一石二鳥

㉖ kind of 稍微；有一點

He's kind of silly, isn't he?

他有點蠢，不是嗎？

 sort of、somewhat

 前兩個片語都是口語用法，kind of 還可以寫成 kinda，但千萬不要與 a kind of 與 a sort of 這兩個正式片語用法搞混，意義完全不一樣。

㉗ knock down **(A)** 撞倒；**(B)** 拆毀；**(C)** 降價

A. His father was in hospital after being knocked down by a car.

他父親被車子撞倒後就在醫院裡。

B. They want to knock the house down and rebuild it.

他們想拆掉屋子重建。

C. The new laptop I bought was knocked down from NT$50,000 to NT$30,000.

我剛買的新筆記型電腦的價格從五萬元台幣降到三萬元了。

 撞倒：knock over

 knock down 做「撞倒」解時，是指「由車輛撞倒」的「撞倒」。

 knock over 撞倒；強盜搶劫

Two young men *knocked over* the bank and killed a guard.

兩個年輕人搶劫銀行，還殺了一個警衛。

㉘ knock out **(A)** 使突然失去效能；**(B)** 擊昏；**(C)** 淘汰出局

A. The air raids were planned to knock out communications on the ground.

空襲是計劃使地面通訊失去功能。

B. The doctor gave him some medicine which totally knocked him out.

醫生給了他一些讓他完全昏死的藥。

C. Our school team was knocked out in the first round.

我們校隊在第一循環賽中就遭淘汰。

㉙ know of 聽說過；知道有

I know nothing of the business.

我對這種生意一無所知。

Unit 12 Exercise

I. 片語選填

join in	knock out	keep pace with	keep one's temper
in the past	intend to	kill time	in the light of

1. _____ the recent situation, the meeting had better be postponed. (91j)

2. It was an important clue to life _____. (90)

3. And iRobot _____ start selling a home-security robot next year for about the cost of a Notebook. (90)

4. She started to dance and we all _____. (86)

5. I found it hard to _____ when he insulted me. (85)

6. Some people think that reading stories is a way to _____ when the real world needs tending to. (87)

7. The new computer virus can _____ your entire system.

8. When they go for a walk, Johnny has to take long steps to _____ his father. (91)

II. 引導翻譯

9. 百分之十四的受訪者說他們通常求助書本而不是上網找資料。(92)

   14 percent of the respondents said they often turned to books for information _____ _____ going online.

10. 擁有 14 天免簽證入境的某些特定國家之國民，應同時申請落地簽證。(85)

    Nationals of the specific countries holding 14-day non-visas entry should apply for a landing-visa in _____ _____.

11. 每年二月，全國的情人都以 St. Valentine 之名互送糖果、花及禮物。(90)

    Every February, across the country, candy, flowers, and gifts are exchanged between loved ones, all _____ _____ _____ _____ St. Valentine.

12. 它可能發源於中國的鄰近地區。(92)

    It probably originated _____ _____ _____ of China.

13. 當時的人在下大雨時，常會想到瀑布。(85)

    People _____ _____ _____ often thought of waterfalls when it rained heavily.

14. Kevin 有麻煩了，因為他今天下午打破客廳的窗戶。(88)

    Kevin is _____ _____ , because he broke the living room window this afternoon.

15. 我國藉著大量投資於電子工業，而躍升為高科技之國。(87)

Our country had become hi-tech by _____ heavily _____ electronic industry.

16. 我和 Jack 一起幫助你學習 ABC，似乎只是昨天的事。(85)

_____ _____ only yesterday that Jack and I were helping you learn your ABC's.

17. 他掙得的錢正和我一樣多。(87)

He makes much money _____ _____ I do.

18. 這些建築上的細節都是「安全措施」，正如一間銀行有的阻止竊賊闖入的那些措施一樣。(84)

These architectural details are "security measures" just like those a bank had to _____ thieves _____ breaking in.

19. 有屋頂的門廊使人們免於日曬雨淋。(83)

The porch _____ the rain and the sun _____ people.

20. 不過那些鐵欄杆顯然就是為了不讓竊賊闖入而做的。(84)

But the iron bars are apparently there for _____ burglars _____.

21. 對不起讓你等我。(85)

Sorry to have _____ you _____.

22. Lucy 與其他同學並駕齊驅有困難。(92)

Lucy's having difficulty _____ _____ with the rest of the class.

23. 當時的醫生們並沒有像現代的我們一樣做紀錄來追蹤病情，雖然他們知道很多人住在一起時，常將疾病互相傳染。(88)

Doctors didn't have the record keeping that we have in modern times to _____ _____ _____ illnesses, although they knew that many people living close together often gave their diseases to others.

24. Judy 昨天被一輛卡車撞倒。(89)

Judy was _____ _____ by a truck yesterday.

25. 然而，我不曾聽說過，有任何父母會因為小孩子說那是他們喜歡吃的東西，就只餵子女加糖的麥片粥和泡泡糖。(87)

However, I don't (k)_____ _____ any parents who feed their children only sugared cereals and bubble gum because that is what the children say they like to eat.

❶ last for 持續

The hot weather lasted for the whole month of July. 　　炎熱的天氣持續了整個七月。

 last out　維持一段時間（沒有被動語態）

Do you have enough coal to *last out* this winter?

你的煤炭足夠你過冬嗎？

❷ lay out **(A)** 設計；**(B)** 展開；**(C)** 打昏；**(D)** 將某事解釋清楚

A. The garden was laid out both as an open concert stage and a place for parties.　　這座花園設計為戶外音樂舞台及宴客的所在。

B. Lay out the table cloth and put all the food on it.　　攤開桌布，將所有食物放在上面。

C. After the guard was laid out, the thief entered the office with ease.　　警衛被擊昏後，小偷輕易地進入辦公室。

D. Dr. Jones laid out the Law of Gravity to us.　　Jones 博士將地心引力完整清楚的解釋給我們聽。

 設計：arrange、design

擊昏：knock out、knock over

 lay off　裁員

This company *laid off* many employees in order to maintain its financial balance.

這家公司解雇許多員工以維持財務平衡。

❸ lead a...life 過…的生活

If the operation is successful, you will be able to lead a normal life.　　如果手術成功，你將可以過正常的生活。

❹ leave/create/make an impression on sb 給某人留下印象

His distinguished performance has created a deep impression on the audience.　　他傑出的表現，已經令觀眾留下深刻的印象。

When it comes to job interviews, making a good first impression on the interviewer is very important.　　提到工作面試，給主試者良好的第一印象是很重要的。

❺ **less than** (A) 少於、不到；(B) 並不很

A. A distance of less than one kilometer can be accepted. 　少於一公里的距離是可以接受的。

B. Her new plan was less than entirely discussed. 　她的計劃並未受到充分的討論。

 in less than no time 　非常迅速

❻ **let go of** 鬆開

The master let go of the leash, and the hound lunged forward. 　主人鬆開狗鏈，獵犬就往前猛撲。

❼ **let in** 允許進入；容許

The device is set up to let in fresh air and let out waste. 　這種裝置的設計，會讓新鮮空氣進入，並排出廢氣。

 let sb in on sth 　讓某人知道某事（秘密）
Would you mind *letting me in on* your secret?
你介意讓我知道你的秘密嗎？

❽ **live a...life** 過…的生活

He's healthy enough to live a normal life after the operation. 　手術之後他很健康，可以過正常的生活了。

 live a + adj + life

❾ **look at** (A) 看待某事；(B) 檢查、檢視；(C) 凝視

A. I hope we can still be friends, but Simon doesn't look at it that way. 　我希望我們還是朋友，但 Simon 不這麼想。

B. We need to look very carefully at the ways of improving the working environment. 　我們必須非常仔細地檢視改善工作環境的方法。

C. The couple looked at each other and smiled. 　那對夫妻彼此凝望然後微笑。

凝視：have a look at、take a look at

❿ **look back (on)** (A) 回顧、回憶起；(B) 回頭看

A. As I looked back on the past, I felt ashamed of what I had done to him. 　當我回顧過去時，我對以前對他的作為感到很羞愧。

B. Later, she looked back in the direction of the sea. 　後來，她回頭往海的方向看。

❶❶ look down upon/on **(A)** 輕視、看不起；**(B)** 俯視

    A. I look down on anyone who always blames other people.

我看不起任何老是責怪別人的人。

    B. The balcony looks down upon the sea.

陽台俯視著海面。

 輕視：despise

 look up to
    = respect
    = admire   尊敬；欽佩
    People always *look up to* heroes for their courage.
    人們一向欽佩英雄的勇氣。

❶❷ look forward to 期望；等待

    I'm really looking forward to your visiting in the summertime.

我真的很期盼你夏天來拜訪。

 look forward to + N/V-ing

辨析 這裡指「愉快興奮的等待某事發生」。

❶❸ look into 調查；研究

    The police are still looking into the brutal murder.

警方仍在調查這宗殘忍的謀殺案。

同義 investigate

辨析 這裡的「調查研究」是「研究某個問題」或「調查某項刑案」。

❶❹ look over **(A)** 瀏覽；**(B)** 從⋯的上面看過去；**(C)** 視察

    A. Please look over all these materials before the lecture takes place.

演講舉行之前，請先看一看這些資料。

    B. This table is low enough for the little girl to look over it by standing on tiptoe.

對小女孩來說這桌子夠低，她踮起腳，就能從桌上望出去。

    C. The president looked each department over.

總裁視察過每個部門。

❶❺ lose one's temper 發脾氣

    I lost my temper when I heard the news.

當我聽到這消息時，我發了脾氣。

❶❻ make a fool of oneself 使自己成為傻瓜

    He's made a fool of himself by getting drunk on the wedding feast.

他在婚宴上喝醉酒，使自己成為笑柄。

觸類旁通 make a fool of sb 愚弄某人；欺騙某人

The aerobics teacher *made a fool of* the old lady. Shame on him!

那個有氧健身教練愚弄那位老婦人，真是可恥！

⓱ make a profit 獲利

Both companies made a huge profit on the deal.

雙方公司在此交易上獲得龐大利益。

⓲ make/deliver/give a speech 發表演說

Each student has to make a short speech to the rest of the class.

每個學生必須對著其他同學發表簡短演說。

⓳ make arrangements for 為…做安排

The Lin family are busy making arrangements for their grandfather's funeral.

林家人正忙著為老爺爺的葬禮做安排。

⓴ make (both) ends meet 使收支平衡

When Father was out of employment, we could barely make both ends meet.

當爸爸失業時，我們幾乎無法收支平衡。

㉑ make friends with 與…交朋友

It's easy to make friends with someone who has similar interests as you.

跟與你有類似興趣的人交朋友很容易。

㉒ make fun of 嘲弄；取笑

My brother keeps making fun of me because I have a big pimple on my nose.

我哥一直取笑我，因為我鼻子上長了顆大痘痘。

同義 poke fun at

㉓ make into 使成為；製造成

The novel made her into a celebrity overnight.

那本小說使她一夜成名。

We can make the baby's room into your study.

我們可將嬰兒房變成你的書房。

用法 make sb/sth into sth

㉔ make it 趕上；成功

If you decide to go by bus, you won't make it in time.

若你決定搭公車，就別想準時趕到。

Unless you work hard, you won't make it.

除非你努力，否則你不會成功。

 辨析 「趕上」不是指「趕上別人」，而是指「及時完成」。

㉕ make/prove one's point　（在爭論中）證明自己意見正確；立論成立

I'd like to make my point before you make a decision.　在你決定前，我想把意見說清楚。

 make a point of doing sth　(A) 堅持做某事；(B) 強調、重視

I *make a point of* getting up at 7 o'clock.
我堅持七點鐘起床。
He *made a point of* my joining his group.
他很重視我加入他的團體一事。

㉖ make resolutions　下定決心

Most students often make great resolutions to study harder at the beginning of the semester.　多數的學生常在學期開始時下很大的決心要更加努力。

㉗ make room for　讓位給…；挪出空間給…

I'm trying to make room for a new set of computer in my study.　我正設法在書房裡挪出空間放一組新電腦。

㉘ make up for　彌補；補償

Tim is anxious to make up for what he has done to her.　Tim 急著要彌補他對她所做的事。

㉙ make up with/to sb　（爭吵後）和解

We should look for a way to make up with her for what we have done.　我們該為我們的所作所為，找個方式與她和解。

Unit 13 Exercise

I. 片語選填

let go of	look down upon	look over	make one's point
last for	make it up with	make room for	
make both ends meet	less than		

1. Alexander Dumas' novels have _____ less than 100 years. (90)

2. Potato chips have been popular in the U.S. for _____ 100 years. (90)

3. The child never _____ my hand until he fell asleep. (88)

4. I've _____ the report, but I haven't studied it in detail. (88)

5. For our family to _____, it is important to minimize living expenses.

6. You've _____; there's no need to go on about it. (88)

7. It's time you _____ your rival. (92)

8. Move along and _____ your brother. (88)

9. Don't _____ those who are inferior to you. (86)

10. 他們看見這房間時覺得有些驚恐，因為房間本是設計為錄音室。(89)

    When they saw the room, they were a bit alarmed, for it was _____ _____ as a studio originally.

11. 大仲馬沒有過著多采多姿的生活。(90)

    Dumas did not _____ a colorful _____ .

12. 這頂帳篷漏雨。我可以換一頂嗎？(88)

    This tent _____ _____ the rain. Can I have another one?

13. 讓我們面對事實：未來的人可能會回顧今日的醫學，正如我們回顧中古時代的醫學。

    Let's face it: people in the future will probably _____ _____ at medicine today as we _____ _____ at medieval medicine.

14. 我們期待見到你。(85)

    We are _____ _____ _____ seeing you.

15. 他們正在調查失業的原因。(85)

    They are (l)_____ _____ the cause of unemployment.

16. 起初他對鳥很溫柔，但漸漸地他會發脾氣。(87)

    At first he was very gentle with the bird, but gradually he _____ his _____ .

17. 但是那位在會議中當眾出糗的年輕人卻不在名單上。(86)

    But the young man who has _____ a fool _____ _____ at the meeting was not on the list.

18. 我對以獲利為主要目的的出版商深感困擾。(87)

    I am deeply troubled by publishers whose main goal is to _____ a _____ .

19. Robot Redford 在 1983 年發表畢業演說。(87)

    Robot Redford _____ a graduation _____ in 1983.

20. Soapy 知道他該為自己一年一度的冬季之旅做安排了。(91)

    Soapy realized it was time to _____ _____ for his annual winter trip.

21. 為了與挪威人交朋友，哪種禮物最能表現你的誠意？(86)

    To _____ _____ _____ Norwegians, what kind of gift can best show your sincerity?

22. 人們嘲笑他，因為他戴那麼奇怪的眼鏡。(86)

    People _____ _____ _____ him because he wears such strange glasses.

23. 岩石被製成建材。(92)

    The rocks were _____ _____ the building material.

24. 很高興你趕得及參加這個派對。(87)

    Glad you could _____ _____ to the party.

25. 有些人總是下了大決心，但從不實現。(90)

    Some are always _____ good (r)_____ but never carry them out.

26. 舉行這個夏日課程的主要理由是彌補在正規教育中錯失的東西。(87)

The main reason for holding the summer school was to _____ _____ for things missing in a regular classroom.

III. 克漏字選擇

About Vincent Van Gogh

Vincent Willem van Gogh (1853-1890) is one of the greatest Dutch painters. He __27__, but found some joy in painting people and landscapes. After having tried many jobs with little success, he decided to be an artist full-time. Vincent's brother Theo was his confidant and best friend. Encouraged by him, Vincent took art lessons. In 1886, he joined Theo in Paris. Vincent __28__ the impressionist painters, especially with Paul Gauguin. His first paintings were sad and dark. His style changed when he was in France and he began to use bright and light colors. In 1888, Vincent went to Provence, in Southern France. He tried to create a community of artists and asked Gauguin to be the head of this community. But following a violent dispute, Vincent __29__ and attacked Gauguin. This event __30__ of regret __30__ Vincent, who decided to cut his own ear and to paint the result: *Self-Portrait with Bandaged Ear* (1889). In June 1890, when he was in Auvers-sur-Oise, Van Gogh painted *The Portrait of Doctor Gachet*. Gachet was his personal doctor. Vincent talked about him in a letter to Theo: "__31__, he is sicker than I am, I think, or shall we say just as much". But Vincent was the one __32__ mental illness and shot himself in July 1890. He almost never __33__ as a painter and died unaware of the admiration later generations would have for his work: in 1990, a Japanese admirer bought *The Portrait of Doctor Gachet* for US$82.5 million.

(   ) 27. (A) lived a difficult life   (B) died a peaceful death
        (C) lead a simple life   (D) put to death in anger

(   ) 28. (A) shook hands with   (B) made a fool of
        (C) made friends with   (D) made fun of

(   ) 29. (A) kept his temper   (B) kept in mind   (C) got lost   (D) lost his temper

(   ) 30. (A) had an impact/on   (B) left an impression/on
        (C) put emphasis/on   (D) made an excuse/for

(   ) 31. (A) First of all   (B) From first to last
        (C) For the first time   (D) For the time being

(   ) 32. (A) escaping from   (B) escaped from   (C) suffering to   (D) suffering from

(   ) 33. (A) made a resolution   (B) made his room
        (C) made a profit   (D) made his point

❶ make use of　利用

You should make good use of this opportunity to learn more English.

你應該好好利用這次機會多學些英文。

 take advantage of、cash in on、capitalize on、avail oneself of、put...to use

The publisher *cashed in on* her fame to make a big fortune.

出版商利用她的名聲賺了一大筆財富。

Sherry *capitalized on* her youth and beauty to attract men.

Sherry 利用她的年輕貌美吸引男人。

We should *avail ourselves of* every possible opportunity to improve our skills.

我們應該利用每一個可能的機會改善自己的技巧。

The money you donate will be *put to* good *use*.

你捐贈的錢會被善加利用。

❷ manage to　設法做到

How do you manage to stay so slim?

你如何做到保持如此苗條的?

❸ merge into　合併成⋯

They tried to merge the three companies into one.

他們設法將現存的三家分店合併為一家。

❹ mind one's p's and q's　謹言慎行

The mother gave her son a frown and told him to mind his p's and q's.

那位母親皺著眉頭告訴兒子要注意言行。

 mind one's manners、mind one's language

❺ mind one's tongue　注意言辭

You've got to learn to mind your tongue in public places.

在公共場合你必須學習注意言辭。

 1. hold one's tongue　謹言

2. bite one's tongue　不說出來

❻ mistake A for B　錯認 A 為 B

I often mistake salt for sugar.

我常把鹽誤認為糖。

❼ more or less **(A)** 幾乎；**(B)** 多多少少、差不多

A. The job is more or less finished.

這工作幾乎完成了。

B. Most people are more or less egoistic.

大部分人多多少少都有點自私。

 幾乎：almost、nearly

 much/still/even less 更別說…（用在否定詞之後）

I don't really like his personality, *much less* fall in love with him.
我不太喜歡他的個性，更別說去愛上他了。

❽ more than once 不只一次

I gave him advice more than once, but he didn't listen to me.

我不只一次勸他，但是他不聽。

❾ most important of all 最重要的是

Most important of all, you need to know what your are doing.

最重要的是，你必須知道自己在做些什麼。

 above all、most importantly

❿ to one's surprise 令某人非常驚訝的是

To our surprise, he can express himself clearly in English.

他能用英文清楚表達，真令我們驚訝。

⓫ next to **(A)** 僅次於；**(B)** 在…的隔壁；**(C)** 幾乎

A. Next to table tennis, I like playing badminton best.

我喜歡打羽球僅次於桌球。

B. The Lins live next (door) to the graveyard.

林家就住在墳場的隔壁。

C. I know next to nothing about economy.

我對經濟幾乎一無所知。

It is next to impossible to be cured.

治癒幾乎是不可能的。

 當「幾乎」解時，只能用在否定詞的前面，表示「幾乎是如此了，只剩一點可能性或希望」的意思。如 next to nothing 表示「幾乎一無所知」。

⓬ no less...than... 與…一樣地

In your report, the second point is no less important than the first.

你的報告裡，第二個重點和第一個一樣重要。

⓭ no more than 僅僅；只不過

Don't be upset. It's no more than bad luck.

別喪氣，只不過是運氣不佳。

 nothing but、only

⓮ no way 表示斷然拒絕或強烈反對

There's no way I'll ever talk to him again.   我絕不再和他說話。

⓯ no/little/small wonder 難怪

The weather suddenly turned cold. No wonder a lot of people got sick.   天氣突然轉冷，難怪很多人都生病了。

⓰ none of your business 少管閒事

It's none of your business how much I weigh.   我體重多少不關你的事。

⓱ not altogether 不能完全

The results were not altogether surprising since he didn't really try very hard.   因為他其實沒有很努力的嘗試，所以結果不完全令人訝異。

同義   not completely

⓲ not...any longer 再也不

The extra forces won't be needed any longer.   不再需要額外的軍力。

同義   no longer、not...any more
It's *no longer* a problem.
它不再是個問題。

⓳ not...but rather... 不是…而是…

The problem is not your lack of education, but rather your lack of experience.   問題不是你缺乏學歷而是你缺乏經驗。

⓴ not to mention 更不用說

Pollution is harmful to the environment, not to mention our health.   污染對環境有害，更遑論我們的健康。

同義   to say nothing of、let alone
My little brother can't even walk, *let alone* run.
我小弟不會走路，更遑論跑步。

㉑ not...until... 直到…才…

He didn't eat lunch until he finished typing the document.   他把文件打好後，才去吃午餐。

用法   Not until 放在句首，該子句需形成倒裝句，請注意下面等號後的例句。
句型：Not until... + aux + S + V + ...; Not until... + be + S + ...
It was *not until* 1972 that the war finally came to an end.
= *Not until* 1972 did the war finally come to an end.
直到 1972 年戰爭才結束。

㉒ nothing but 只不過

We need nothing but a peaceful life.　我們需要的不過是平靜的生活。

 only、no more than、nothing more than

㉓ number in 總計；多達…之多

The population of koalas once numbered in one million here.　此地無尾熊的數量曾經高達一百萬隻。

 number in + 數量

 be numbered　有限；屈指可數

His sickness is getting worse and worse. His days *are numbered*.
病勢逐漸惡化，他的日子不多了。

㉔ on a charge of 被指控…的罪名

The following morning, he was arrested on a charge of murder.　第二天早上他以謀殺罪名遭到逮捕。

㉕ on account of 因為；由於

She was told to stay in bed for a few days, on account of her back injury.　因為背部受傷，所以她必須臥床數日。

 because of、owing to、due to、as a result of

㉖ on and on 不斷地；持續地

She talked on and on all night about her adventure in Africa.　她整晚不停地說著關於她在非洲的冒險。

 on and off
= off and on　斷斷續續

She's been in and out of the hospital *on and off* for three years.
過去三年她斷斷續續地進出醫院。

㉗ on board **(A)** 在飛機、船、火車上；**(B)** 參與計畫、為某公司工作

A. There are about 300 passengers on board the plane.　大約有三百名乘客在機上。

B. We welcome you to be on board this medical research.　我們歡迎你加入這項醫藥研究工作。

 1. take sth on board　理解、接受某事（點子、問題等）

The editors agreed to *take* your writing proposal *on board*.
編輯群們同意接受你的寫作計畫。

2. board (vi, vt)　登機、船、公車

　　Please *board* your plane through Gate 15.

　　請在十五號登機門登機。

3. boarding pass/card　登機證

❷❽ **on duty**　值班中

When on duty, he is always on the alert.　　　　　值班時，他總是保持戒備狀態。

觸類旁通　off duty　下班；不值勤

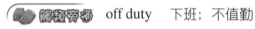

I. 片語選填

make good use of	on board	on a charge of	not to mention
next to	mind one's tongue	more or less	nothing but

1. Try to _____ your time during the summer vacation. (92)

2. Be polite and _____ while talking to your boss. (85)

3. Everyone has his own weaknesses, _____ . (85)

4. _____ knowledge, we must retain, and never lose, a taste of life. (87)

5. I'm much afraid of mice, _____ spiders and snakes.

6. The owner was demanding. He expected _____ perfection from his employees. (89)

7. At this moment, the policeman appeared again, arresting him _____ vandalism. (91)

8. In all three cases, the terrorists weren't _____ . (92)

II. 引導翻譯

9. 因此，眼淚在情緒上，以及生理上的功能合而為一，讓我們比不流淚時更加「人性化」。

　　And thus the emotional and the biological functions of tears _____ _____ one and make us even more "human" than we would otherwise be.

10. 別把知識錯認為智慧。(86)

　　Don't _____ knowledge _____ wisdom.

11. 那個學生說謊不只一次。(85)

　　The student has told lies _____ _____ _____ .

12. IMO 的第一個目標就是發掘、鼓勵，最重要的是，挑戰世界各地有數學天賦的年輕人。

　　The first aim of the IMO is to discover, to encourage, _____ _____ of _____ , to challenge mathematically gifted young people all over the world.

13. 令他非常驚訝的是，這名他試著用言語騷擾的婦女甚為感動；事實上，她還感謝他，因為他是第一個對她甜言蜜語的男人。(91)

The woman he tried to harass verbally was, _____ to _____ _____ overwhelmed and in fact thanked him for being the first man ever to say such sweet words to her.

14. 我幾乎不可能在三天之內完成家庭作業。(85)

It's _____ _____ impossible for me to finish the homework in three days.

15. 「注意言辭，他是公司的總裁。」「沒什麼大不了的!」(86)

"Mind your tongue; he's the company's president." "_____ _____ _____!"

16. 藝術、宗教、文學和哲學與科學一樣地重要。(87)

Art, religion, literature and philosophy are _____ _____ important _____ science.

17. 當我只是匆匆瀏覽了書本一眼就準備要說「這裡有一本好書」時，這似乎是錯的嗎？

Does it seem wrong that I am prepared to say, "Here is a good book," when I have done _____ _____ _____ glance at it?

18. 「我可以搬過去住幾天嗎？」「不行!」(89)

A: Can I move in with you for a few days? B: _____ _____!

19. 少管閒事，少說話! (89)

It's _____ _____ _____ _____. Hold your tongue!

20. 作者對於人們不再需要的物品的看法為何？(86)

What is the author's opinion of an item that someone _____ need _____ _____?

21. 它們出聲並非為了溝通，而是為了警告捕食者不得靠近。(90)

They produce the sound not for communication, _____ _____ for warning off predators.

22. 中國人於十一世紀發明了活字印刷，但是直到大約一四四〇年，歐洲才知道這種印刷術。(83)

The Chinese discovered the use of the movable type in the 11th century, but it was _____ known in Europe _____ about 1440.

23. 紅毛猩猩曾經多達好幾十萬隻，但由於火災，它們的總數已減至約略兩萬五千隻。(87)

Orangutans once _____ _____ hundreds of thousands, but their population has dropped to roughly 25,000 due to fire.

24. 培養兒童對讀物的愛好，最好的方法就是唸給他聽，從呱呱落地開始，持續地唸給他聽。(87)

The best way to cultivate children's tastes in reading is to read to them, starting at birth and keeping _____ _____ _____.

25. 耶誕節後幾天的一個早上 Dr. Schwarts 在醫院當班時，一名男子走進來只是抱怨臉上出現了一個小時的青印。(84)

Dr. Schwarts was _____ _____ at a hospital one morning a few days after Christmas when a man came in complaining only of blueness to his face of one hour's duration.

26. 在公共場合你最好注意自己的言行。(87)

You'd better mind your _____ _____ _____ in public places.

❶ on one's way to　某人去…的途中

I bumped into an old friend on my way to school.　　　　上學途中我遇到一位老朋友。

　all the way　完全地；盡全力；一路上；從遠處

His ambition is to destroy his opponents *all the way*.

他的野心是要把對手完全的摧毀。

The players have played *all the way* in this game.

球員們在這場比賽中都已竭盡全力。

He came *all the way* from New York.

他千里迢迢從紐約來。

❷ on the contrary　相反地

It's not a good essay; on the contrary, it has lots of
mistakes.

它不是一篇好論文；相反地，還有
多處錯誤。

　1. to the contrary　與之相反的

There was no evidence *to the contrary*.

沒有任何與之相反的證據。

2. contrary to　違反；相悖

The result was *contrary to* our expectation.

這個結果大出我們意料之外。

3. by contraries　完全相反地；與預期相反地

Dreams go *by contraries*.

夢境預言相反的事。

❸ on the move　**(A)** 遷移不定；**(B)** 不斷改進；**(C)** 不斷活動中

A. The migrating birds are on the move now.　　　　候鳥正在移動居所。

B. Theaters are on the move, adding performances that
entertain and educate people.

劇院不斷發展,增加許多寓教於樂
的演出。

C. Jerry is constantly on the move; in other words, he's
very busy and active.

Jerry 不停地有活動；換言之,他既
忙碌又活躍。

❹ on the outside　外面

To anyone on the outside, our performance is perfect.　　對任何門外漢而言,我們的演出很
完美。

Jimmy felt happy for your success on the outside, but actually he despised your achievement.

Jimmy 表面上為你的成功感到高興，但事實上他輕視你的成就。

The steak was awfully prepared. Look! It is black on the outside, but raw on the inside!

這牛排料理得真糟糕！看吧！表面焦黑，裡面竟然還是生的！

Being in prison for more than 10 years, he can no longer imagine how life is on the outside.

在監獄裡待了十年，他已經無法想像外面的生活會是什麼樣子了。

 辨 析　on the outside 的「外面」，有好幾種意思：
(1) 指「某種領域的門外漢或局外人」。
(2) 指「表面上如此，真實情況並非這樣」。
(3) 指「物體的表面」。
(4) 當某人在監獄或必須久待在一個地方，如醫院，時，外面的世界就是 on the outside。

❺ **on (the) set**　在拍片現場

Tom Cruise met Nicole Kidman on the set of *Days of Thunder*.

Tom Cruise 在 *Days of Thunder* 的片場與 Nicole Kidman 相遇。

❻ **on the spot**　(A) 當場；(B) 立即

A. He had to make a decision on the spot.

他必須要當場作決定。

B. The crazy drunken driver was arrested on the spot, because he hit a passer-by.

這個瘋狂的酒醉駕駛立刻被逮捕，因為他撞倒一個路人。

同 義　立即：immediately

❼ **on the verge of**　瀕臨；即將；接近於

Condors are on the verge of extinction.

禿鷹瀕臨絕種。

The variety show was on the verge of being cancelled due to low television rating.

由於收視率低，該綜藝節目即將取消了。

同 義　on the edge of
After repeated failures, he felt he was *on the edge of* madness.
重複的失敗之後，他覺得快要發瘋了。

❽ **on the whole**　大體上；整體來說

On the whole, I thought the leading actor did a good job.

大體上，我覺得男主角演得不錯。

同 義　in the main、in general、generally speaking、on average
His job *in the main* consists of filing away documents and delivering mail.
總的說來，他的工作包括歸檔和送郵件。

On average, women live longer than men.

大體上，女性比男性壽命長。

 as a whole　總體上（的）；總而言之

As a whole, they've done a good job.

總而言之，他們作得很好。

His idea of delaying this party didn't consider the guests *as a whole*.

他那個把派對延期的意見，整體而言，根本沒有考慮到所有的客人。

❾ (skate) on thin ice　做冒險的事

Doing something risky is just like skating on thin ice.

做危險的事就像在薄冰上溜冰。

❿ on time　準時

My father usually gets home on time to have dinner with us.

爸爸通常會準時回到家和我們吃晚餐。

 1. in time　及時；遲早

in time + to V/for N

I'm rather worried about whether we can arrive there *in time*.

我很擔心我們是否能及時到達。

Will you be *in time* for the plane?

你來得及趕上飛機嗎？

2. over time　漸漸

Don't worry about her injury. She'll recover *over time*.

別擔心她的傷勢，她會漸漸康復的。

3. out of time　沒時間

We need to hurry up, because we are almost *out of time*.

我們得快點，因為我們快沒有時間了。

⓫ once more　再一次

The teacher asked all the students to do the exercise once more before she dismissed the class.

老師在下課之前要求所有學生再做一次練習。

 once again

⓬ one at a time　每次一個

I'll answer your questions one at a time.

我會一次回答你們一個問題。

 two/three/four/... at a time　一次兩／三／四…個

❸ one day 有一天

One day she hopes to return to her hometown.

她希望有一天能回到家鄉。

One day she heard Beethoven's Symphony No. 9, and fell in love with classical music from then on.

有一天她聽到貝多芬的第九號交響曲，從那時起就愛上了古典音樂。

 用法 one day 可以指「未來的某一天」，也可以指「過去的某一天」。

❹ open up **(A)** 暢談、傾吐心事；**(B)** 開創機會；**(C)** 打開、開啟

A. This is the first time that I open up about my true feelings.

這是我第一次說出我真正的感受。

B. The deal opens up the possibility of cooperation to make more profits.

這項交易開創謀取更高利潤的合作可能。

C. He opened up his case, and took out his cell phone.

他打開箱子然後取出手機。

❺ originate in/from 起源於

The tango is a kind of dance which originates in/from South America.

探戈是一種源自於南美的舞蹈。

❻ out of 由於；從…出來

Out of interest he gave up his business and took up painting.

因為興趣，他放棄事業，開始學畫。

We obeyed him out of fear rather than respect.

我們服從他是因恐懼而非尊敬。

He opened the box out of curiosity.

他因為好奇打開了盒子。

❼ (be/go) out of one's mind 發瘋

You must be out of your mind to buy the lousy car.

買下這部爛車，你一定是瘋了。

❽ out of order 故障

The elevator is out of order. Please take the stairs.

電梯故障了。請走樓梯。

 辨析 這個「故障」常指「小東西的故障」。

 觸類旁通 break down 大物件的故障

The car just *broke down* on the slope.

汽車剛剛在斜坡上拋錨了。

⓳ out of stock 貨賣光了；缺貨

I'm sorry. That kind of shoe is completely out of stock in your size.

對不起，那款鞋子你的尺寸完全缺貨。

 in stock　現有存貨

Do you have any mouth mask *in stock*?

口罩有現貨嗎？

⓴ out of style 不時髦；不再流行了

Curly hair is out of style now.

捲髮不流行了。

 out of fashion、out of date

 in style

= in fashion　時髦；流行

Mini-skirts are back *in style* again.

迷你裙又再度流行。

㉑ out of the question 不可能

It's out of the question to make all these figures accurate.

要這些數據都正確是不可能的。

 impossible

 beyond question　無庸置疑

Why do you still doubt his ability? His achievement is *beyond question*.

你為何還在質疑他的能力呢？他的成就是無庸置疑的。

㉒ over and over again 一而再、再而三

He made the same mistake over and over again, which made his parents quite angry.

他一再犯相同的錯誤，頗令父母生氣。

 again and again、repeatedly

 over and above

= besides

= as well as　除…之外；再加上

We should add the fee of traveling *over and above* the entertainment cost.

除了娛樂支出外，我們也該加上旅行的費用。

㉓ owe...to 歸功於

I owe my success to your assistance.

我的成功歸因於你的協助。

觸類旁通 owe 還有「欠」的意思，可以視同一般的「使役動詞」來寫句型。

He owes $10,000 to John.

= He owes John $10,000.

他欠 John 一萬美元。

❷ **part of** 一部份

Part of the money will be spent on your reference books. 一部份的錢會花在你的參考書上。

❷ **pass on** **(A)** 傳遞；**(B)** 傳染（疾病）；**(C)** 轉嫁（某人身上）；**(D)** 死亡

A. He said he would pass the message on to his friends. 他說他會把這個消息傳給他的朋友。

B. One catches SARS and then passes it on to the rest. 一個人感染 SARS 然後再傳染其他人。

C. Any increase in costs will have to be passed on to the customer. 任何成本上的增加都將轉嫁到消費者的身上。

D. My grandfather passed on yesterday. 我祖父昨天過世了。

❷ **pass out** **(A)** 失去知覺；**(B)** 散發（傳單、小冊子等）

A. I nearly passed out when I witnessed the accident. 當我目睹意外時差點失去知覺。

B. The examiner began to pass the papers out. 試務人員開始分發考卷。

❷ **pay for it** 為它付出代價；為它得到報應

If the government keeps ignoring educational development, someday we will pay for it. 如果政府持續忽視教育的發展，有一天我們會為此付出代價。

觸類旁通 pay for 付錢買

You may *pay* another one dollar *for* that ice cream.

要買那個冰淇淋你必須再付一塊錢。

❷ **pay off** **(A)** 還清（債務）；**(B)** 看見成效；**(C)** 資遣；**(D)** 收買；行賄

A. I'll pay off all my debts first, and then travel around the world. 我會先還清所有債務，然後再去環遊世界。

B. All the practice will pay off when you join in the competition. 當你參加競賽時，先前所有的練習都會顯出其成果。

C. This company closes and pays off all the employees. 這家公司關門大吉，資遣所有員工。

D. They paid off the Senator. 他們收買了參議員。

㉙ pay sb a visit = pay a visit to sb　拜訪某人

I decided to pay him a visit in the hope that we could cooperate.

我決定去拜訪他，希望我們能合作。

 同義

call on sb

We'll *call on* Larry on the way home.

回家路上我們會去拜訪 Larry。

 觸類旁通

pay a visit to (place)

= call at (place)　到某地

I *call at* his office for news every afternoon.

我每天下午到他辦公室等新消息。

Unit 15 Exercise

I. 片語選填

pass out	on the spot	on the contrary	originate in
pay off	at a time	out of the question	on the outside
out of one's mind			

1. People with low self-esteem are shy. _____, people with high-esteem tend to be optimistic. (88)

2. These were thickly cut potatoes, fried until golden brown and crisp _____. (90)

3. Kevin burst into tears _____ because his teacher punished him in front of the whole class. (92)

4. The first printing was done from wood blocks one letter _____ by hand.

5. Human beings may have _____ the sea. (89)

6. He must be _____ to have done such a crazy thing. (87)

7. Skiing in Taiwan is _____ most of the time because there is very little snow here. (86)

8. When Ms. Jones was told that her husband was dead, she _____.

9. All his hard work in the past three years has _____ now that he has graduated with top honors. (92)

II. 引導翻譯

10. 在去垃圾場的途中鈴聲響了。(88)

_____ his _____ _____ the dump, the bell rang.

11. 候鳥正在移動居所。(92)

The migrating birds are _____ _____ _____ now.

12. 別做冒險的事，它可能會讓你惹上麻煩。(92)

Don't _____ on _____ _____ . It might get you in trouble.

13. 這名男子已瀕臨嚴重的精神崩潰，因為他無法處理來自日常生活的壓力。(91)

The man is _____ _____ _____ _____ a serious breakdown because he is unable to deal with pressure from daily life.

14. 人們對於什麼是準時和遲到有不同的看法。(89)

People have different ideas about what exactly is being _____ _____ and being late.

15. 如果你再對我說一次謊，我就不原諒你。(85)

If you lie to me _____ _____ , I won't forgive you.

16. 有一天當他坐在小鎮上的咖啡館裡，他想到了一個點子。(85)

_____ _____ , as he sat in a café in a small town, he had an idea.

17. 如果有人覺得你不僅只是聽聽，而且是正在仔細地傾聽他說的話和體會他的感受，他就更有可能和你傾吐心事，甚至與你溝通。(89)

If a person feels you are not just listening, but you are listening carefully to his words and feelings, he is more likely to _____ _____ and communicate with you even more.

18. 許多人因為不理性的恐懼而殺害蝙蝠。(85)

Many people kill bats _____ _____ unreasonable fear.

19. 但是因洋芋須靠手工削皮，故這是非常費時的雜事，且洋芋片常常缺貨。(90)

But because the potatoes had to be peeled by hand, it was a time-consuming chore and potato chips were often _____ _____ _____ .

20. 一般來說它不流行了。(86)

It's generally _____ _____ _____ .

21. 年輕人所觀看的搖滾音樂錄影帶一再地以飲酒為特色。(84)

The rock videos young people watch _____ and _____ _____ feature alcohol.

22. 那個年輕人將他的成功歸功於許多人，特別是他的父母。(88)

The young man _____ his success _____ many people, his parents in particular.

23. 那對夫妻看到死亡是人生的一部份。(89)

The couple saw that death was _____ _____ life.

24. 說故事是傳遞家族史及讓經驗有意義的一種知識。(87)

Storytelling was a knowledge of _____ _____ family history, and of giving meaning to experience.

25. 如果我們對培養想像力一事漠不關心，世人將為此付出代價。(87)

If we are careless in the matter of nourishing the imagination, the world will

_____ _____ _____ .

26. 那對夫妻衝去參拜佛陀。(89)

The couple rushed to _____ the Buddha a _____ .

III. 克漏字選擇

Christmas Madness

Unfortunately, many Americans who celebrate Christmas these days feel that the holiday is more about gifts __27__ anything else. Children are warned to mind their __28__ , or Santa will not bring them presents. During the Christmas season, it is hard to pay a visit __29__ a neighbor without feeling guilty if you didn't bring a little gift. __30__ , it seems that Americans spend more time in December in shopping malls than they do with their family. The mall scene is crazy: one person is __31__ the verge of tears because an item she needs has been __32__ for weeks; another is going __33__ trying to find the perfect gift for his wife; still another is about to __34__ because she has been on her feet shopping all day without stopping to eat. What madness! True, Christmas is the season of giving, but is it really meant to be a time for people to be under stress to buy stuff? __35__ , Christmas is a time of peace. Americans would do well to forget about the malls and bring a little more peace into the lives of their loved ones instead.

( ) 27. (A) then   (B) but   (C) than   (D) and
( ) 28. (A) p's and q's   (B) pros and cons
        (C) ups and downs   (D) haves and have-nots
( ) 29. (A) for   (B) on   (C) to   (D) with
( ) 30. (A) On the move   (B) On the main (C) On the spot   (D) On the whole
( ) 31. (A) in   (B) on   (C) to   (D) by
( ) 32. (A) out of stock   (B) out of the question
        (C) out of order   (D) out of sight
( ) 33. (A) out of style (B) out of his date (C) out of fashion (D) out of his mind
( ) 34. (A) pass away   (B) give away   (C) pass out   (D) give out
( ) 35. (A) By contrast   (B) On the contrary (C) In general   (D) Out of curiosity

❶ pick sb up 讓某人搭便車

I'll pick you up at the station after work.　　　　下班後，我會開車去車站接你。

 觸類旁通 pick up 把…撿起；收拾；零零星星自然學習；改進

The phone rang, and he *picked* it *up* in no time.

電話響了，他立刻去接。

Pick up your room before your parents come home.

你爸媽回來之前，把房間收拾好。

I *picked up* a little Italian when I was there last year.

去年我在那裡時，順道學了一些義大利文。

The economy is beginning to *pick up* again this summer.

今年夏季經濟再度開始改善。

❷ pick up the check 付帳

The stingy man didn't want to pick up the check, so he sneaked out.　　那個吝嗇鬼不想付帳，所以悄悄溜出去。

 同義 pay/foot the bill

❸ pie in the sky 畫餅充飢；不太可能實現的計劃

The hope of a cure for his illness is just pie in the sky.　　希望治癒他的病是不太可能的。

 同義 castle in the air

❹ pile up **(A)** 疊放成一堆；**(B)** 增加

A. Those old newspapers and magazines piled up on the floor.　　舊報紙和雜誌在地上堆成一堆。

B. The work will pile up if you keep talking.　　如果你繼續談天，工作就會累積增加。

❺ play with **(A)** 與…玩；**(B)** 玩弄

A. The children are playing with their toys happily.　　孩子們開心地玩玩具。

B. It's not acceptable to play with other people's emotions.　　玩弄他人的感情是不被接受的。

❻ plenty of 許多

There is no hurry—you still have plenty of time.　　不急，你還有很多時間。

 用法 plenty of 後面可以接單數名詞，也可以接複數名詞。

❼ point out 指出來

This passage points out that Wearing is sad because part of his memory is lost.

這篇短文指出，Wearing 對於他喪失了部分記憶感到難過。

The teacher pointed out three mistakes in my composition.

老師在我的作文裡指出三個錯誤。

❽ point to 指向；指明、表明

He was pointing to a truck that was approaching the toll-gate.

他正指著一輛接近收費站的大卡車。

All the evidence pointed to his involvement in the murder.

所有證據都指明他涉及這件謀殺案。

 觸類旁通 point up 強調某物或極力主張某種觀點

Dr. King *pointed up* that men are created equal, whatever the color of their skin is.

金恩博士極力主張，不論人的膚色為何，人皆生而平等。

❾ pop up 突然蹦出；到處不斷出現

His name keeps popping up in the news these days.

最近，他的名字突然不斷出現在電視新聞裡。

❿ prefer to 較喜歡；偏好

I prefer to wear clothes made of cotton.

我比較喜歡穿棉質的衣服。

用法 prefer to + V/N
這個用法要小心，不能與下面「觸類旁通」所提示的用法混為一談。

 觸類旁通 1. prefer A to B 喜歡 A 甚於喜歡 B
句型：prefer + N/V-ing + to + N/V-ing
I *prefer going* to the movies *to watching* TV.
我比較喜歡看電影甚於看電視。

2. prefer to + V... rather than + V...
= would rather/sooner + V...than + V... 寧願…而不願…
I *would rather/sooner* stay in *than* go out this evening.
= I *prefer to* stay in *rather than* go out this evening.
今晚我寧願在家也不願外出。

⓫ present sb with sth **(A)** 送某人某物；**(B)** 造成某人某問題

A. She was presented with an award on account of her kindness.

她因為善心而獲獎。

= An award was presented to her on account of her kindness.

B. The noise of train has presented the residents with great annoyance.　火車的噪音已經造成居民的嚴重困擾。

= The noise of train has presented great annoyance to the residents.

 用法　這兩種意思都還可以寫成 present sth to sb

❷ **prior to**　早於

All the arrangements should be set prior to the ceremony.　所有的安排應該在典禮前就緒。

❸ **provide sth for sb**　提供某人某物

How can he provide the necessities of life for his children without work?　沒有工作，他如何供應孩子日常生活所需？

 用法　這個片語也可以寫成 provide sb with sth

The project is designed to *provide* the middle-aged *with* work.

該方案是為提供中年人工作而設計的。

❹ **pull down**　(A) 拆除；(B) 拉下

A. The old library was pulled down yesterday, and will be rebuilt in three years.　老圖書館昨天被拆了，三年內會重建起來。

B. The actor pulled down the hat to hide his face.　那名演員把帽簷拉低以遮住臉。

❺ **pull out**　(A) 拉開、拉出；(B) 開（車）到另一個車道；
(C)（軍隊）撤離、退出（市場、競爭、事件或活動等）

A. The girl struggled fiercely, trying to pull her arm out of her father's grasp.　女孩用力掙扎，設法把手臂掙脫出父親的緊抓。

B. Don't pull out! There's a truck coming.　別換車道，有一輛卡車來了。

C. Most of the troops have been pulled out since July.　七月之後，多數的軍隊已撤離。

This firm decided to pull out of the Internet business because of some financial problems.　因為財務問題，這間公司決定退出網路市場。

 同義　撤離、退出：withdraw

觸類旁通　pull in　（火車等）進站、（車子等）停下、駛向路邊；賺錢；吸引（人群等）

The train *pulled in* on time.
火車準時到達。

Whenever you feel tired, *pull in* and take a small rest.
只要你感到疲累，就停到路邊休息一下。

He *pulls in* at least six figures by translating this popular modern novel.

他藉著翻譯這本當代受歡迎的小說，賺進至少六位數的錢。

Mr. Wang *pulled in* many votes in the election.

王先生在選舉中贏得許多選票。

❶⑥ put away　**(A)** 把…收起來，放回原處；**(B)** 存錢、儲蓄

A. Put your toys away before going to bed.　　睡覺之前把玩具收拾好。

B. I'm putting some money away for my daughter's tuition in college.　　我正在為女兒的大學學費存些錢。

❶⑦ put...in jail　送入監牢

The government put him in jail because he betrayed our country.　　他因為叛國而被政府送進監牢。

❶⑧ put...into operation　實施

A scheme is being put into operation to see how the new medicine works.　　一項計劃正在實施，以了解新藥的功能。

❶⑨ put...into practice　將…實現

My boss gave me the chance to put my ideas into practice.　　我的老闆給了我機會將想法實現。

 同義　　carry sth out、realize sth

Will the government *carry out* its promise to reform education?

= Will the government *realize* its promise to reform education?

政府會實踐諾言從事教改嗎？

 **觸類旁通**　sth come true　實現

這裡的「實現」是指夢想、希望與期待實現，而 put into practice 則是指計畫的實行，兩者仍有差別。

Winning the Oscar Award to her is like a dream *coming true*.

她獲得奧斯卡獎，就像是夢想實現了。

❷⓪ put off　**(A)** 延期；**(B)** 使討厭

A. Do not put off until tomorrow what you can do today.　　（諺）今日事今日畢。

B. The actor put me off the movie.　　那個演員使我討厭那部電影。

 同義　延期：postpone

用法　延期：put off + N/V-ing

使討厭：put sb off + N/V-ing

㉑ put on (A) 穿上、戴上; (B) 假裝

A. He took off his uniform and put on a sweater and jeans. 　他脫下制服,換上毛衣牛仔褲。

B. Jimmy isn't that upset; he's just putting it on. 　Jimmy 沒那麼不高興;他是裝的。

 同義　假裝: put on a pretense、pretend

觸類旁通　put on a brave face/front　假裝勇敢

㉒ put to death 判死刑; 處死

Legend has it that Lisa was put to death for practicing witchcraft. 　傳說 Lisa 因施行巫術而被判死刑。

㉓ rain cats and dogs 下豪大雨

It's raining cats and dogs outside. You'd better stay here for a while. 　外面正在下大雨,你最好在此待上一會。

㉔ rain down 像下雨般降下來

Bombs rained down on the city, causing great loss of lives. 　炸彈如雨般投向城市,造成重大生命的損失。

㉕ recognize A as B 承認 A 為 B

The WHO has recognized SARS as a disease since March, 2003. 　世衛組織自 2003 年三月起,承認嚴重急性呼吸道症候群為疾病。

㉖ recover from 從…中恢復

His father is in hospital, recovering from a heart attack. 　他的父親在住院,心臟病逐漸康復。

㉗ refer to A as B 視 A 為 B

He likes to be referred to as a big brother. 　他喜歡被人視為大哥哥。

 同義　look upon A as B、think of A as B

 用法　refer to + N + as + N/V-ing

 觸類旁通　refer to　談到; 參考

When he came, he didn't *refer to* you in our conversation.

他來的時候,在我們的談話中沒有提到你。

I often *referred to* a dictionary for information on my papers.

我常常參考字典,以獲得報告的資料。

❷❽ reflect on/upon　(A) 反省；(B) 招致…的影響（好或壞均可）

A. After retirement, he had time to reflect on his success and failure in life.

退休之後，他有時間去反省一生的成功與失敗。

B. The unemployment figures last year reflected badly on the government's image.

去年的失業數字給政府的形象帶來很壞的影響。

❷❾ regard A as B　視 A 為 B

Everyone regards him as the smartest man in the company.

每個人都認為他是全公司最聰明的人。

 view A as B、take A as B、label A as B、describe A as B

The magazine has unjustly *labeled* him *as* a troublemaker.

該雜誌很不公正地將他視為麻煩製造者。

 regard + N + as + N/adj

這個片語通常會使用被動語態來表現。

Beethoven is *regarded as* the best composer of all.

貝多芬被視為最好的作曲家。

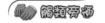 as regards

=with/in regard to

= regarding　關於；至於

As regards wheat, price is shooting up.　至於小麥，價格正在飆漲。

❸⓿ regardless of　不管

Everyone was born equal under the law, regardless of race, religion, or sex.

人人在法律之下生而平等，無論其種族、宗教或性別。

 Unit 16 Exercise

I. 片語選填

reflect on	put to death	pie in the sky	pull down
regardless of	refer to as	put off	prior to
plenty of			

1. I cannot agree to your idea, for it is just _____ . (88)

2. Besides, being an early bird, you have _____ time to take exercise or do a lot of work. (86)

3. All the preparations should have been completed _____ the vacation.

4. The old houses will soon be _____ and rebuilt because of the severe damage caused by the earthquake. (89)

5. The outdoor concert was _____ because of the rain. (85)

6. The emperor ordered that the slaves be _____ . (90)

7. Positions are open to everyone, _____ age and sex. (91)

8. And if you can _____ the mistakes you have made, you can avoid making the same mistakes again and again. (86)

9. We were each separately sent on what was grandly _____ a cruise loaded down with enough food for a week. (87)

II. 引導翻譯

10. 大約七點左右，我會開車接你。(87)

    I'll _____ _____ _____ around seven o'clock.

11. 聚集一堆的「無著落信件」時，「無著落信件辦公室」會舉辦公開拍賣會。(89)

    When a lot of dead mail has _____ _____, the dead mail offices would hold public auctions.

12. 不久牠將學會：當牠咬的時候，你就不和牠玩。(88)

    He will soon learn that when he bites, you will not _____ _____ him anymore.

13. 然後老闆笑著指出，同樣的提議幾分鐘前才提出，且被否決了。(86)

    The boss then laughingly _____ _____ that the same proposal had been made and turned down some minutes before.

14. 不管如何，若你想精通英文，你就必須熟悉這些似乎隨處會蹦出來的電腦新詞彙。(91)

    In either case, if you want to master English, you will need to be familiar with those new computer words that seem to be _____ _____ everywhere.

15. 對偏好待在鎮上的人來說，觀光客可以瀏覽許多有趣的商店。(84)

    For those who _____ to stay in town, tourists can browse through a number of interesting shops.

16. 在挪威，要結交新朋友，或向鄰居介紹自己，有個好方法，那就是送他們一份簡單的禮物，比方說，蛋糕或一條土司。(86)

    A fine way to make friends and introduce yourself to your neighbors in Norway is to _____ _____ _____ a simple gift like a cake or a loaf of bread.

17. 該計劃提供家畜給這些貧窮的非洲家庭。(90)

    This program _____ livestock _____ these poor African families.

18. 顯然他們將後車座拉開，爬到後車箱，之後又無法再向前推開座椅。(89)

    They had apparently _____ _____ the back seat, crawled behind it, and then had not been able to push the seat forward again.

19. 在你學到某個新事物後，重要的是設法實行它。(88)

After you have learned something new, it is important that you try to _____ it _____ _____ .

20. 讀完之後，將那些書收到箱子裡。(90)

After finishing reading, _____ those books _____ in the box.

21. 他穿上外套，立即出去。(88)

He _____ _____ his coat and went out in no time.

22. 之後他們把他關進牢裡，並控告他未經許可，攀爬這棟大樓。(83)

Then they _____ him _____ _____ and charged him with the violation of law for climbing the building without a permit.

23. 公司決定實施這項計劃，因為它是最切實可行的一項。(89)

The company decided to _____ the plan _____ _____ because it was the most feasible one.

24. Glenn 第一次的遊行，預估有 3474 噸的五彩碎紙，在七英里的路線中像雨般灑下，被視為規模最大的一次。(88)

Glenn's first parade, an estimated 3474 tons of confetti _____ _____ along a seven-mile route, was considered the largest ever.

25. 市場商人將嘻哈文化視為年輕人文化的一部份。(92)

Businessmen _____ hip-pop culture _____ a part of youth culture.

26. 你知道快樂的人生病時比沮喪或喜歡抱怨的人恢復健康來得快嗎？(86)

Do you know that happy folks _____ _____ illness much more rapidly than those who are depressed and always complaining?

27. 他們不把批評視為對個人的拒絕。(83)

They do not _____ criticism _____ personal rejection.

❶ relieve oneself 上廁所（舊式用法）

Just go straight and you will see a restroom to relieve yourself.

直走就可以看到洗手間。

 這是「上廁所」的「嚴肅講法」，一般口語上，go to the restroom/bathroom 就可以了。

 relieve one's feeling 發洩感情；洩憤

I know you're sad about your mother's passing away. If you need time to *relieve your feeling*, just go ahead.

我知道你母親過世，你很難過。如果你需要時間去發洩一下，你就去吧。

❷ remind A of B 使 A 想起 B

The landscape here reminds me of my hometown Hualien.　此地的風景，使我想起家鄉花蓮。

 may/can I remind sb... 容我提醒某人（一些已經知道的事情）

Before you go mountain climbing, *may I remind you* that be sure to pay attention to the weather forecast, especially the movement of typhoon No. 21.

在你們登山前，請容我提醒你們，務必注意氣象預報，特別是 21 號颱風的動向。

❸ report for...duty 報到上班

Mr. Harrison was told to report for military duty as a general.

Harrison 先生被通知報到擔任將軍的軍職。

 report for duty 到班

The teachers are required to *report for duty* before 8:00 in the morning.

教師們被要求要早上八點以前到班。

❹ rest on/upon (A) 根據；(B) 停留在；(C) 依賴、信賴

A. Success in management entirely rests on good judgment.

管理的成功，完全基於正確的判斷。

B. My eyes rested on his hair.

我盯著他的頭髮瞧。

C. Do you rest upon his promise?

你相信他的承諾嗎?

 根據：depend on、be based on

The case *is* ultimately *based on* circumstantial evidence.

這個案子，終究要靠間接推測的證據。

 這裡的「停留在」是指「眼神停留在…」。

❺ retire from 從…退休

My mother retired from teaching three years ago.　我母親三年前從教職退休。

❻ ride out 安然度過

Only about half of the small companies were able to ride out the recession.　只有約半數的小公司能夠安然度過此經濟衰退。

❼ right away 立刻；馬上

I'll phone him right away just in case.　我會馬上打電話給他，以防萬一。

 immediately、right now、at once、in no time

❽ run down　**(A)** 把…撞倒；**(B)** 不公平的批評他人；**(C)**（電池、鐘、機器）停擺；**(D)**（公司的規模）變小；**(E)** 往下流；**(F)** 快速瀏覽列表上的東西

A. A motorcycle ran his wife down.　他的太太被摩托車撞倒。

B. I think he is just jealous of you, or he wouldn't run you down.　我想他不過是嫉妒你吧！不然他不會這樣不公正的批判你的。

C. If a clock runs down, it has no power and stops working.　如果鐘停了，它就沒有作用而停擺了。

D. Many smaller companies are being run down.　許多較小的公司規模變更小了。

E. Tears are running down her cheeks.　眼淚從她的臉頰流下。

F. Before going out to the mall, please run down the list of what you want to buy again.　出門去購物中心前，請再很快的看一遍你的購物清單。

 「把…撞倒」是指「駕駛汽機車時撞倒別人，還讓他受傷或死亡」，情況比 knock down 來得嚴重，不過與 run over 的「輾過」相比似乎好一點。

❾ run into　**(A)** 與…不期而遇、遭遇；**(B)** 撞上

A. I ran into my classmate, Jane, on the bus.　我與 Jane 在公車上不期而遇。

His business ran into financial difficulties.　他的事業遭遇財務困難。

B. The car ran into the fence.　車子撞上駕駛柵欄。

 不期而遇：bump into、come across、encounter

 run into sb/sth

 run into trouble/difficulty/problems　碰上麻煩

⑩ run off　(A) 逃離、逃跑；(B) 流出；(C) 迅速寫出

A. Upon seeing the police, the thief ran off rapidly.　　一看到警察，小偷快速逃離。

B. The rain ran off the eaves.　　雨水流下屋簷。

C. I can just run off an e-mail now.　　我現在可以馬上打一封電子郵件。

⑪ run out (of)　(A) 用光；(B) 跑出去；(C) 流出；(D)（法律）到期

A. We are running out of money.　　我們的錢快用光了。

Their money ran out because they didn't use their budget wisely.　　他們因為沒有明智的運用預算而把錢用完了。

B. Students ran out the door when the bell rang.　　鈴聲響起，學生跑出門外。

C. The jar broke and the jam ran out.　　瓶子破了，果醬流了出來。

D. Our contract runs out at the end of this year.　　我們的契約今年底就到期了。

 用法　只有當「用光」解時，才會用到 run out of + N，其他的用法都不加 of。

⑫ run over　(A) 輾過；(B) 演練（演說或表演）；(C) 大略看過

A. The dog was almost run over by a truck.　　小狗差點被卡車輾了過去。

B. Let's run over the whole program before the concert begin.　　音樂會開始前，再把整個節目演練一次吧！

C. He quickly ran over his notes before the test.　　他考試前很快瀏覽了筆記。

同義　演練：rehearse
大略看過：run through

⑬ rush into　（不加思索的）衝進；倉促從事

When the bell rang, we rushed into the classroom.　　當鐘聲響起，我們衝進教室。
He often rushes into decisions and regrets afterwards.　　他常匆促下決定又事後反悔。

⑭ save...from...　(A) 挽救；(B) 免於；(C) 省去

A. Only by down sizing can save this company from bankruptcy.　　只有藉著縮小規模，這家公司才能免於破產。

B. Don't go out when a typhoon hit. This would save you from every possible harm.　　颱風來襲時不要出門。這會使你免於任何可能的傷害。

C. If you lend me five thousand dollars, it will save me a trip from going to the bank.　　如果你借我 5000 美元，我就可以省得多跑銀行一趟。

 辨析　「免於」是指「免於任何形式的危險」。

128

⓯ save one's skin/neck/bacon   逃脫危險；免遭傷害

He didn't tell the police the truth to save his skin.

他沒對警察吐實，免得被傷害。

To save your skin, you'd better hold your tongue.

為了避免皮肉之苦，你最好什麼都不說。

 save one's breath   多說無益

We may *save our breath* upon this plan, and just put it into operation to see the outcome.

我們繼續討論這個計畫，並沒有多大意義，乾脆直接付諸實行，然後看看結果如何。

⓰ scare off   嚇跑；嚇走

Rising prices in tickets are scaring off many potential tourists.

票價日益高漲，嚇走了許多潛在觀光客。

 1. scare + the life/the hell/the living daylights + out of sb
把某人嚇得魂飛魄散
The alarm at midnight *scared the hell out of* me.
半夜的警鈴把我嚇得魂飛魄散。

2. scare the pants off sb   嚇得屁滾尿流

⓱ see A as B   視 A 為 B

I see the opportunity of hosting the conference as a challenge.

我將這次主辦研討會的機會視為一項挑戰。

 consider A (to be) B

 這個片語沒有現在進行式。

 see A for B   看清某人或某事的真面目

He didn't *see* this woman *for* a liar until she ran away with his money.

直到這個女人捲款潛逃，他才知道這女的根本是個騙子。

⓲ see through   看穿

I could never lie to my mother, because I know she'd see me through straight.

我永遠不能對媽媽說謊，因為我知道她能一眼就看穿我。

 這個「看穿」有「拆穿某人的謊言或面具」的意思。

❶ sell out 售完

We've completely sold out of this kind of jeans in your size.

這款牛仔褲，你的尺寸完全銷售一空。

 sell off　降價求現

He *sold off* these products to pay back the loan.

他把這些產品降價賣出，以償付貸款。

❷ separate...from...　**(A)** 把…與…分隔開來、區隔；**(B)** 把…和…分開思考

A. They separate the aluminum cans from the rest of the garbage for recycling.

他們為資源回收把鋁罐從其餘垃圾分開出來。

B. It is impossible for me to separate morality from success.

要我把道德和成功分開思考，是不可能的。

　separate + N + from + N

❸ serve as　充當

This anti-war treaty serves as symbol of peace.

這項反戰協議成為和平的象徵。

　1. serve A with B　**(A)** 以 B 供給給 A；A 餐附 B（如水果、沙拉等）

The river *serves* the city *with* water.

這條河流供給該市水源。

All steaks are *served with* salad, fruit and juice.

所有的排餐都附沙拉、水果與果汁。

2. serve out　分配；供給

The waiters *served out* the last course.

服務生端上了最後一道菜。

❹ set aside　**(A)** 保留；（為某一目的）存下時間、金錢；**(B)** 擱置

A. Try to set aside some time to care for your sick father.

你該設法挪時間照顧生病的父親。

B. We should set aside our personal feelings at work.

工作時我們應把個人情感放一邊。

　存下金錢、時間：put aside

　這裡的「擱置」是指「把人的情感、意見與信仰放到一旁，不因為這些事情影響到某件事情的完成。」

❺ set free　釋放

The landlord finally set the slaves free.

那位地主最後終於釋放這些奴隸。

　release

　set sb free

❷❹ set off **(A)** 出發；**(B)** 放煙火、鞭炮；**(C)** 使⋯更為出色；
(D) 使某人產生某活動（開始笑、哭或說話）

A. We'd better set off early to avoid the traffic.　　我們最好早點出發，避開車潮。

B. They set off fireworks in celebration of National Day.　　他們施放煙火以慶祝國慶。

C. The diamond ring set off her beauty.　　鑽戒更襯托出她的美。

D. Don't mention her parents—you'll set her off again.　　別提她的父母，你會再勾起她的情緒。

 出發：set out、start out

放煙火、鞭炮：let off

❷❺ set on **(A)** 唆使襲擊或追趕；**(B)** 攻擊；襲擊

A. The vineyard's master threatened to set dogs on thieves.　　葡萄園主人威脅要放狗追小偷。

B. If Jimmy keeps on running you down, I'll certainly set him on!　　要是 Jimmy 繼續不公正的批評你，我一定會痛扁他一頓！

 唆使：set A on B

 第一個「唆使」，是指「唆使 A 去襲擊或追趕 B」；第二個「攻擊」是說話者親自上陣攻擊。

❷❻ set out (for) 往⋯出發

They set out for Kengting last night.　　他們昨晚出發到墾丁去了。

 set off (for)

 set out for + 地方

 set out + to V/with sth　開始做某事

We *set out to look* for related information but found merely part of it.
我們開始尋找相關資料，但只找到一部份。

He *set out with the intention* of laying off one third of the employees.
他著手的意圖在資遣三分之一的員工。

❷❼ shake hands with 與⋯握手

On entering the chamber, he shook hands with me.　　一進入會議廳，他就和我握手。

 shake hands with 與 make friends with 的 hands 和 friends 一定要用複數形。

㉘ shed tears 流淚

There is no use shedding tears now. You just have to work harder.

現在掉眼淚也沒用。你只得更努力做才是。

 shed blood （在戰爭中）受傷或死亡
Too many youths *shed* their *blood* in World War II.
太多的青年人在第二次世界大戰中喪失生命。

㉙ slip (out of) one's mind/memory 被遺忘；被忘掉

I should have mailed the letter, but it completely slipped my mind.

我早該寄這封信，但我把它完全忘了。

 slip through one's fingers 讓（機會、獎賞）從手中溜走
Even though she really did a good job in this movie, the Oscar Award still *slipped through her fingers* yet again.
雖然她在這部電影中表現精采，仍然與奧斯卡小金人無緣。

㉚ slow down 放慢速度；減速

You have to slow down your car when you turn.

開車轉彎時要減速。

Unit 17 Exercise

I. 片語選填

set out	see through	shed tears	serve as	relieve oneself
save one's skin		run into	ride out	slip one's mind

1. His flight in the universe was supposed to last only 15 minutes, so there was no provision made for him to _____ in the capsule. (92)

2. If you can _____ this crisis, you will have a good chance of success.

3. She _____ severe criticism after the article she wrote in the newspaper.

4. He didn't tell the police the truth to _____ .

5. I'm really sorry I forgot your birthday; the date just completely _____ .

6. To _____ a symbol of environmental concerns, the new tower is made of wood. (87)

7. A woman can _____ her husband's secrets before he realizes it. (85)

8. They _____ to look for the mustard seeds. (89)

9. Animals also experience emotions — fear, pleasure, loneliness — but they do not _____ . (89)

10. 曼谷令 Warren 想起家鄉。(92)

    Bangkok (r) _____ Warren _____ home.

11. 我會馬上向傳真辦公室求證。(88)

    I'll check the fax office _____ _____.

12. 他不小心撞倒三輛摩托車。(89)

    He _____ _____ three motorcycles in a careless manner.

13. Eric 逃走了，留下兩個孩子讓妻子養育。(87)

    Eric _____ _____ and left his wife with two kids to bring up.

14. 他們的錢用光了，不得不放棄旅行的計劃。(87)

    They _____ _____ _____ money and had to abandon their plan for a

    trip.

15. 在午餐時間，Jane 翻閱她的筆記，免得在考試時忘掉。(87)

    During the lunch hour, Jane _____ _____ her notes so she would remember

    them for the test.

16. 開始下大雨了，所以我決定把小孩留在車上，我自己衝進店裡。(89)

    It began to rain heavily, so I decided I would leave the children in the car, while I

    _____ _____ a shop.

17. Carnegie 聽說，一個叫 William Hunter 的青年，在救其他兩個快滅頂的男孩時喪生。

    Carnegie heard about a young man by the name of William Hunter, who lost his life trying

    to _____ two other boys _____ drowning.

18. 將語言中的文字，視為像生命有機體中的細胞，是一個容易的步驟。(89)

    It is an easy step to (s)_____ the words of a language _____ being like the

    cells of a living organism.

19. 對不起，你的尺寸賣完了。(89)

    I'm sorry, but your size is _____ _____.

20. 英法兩國被海分隔。

    England is _____ _____ France by the sea.

21. Carnegie 成為非常有錢的商人，並存錢獎勵像 William 這樣的英雄。(83)

    Carnegie became a very rich businessman and _____ _____ money to honor

    heroes like William.

22. 在距離釋放地點 60 英里處，牠們被發現與為數 50 隻的鯨魚群在一起。(84)

    They were found in a group of 50 whales about 60 miles from where they had been

    _____ _____.

23. Vladimir 父子將再度開拔，繼續他們航行世界的旅程。(86, 90)

    The Vladimirs will be able to _____ _____ again and continue their

    round-the-world voyage.

24. 有些人仍然誤信，人們會經由與同性戀者握手而得到愛滋病。(92)

Some people still believe, quite mistakenly, that one can get AIDS by _____ _____ _____ homosexuals.

25. 設計公車專用道的理由是有助於交通流量，而非使其減速。(89)

The reason for designing the special bus lane is to facilitate the traffic flow, not to _____ it _____ .

III. 克漏字選擇

Nelson Mandela, a life in prison

Nelson Mandela was born in South Africa in 1918. In the 1940s, he joined a movement that tried to __26__ the black people in his country. __27__ the white population, the nonwhites were refused the right to vote. Mandela __28__ as an activist and fought to obtain full citizenship for all South Africans. In 1962, he went to a conference in Ethiopia to promote African freedom, but __29__ . When he returned, he was arrested for illegal exit. Judged a second time for having betrayed his country, he was sentenced __30__ life imprisonment. When he was in prison, he didn't __31__ his laurels: he continued to have contacts with the ANC and wrote his autobiography. He refused to be released from prison and to __32__ by giving up his fight for a free South Africa. As a result, he spent almost 30 years in jail and became a symbol of courage around the world. In 1990, President F. W. de Klerk abolished the racist laws and freed many political prisoners, __33__ Mandela. Three years later, he won the Nobel Peace Prize and in 1994 became the first black president of South Africa. He __34__ Public life in 1999. He lives now in his birth place and can enjoy the fruits of his sacrifice: freedom for all South Africans.

( ) 26. (A) set up   (B) set free   (C) set aside   (D) set off

( ) 27. (A) Known as   (B) Apart from   (C) Notorious for   (D) Separated from

( ) 28. (A) played an important role   (B) referred to

       (C) was badly treated   (D) was mistaken for

( ) 29. (A) without a doubt   (B) without hesitation

       (C) without authorization   (D) without delay

( ) 30. (A) to   (B) for   (C) in   (D) by

( ) 31. (A) look upon   (B) depend upon   (C) feed upon   (D) rest upon

( ) 32. (A) skin him alive   (B) save his skin   (C) sack out   (D) scare the hell

( ) 33. (A) including   (B) included   (C) inclusive   (D) exclusive of

( ) 34. (A) retired as   (B) retired from   (C) served as   (D) saved from

❶ smile at　**(A)** 對…微笑；**(B)** 對…一笑置之

A. Ann always smiles at me whenever she sees me.　每次 Ann 見到我都會對我微笑。

B. She smiled at the ridiculous comments he made.　她對他作出的荒謬評論一笑置之。

❷ so much for　到此為止；就只有這些

So much for winning the championship since we already lost the first round.　要贏得冠軍賽就到此為止了，因為我們已經輸了第一回合比賽。

 and so on/forth　…等等

He sells old furniture, secondhand clothes, *and so on*.

他販賣舊家具、舊衣服等等。

❸ so...that...　如此…以致於…

He was so weak that he could hardly get out of bed.　他太虛弱，幾乎不能下床。

❹ sooner or later　遲早

If you keep gambling like this, sooner or later you'll be in big trouble.　如果你繼續這樣賭下去，遲早會有大麻煩。

　1. no sooner...than...

= as soon as　一…就…

I had *no sooner* arrived *than* it began to rain.

= *No sooner* had I arrived *than* it began to rain.

我一到就開始下雨。

2. The sooner, the better.　越快越好

❺ sort of　稍微；有一點

I'm sort of afraid of him, but I don't know why.　我有點怕他，但不知為什麼。

　kind of、somewhat

　前面在談到 kind of 時已經提過，這三個片語全部屬於口語上的用法，不能與 a kind of、a sort of 等的正式用法搞混。

 out of sorts　輕微的生病、沮喪或不開心

I'm ok, just a little bit *out of sorts*. Thank you.

我還好，只是有一點不舒服，謝謝你的關心。

❻ speak out 大膽公開說出來

No one dared to speak out against his unreasonable demands on us.

沒有人敢公開反對他對我們的不合理要求。

 1. speak to 說到；言及

Please *speak to* the point; time is almost up.

請說重點；時間快到了。

2. speak of

= mention 談到

He seldom *speaks of* his family.

他很少提到家人。

❼ speak up **(A)** 大聲說話；**(B)** 表達意見

A. I can't hear you. Could you please speak up?

我聽不見你說話，請大聲一點。

B. Now let's talk about this agenda. Please speak up.

現在我們來聊聊這項議題。請各位談談自己的看法。

 speak up for 為支持某人而說話

It's about time someone *spoke up for* the poor.

該是有人替窮人發聲的時候了。

❽ speed up **(A)** 加速前進；**(B)** 使某事加速進行

A. You can't speed up when passing by a hospital or a school.

經過學校或醫院時，不可以加速。

B. The use of machinery in the late 19th century speeded up the producing process in many factories.

十九世紀後期，機器的使用加速了許多工廠的生產程序。

 「使某事加速進行」可以寫成 speed sth up

❾ split off 使裂開；使分開

A huge lump of rock split off from the cliff face after the earthquake.

地震之後，一塊大岩石從懸崖表面裂開。

 split off 常接介系詞 from。

❿ stand for **(A)** 代表；**(B)** 容忍；**(C)** 支持、主張

A. The national anthem and the national flag both stand for a country.

國歌和國旗都是一個國家的代表。

B. You shouldn't stand for his rude words.

你不該容忍他粗魯的言語。

C. He stands for equality and non-violence.

他主張平等與非暴力。

代表：represent

容忍：tolerate

 這裡的「容忍」通常用在否定句裡，意味著「不能容忍」。

❶ stand on one's own feet 靠自己獨立

Though she is twenty, she's never learned to stand on her own feet.

雖然她 20 歲了，卻從未學習過獨立。

❷ stand up for 保衛；支持

I always stand up for what I believe in.

我總是會保衛自己的信念。

 1. stand up 起立；耐久

We *stood up* when the honored guest entered.

貴賓進入時，我們站起來。

The laptop won't *stand up* under hard use.

筆記型電腦無法承受粗暴的使用。

2. stand up to 勇敢的抵抗；（物）經得起

The little boy *stood up to* the bigger boy.

小男孩勇敢的面對這個大男孩。

This metal will *stand up to* high temperatures.

這金屬耐高溫。

❸ start...off (A) 幫助某人展開一項活動；(B) 使某事發生

A. The coach started us off with some stretching exercises.

活動前，教練指導我們先做一些伸展操。

B. It's your support that started the parade off.

是你的支持使這個遊行能進行。

❹ start out (A) 出發；(B) 開始生活、展開創業

A. Stanley started out at dawn and reached home at midnight.

Stanley 黎明出發，半夜回到家。

B. Serene started out as a sales assistant before turning to the music.

轉到音樂這條路上之前，Serene 是以業助一職展開她的生活。

 start over 重新開始

The divorce didn't defeat her. She has *started over* her career from a coffee shop.

離婚並沒有打倒她。她從一間咖啡店開始，重新展開她的職場生涯。

⓯ start up　**(A)** 發起、開創、建立；**(B)** 發動（引擎等）

A. Mike decided to start up a photo studio of his own.

Mike 決定開設自己的攝影工作室。

B. You guys wait for me here. I'll go to the parking lot and start up my car.

你們在這裡等我，我去停車場發動車子。

⓰ stay away from　遠離

Stay away from Kate. She's in a bad mood now.

離 Kate 遠一點；她現在心情不好。

⓱ stay up　熬夜

We are allowed to stay up on Fridays.

星期五我們可以熬夜。

 sit up

 1. sit up　坐起來；坐直；熬夜

She *sat up* in bed, looking out of the window.

她從床上坐起身，看著窗外。

Sit up straight, everybody.

大家坐直。

2. stay over　在別人家過夜

Before deciding to *stay over* in my house, you'd better call back home first.

你決定在我家過夜之前，最好先打個電話回家。

⓲ stem from　源於；來自；肇因於

Your headache stemmed from too much tension.

你會頭痛，是因為過度緊張。

⓳ strike a balance　達到平衡；達到均勢

Parents should learn to strike a balance between work and family.

父母應學習在工作與家庭間找到平衡。

⓴ such as　諸如…之類

Cartoon characters such as Snoopy and Garfield are still popular.

像 Snoopy 及加菲貓等卡通人物仍然受歡迎。

㉑ such...that...　如此…以致於…

It was such an interesting movie that it appealed to a lot of audience.

那是一部相當有趣的電影，所以吸引了很多觀眾。

= This movie was so interesting that it appealed to a lot of audience.

 such + adj + N + that...

而 so + adj + that... 也有「如此…以致於」的意思

㉒ sue...for... 起訴；控告

This superstar sued the magazine for reporting his private life without his permission.

這位超級巨星控告雜誌社，未經他允許，就報導他的私生活。

 同義 charge...with...

 觸類旁通 sue for divorce 訴請離婚

Lori and her husband *sued for divorce*.
Lori 和她的老公要訴請離婚。

㉓ sum sth up **(A)** 總結、歸納；**(B)** 合計、總計

A. You open up the debate and I sum it up.

你開始辯論，我做總結。

B. The accountant summed up the expense of this year.

會計師加總今年的支出。

 **觸類旁通** to sum up 總之

To sum up, you can improve your health by taking more exercise.
總之，你可以藉著多運動改善健康。

㉔ take a risk 冒險

He took a big risk to walk across the stream.

他冒極大風險走過溪流。

 同義 run a risk、take a chance

㉕ take along 攜帶

He always takes along his dictionary when traveling abroad, for he doesn't know much English.

他出國旅行時，都會帶著字典，因為他不太會英文。

㉖ take apart 拆開

The mechanic took the computer apart to repair it.

技工把電腦拆開來修理。

㉗ take care of **(A)** 照顧（某人等）；**(B)** 處理（某事）

A. Who will take care of the business when Father is out of town?

爸爸出城時，誰來照顧生意？

B. Don't worry. I'll take care of the waste materials.

別擔心，我會處理這些廢棄物。

 同義 照顧某人：look after、care for

處理某事：deal with、cope with、handle

 **觸類旁通** take care 小心；注意

Take care not to eat too much every meal.
小心每一餐不要吃過多。

❷❽ **take delight in** 以…為樂

Carl takes delight in playing tricks on others.　　　　Carl 以在別人身上惡作劇為樂。

 同　義　be fond of、care for、like、take to

Little girls *are fond of* listening to fairy tales.

小女孩喜歡聽童話故事。

❷❾ **take/have exercise** 運動

You can take more exercise to strengthen your muscles.　　你可以多運動來強化肌肉。

❸⓿ **take heart (from)** （自…）獲得信心、勇氣

The actor took heart from the audience's positive
feedback.

這名演員從觀眾的正面回應中獲
得信心與勇氣。

觸類旁通　take sth to heart　把某件事看得很嚴重（結果是讓自己很沮喪）

His criticism upon your performance is his own prejudice. Don't *take it to heart*.

他對你的表演所做的評論，不過是他的偏見，別放在心上。

Unit 18 Exercise

 I. 片語選填

sum up	stand up for	stay away from	take delight in
split off	take heart	so much for	sooner or later
strike a balance	speak up		

1. ＿＿＿＿＿＿＿＿＿＿ our discussion of movies. Let's get back to work now. (90)

2. His boss is bound to find out the truth ＿＿＿＿＿＿＿＿＿＿. (88)

3. Try to ＿＿＿＿＿＿＿＿＿＿ in front of your class while doing the drill. (90)

4. This part of the project has now been ＿＿＿＿＿＿＿＿＿＿ from the main team.

5. In a democratic society, everyone can ＿＿＿＿＿＿＿＿＿＿ his or her human rights.

6. Mary and I had a quarrel, so she ＿＿＿＿＿＿＿＿＿＿ me. (86)

7. It is hard for a country to ＿＿＿＿＿＿＿＿＿＿ between economic development and environmental protection. (88)

8. In your final paragraph, ＿＿＿＿＿＿＿＿＿＿ your argument. (86)

9. Booksellers ＿＿＿＿＿＿＿＿＿＿ having books around them. (88)

10. ＿＿＿＿＿＿＿＿＿＿ and hang on to your goal for as long as it takes. (87)

II. 引導翻譯

11. 有些人對我微笑，但其他人只是忽略我。(92)

    Some people _____ _____ me, but others just ignore me.

12. 車子移動太快，以致闖過高速公路分隔柵欄，造成對撞，而死了五個人。(84)

    The car was moving _____ fast _____ it went through the highway-driving fence, resulting in a collision in which five people died.

13. 人們對那些公開反對改革者破口大罵。(90)

    People shouted insults at those who _____ _____ against the reform.

14. 在病人的窗外種樹，可以加快病人的恢復速度。(90)

    Planting trees near patients' windows can _____ _____ recovery rates.

15. 每個台灣學生都應知道 M.I.T. 代表什麼。(86)

    Every Taiwanese student should know what "M.I.T." _____ _____ .

16. 他的父母要他在大學畢業之後自己獨立。(86)

    His parents want him to _____ on his own _____ after graduating from college.

17. 就早餐來說，它使你展開漫長一天的工作，所以你需要充足的食物來提供你足夠的精力。(87)

    For breakfast, which _____ you _____ on a long day's work, you need sufficient food to provide you with enough energy.

18. 這些花十一月開始泛黃，後來就枯萎了。(90)

    The flowers _____ _____ with a pale yellow in November, and later faded away.

19. 我要知道是誰造的謠。(87)

    I want to know who _____ _____ that rumor.

20. 多數學生都有熬夜準備考試的經驗。(90)

    Most students have the experience to _____ _____ preparing for the exam.

21. 另一則傳說源自於古老氣象先知的信念，他們認為，雨是貓狗的惡靈在作怪。(85)

    The other legend _____ _____ the beliefs of ancient weather prophets that rain was caused by the evil spirits of cats and dogs.

22. 我們個人的慶祝會，譬如婚禮、升遷、畢業、週年等，也與飲酒關係密切。(84)

    Our personal celebrations, _____ _____ weddings, promotions, graduations, and anniversaries, are closely linked with drinking.

23. 那個英雄擁有如此的勇氣，所以他敢衝入火場。(84)

    The hero had _____ courage _____ he dared to rush into the fire.

24. 那位七十歲的教授控告大學年齡歧視，因為他的教書合同未被續約。(92)

    The 70-year-old professor _____ the university _____ age discrimination, because his teaching contract had not been renewed.

25. 當你計畫參觀一個國家時，如果你知道特定季節有的天氣狀況，你就能攜帶適當的衣服。(87)

If you know the weather of a particular season when you plan to visit this country, you can _____ _____ suitable clothes.

26. 中國父母通常很保護孩子，他們要確定孩子是安全的，而且一直受到良好照顧。(92)

Chinese parents are usually very protective of their children. They want to make sure their children are safe and well _____ _____ _____ all the time.

27. 印刷完之後，字母可以拆卸，再重新組合，印刷其他的東西。(83)

When the printing was finished, the letters could be _____ _____ and rearranged to print something else.

28. 此外，因為是早起的鳥兒，所以你有大量的時間運動，或做很多工作。(86)

Besides, being an early bird, you have plenty of time to _____ _____ or do a lot of work.

❶ take one's word 相信某人的話

If I don't trust you, I won't take your word.

如果我不信任你，我就不會相信你的話。

❷ take out **(A)** 取出、拿走、帶走；**(B)** 帶…出去

A. You can take out six books at a time from the library.

你一次可以從圖書館借出 6 本書。

B. A red-faced guy took this little girl out an hour ago.

小女孩一小時前被一個紅臉男子帶出去。

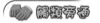 take sth out on sb　發洩不好的情緒到某人身上

We all know the boss' laying the blame on you makes you mad, but you can't *take it out on* us!

我們知道老闆究責於你令你生氣，但你也不能把不滿的情緒發洩在我們身上啊！

❸ take/feel/express pride in 以…為榮；自傲於

The actress takes great pride in her appearance.

那名女演員以其外貌為榮。

 pride oneself on、be proud of

I *pride myself on* my son's performance at school.

我以我兒子在學校的表現為榮。

❹ take responsibility (for) 負責任

The manager took responsibility for his employee's mistake.

這位經理為他員工的錯誤負責任。

❺ take the place of 取代；代替

Natural methods of pest control are now gradually taking the place of chemicals.

天然的昆蟲控制法正逐漸取代化學藥品的地位。

 replace、take one's place

I *took her place* as secretary yesterday.

我昨天代替她當秘書。

❻ take to **(A)** 開始做；**(B)** 開始喜歡

A. Lots of teenagers take to hip-pop nowadays.

當前很多青少年喜歡嘻哈音樂。

Computer games are so exciting that many teenagers take to them at once.

電腦遊戲這麼刺激，很多青少年一下子就喜歡上了。

B. He immediately took to car-racing after seeing the movie.

看完電影之後，他立刻喜歡上賽車。

 同義 take a liking to、have a liking for、care for、be fond of、take delight in、like

 用法 take to + V-ing/N

❼ **take turns** 輪流

The students are taking turns reading the story out loud in class.

學生們在課堂上輪流大聲朗讀故事。

= The students are reading the story out loud by turns in class.

They take turns taking care of their sick mother.

他們輪流照顧他們生病的母親。

= They take care of their sick mother by turns.

 同義 by turns

 用法 S + take turns + V-ing = S + V + … + by turns

❽ **take up** (A) 接受（挑戰、職務等）；(B) 養成…的習慣；(C) 佔去（時間、空間）

A. Jack took up the challenge to go abroad alone.

Jack 接受挑戰，獨自出國去。

B. Martha took up jogging every morning when she was only 15.

Martha 早在十五歲就養成晨跑的習慣。

C. The computer takes up half of my desk.

電腦佔去我書桌的一半。

 用法 take up + V-ing/N

 辨析 「養成習慣」在這裡有時還會指「開始養成這個習慣」。

 腦筋旁衝 1. take up arms 開戰

2. take up residence 開始居住於某處

3. take sb up on 接受某人所提供的工作或邀請

Mr. Bergman *took John up on* his wedding feast.

Bergman 先生接受 John 的邀請參加他的婚宴。

❾ **take...with...** 隨身攜帶

Take an umbrella with you in case of rain.

隨身帶把傘，免得下雨。

❿ **thank sb for sth** 為某事感謝某人

The host made a toast to thank everyone for coming.

主人舉杯，感謝大家的光臨。

⓫ thanks to 幸虧；由於

Thanks to the generosity of the public, the aim of the fund has been reached.

幸虧大家的慷慨，基金的目標已經達成。

 thanks to 只限用於好的方面。

⓬ that is (to say) **(A)** 換言之；**(B)** 應該這麼說

A. She is a perfectionist; that is to say, she always wants things to be as good as possible.

她是個完美主義者；換句話說，她總是想要每件事都能盡善盡美。

B. I've always enjoyed watching news report—that is, I did until so many gossip showing on the news.

我一直很喜歡看新聞一喔，應該這麼說，到前一陣子一堆八卦新聞出現前，我很喜歡看新聞。

 換言之：in other words、to put it differently、namely

 「應該這麼說」其實就是「針對自己剛剛說的事情做一點修正」。

⓭ the minute 一⋯就⋯

Tell him to call me back the minute he arrives.

他一到，就叫他打電話給我。

 the moment、the instant、as soon as

⓮ the rest 其餘的；剩下的

The doctor said that he would be in the wheelchair for the rest of his life.

醫生說，他將在輪椅上度餘生。

⓯ the same as 和⋯一樣

As far as I know, he has the same idea as you.

據我所知，他的想法與你一樣。

⓰ these days 最近

The price of housing in Kaohsiung is declining these days.

最近高雄地區的住宅價格下跌。

 recently

⓱ think of A as B 視 A 為 B；把 A 看作是 B

Many people think of America as a melting pot.

很多人視美國為大熔爐。

 think of + N + as + V-ing/N

 think of　思索；想起

What do you *think of* Robert as a boyfriend?

你覺得 Robert 這個男朋友怎麼樣？

Whenever I see you, I always *think of* my mother.

每次見到你，我總是想起我的母親。

⓲ thrive on　在…之下興盛／成長

He is the kind of person who thrives on pressure and challenges.

他是那種在壓力跟挑戰之下能成長茁壯的人。

⓳ through and through　徹底地；完全地

He lost the competition and felt disappointed at himself through and through.

他輸了比賽而對自己徹徹底底的感到失望。

　completely、thoroughly

⓴ throw away　(A) 丟棄；(B) 斷送

A. You can't throw away the broken furniture here.

你不能把壞家具丟棄在此。

B. You are throwing away your chance of becoming a promising singer.

你在糟蹋成為知名歌手的機會。

　丟棄：throw out

 throw out　丟棄；要求某人離開；駁回（提案、申請）

Ted didn't expect Amy to be one of the members in his group, but he couldn't directly *throw her out*.

Ted 雖然一開始就不希望 Amy 進入他那一組，但他也不可以就直接的要求 Amy 離開啊！

The boss *threw out* Jone's plan of investing in Mainland China.

老闆駁回了 Jone 投資大陸的計畫案。

㉑ throw off　(A) 擺脫某人的追逐；(B) 脫離桎梏、統治；(C) 快速脫去衣物

A. I ran all out for about 500 meters before I could throw him off.

我全速跑了約 500 公尺才擺脫掉他。

B. Finally Taiwan threw off the yoke of Japan in 1945.

1945 年，台灣終於脫離日本統治。

C. He threw off his coat and sat down.

他脫掉外套坐下來。

㉒ throw sth/sb into...　丟入；投入

After a long day's working, he threw himself into the couch.

一天漫長的工作之後，他一頭栽進沙發中。

146

 throw in 　附贈

If you purchase our CD player, we'll *throw in* a pair of headphones to you.

如果您選購我們的 CD 音響，我們就附贈您一副耳機。

㉓ tie together with 　與⋯符合；內容一致

The thesis you wrote does not tie together with the title we discussed.

你所寫的論文與我們討論的主題不相符合。

㉔ to (good/best) advantage 　有效地

How could he turn the situation to good advantage?

他如何有效地轉換情勢？

㉕ to and from 　來回（兩地）

Most commuters to and from Tamshui prefer to take the MRT.

大部分往返淡水的通勤族都偏好搭捷運。

㉖ top priority 　優先考慮

The top priority of the government is economy.

政府的第一優先考慮是經濟。

㉗ touch on/upon 　觸及

The thesis touches on the relationship between poverty and crime.

這篇論文觸及貧窮與犯罪之間的關係。

㉘ transform into 　轉變為

The novel transformed her from a nobody into a famous writer in the world almost overnight.

這部小說讓她幾乎在一夜之間成為世界知名作家。

㉙ translate into 　翻譯為

Translate the following sentences into English.

將下列句子翻譯為英文。

 　translate + N + into + N

㉚ try on 　試穿

Can I try on these sneakers?

我可以試穿這些運動鞋嗎？

 　凡指試穿衣服、鞋子、帽子、耳環等穿戴在身上的物件皆可用此片語。

 try out 　試用（通常指試用點子）

His idea sounds good; let's *try* it *out*! 　他的點子聽起來不錯；咱們試試看吧！

Unit 19 Exercise

I. 片語選填

touch on	the minute	translate into	take responsibility
take turns	throw off	take to	through and through

1. In modern times, we also need to _____ to avoid spreading illness.

2. After retirement, Mr. Wang _____ ice skating, which he had always loved but had not had time for. (92)

3. They _____ looking after their sick mother. (88)

4. The empty boxes and many other things fell all over _____ he opened the door. (88)

5. These fires continue until heavy rainfall soaks the peat _____ . (87)

6. I did everything I could to _____ his sense of direction. (92)

7. If you carelessly _____ this topic, they will feel quite uneasy or upset.

8. Alexander Dumas' novels have been _____ more than 100 languages.

II. 引導翻譯

9. 今晚我帶你出去吃晚餐。(90)

I'll _____ you _____ for dinner tonight.

10. Boll 和他太太以曼哈頓計劃的成功為傲。(91)

Boll and his wife _____ great _____ _____ the success of the Manhattan Project.

11. 甚至 iRobot 公司也承認,家庭安全機器人不能取代家庭警衛系統。(90)

Even iRobot acknowledges that a home-security robot can't _____ the _____ of a household alarm system.

12. 如果你接受一份工作,要盡全力完成。(86)

When you _____ _____ a job, do your best to carry it out.

13. 他隨身攜帶很多貨物,包括大量的帆布。(85)

He _____ many goods _____ him, including a large quantity of canvas.

14. 有時,日常生活中令人恐懼的事件就會在夢中以真實的方式呈現,也就是說,這個小男孩夢到被那個大男孩欺負。(89)

At other times the dreaded event from daily life simply occurs in a dream in its real-life form; _____ _____ , the boy dreams of being bullied by the bigger boy.

15. 孤獨的 Victoria,終其餘生都在哀悼失去 Albert。(91)

For _____ _____ of her life, the lonely Victoria mourned for the loss of Albert.

16. 黑猩猩的腦與人類的腦擁有相同的內部構造，雖然牠的腦是人類的三倍大，但其腦表面的皺摺規律與人腦類似。(90)

The brain of a chimpanzee has the same internal structure and in its surface _____ _____ pattern of folds _____ the human brain, which, however, is three times as large.

17. 最近我都沒有他的信息，連電子郵件或電話都沒有。(85)

I haven't heard from him _____ _____, either e-mail or phone.

18. 電腦業充滿自認為和傳統西裝畢挺的生意人不一樣的年輕人。(91)

The computer industry is full of young people who _____ _____ themselves _____ very different from traditional business people in suits.

19. 將無人信件丟掉，不是處理的方法。(89)

To _____ dead mail _____ is not a way to deal with it.

20. 他撿起鸚鵡，把牠丟進雞舍中。(87)

He picked the parrot up and _____ the bird _____ the chicken house.

21. 在現代世界中，這些事似乎不能和科學相結合。(87)

These things do not seem to tie _____ _____ science in the modern world.

22. 蜂鳥有效地運用牠獨特的飛行能力。(84)

The hummingbird uses its unique flying abilities to _____ _____ .

23. 因為雷雨交加，所有往返高雄的班機都取消了。(92)

All the flights _____ _____ _____ Kaohsiung were cancelled because of the heavy thunderstorm.

24. 這次慶祝會，將會使巴黎由「光的城市」轉變成為「光的首府」。(87)

The celebration would _____ Paris the "city of light" _____ the "capital of light."

25. 你為何不先試穿看看？(89)

Why don't you _____ them _____ first?

III. 克漏字選擇

Hercules

The queen of the gods, Hera, was angry at Hercules because he was the son of his husband Zeus and a mortal woman. She tried to kill him, but __26__ his extraordinary strength, Hercules escaped death many times. However, one day, Hera made him so mad that he killed his wife and children. Hercules decided to __27__ the murder of his family. Apollo's priestess told him that he had to be his cousin's servant for 12 years __28__ a punishment. Influenced by Hera, Hercules' cousin gave him very dangerous and difficult labors to perform. Zeus could __29__ his son's attitude: Hercules showed courage and strength by fighting terrible monsters, __30__ a nine-headed snake. As Hercules __31__ finish his labors, Hera tried again to harm him. His ninth labor was to __32__ the girdle of Hippolyta, queen of the Amazons. Hippolyta was ready to give him the girdle, but Hera ___33___ his easy victory into a tragedy. She persuaded the Amazons that Hercules wanted to kidnap Hippolyta. They attacked him. He thought the queen had betrayed him; he killed her and escaped with the girdle. Hercules eventually accomplished ___34___ of his labors. Later, when he died, he was accepted among the gods on Mount Olympus.

(　　) 26. (A) in addition to　(B) when it comes to (C) thanks to　　(D) up to

(　　) 27. (A) take advantage of　　　　　(B) take responsibility for
　　　　 (C) make use of　　　　　　　　(D) make up for

(　　) 28. (A) as　　　　(B) of　　　　(C) into　　　(D) from

(　　) 29. (A) be proud on　(B) pride himself in (C) take pride in　(D) take proud on

(　　) 30. (A) including of　(B) such as　　(C) as such　　(D) inclusive

(　　) 31. (A) was rarely　(B) was to　　(C) was able to　(D) set on

(　　) 32. (A) bring in　　(B) bring off　(C) bring down　(D) bring back

(　　) 33. (A) transcended　(B) transcribed　(C) transformed　(D) translated

(　　) 34. (A) the rest　　(B) the other　(C) all kinds　(D) the first

❶ turn a deaf ear to 充耳不聞

Many teenagers turn a deaf ear to their parents.　　　許多青少年對父母的話充耳不聞。

 辨析　　turn a deaf ear to 是指「拒絕接受所有的忠告或建議」。

觸類旁通　　fall on deaf ears　將（警告、忠告、建議等）拋在腦後

這是指「雖然接受了建議，但一下子這個人就完全忽略掉了」。

❷ turn into　　**(A) 轉變為；(B) 把⋯駛進**

A. A few weeks later, a hot summer turned into a pleasant fall.　　　幾星期之後，炎熱的夏天變成宜人的秋天。

B. Don't turn the car into that narrow lane.　　　別把車開進那條窄巷中。

同義　　轉變為：turn to

觸類旁通　　turn to　朝⋯方向、轉變；參照⋯；求援

To get more information about Culture Industry, please *turn to* Chapter 8.

如需要更多有關文化工業的資料，請參照第八章。

I couldn't repair the car by my own. I had to *turn to* the factory.

我自己沒辦法把車修好。我得向工廠求助了。

❸ turn off　　**(A) 關閉；(B) 從⋯轉進岔路**

A. Remember to turn off the light before you leave.　　　記得在離開前關燈。

B. Turn off the main road here, and you will come to the nursery home.　　　在這離開幹道轉進岔路，你就會到達安養院。

❹ turn on　　**(A) 打開；(B) 取決於⋯；(C) 突然襲擊**

A. If you feel hot, turn on the air-conditioner.　　　如果覺得熱就把冷氣打開。

B. The solution to the problem turns on a matter of money.　　　這個問題能否解決，是錢的問題。

C. The bear suddenly turned on the little boy.　　　熊突然攻擊小男孩。

觸類旁通　　turn A on B　把 A 事物朝向 B

He *turned* his criticism *on* me.

他把批評的矛頭對準我。

❺ turn one's back on　　某人背棄⋯

How can you turn your back on your parents when you succeed?　　　當你成功時，豈可背棄父母？

❻ turn over a new leaf 改頭換面；重新做人

After failing the math test, he decided to turn over a new leaf instead of fooling around all day long.

數學考試不及格之後，他決定捲土重來，不再終日打混。

 turn over 讓渡、引渡；發動（引擎）；深思熟慮；把…翻過來

He *turned over* his business to his son.

他將自己的事業移轉給他的兒子。

Derek *turned over* the engine to see if the car was broken.

Derek 發動引擎，想知道車子是不是故障了。

We have to *turn* this proposal *over* in this meeting.

在這次的會議中，我們必須把這個提案好好考慮一下。

I *turned* the china *over* to see who made it.

我把陶器翻過來，看看是誰製作的。

❼ turn up **(A)** 出現；**(B)** 突然發現；**(C)** 使…向上；
(D) 調強（如瓦斯爐的火）、開大（如音量）

A. She turned up at the dance party and surprised everyone.

她突然出現在舞會上，讓大家都很驚訝。

B. The police turned up the robber hiding behind the safe.

警方突然發現搶匪躲在保險箱之後。

C. Feeling chilly, she turned up the collar of her coat.

她覺得冷，所以把外套領子豎起來。

D. I can't hear the radio clearly. Would you mind if I turn the volume up?

我聽不清楚收音機的聲音，你介意我把聲音調大聲嗎？

 turn up 的「出現」是指「未經預期或未事先安排好」的出現，而 show up 與 appear 雖然中文上也有「出現」之意，但卻是「安排好或預期中」的出現。

❽ under pressure 在壓力之下

He eventually broke down under pressure.

他最後在壓力下崩潰了。

❾ under the care of 在…的照顧之下

I grew up happily under the care of my grandparents.

我在祖父母照顧之下快樂地長大。

❿ up and down **(A)** 上下；**(B)** 到處

A. I saw many boats sailing up and down the river.

我看到許多船隻在這條河流來回穿梭。

B. She is looking up and down for her lost child.

她四處找尋她走失的孩子。

⓫ use up　用光

Try not to use up all your money at the end of every month.

試著別當「月光族」。

⓬ wander about　徘徊；流浪；漫遊

I wandered about the shopping mall alone for three hours.

我一人在購物中心閒逛了三小時。

⓭ ward off　避開

Many people believe that Feng Shui can help ward off evil spirits.

很多人相信風水可以幫助避開邪靈。

⓮ warn sb of/about sth　警告某人某事

The message warned us of the possible danger cigarettes would bring.

信息中警告我們香煙可能會帶來的危險。

⓯ warn sb off　警告某人勿從事某種行為

Anti-smokers try to warn people off smoking cigarettes.

反菸者試圖警告人們不要抽煙。

⓰ watch one's back　注意安全

While walking in the dark, watch your back all the time.

在黑暗中行走時，隨時注意安全。

 watch your weight　注意體重

watch your step　小心謹慎

Watch your step while walking on the muddy road.

走在泥濘的路上要小心步伐。

⓱ what a pity　好可惜

What a pity we missed the celebration.

真可惜我們錯過了慶祝會。

 what a shame

⓲ what if　如果…怎麼辦?

What if he doesn't show up?

如果他沒有出現怎麼辦?

What if John sends you back? Then you can stay with us without having to worry about the bus schedule.

讓 John 送你回去如何? 這樣你就能留下來，不用擔心公車時刻了。

 這個片語主要用在口語上。

 這個片語除了「如果…怎麼辦?」這種用在比較負面情況的場合外，還可以用在當你要「給人家一個有用的建議」時。

❶❾ when it comes to   一提到

When it comes to traffic, safety cannot be emphasized too much.

一提到交通，安全最重要了。

 when it comes to + N/V-ing

❷⓿ wipe out   擦拭掉；除掉

The whole army was wiped out after the explosion.

在爆炸之後整支軍隊都滅亡了。

❷❶ with all one's heart   (A) 某人全心全意地；(B) 強調非常強烈的感覺

A. He worked with all his heart to help the poor woman.

他全心全意地工作以幫助那可憐的女人。

B. Sandy wished with all her heart that her boyfriend would call her last night.

Sandy 非常期待她的男友昨天會打電話給她。

 with all one's heart and soul

❷❷ with the help of   有了…的幫助

I completed my report smoothly with the help of Professor Lin.

在林教授的幫助之下，我順利完成報告。

❷❸ work for   為…工作

We should be loyal to the company we work for.

我們應對我們任職的公司忠誠。

❷❹ work with   和…一起工作

People in modern times should learn to work with computers.

現代人應學習與電腦為伍一塊工作。

❷❺ worry about   擔心；憂慮

There's no reason why you should worry about him; he is quite competent.

你實在沒有理由擔心他；他很有能力。

 be worried about

 worry about+ N/V-ing

❷❻ You can say that again.   我非常贊同。

A: John shouldn't work for that commercial bank.
B: You can say that again.

A:「John 不應該去那家商業銀行上班。」B:「我完全同意。」

 I can't agree with you more.

154

❷ **You deserve it.**　你活該。

A: "Hey! Why did you kick me?"

B: "You deserve it, teasing me like that."

A:「嘿，你踢我幹嘛?」B:「你活該，誰叫你取笑我?」

 同義　It serves you right.

I. 片語選填

| turn off | ward off | with all one's heart | use up |
| work with | turn over a new leaf | up and down | |

1. When the meeting was over, I＿＿＿＿＿＿＿＿ the tape-recorder and brought around the drinks. (89)

2. Soapy was put in jail though he had decided to ＿＿＿＿＿＿＿＿. (91)

3. When the landlord opened the door, he looked at me ＿＿＿＿＿＿＿＿ before asking who I was. (89)

4. Stricter measures have been taken to ＿＿＿＿＿＿＿＿ potential dangers brought by cigarette-smoking. (87)

5. They loved him ＿＿＿＿＿＿＿＿. (89)

6. They would have to learn to ＿＿＿＿＿＿＿＿ robots and technology to solve society's problems. (87)

7. She's ＿＿＿＿＿＿＿＿ all the money her parents gave her in two weeks.

II. 引導翻譯

8. 林太太對她先生的抱怨充耳不聞，對她來說，面對現實比終日抱怨來得有建設性。(91)

Mrs. Lin ＿＿＿＿＿ a ＿＿＿＿＿ ＿＿＿＿＿ to her husband's complaints because, to her, facing the music is more constructive than complaining all day.

9. 我打開錄音機，每一個人很嚴肅地輪流以最好的口音從一數到二十。(89)

I ＿＿＿＿＿ ＿＿＿＿＿ the tape-recorder and each in turn solemnly counted from one to twenty in their best accent.

10. 我和 Mary 發生爭執，所以她背棄了我。(86)

Mary and I had a quarrel, so she ＿＿＿＿＿ ＿＿＿＿＿ ＿＿＿＿＿ on me.

11. 許多商人承受重大壓力去爭取可能最大的市場佔有率。(86)

Many businessmen are ＿＿＿＿＿ ＿＿＿＿＿ ＿＿＿＿＿ to gain the largest market share possible.

12. Zoe 被發現時相當健康，在孤兒院細心地照顧下，她非常開心。(90)

Zoe was rather healthy when she was found, and once _____ _____ _____ of the orphanage she was very happy.

13. 他四處徘徊，直到他發現自己站在一座教堂前面。(91)

He _____ _____ until he found himself standing in front of a church.

14. 水中生物已經演化出獨特的聲音製造方式，用以與同類溝通，並警告捕食牠們的掠食者。(90)

Underwater creatures have evolved remarkable ways of producing sound to communicate with each other, and to _____ _____ predators that feed on them.

15. 醫生不斷地警告人們噪音的嚴重影響。(85)

Doctors have repeatedly _____ people _____ the serious effect of noise.

16. 這個城市相當安全。你散步時，即使晚上也不必擔心你的背後有什麼。(92)

It's quite safe here in the city. You don't need to _____ _____ _____ when taking a walk—even at night.

17. 今晚你不能加入我們，真是可惜！(86,89)

_____ _____ _____! You can't join us tonight.

18. 如果我期末考失敗了怎麼辦？

_____ _____ I fail the final exams?

19. 我們能夠做許多高科技的手術等等，但一旦談到了解心靈和身體如何合作時，我們真的就不太清楚了。(86)

We can do many high-tech operations and so on, but _____ _____ _____ _____ understanding how the mind and body work together, we are really not very well-informed.

20. 司機必須不斷地走出街上電車，去清除掉累積在擋風玻璃上的冰雪。(91)

Repeatedly, the motorman had to get out of the streetcar to _____ _____ the snow and ice collected on the windshield.

21. 有了地圖相助，我將小狗 Derek 留在三十分鐘路程處，但 Derek 又比我先到家。(92)

_____ _____ _____ of a map, I left Derek the doggie 30 minutes away, but Derek beat me home again.

22. 雖然 Siegel 先生和 Shuster 先生創造了這個超級英雄，但真正賺到錢的卻是他們任職的公司。(89)

Though Mr. Siegel and Mr. Shuster invented this superhero, it was the company they _____ _____ that actually made the money.

23. 別擔心成績。只要專注於課業上。努力常會使你發揮到極致。(88)

Don't _____ _____ your grades. Just concentrate on your studies. Hard work often brings out the best in you.

Key Idioms & Phrases 800

Section Two

Unit 21 ～ 29

超高頻片語

❶ a number of　一些；許多

We have been friends for a number of years.　我們已是多年老友。

Every summer a great number of tourists crowd into the town.　每年夏天，大量觀光客湧入此鎮。

 a great many、a good many、many

 number 之前可加上不同的形容詞，如：a large/great/good number of 表示很多。

❷ a (wide, great) variety of　多樣的；多種的

Based on the passage, in order to break into computer code, one needs a thorough understanding of a variety of computers.　根據短文所述，要侵入電腦密碼，必須對各種電腦徹底了解。

The students in my class come from a variety of backgrounds.　我班上的學生來自各種不同的背景。

 different kinds of、various kinds of

❸ according to　**(A)** 根據；**(B)** 依照

A. According to my experience, it takes three months to read this novel.　根據我的經驗，看這本小說要花三個月的時間。

B. Cut your coat according to your cloth.　（諺）量入為出。

 in accordance with

 according to + N

 according as + S + V, ...　根據；取決於
You could get there without delay *according as* he told me.
根據他告訴我的，你會準時到達而沒有耽誤。

❹ achieve/reach/attain one's goal　達成目標

A person of great determination usually can achieve his goal.　具有極大決心的人，通常能夠達成目標。

She eventually achieved her goal of becoming a professor.　她最後達成了當教授的目標。

 set a goal　設定目標
They *set a goal* of increasing sales by five percent every month.
他們設定目標，每個月的銷售要增加百分之五。

❺ add A to B   將 A 加入 B

She added John and his girlfriend to the guest list.

她將 John 跟他女朋友加入賓客名單裡。

 1. add to   增加

The hat with purple ribbon *adds to* her charm.

那頂有紫色緞帶的帽子增加了她的嫵媚。

2. to add insult to injury   在傷口灑鹽

She not only deceived him but, *to add insult to injury*, took away all his money in the bank.

她不僅欺騙他，還拿走他銀行裡所有的錢，簡直是傷口上灑鹽。

3. to add fuel to the flames   火上加油

Rather than providing a solution, their statements merely *added fuel to the flames*.

他們所陳述的，非但不能解決問題，反而是火上加油。

❻ adjust (oneself) to   (A) 適應、習慣於；(B) 調整…以配合…

A. It seems that he can't adjust himself to country life.

他似乎無法適應鄉間生活。

B. The speaker adjusted his lecture to his audience.

演講人配合聽眾口味來調整內容。

    adapt (oneself) to、accustom oneself to、get used to、be used to、be accustomed to

It took a few seconds for my eyes to *adapt to* the darkness.

我的眼睛經過數秒，才適應黑暗。

    adjust to + N/V-ing

❼ after all   畢竟

Don't blame the whole thing on him; after all, he is only an eight-year-old boy.

別把整件事都怪罪在他的身上；畢竟，他只是個八歲大的孩子。

I don't know why you are so concerned—it's not your problem after all.

我不明白你為何那麼擔心，畢竟那不是你的問題。

❽ agree with   (A) 同意；(B) 和…一致；(C) 適合

A. I agree with her about the best age for getting married.

我跟她對於適婚的年齡看法一致。

B. The film version agrees with the original novel.

電影版和原著小說一致。

C. Drinking does not agree with such a lady like you.

喝酒不適合像你這樣的淑女。

Unit 21

A

 1. agree on　就…達成協議

We *agreed on* the price for the villa.
我們就別墅的價格達成協議。

2. agree to V/N　同意

We *agreed to* leave at once.
我們同意立刻離開。

People with common sense will *agree to* it.
有常識的人會同意的。

❾ **ahead of**　早於；在…之前

Thanks to his help, we finished the work ahead of schedule.

由於他的幫助，我們提前完成這個工作。

 before

You'd better take a small rest *before* driving on the highway.
在上高速公路開車前，你最好先休息一下。

❿ **all over**　**(A)** 遍及；到處；**(B)** 完全結束；完蛋

A. He ached all over after falling off the bike.

從腳踏車上摔下後他全身都酸痛。

This bank has put up branches all over the world.

這家銀行已在世界各地設立許多分行。

B. It's all over with you now.

你現在完蛋了。

 all over the world

= the world over

= throughout the world　遍及全世界

The first aim of the IMO is to discover, to encourage, and, most important of all, to challenge mathematically gifted young people *all over the world*.
國際奧林匹亞數學競賽的第一個目標就是發掘、鼓勵，最重要的是挑戰世界各地有數學天賦的年輕人。

⓫ **all the time**　一直；始終；總是

The businessman seems to be busy all the time.

這位商人似乎一直都很忙碌。

I keep practicing the violin, so I'm still improving all the time.

我保持練琴，所以我仍能不斷進步。

 the whole time、always、all the while

⓬ amount to　　**(A)** 數量達到⋯、高達；**(B)** 等於

A. The whole set of home theater amounts to two hundred thousand NT dollars.

這一整套家庭劇院組合一共是台幣二十萬元。

Money lost through illness amounts to one million dollars.

因疾病造成的財產損失高達一百萬美元。

B. What she says always amounts to nothing.

她說的話一向等於空談。

 等於：come to

 amount to + N

⓭ appeal to　　**(A)** 要求、訴諸；**(B)** 吸引

A. My neighbor, John, just appealed to me for taking care of his son 20 minutes ago.

我的鄰居，John，20 分鐘前才請我幫忙照顧他兒子。

B. The idea of working abroad really appeals to me.

出國工作的點子真的很吸引我。

　　1. appeal to + sb + for + N
　　　　　　　　2. appeal to + sb + to V

⓮ apply for　　申請

We need to apply for planning permission to build a garage.

要建立車庫，我們必須申請（建築）計劃許可書。

　　1. apply to (college/university) for admission　申請入學；向⋯報名

The college in question is one of the best in our country. You may *apply to it for admission*.

談論中的這所大學是我國最棒的學校之一。你可以申請入學。

I *applied to* five universities and was accepted by all of them.

我申請五所大學，而且都獲准了。

　　　　　　　　2. apply to + N　適用於

The rule does not *apply to* the case.

本規定並不適用於該情況。

⓯ as a result　　因此

The snow was too heavy; as a result, all the flights were cancelled.

雪下得太大了，因此，所有班機都取消。

　　in consequence、therefore、thus、consequently、accordingly

❶ as a result of　因為

He was late for the meeting as a result of the heavy rain.　因為豪大雨，所以他開會遲到。

As a result of his laziness, he ended up achieving nothing.　由於懶惰，他到頭來一事無成。

 because of、due to、owing to、on account of
Because of his timely help, I finally achieved success.
由於他即時的幫助，我終於成功。

❷ as far as　和…一樣遠；一直到…的程度

I'll answer you as far as I am able to.　我將盡我所能的回答你。

 1. as/so far as one be concerned　對…而言
As far as I am concerned, this problem is too difficult to solve.
對我而言，這個問題太難解了。

　　2. as far as one know
　　= to one's understanding
　　= to one's knowledge　據…所知
　　As far as I know, David has left for Paris.
　　就我所知，David 已經前往巴黎了。

❸ as much as possible　盡可能多…

Barbara always does as much work as possible.　Barbara 總是盡可能多做工作。

To have the best performance next week, you should have as much practice as possible.　為了下週能有最成功的演出，你應該盡可能多練習。

 as much (+ N) + as possible

 as...as possible　盡可能
Please hand in your final paper *as soon as possible*.
請儘速繳交你的期末報告。

❹ as soon as　一…就…

As soon as you finish your work, I'd like to talk to you for a minute.　當你做完工作時，我想和你談一下。

As soon as she entered the room, she knew there was something wrong.　她一進房間，就知道不對勁。

❺ as though/if　彷彿

It looks as though everyone else has gone home.　看起來，似乎每個人都已經回家了。

She stared at me coldly as if I were a complete stranger.

她冷冷地瞪著我，彷彿我完全是個陌生人。

 用法　as if/though 後面接一般敘述或假設句，完全看後面句子的情況而定：
1. 如果是「敘述一件應該是真實的事情」，就接一般的敘述句，如上面第一個例句。
2. 如果是「用假設來解釋一種事件或情況，但是很明顯這個假設與事實不合」時，就接假設句，如上面第二個例句。

㉑ as to　　**(A)** 說到；**(B)** 至於、關於

A. As to the picnic, we must decide the destination later.

說到野餐，我們待會兒一定要決定目的地。

B. He has no idea as to what he should do next.

下一步該如何，他完全沒概念。

 同義　至於、關於：about

 用法　放句首時表「說到」，放句中則是引導受詞。

 觸類旁通　as for　至於
He will have a cup of coffee; *as for* me, I'll just have a glass of water.
他要喝一杯咖啡；至於我，只要一杯水就可以了。

㉒ as well　　**(A)** 也；**(B)** 最好

A. There were guitars in ancient Egypt and Greece as well.

在古埃及和希臘也有吉他。

Not only can he sing, but he can play the guitar as well.

他不僅會唱歌，還會彈吉他。

B. You might as well move out because you're always fighting with your roommates.

你不如就搬出去，因為你老在跟室友吵架。

 同義　也：too

 用法　表「也」時放在句尾。

㉓ as well as　　不但…而且；和

Exercise regularly can help strengthen your body as well as your mind.

規律的運動可以幫助增強你的身體以及你的心智。

He as well as I is happy about the result.

他和我對這個結果感到高興。

 同義　as well as 連接兩個主詞時：A together with B、A along with B
　　　　　　　　　　　　　　A no less than B

 用法　1. as well as 可用來連接對等的單字、片語及子句，就等於 and。
2. as well as 連接兩個主詞時，動詞以第一個主詞來做變化。

Unit 21

A

❷⁴ **at all costs** 無論如何；不惜代價

at any cost 不管怎樣

We should avoid war and maintain world peace at all costs.

我們應該不惜任何代價來避免戰爭，並維護世界和平。

It may rain tomorrow, but we are still going camping in any case.

明天可能會下雨，但不管怎樣，我們仍要去露營。

 無論如何: anyway

不管怎樣: at any rate、in any case

At any rate, you must have a complete physical checkup.

不論如何，你必須做一次徹底的健康檢查。

❷⁵ **at best** 充其量

Decreasing income tax, at best, is a temporary solution to recent economic situations.

減免所得稅，充其量不過是暫時解決目前經濟情況的辦法。

The campaign was at best partially successful.

這次活動，充其量只是部分成功。

I. 片語選填

all the time	as well	ahead of	a variety of	at all costs
as a result of	add to	as soon as	at best	as a result
appeal to	apply for	as to	adjust to	
as much as possible		a good number of		

1. The author recommends that we should avoid failure _____ . (87)

2. Drinking is part of our national celebrations _____ . (84)

3. _____ the couple realized that they didn't love each other anymore, they broke up. (92, 85)

4. _____ , an e-mail writer enjoys a great deal of freedom in communicating with anyone in any place of the world at any time. (88)

5. The idea of becoming famous _____ many people. (86)

6. Graduation from high school means that a new stage of life is _____ you. (86)

7. It was also because of Robert Houdin that many magicians were able to _____ Dr. or MD _____ their names. (92)

8. The lake produces _____ bass each season.

9. The staff of the dead mail offices has _____ ways to deal with all of these pieces of dead mail. (89)

10. At Tasvo National Park, Zoe has been taught to _____ life in the wild.

11. Generally speaking, all foreigners coming to Taiwan should _____ entry visas through the embassies or consulates of the R.O.C. (85)

12. The 60 pilot whales swam ashore _____ a behavior currently unknown to scientists. (84)

13. Living in a highly competitive society, you definitely have to arm yourself with _____ knowledge _____ . (92)

14. There are two more explanations _____ how this idiom came into being. (85)

15. These batteries are not good. _____ they will last only for two months.

16. She talks and talks _____ . She is talkative. (90)

II. 引導翻譯

17. 每當他看到她時，距上回看見她也許只隔五分鐘，他仍會非常欣喜地迎接她，歡迎她回到他的生命之中，彷彿她已經離開許多年似的。(88)
Every time he sees her, which may be five minutes since he last saw her, he greets her with great joy, welcoming her back into his life _____ _____ she had been gone for years.

18. 中國父母通常很保護孩子，他們要確認孩子是安全的，且一直受到良好的照顧。(92)
Chinese parents are usually very protective of their children. They want to make sure their children are safe and well taken care of _____ _____ _____ .

19. 社工人員要求整個社會遏止藥物的濫用。(86)
The social workers _____ _____ the whole society to help stop drug abuse.

20. 一份均衡的飲食，包含了一天三餐適量的食物，和各式各樣的食物，如蔬菜、水果、蛋、牛奶、穀物和肉類。(87)
A balanced diet contains adequate amounts of food for the three meals of a day and a _____ _____ foods such as vegetables, fruits, eggs, milk, cereals and meat.

21. 由於有更便宜、更有效率的電腦，有些公司已經開始生產機器人來做家事。(90)
Some companies have begun to produce robots for doing household chores _____ a _____ of cheaper and more efficient computers.

22. 但是當歌手一開始唱，他的臉立即為之一亮，而且開始唱著並指揮一首莫札特的曲子。
But _____ _____ _____ the singers start to sing, his face immediately brightens and he begins to sing and conduct a song by Mozart.

23. 理由可能是因為他們認為，人們的薪水是依其身價而定，他們不想讓自己的身價曝光。
The reason may be that they think people are paid _____ _____ their worth, and they don't want to have their worth known by others.

24. 如果談工作不能製造話題，試試別的主題，像是嗜好等。(88)

If work does not prove to be a productive topic, try other topics _____ _____ hobbies.

25. 機器人的消費市場似乎越來越看好，雖然這充其量只是個緩慢的轉變。(90)

The customer market for robots appears to be changing for the better, though it's a slow change _____ _____.

26. 建築師的工作，無論如何要滿足使用者的需求。(87)

The job of an architect is to satisfy the needs of the users _____ _____ _____.

27. 這個系統必須不斷調整適應新環境及情勢，才能繼續存在並繁衍興盛。(89)

This system must constantly _____ _____ a new environment and new situations to survive and flourish.

28. 數年後他們在全美販售。(90)

A few years later, they were selling _____ _____ the United States.

29. 成語和諺語增添語言的色彩，它們也透露出一些語言的文化背景。(85)

Idioms and proverbs _____ color to a language, and they also reveal some of the culture behind the language.

30. 因此，澳洲大約百分之九十五的哺乳動物和百分之九十四的青蛙，在世界其他地方已不見蹤影。(92)

_____ a _____, about 95% of Australia's mammals and 94% of its frogs are found nowhere else in the world.

31. 事實上，一隻蝙蝠每晚所吃的食物量高達它體重的四分之一。(85)

In fact, the food a bat eats every night _____ _____ one quarter of its own body weight.

32. 我們必須幫他，畢竟他是我們的親戚。(86)

We have to help him. _____ _____, he is our relative.

33. 我會盡全力幫助你。(88)

I'll help you _____ _____ _____ I can.

34. 女人易於比男人有技巧，因為女人通常比較圓滑，且會運用間接的策略來達成她們的目標。(85)

Women tend to be more skillful than men, because they are often more tactful and can use indirect strategies to _____ _____ _____.

35. 她老是以為自己是對的，期望每個人都贊同她。(91, 92)

She always thought that she was right, and expected everyone to _____ _____ her.

36. 他們將某人安全置於自己之前。(83)

They put someone's safety _____ of _____ own.

37. 對於喜歡待在市區裡的人，遊客可以逛逛許多有趣的商店。(84)

For those who prefer to stay in town, tourists can browse through a _____ _____ interesting shops.

38. 到了這個時候，廚師非常生氣，決定完全依照這位客人的要求：盡可能地將這些洋芋切得越薄越好。(90)

By this time the cook was angry and decided to do exactly what the guest wanted: slice the potatoes _____ _____ _____ _____.

III. 克漏字選擇

Leonardo da Vinci (1452-1519)

Leonardo was the son of a notary and a peasant girl. He was born in the small city of Vinci, Italy. __39__ his biography, Leonardo studied painting in a workshop until 1478, when he became an independent painter. He produced his first masterpiece, *The Last Supper* (1495-97), when he was in Milan. When the French attacked Milan in 1500, Leonardo went back to Florence and began his second masterpiece: the portrait of a Florentine lady: *Mona Lisa* (1503-1506). But Leonardo was __40__ a painter. As a scientist, he was centuries __41__ his time. He invented __42__ civil and military machines, designed buildings and studied geology and astronomy __43__ equal success. Leonardo made __44__ incredible inventions, such as the bicycle, flying machines, submarines, and tanks. His study of the human body caused him some serious trouble with the Catholic Church. Leonardo was very unhappy __45__ the way he was treated in Italy. __46__, when the French king Francis I offered him to come to France, he accepted and __47__ him many of his works, including the *Mona Lisa*. Leonardo spent the last years of his life in the famous Loire Valley and is said to have designed the plan for the greatest castle of the Renaissance: Chambord. He died in France in 1519.

( ) 39. (A) According to   (B) According as   (C) In accordance to   (D) In addition to
( ) 40. (A) not merely   (B) other than   (C) nothing but   (D) more than
( ) 41. (A) proud of   (B) in the way of   (C) ahead of   (D) open to
( ) 42. (A) a flock of   (B) a variety of   (C) a sense of   (D) a shortage of
( ) 43. (A) of   (B) by   (C) with   (D) in
( ) 44. (A) a burst of   (B) a herd of   (C) a great deal of   (D) a number of
( ) 45. (A) with   (B) by   (C) in   (D) on
( ) 46. (A) After all   (B) Above all   (C) As a result   (D) In a nutshell
( ) 47. (A) took with   (B) brought with   (C) took to   (D) brought in

Unit 22

❶ at least　至少

I have to read at least 2 acts of the play tonight.

我今晚至少得看完這本劇本兩幕。

Ted is poor, but at least he works very hard.

Ted 很窮，但至少他努力工作。

　at most　至多

❷ at times　有時候

I drink coffee at times while I read literary pieces.

在我讀文學作品時，會喝點咖啡。

　(every) now and then、once in a while、from time to time、occasionally

❸ based on　根據；建基於

Based on the second aim of this proposal, more international exchanges are encouraged and established.

根據此計劃的第二個目標，更多的國際交流將受到鼓勵並建立起來。

Their relationship is based on mutual respect.

他們的關係植基於互相尊重。

❹ be accused of　被控…的罪名

The professor was accused of stealing his student's ideas and publishing them.

那名教授被指控竊取學生的點子，並將它們出版。

❺ be aware of　了解；察覺

These folk healers also use observation and logic, but they are not aware of it.

當地的醫治者也使用觀察與邏輯方法，但他們並不知道。

The children are aware of the danger of taking drugs.

孩子們了解吸毒的危險。

❻ be concerned about/with　關心

All of us should be concerned about public affairs to make our society a better place.

為使我們的社會變成更好的地方，我們都應該關心公共事務。

　be concerned about + N；be concerned that + cl

　be concerned with/in　與…有關

The background of the novel *is concerned with* the Civil War.

這部小說的背景，與美國內戰有密切的關係。

❼ be covered with　覆蓋

The pit was covered with branches and dirt.

這個洞被覆蓋上樹枝和泥土。

The bulletin board was covered with messages.

通報蓋滿了佈告欄。

❽ **be crazy about**　對…瘋狂；醉心於…

He's crazy about her; in other words, he likes her very much.

他為她瘋狂。換言之，他非常喜歡她。

❾ **be familiar with**　熟悉

I am not familiar with what he is doing.

我對他正在做的事並不熟悉。

Are you familiar with this type of laptop?

你熟悉這一型的筆記型電腦嗎?

Almost every Chinese is familiar with Confucianism.
= Confucianism is familiar to almost every Chinese.

幾乎每個中國人對儒家學說都耳熟能詳。

　sb be familiar with sth = sth be familiar to sb

❿ **be fond of**　喜歡

The Earl Sandwich, an English aristocrat, was very fond of gambling at cards.

Sandwich 爵士是英國貴族，非常喜歡賭紙牌。

　care for、take to、take a liking to、have a liking for

⓫ **be made of**　由…製成（成品可以看出其原先的材料）

Some 20th century chairs are made of steel and plastic.

一些二十世紀的椅子是由鋼及塑膠所製造而成的。

The shirt is made of silk.

這件襯衫是絲製品。

　be made from　由…製成（成品看不出其原先的材料）
The wine you are drinking now *is made from* peaches planted by my father.
你現在喝的酒，是用我爸爸種的桃子所釀的。

⓬ **be proud of**　因…而引以為榮

Your past records are certainly something to be proud of.

你過去的紀錄的確是值得驕傲的。

　take pride in、pride oneself on
She *takes pride in* her children's achievements.
她以孩子的成就為榮。
She *prides herself on* being a good teacher.
她以身為好老師為榮。

⓭ **be related to**　**(A)** 與…有關；**(B)** 與…有親戚關係

A. We can conclude that tears are closely related to the emotional and biological makeup of the human species.

我們可以斷定：眼淚和人類的情感及生物構造是息息相關的。

B. The report says that she is related to the President.

該報導指出，她與總統有親戚關係。

　be related to + N

Unit 22

B

❹ be responsible for   (A) 為…負責；(B) 造成

A. Neumann is also responsible for her students' physical safety and moral welfare.

Neumann 也必須負責學生的人身安全和精神上的福祉。

Jack is responsible for interviewing and training new staff.

Jack 負責面試並培訓新員工。

B. The severe typhoon was responsible for many deaths.

嚴重的颱風造成多人死亡。

 take/have responsibility for   對…負責

Who do you trust to *take responsibility for* the new project?

你信賴誰來負責新的企劃案？

❺ be sensitive to   對…敏感

Their skin is very sensitive to temperature changes.

他們的皮膚對溫度變化很敏感。

Many people are sensitive to criticism from their close friends.

許多人對來自好朋友的批評很敏感。

    be sensitive to + N

❻ be similar to   與…類似

Richard is quite similar to his brother in personality.

Richard 個性和他弟弟非常相像。

    be similar to + N

❼ because of   因為；由於

She has to retire because of age.

她因為年紀而必須退休。

    due to、owing to、as a result of、on account of

❽ begin with   以…開始

The slogan "Just do it!" begins with the letter "j".

「就做吧！」這句廣告詞由 j 字母起首。

   1. end in   以…結束

Their marriage *ended in* divorce.

他們的婚姻以離婚結束。

2. to begin with   首先

To begin with, you shouldn't cheat in the test.

首先，你不該考試作弊。

⑲ break down　**(A)** 感情失去控制；**(B)**（機器）停止運轉；**(C)** 把…分解為；**(D)** 破壞；**(E)** 失敗

A. Hearing her father's death, she totally broke down.　　聽聞父親的噩耗，她完全崩潰了。

B. The car broke down in the middle of nowhere.　　車子在不知名的地方拋錨了。

C. Food is broken down in the stomach.　　食物在胃中分解。

D. It takes a long time to break down prejudice.　　消弭偏見得花上一段時間。

E. All our plans broke down just because of your carelessness.　　只是因為你的粗心，所有的計劃都失敗了。

⑳ break in/into　**(A)** 闖入；**(B)** 突然開始；**(C)** 打斷（談話）

A. The thief broke into his house and stole a gold watch.　　這賊闖入他家，偷走一只金錶。

B. Much to our amazement, the teacher broke into tears.　　老師突然大哭，真令我們驚訝。

C. The telephone broke into our discussion.　　電話中斷了我們的討論。

 觸類旁通　break out
= erupt 　（瘟疫、災難、戰爭等）爆發
The war in Iraq *broke out* two days ago.
兩天前伊拉克戰爭爆發了。

㉑ bring out the best/worst in sb　發揮／帶出某人最好的或最差的

Alcohol always brings out the worst in my father.　　我父親酒後總會露出他最壞的一面。

㉒ bring up　**(A)** 養育；**(B)** 提出

A. He was born in Taipei but brought up in Japan.　　他出生於台北，但在日本長大。

B. She brought up the subject of divorce to her husband again.　　她再次向她丈夫提出離婚的要求。

 同義　養育：rear

㉓ by all means　當然；盡一切辦法

"Can I use your car?" "By all means."　　「我可以用你的車嗎?」「當然可以。」

 同義　of course、certainly

 by no means

= never

= in no way

= under no circumstances

= not in the least　　絕不

It is *by no means* that the meeting will take place.

會議絕對不會舉行。

㉔ by and large　大體上；一般說來

By and large, men are paid higher than women.　　　一般說來，男性待遇比女性高。

　　in general、generally speaking、on the average、on the whole、in the main

㉕ by hand　手工的

The silk shirt had better be washed by hand.　　　絲質襯衫最好用手洗。

　1. in hand　手頭現有的；在掌握中的

We still have money *in hand*.

我們手頭上仍有錢。

2. on hand　在手邊；在旁邊

The nurse will be *on hand* if you need her.

如果你需要，護士隨時在你身邊。

3. at hand　即將到來

The summer vacation is *at hand*.

暑假快到了。

Unit 22 Exercise

I. 片語選填

break into	break down	be made of	be accused of	by hand
begin with	be sensitive to	based on	because of	be related to
be similar to	be proud of	be familiar with	be crazy about	
at least	be concerned with			

1. The first printing was done from wood blocks one letter at a time _____.

2. My computer's _____. No idea what's wrong with it. (84)

3. He didn't come to the meeting on time _____ the traffic jam. (89)

4. Many women are more observant than men, because they _____ tiny things. (85)

5. Much of your success, both in your work and social life, _____ how you listen. (86)

6. Stone Age hunters had only crude weapons that _____ stone and wood.

7. Perhaps most of us _____ the saying "Laugh and the world laughs with you; weep and you weep alone." (87)

8. These bats have _____ attacking humans and carrying infectious diseases. (85)

9. _____ this article, a Taiwanese temple is partly designed to prevent bad spirits and people from entering. (84)

10. 45 percent of the school children read _____ five books every month.

11. The design of a building is creative rather than a mathematical process, but unlike other art-forms, it _____ a positive search for solutions. (87)

12. These products can attract only those consumers who _____ already _____ robots. (90)

13. We should _____ the result. (90)

14. According to the research, the brain waves of a sleeping person _____ those of a walking person. (89)

15. Magic is believed to have _____ the Egyptians, in 1700BC. (92)

16. _____ the computer codes of banks, large companies or even government departments is the latest game for super-intelligent teenagers. (84)

II. 引導翻譯

17. 為了預防 SARS，我們必須用肥皂和水洗手，用力摩擦雙手至少 30 秒。
   To Prevent SARS, we must wash hands with soap and water, scrubbing all the surface of our hands for _____ _____ 30 seconds.

18. 林先生的評論非常難懂，因為它們與正在討論的主題相關性不夠。(92)
   Mr. Lin's comments were very difficult to follow because they _____ loosely _____ _____ the topic under discussion.

19. 若他們全然察覺存在於人類與這些動物間所有類似之處，觀察者將更感到驚訝。
   The visitors would be even more startled if they _____ fully _____ _____ all the existing similarities between them and these animals.

20. 有時候似乎我們沒有許多東西可以給擁有所有事物的學生。(90, 85)
   _____ _____, it seems like there are not many things that we can give a student who has everything.

21. Petek 博士報導龍蝦發出一種類似於小提琴手以弓拉弦的聲音。(90)
   Dr. Petek reported that the lobster produces sound in a way _____ _____ a violinist drawing a bow across strings.

22. 醫生可能會因為太關心如何治療疾病，以致於沒有注意到，有時候，困擾病人的，其實根本不是疾病。(84)

Doctors can _____ so much _____ about curing diseases that they may fail to notice that sometimes what troubles a patient is not really a disease at all.

23. 由於它的強度，鋼不久就成為一種有用的建材。(92)

_____ of its strength, steel soon became a useful building material.

24. 那個九個月大的男孩臉上蓋著一塊白布。(92)

The nine-month-old boy's face _____ _____ _____ a white cloth.

25. Tom，我們以你為榮。(85)

We _____ _____ _____ you, Tom.

26. 雖然被指責疏忽了我們的教育，父親仍然為我和弟弟擬定了一套夏日課程。(87)

(A)_____ _____ neglecting our education, my father still instituted a summer school for my brother and me.

27. 工作與嗜好是展開談話的好起點，但當然要避開年齡和金錢。(88j, 87)

Work and hobbies are good starters for conversations, but by _____ _____ avoid talking about age and money.

28. 它們的範圍包括分解天然廢棄物進入空氣、土壤和水中的細菌、菌類和較小動物。(88)

They include a range of bacteria, fungi, and smaller animals that _____ _____ nature's wastes into the air, the soil, and the water.

29. 好的聆聽者往往傾向聽得多且對週遭發生的事物比其他人更敏銳。(88)

Good listeners tend to listen more and to _____ more _____ to what is going on around them than other people.

30. 別擔心你的成績；只要專心課業。努力常常會使你發揮你的極致。(88)

Don't worry about your grades. Just concentrate on your studies. Hard work often (b)_____ _____ the best in you.

31. 不管是哪種情況，若你想要精通英文，你就必須熟悉那些似乎隨處會迸出來的電腦新詞彙。(91)

In either case, if you want to master English, you will need to _____ _____ _____ those new computer words that seem to be popping up everywhere.

32. 現今超大型汽車的設計應該為公路上與日俱增的死亡人數負大部分責任。(84)

The present design of the oversized automobile should _____ largely _____ for the increasing death toll on the highway.

33. 許多美國成人極渴望看起來年輕，所以總是保守年齡的秘密。(88)

Many adult Americans _____ _____ about looking young, so they always keep their age a secret.

34. 他們的基本造型，與選用來構築室內空間的建材，和所設計的功能有直接的關係。(87)

Their basic shape is directly _____ to the materials chosen to form that inner space and to the functions it is designed to serve.

35. 她所受的養育使她相信人是善良的。(88, 89, 90)

She was (b)_____ _____ to believe that humans are kind.

36. 兩個俄國人船隻壞掉之後開始漂流，並於星期六在台灣西南方澎湖群島附近獲救。(86)

Two Russians were rescued Saturday near the Penghu Islands off southwestern Taiwan after their sailboat _____ _____ and began drifting.

37. 這些建築的細節是「安全措施」，正如一家銀行有的阻止竊賊闖入的那些措施一樣。(84)

These architectural details are "security measures" just like those a bank had to keep thieves from _____ _____ .

38. 巴黎為慶祝千禧年而被贈予一座新的艾菲爾鐵塔，但是木頭造的。(87)

Paris was given a new Eiffel Tower—but _____ _____ wood—for the millennium.

39. 傳統的信通常以地址、日期、或收信人的地址為開頭。(88)

A traditional letter usually _____ _____ an address, the date and perhaps the address of the addressee.

40. 一般地說，這個電視節目會把非洲不同種類的動物介紹給你。(90, 84)

This TV program, _____ and _____ , will introduce you to different species of animals in Africa.

❶ by means of 藉著；應用

The stages are put up by means of pulleys.　　這些舞台藉由滑輪架設起來。

❷ by the way 順便一提；對了

I'm going to Kaohsiung now. By the way, do you want me to bring anything back for you?　　我要到高雄去了。對了，要我幫你帶什麼東西回來嗎？

❸ call on/upon **(A)** 要求某人做某事；**(B)** 對某人做短時間的拜訪

A. The environmentalist called on the whole world to protect the ozone layer.　　環境保護者要求全世界保護臭氧層。

B. Why didn't you call on my brother when you were in Texas?　　當你在德州時，為什麼沒去拜訪我哥哥？

 要求某人做某事：request

用法 1. call on + N + for + N

2. call on + N + to V

辨析 「要求某人做某事」這裡是用在正式場合上，被要求的對象可以包括組織。

❹ care for **(A)** 照顧；**(B)** 喜歡

A. Women's intuition can be found in mother's caring for their babies.　　女性的直覺可以在母親照顧她們的小嬰兒這點被發現。

B. Would you care for a cup of coffee?　　要不要來杯咖啡？

Martha likes all kinds of music, but she doesn't seem to care much for jazz.　　Martha 喜歡所有的音樂，不過她對爵士樂似乎不那麼喜愛。

 照顧：take care of、look after

喜歡：have a liking/fancy/preference/taste for、take a liking to

❺ carry out **(A)** 完成；**(B)** 實行；**(C)** 執行

A. It took him ten days to carry out the mission.　　他花了十天的時間完成任務。

B. He didn't carry out his promise to us.　　他並未實現對我們的承諾。

C. Soldiers are here to carry out orders, not to act on their own.　　軍人在此是執行命令，而非為所欲為。

Unit 23
B
C

❻ **cater to sb/sth**　投合、迎合；滿足…的需求

Most movies are made with the goal of catering to the mass public's taste.

多數電影的製作目的在迎合大眾的口味。

❼ **check out**　**(A)** 查證；**(B)**（旅館、超市）結帳離開；**(C)** 從圖書館借出書

A. I made a phone call to check out the company's address.

我打電話去查公司的地址。

B. We'll check in on Monday and check out on Wednesday.

我們星期一進旅館，星期三退房。

When you check out in Carrefour, you can use a credit card.

當你在家樂福結帳時，你可以使用信用卡。

C. If you need more information, you may have to check out more references from the library.

如果你需要更多資料，你可能必須從圖書館借更多參考資料。

❽ **close to**　接近；從近處

He is close to sixty.

他大約60歲左右。

I don't mind where we go on a vacation as long as it is close to a beach.

只要靠近海灘，我並不介意到何處去渡假。

　close to + N

❾ **come about**　（以難以防止的方式）發生

I have no idea how this confusion has come about.

我不知道這個混亂的狀況是如何發生的。

　happen、spring up
No one knows when tragedy will *spring up*.
沒有人可以預知悲劇何時發生。

　spring up　跳起
All the kids *sprang up* with a howl.
所有的孩子大叫一聲跳了起來。

❿ **come off**　**(A)**（照計畫）進行；**(B)** 達到預期效果；**(C)** 結果是

A. The wedding came off in the yard as planned.

婚禮按計劃在院子裡進行。

B. What you said was humorous, but it didn't quite come off.

你說得滿幽默，可惜沒達到預期效果。

C. They came off rather badly in the game.

他們在比賽中輸得很慘。

⓫ come to 演變成

After years of searching, they have come to believe that they will never be able to find their son.

經過多年搜尋之後，他們已經變得相信他們將再也無法找到兒子。

 用法　come to + V（come to 的其他意義與用法，請參照 Unit 6）

 觸類旁通
1. come to + N　達到；結果是

All those years of studying *came to* nothing.

那些年的努力落得一場空。

2. come to an end　結束

I promised Allen to call him as soon as the movie *came to an end*.

我答應 Allen，電影一散場，我就會打電話給他。

3. come to a conclusion/decision　達到結論；下決定

If you don't *come to a decision* by five o'clock, the talks will be abandoned.

五點之前如果你們不做出決定，就放棄談判。

⓬ come up　(A) 被提出；(B) 發生；(C) 走近

A. This question came up several times at the meeting.

這個問題在會議中被提出討論多次。

B. Please call me if anything comes up.

若發生任何事，請打電話給我。

C. A stranger came up and asked me the time.

一位陌生人進前來問我時間。

⓭ come up with　提出；想出

Is that the best suggestion you can come up with?

那是你所能想到最好的建議嗎？

⓮ communicate with　(A) 與…溝通；(B) 和…相通

A. Parents find it hard to communicate with their teenage children sometimes.

父母親有時會覺得很難與青春期的孩子溝通。

B. The baby room communicates with our bedroom.

嬰兒房和我們的臥室相通。

 用法　communicate with + N

⓯ complain about/of　(A) 抱怨；(B) 抗議

A. Two days later, men began to complain of having very bad colds.

兩天之後，人們開始抱怨感冒嚴重。

Stop complaining about life.

別再抱怨人生了。

B. The residents complained about the workers' demonstrations.

居民對工人示威遊行提出抗議。

⑯ concentrate on 專心；專注

Left-brained learners usually concentrate on memorizing rules and lists.

左腦學習者通常專注於記憶規則和列表。

Don't bother him. He is concentrating his efforts on his report.

別打擾他。他正努力專注於報告。

⑰ consider A to be B 視 A 為 B（**to be** 可省略）

77% of the students consider the Internet to be the most convenient source of information.

百分之七十七的學生視網路為最方便的資訊來源。

I consider the invitation to be a great honor.

我認為受邀是莫大的光榮。

 regard A as B、view A as B、think of A as B、look upon A as B, as 不可省略。

⑱ consist of 由…組成；包括

My life can be described as consisting of a series of "ups" and "downs."

我的生活可稱得上是由一連串的「起」、「落」所組成的。

Human life consists of a succession of small events.

人生是由一連串的小事件組成的。

 be composed of、be made up of
The committee *is made up of* parents and teachers.
委員會由家長與老師所組成。

⑲ cope with 應付；處理

Local authorities have to cope with the problems of waste and garbage.

地方政府必須處理廢棄物和垃圾的問題。

 deal with、handle

⑳ couldn't be better 好得不能再好了

A: Hi, Mary. It's been a while since we saw each other. How are you?

B: Couldn't be better.

A：嗨，Mary 好久不見，你好嗎?
B：非常好啊!

㉑ deal with 應付；處理

Your problem is hard to deal with.

你的問題很難處理。

He has no idea about how to deal with this problem.

他一點都不知道該如何處理這個問題。

 cope with、handle

 1. deal with sb

= get along with sb

= associate with sb　與某人相處

You should be honest when *dealing with* other people.

與人交往時要誠實。

2. deal in　從事…的買賣

My father has been *dealing in* used car sales for years.

我父親從事中古車的買賣已經好幾年了。

㉒ describe A as B　描述 A 成 B

Mozart is described as one of the greatest musicians in the world.

莫札特被描述成世界上最偉大的音樂家之一。

㉓ die of (hunger, disease, etc)　死於（飢餓或疾病等等）

The tourists died of starvation in the snow.

那些觀光客在雪地中死於飢餓。

His mother died of breast cancer.

他的媽媽死於乳癌。

 1. die from　死於（間接的原因）

It is reported that the young man *died from* overwork.

根據報導，那個年輕人死於過勞。

2. die for　在抵抗中死亡

Do you believe he *died for* freedom?

你相信他為了爭取自由而死嗎？

㉔ die out　絕跡；完全消失

What suggestion about protecting bats from dying out is given in this article?

這篇文章中提出什麼建議來阻絕蝙蝠的滅種？

Will old words die out while new words are constantly added?

當新字不斷地增加時，舊字會完全消失嗎？

㉕ dispose of　處理；除去

They disposed of the animals' waste matter by burning it.

他們以焚燒法處理動物的排泄物。

Would you please help me dispose of the litter in the kitchen tonight? I won't be home.

能麻煩你今晚幫我丟掉廚房裡的垃圾嗎？我今晚不在家。

 處理：deal with、cope with、handle

除去：throw away

 dispose of 接「物」是指「處理」或「除去」，但接「人」的話卻是指「殺了某人」或「擊敗某人」，不能亂用。

Unit 23

D

I. 片語選填

deal with	complain about	consist of	call on	dispose of
describe as	by the way	die out	close to	carry out
come up with				

1. Once used, the bags are sealed and stored for the flight back to the earth, where they are _____ . (92)

2. Since catadupa sounds like "cats and dogs," heavy rains came to be _____ _____ falling cats and dogs. (85)

3. The left hemisphere _____ rules, lists of information, and short-term memory. (85)

4. Don't waste time _____ it, no matter how difficult and boring it is.

5. After thinking about this problem for a long time, I still cannot _____ any solution. (86)

6. Fiction can be so _____ the truth that it seems as real as something that happened to you this morning. (91)

7. People in this village have _____ many welfare programs. (90)

8. Child protection groups _____ the German police to take action against the pop legend. (92)

9. I'll pick you up at seven. _____, is your guest still staying with you?

10. Part of the course _____ tying several knots in a given time limit. (87)

11. Without the carbon dioxide released from the process, all plant life would _____ . (88)

II. 引導翻譯

12. 根據這個段落，因為可重複利用，所以移動式鉛字的使用被視為「重大的進步」。(83)
According to the passage, the use of movable type was (c)_____ _____ _____ a "great step forward" because they could be reused.

13. 在冗長的討論之後，專家們終於提出解決經濟危機的建議。(89)
After a lengthy discussion, the experts finally _____ _____ _____ suggestions for resolving the economic crisis.

14. 絕大部分的建築物包含有防止外人妄入的外牆，及提供住戶一躲風避雨、覆以屋頂的內部空間。(87)
The vast majority of buildings _____ _____ external walls to keep people out and an interior space covered by a roof providing shelter for the residents.

15. 人類可以藉著語言表達自己。(87, 88)

Men can express themselves _____ _____ _____ language.

16. 你甚至可以定期去借書。(85, 87)

You may even go there regularly to _____ _____ books.

17. 這名男子已經瀕臨嚴重的精神崩潰，因為他無法處理日常生活的壓力。(91)

The man is on the verge of a serious breakdown because he is unable to _____ _____ pressure from daily life.

18. 經過數個月的尋找，他們漸漸變得體會到佛祖的要求是不可能達成的。(89)

After months and months of searching, they _____ _____ realize that the Buddha's request was impossible to fulfill.

19. 在執行這個程序時，應該將試管插入鼻子或口腔去看看肺部。(90)

In (c)_____ _____ this procedure, tubes should be inserted through the nose or mouth to see the lungs.

20. 我想知道你們家每隔多久會購買新傢俱、窗簾、或是廚具，我也想知道，你們是如何處置那些仍然很有用的舊物品。(86)

I wonder how often your family buys new furniture, curtains or kitchen equipment and then wonder how you _____ of the old items that still have quite a lot of life left in them.

21. 我們希望你八點到；順便說一下，這是個非正式晚餐。(87, 88)

We shall expect you at eight o'clock; _____ _____ _____, it's an informal dinner.

22. 一名女子在開旅行車時，因心臟病發而死亡。(84, 90)

A woman _____ _____ a heart attack while driving her station wagon.

23. 我們為什麼要忍受 Sue 自私的行為？我們必須教她照顧他人。(92)

Why do we have to put up with Sue's selfish behavior? We have to teach her to _____ _____ others.

24. 而冥想法也廣泛被應用在對付焦慮不安與壓力。(90, 86)

And meditation methods are widely practiced in _____ _____ anxiety and stress.

25. 下午五點半，男子打電話給醫生說，他已經洗過臉，且藍印脫落了。(84)

At 5:30 p.m. the man called the doctor to report that he had "washed his face and the blue _____ _____."

26. 曼谷迎合各種不同的興趣：有廟宇、博物館和其他歷史遺跡提供給那些對傳統泰國文化有興趣的人。(92)

Bangkok _____ _____ diverse interests: there are temples, museums and other historic sites for those interested in traditional Thai culture.

27. 社會工作者要求整個社會一起幫助杜絕毒品濫用。(86, 86)

The social workers _____ _____ the whole society to help stop drug abuse.

28. 別擔心你的成績。只要專心課業，努力常常會使你發揮到極致。

Don't worry about your grades. Just _____ _____ your studies. Hard work often brings out the best in you.

29. 水中生物已經演化出獨特的聲音製造方式，用以與同類溝通。(90, 85)

Underwater creatures have evolved remarkable ways of producing sound to _____ _____ each other.

30. 雖然寫於 150 年以前，且被譯成近百種語言，大仲馬的動作小說仍然鼓動了世界上數以百萬個讀者的心。(90)

Even though they were written 150 years ago, Alexander Dumas' action novels still excite millions of readers around the world, in _____ _____ a hundred languages.

31. 耶誕節後幾天的一個早上，Schwarts 博士在醫院當班時，一名男子走進來，只是抱怨他臉上出現了已持續一小時的青印。(84)

Dr. Schwarts was on duty at a hospital one morning a few days after Christmas when a man came in _____ only _____ "blueness to his face of one hour's duration."

32. 這場車禍是怎麼發生的？(87, 92)

How did the traffic accident _____ _____?

33. 當我走去海邊時，一個陌生人走近我，且試著和我握手。(88)

As I was walking to the beach, a stranger _____ _____ to me and tried to shake my hand.

34. 可是書本告訴我生存之道，處世之道和人事的應對方法，以及靠我一個人是永遠想不到的問題。(87)

But books show me ways of being, ways of doing, ways of _____ _____ people and situations and problems that I could never have thought up on my own.

35. 機器人描述它自己如一個人能力的擴大，幫助人們增加工作量。(87)

The robot _____ itself _____ an extension of a person to help humans increase the workload.

36. 當信風吹來時，印尼的大火在幾天之內會完全熄滅掉。(87)

Fire in Indonesia will _____ _____ in a few days when the trade winds blow.

III. 克漏字選擇

The Hardest Question

I was struggling to __37__ the demands of medical school. I wanted to __38__ my dreams of becoming a doctor, but I was not sure my plans would __39__ as I hoped. It took all my effort to __40__ the facts that I needed to learn for my classes. But then I had an experience that shifted my attitude. I was taking a test that __41__ only twenty questions. The last question asked, "What is the name of the cleaning lady who __42__ this building?" I thought it must have been a mistake. I had seen the cleaning lady almost every day as she __43__ trash or swept the floors, but I would never be able to __44__ her name. I complained to the professor that it was an unfair question. He replied that as a doctor I would need to __45__ many different people and that they are all significant and deserve my time and respect. Therefore, the cleaning lady's name was important. I realized then that medical school wasn't just about learning the facts; it was about learning to care. And that gave me a purpose that made the whole process easier.

(　　) 37. (A) cater to   (B) cope with   (C) call on   (D) check out

(　　) 38. (A) come true   (B) carry out   (C) put into   (D) carry with

(　　) 39. (A) come to   (B) come up   (C) come off   (D) come about

(　　) 40. (A) concentrate on   (B) close to   (C) come up with   (D) focus in

(　　) 41. (A) consisted in   (B) made up of   (C) composed of   (D) consisted of

(　　) 42. (A) cares for   (B) responsible for   (C) looking after   (D) took care

(　　) 43. (A) dealt in   (B) disposed of   (C) died of   (D) came to

(　　) 44. (A) call upon   (B) check in   (C) come up with   (D) put up with

(　　) 45. (A) communicate to   (B) contribute with   (C) communicate with (D) donate to

❶ **do one's best** 盡全力

As long as you do your best in this contest, we will be happy.

只要你在比賽中盡力了，我們都會很開心。

 try one's best、bring out the best in one

❷ **do the/some/one's/a little/a lot V-ing** 從事⋯的活動／事務

They decided to do some fishing a few minutes later.

他們決定過幾分鐘後去釣魚。

My grandfather used to do some jogging in his leisure time.

我祖父以前常常在空閒時間去慢跑。

❸ **due to** 由於；因為

His success was due to hard work.

他的成功是由於努力。

He didn't show up due to laziness.

他因為懶惰而沒有出現。

 owing to、because of、on account of、as a result of

❹ **end up in sth** 結果為⋯；以⋯收場

His plan ended up in failure though it had been supported by many people.

雖然獲得眾人的支持，他的計劃仍以失敗收場。

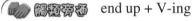 end up + V-ing 結果

Most slimmers *end up putting* on weight back.
多數的瘦身者後來都復胖。

❺ **even if/though** 即使

She has to ask her students to leave the set even if the shooting schedule runs late.

即使拍攝的進度落後，她也必須要求她的學生離開拍攝現場。

Even if he doesn't listen to you, you shouldn't find fault with him.

即使他不聽你的話，你也不該找他的麻煩。

Even though he couldn't swim, he jumped into the lake to save his daughter.

儘管他不會游泳，他還是跳進湖裡去救女兒。

❻ **face the music** 承擔後果；面對現實

He killed a boy without any reason. He has to face the music now.

他沒來由的殺了一個男孩，現在他得自己承擔後果。

 face the reality

❼ fall ill   生病

To avoid falling ill on such a cold day, you have to wear enough clothes.

在這種冷天裡要避免生病，你就得穿足夠的衣服。

 同　義   fall sick、get sick

❽ far from   (A) 一點也不；(B) 離…很遠

A. Your statements are far from clear.

你的說明一點都不清楚。

B. My home is far from the library.

我家離圖書館很遠。

❾ figure out   理解；想出

That's what I'm trying to figure out.

那就是我試著要了解的事。

From this book they figured out what treatments might work.

從這本書中他們了解到，什麼樣的治療方式可能有效。

I really can't figure out what he said.

我真的無法理解他的話。

 同　義   make sense of

❿ fill in/out   (A) 填上；(B) 把…補好

A. Please fill in this application form before entering the immigration office.

進入移民局之前，請填寫這張申請表。

B. The worker filled the hole in three days later.

三天後工人填好那個洞。

 辨　析   「填上」這個動作，fill in 與 out 均可，都是「在正式表格裡填上資料」的意思。但「把…補好」只有 fill in 可以表達。

⓫ find out   (A) 找出；發現；(B) 識破

A. You must find out the answer to the question now.

你必須現在找出這個問題的答案。

B. I'm afraid that you will be found out by the enemy.

我很擔心你會被敵人識破。

⓬ first of all   首先

First of all, they have to look for clues to the murderer's motive.

首先，他們必須找尋謀殺動機的線索。

 同　義   to begin with

I can't go—*to begin with*, it's too late now; besides, my feet hurt.
我無法去，首先，現在太晚了，其次，我的腳痛。

 觸類旁通   in the first place   第一步；首先

In the first place, we will talk about the subject.
首先，我們先談談主題。

⑬ focus on　專注於；集中（注意力）在…

He focused his study on parrots' ability of imitating sounds.

他專注他的研究在鸚鵡模仿聲音的能力上。

　concentrate on

⑭ for example　舉例

He doesn't know the importance of saving money. For example, he uses up his pocket money every day.

他不知道存錢的重要性。舉例來說，他每天都花光零用錢。

　for instance

Steel, *for instance*, was developed by engineers in the 19th century.

舉例來說，鋼是由十九世紀的工程師所發展而成的。

　take sb/sth for example　舉…為例

Take myself for example: I seldom eat anything after nine o'clock.

舉我自己為例：我九點之後很少吃東西。

⑮ for good　永遠地

The hero's brave deed will be memorized for good.

這位英雄英勇的行為會永遠被記得。

　forever、for ever、permanently

⑯ for one thing...for another　一則；一方面…再則；另一方面

He felt depressed. For one thing, he had no money, and for another, none of his family was alive.

他覺得沮喪，一則他沒有錢，再則他的家人都亡故了。

⑰ for the first time　第一次

When you meet an American for the first time, it is correct to ask "How do you do?" instead of "How are you?"

當你第一次遇到美國人時，問 "How do you do"？（你好嗎？）而不是 "How are you" 才是正確的。

⑱ get along with　(A) 與某人和睦相處；(B) 進行（工作）

A. A person who likes to pick on others is definitely not easy to get along with.

一個喜歡挑剔他人的人，肯定不易相處。

It's hard to get along with a selfish person.

和自私的人相處是很困難的事。

B. How are you getting along with your new job?

你的新工作進行得如何？

⑲ get over (A) 克服…的痛苦（包括驚慌、疾病等）；(B) 渡過

A. Mr. Huang hasn't got over the death of his wife yet.　　黃先生仍未克服喪妻的痛苦。

It took her a long time to get over the shock.　　她很久才從打擊中站起來。

B. He stood still by the river and wondered how to get over to the other side.　　他靜靜地站在河邊，思考如何過河到對岸。

同義 克服…的痛苦：overcome

⑳ get over with 做完；結束（不愉快的事情）

Do your home work right after school to get it over with.　　放學回家後馬上把功課做完。

㉑ get rid of 擺脫

Oh, how did you get rid of her?　　喔，你是如何擺脫她的？

Nancy got rid of her old car and bought a new one.　　Nancy 賣掉舊車，另外買台新的。

㉒ give away (A) 捐贈；分送；(B) 暴露（真面目、秘密）

A. He decided to give away all his money to charities after death.　　他決定死後捐出所有的錢給慈善團體。

B. If a spy gives himself away, his life would certainly be in danger.　　如果一個間諜暴露了自己的身份，他的性命可就危險了。

㉓ give in (A) 屈服；讓步；(B) 交出

同義 屈服：surrender

A. I won't give in to his unreasonable demand.　　對他不合理的要求，我不會讓步。

B. You'd better give in the money as requested.　　你最好一如要求交出那筆錢。

Unit 24 Exercise

I. 片語選填

end up in	get over	due to	even if	do one's best
figure out	for one thing	focus on	for example	get rid of

1. As long as a language is alive, its cells will continue to change, forming new words and _____ the ones that no longer have any use. (89)

2. _____, in the US, it is very important to be on time for almost all occasions. (89, 89)

3. The traffic on Main Street was obstructed for several hours _____ a car accident in which six people were injured. (91)

4. _____, and when you think your creation is good enough to give away, do just that. (86)

5. _____ her friends teased her about her awkward invention attached to a streetcar, Mary didn't give in to peer pressure. (91)

6. Sam couldn't _____ how to print out the document until the teacher showed it to him. (91)

7. America encourages its young people to drink. _____, their society makes drinks a part of every celebration. For another, actors usually drink in the movies.

8. Peter's sudden death was a great blow to Jane and it took her a long time to _____ the grief. (89, 91)

9. All thinking must _____ what was happening at the moment, and the mind and the body became one. (86)

10. His plan _____ failure though it had been supported by many people.

II. 引導翻譯

11. 一則，牠們的天然居所—洞穴、廢棄的礦坑、以及特定種類的樹木—正在急速消失中。
For _____ _____, they are fast losing their natural homes—caves, abandoned mines, and certain kinds of trees.

12. 舉例而言，有自尊的人通常表現得有信心。(83)
_____ _____, people having a sense of self-esteem usually act with confidence.

13. 他們會珍惜你真誠表示友誼的動作，就算你所做的麵包有點硬，蛋糕看起來又很…嗯…「有趣」。(86)
They will appreciate your honest gesture of friendship, _____ _____ your bread is kind of hard, and the cake looks..."interesting."

14. 一個懂變通的人常能和別人好好相處，因為他不會堅持己見。(86)
A flexible person usually can _____ _____ _____ with other people, because he does not insist on his own opinion.

15. 這項作業非常無趣，我希望盡快完成。(87)
This assignment is very boring. I want to _____ it _____ as soon as possible.

16. 總計四千零一十七份問卷由受訪者適切地填入。(92)
A total of 4,017 questionnaires were properly _____ _____ by the respondents.

17. 即使朋友嘲笑她裝在擋風玻璃上的怪異發明，Mary 並未屈服於同儕壓力。(91)

Even though her friends teased her about her awkward invention attached to the windshield, Mary didn't _____ _____ to peer pressure.

18. 英國探險家發現：印地安的王子們在北美東岸也攜帶雨傘。(83)

English explorers _____ _____ that Indian princes also carried umbrellas on the east coast of North America.

19. 首先，恭喜你畢業了！(86)

_____ _____ _____ _____, congratulations on your graduation!

20. 如果這些「不做夢者」在實驗室進行睡眠實驗，當研究者喚醒他們並問他們之前是否有作夢時，結果發現他們作夢與其他人一樣多。(89)

If these "non-dreamers" _____ their _____ in a laboratory where researchers can wake them up and ask them whether they were having dreams before, it turns out that they dream as much as others.

21. 八個月之後，袋鼠永遠地離開家。(92)

After eight months, the kangaroos leave home _____ (g)_____.

22. 領航鯨死於鱈角海灘，是因出水面後，他們的身體構造無法支撐體重。(84)

The pilot whales died on the beaches of Cape Cod (d)_____ _____ their body structure which is unable to support their body weight out of water.

23. 他收到的耶誕禮物是藍色的毛巾，那天早上他第一次拿其中一條來使用。(84)

He had received blue towels as Christmas gifts and had used one of them that morning _____ _____ _____ _____.

24. 我被要求正式地在航海桌上繪製航程圖，即使我們的目標是一個在遠處海上我可以看得相當清楚的小島。(87)

I was required to formally plot our course, using the tide table, _____ _____ our goal was an island I could see quite clearly across the water in the distance.

25. 你把客廳弄得亂七八糟的，媽媽回家時，你就得自己承擔後果。(88)

You messed up everything in the living room. When Mom comes home, you'll have to _____ _____ _____.

26. 如果這對年輕夫婦繼續把焦點放在嬰兒的死亡，將無法回復往常的生活。(89)

The young couple would not be able to return to their old way of life if they continue to _____ _____ the death of the baby.

27. 每一個人都應該竭盡全力做到最好，同時，在獲得部分成果或遭遇部分失敗之際，必須對自己說：「我已盡了全力。」(87)

One must try to _____ _____ _____ and at the same time, one must, when rewarded by partial success or confronted with partial failure, say to oneself, "I have done my best."

28. 領航鯨死於鱈角的海灘上，是由於一種科學家尚未理解的現象。(84)

The pilot whales died on the beaches of Cape Cod due to a phenomenon not yet to be _____ _____ by scientists.

Unit 24

29. 盡力就好，當你自認你的創作夠好可以<u>送給</u>別人時，就送吧! (86)

Do your best, and when you think your creation is good enough to _____ _____ , do just that.

❶ give off　散發（氣體、液體）

The flowers would give off unique odor at night.

這些花晚上會散發出獨特的味道。

 同義　emit

❷ give up　放棄；認輸

He who gives up hope easily will never succeed.

凡輕易放棄希望的人不會成功。

❸ go on　(A) 繼續做；(B) 發生

A. He went on playing the cello after dinner.

晚餐後，他繼續拉奏大提琴。

B. The manager, realizing what was going on, asked Mary to follow him into the kitchen.

那位經理了解所發生的狀況，就要求 Mary 跟他進入廚房。

 go on an errand　跑腿（買東西、寄信、搬東西等）

I often *go on an errand* for my mother.

我常為媽媽跑腿。

❹ go through　經歷

Lucy had gone through many hardships before she became what she is today.

Lucy 歷經千辛萬苦，才有今日的成就。

 同義　undergo

❺ hang up (the phone)　掛電話

Father was very angry when I hung up on him last night.

當我昨晚掛我爸爸電話時，他非常生氣。

 用法　hang up + on + 人，表「掛掉誰的電話」。

 1. be hung up on/about　一心一意想；熱切希望

She's *hung up about* being independent.

她一心一意想獨立生活。

2. hang-up (n.) 苦衷；苦惱

❻ have an effect on　對…有影響

The way people think about themselves has a profound effect on all areas of their lives.

人們對自己的看法，對他們生活上各方面都有深刻的影響。

 同義　affect、influence、impact、have an impact on、have an influence on

❼ have confidence in   對…有信心

She has great confidence in herself.

她對自己很有信心。

 同 義   be confident in/of

❽ have no idea   不知道；沒有概念

It was getting dark, and I had no idea where I was.

天色漸暗，而且我不知道自己身在何方。

Celebrities in the rally probably have no idea about how much a CD of their music albums costs.

參加這場集會的名人，大概不知道他們的音樂專輯 CD 一張多少錢。

❾ have sth in common   有共通點

Jane and Sue are twins, but they seem to have nothing in common.

Jane 和 Sue 是雙胞胎，但她們似乎完全沒有共通點。

❿ hold up   (A) 耽擱；(B) 支撐

A. I was held up by a traffic jam on the freeway for about one hour.

我在高速公路上被塞車給耽擱了約一小時。

B. I'm afraid that I'm not able to hold this barbell up.

我恐怕不能支撐這根槓鈴。

⓫ in a hurry   匆忙

Sometimes people are in such a hurry that they cannot wait for the bus to come.

人們有時很匆忙，所以不能等到公車來。

I am in a hurry to enter the chamber.

我很匆忙的要進入會議室。（不可用 in haste）

 同 義   in a rush、in haste

 用 法   in a hurry, in a rush 及 in haste 可做副詞片語，修飾句中動詞。然而 in a hurry 及 in a rush 可做形容詞片語，置於 be 動詞之後，做主詞補語，in haste 則無此用法。

⓬ in addition   此外

We should love our country. In addition, we should respect our national flag.

我們應該愛國；此外，我們應尊重國旗。

 同 義   besides、moreover、furthermore、what's more、additionally

 用 法   in addition 是指「針對已經提出的說法或內容，增加額外的資訊」，屬於轉折詞，與 moreover、furthermore 等雷同，但與 in addition to 用法有別。

Unit 25 **H I**

⓭ in case　萬一

Take your cell phone with you in case you need to call for help.

隨身帶著手機，以防萬一你需要打電話求救。

 同義　if

 解類旁通　in case of　要是…；在…的時候

Dial 119 *in case of* emergency.

緊急時撥一一九。

⓮ in contrast　相對地；相比之下

The weather in summer is hot, but in contrast, the weather in winter is cold.

夏天的天氣炎熱，相對的，冬天天氣寒冷。

 同義　by contrast

⓯ in fact　事實上

In fact, my life can be described as consisting of a series of "ups" and "downs."

事實上，我的生活可稱得上是由一連串的「起」、「落」所組成的。

 同義　in effect、in practice、in reality、in actuality、as a matter of fact

He is, *in effect*, not the one you can trust.

事實上，他不是個可信賴的人。

Denny always tells the truth. *As a matter of fact*, he is a man of his word.

Denny 總是說實話。事實上，他是個言而有信的人。

⓰ in front of　在…之前

The teacher is standing in front of the classroom and talking to my father.

老師站在教室前面與我的父親談話。（老師並不在教室裡）

 辨析　in the front of 是「主詞包含在這個空間裡」，但 in front of 是指「主詞不包含在這個空間裡」，請從下面的例句去體會差別。in back of 與 in the back of（在…之後）的區別原則是相同的。

The teacher is standing *in the front of* the classroom and writing on the blackboard.

老師站在教室前面寫黑板。（老師在教室裡面）

⓱ in general　大體上；一般而言

People in general believe that nothing in life can be permanent.

一般人都認為：生命中沒什麼是永恆的。

 同義　generally speaking、by and large、on (the) average、on the whole、in the main

❶ in keeping with　和…一致；跟得上

He studies very hard in keeping with times.

他為了跟上時代而努力。

❷ in order to　為了

She throw away many things in order to travel lighter.

她為了較輕便的旅行而丟掉很多東西。

 so as to、to + V

 with an eye to
= with a view to
= for the purpose of
= for + N/V-ing　為了

With a view to improving traffic, they took many new measures.
為了改善交通，他們採取許多新措施。

❷ in part　一部份（地）；在某種程度上

Your failure is due in part to carelessness, but mainly to bad luck.

你的失敗，一部份是因為粗心，但主要是運氣不好。

❷ in particular　尤其是

The young man owes his success to many people, his parents in particular.

那個年輕人將成功歸功於許多人，尤其是他的父母。

❷ in person　本人；親自

I'll tell her the news in person rather than over the phone.

我會親自告訴她這個消息，而不會打電話告訴她。

❷ in response to　回應；因應

In response to John's inquiry yesterday, I wrote an e-mail to him this morning.

為了回應 John 昨天的質問，我今早寫了封電子郵件給他。

 in reply to

In reply to your letter dated July 4, I regret to tell you that the deal is canceled.
針對你七月四號的來信，我很抱歉告訴你我們將取消這項交易。

❷ in spite of　儘管

In spite of the heavy rain, they arrived at the destination on time.

儘管下大雨，他們仍準時到達目的地。

 despite、notwithstanding

㉕ in terms of　由…觀點來看；以…方式來說

The expression "women's intuition" can be better explained in terms of concrete examples.

「女性的直覺」這個用語以具體例子的方式來解釋比較好。

Unit 25 Exercise

I. 片語選填

have nothing in common	in order to	in terms of	in response to
have a profound effect on	in person	have no idea	in such a hurry
go on	in part		

1. It was ＿＿＿＿＿＿＿＿＿＿ this situation that the Carpenter's Shop was opened. (86)

2. Did she throw away goods that she didn't need ＿＿＿＿＿＿＿＿＿＿ travel lighter?

3. But sometimes people are ＿＿＿＿＿＿＿＿＿＿ that they cannot wait for the mail to come. (86)

4. Jane and Sue are twins, but they seem to ＿＿＿＿＿＿＿＿＿＿ . (87)

5. The manager, realizing what was ＿＿＿＿＿＿＿＿＿＿ , asked Soapy to follow him into the kitchen. (91)

6. The way people think about themselves ＿＿＿＿＿＿＿＿＿＿ all areas of their lives.

7. Those unnecessary deaths are attributable ＿＿＿＿＿＿＿＿＿＿ to the woman's choice of a large automobile. (84)

8. For this last case, Jack had to go ＿＿＿＿＿＿＿＿＿＿ to Thatcher's office for security reasons! (86)

9. The expression "women's intuition" can be better explained ＿＿＿＿＿＿＿＿＿＿ concrete examples. (85)

10. Celebrities in the rally probably ＿＿＿＿＿＿＿＿＿＿ how much a CD of their music albums costs. (91)

II. 引導翻譯

11. 由 Einstein 對物理研究影響的角度來看，他被視為二十世紀最偉大的科學家之一。(89)
　　Einstein was considered one of the greatest scientists of the 20th century in ＿＿＿＿＿＿ ＿＿＿＿＿＿ his influence on the study of physics.

12. 如果你不知道對方的作息時間，就儘量不要在晚上十點以後，或早上八點之前打電話給對方。(86)
　　If you ＿＿＿＿＿ ＿＿＿＿＿ ＿＿＿＿＿ what sort of hours somebody keeps, you should probably try not to call after 10 p.m. or before 8 a.m.

13. 請掛上電話。(86)
　　＿＿＿＿＿ ＿＿＿＿＿ the phone, please.

14. 你是一個幾乎可說是生活在電腦前面的人嗎？所謂的「滑鼠馬鈴薯」? (91)

Are you someone who practically lives _____ _____ _____ the computer—a mouse potato?

15. 帶著傘吧! 免得下雨。(85)

Take your umbrella _____ _____ it should rain.

16. 這條電線發出低電力無線電信號。(90)

The wire _____ _____ a low-power radio signal.

17. 最近一項名為「送一頭母牛」的福利計劃，就是一些公益團體為響應這種需要而舉辦的。(90)

Recently, a welfare program called "Send a Cow" has been organized by some social services _____ _____ _____ this need.

18. 直覺式的思維是一種帶點溫暖、情緒化和半幽默、混著幾分的理想主義與幾分令人愉快的無理之類型的思維。(87)

Truly intuitive thinking is always the type of thinking that is sort of warm, emotional, and half-humorous, mixed _____ _____ with idealism and _____ _____ with delightful nonsense.

19. 我很匆忙，所以這件事情我只能和你簡單地討論。(88)

I am _____ _____ _____, so I can only discuss this matter with you briefly.

20. 醫生要他戒酒。(85)

The doctor told him to _____ _____ alcohol.

21. 這筆錢將用來償付那些為了要救他，而急速送達的特殊設備，與火速趕往現場的八十位警官。(83)

The amount would pay the costs of rushing special equipment and eighty police officers _____ _____ _____ save him.

22. 我在高速公路上被交通阻塞給耽擱了約一小時。(85)

I was _____ _____ by a traffic jam on the freeway for about one hour.

23. 相對地，右半球負責感覺、色彩和長期記憶。(85)

_____ _____, the right hemisphere deals with feelings, colors and long-term memory.

24. 然而所有的英雄都有一個共通點。(83)

All these heroes _____ one thing _____ _____, however.

25. 我們教育體系的目標和社會發展一致。(90)

The goals of our education system are _____ _____ _____ the development of our society.

26. 我知道科學的限制，但基於我對科學的崇拜，我總是讓科學家去做基礎的工作，而且對他們完全有信心。(87)

I know science's limitations, but with my worship of science I always let the scientists do the groundwork, _____ complete _____ in them.

27. 根據最近的調查，人們正喪失笑的藝術，這對我們的健康有<u>嚴重的影響</u>。(87)

According to the recent research, people are losing the art of laughter, which could _____ a _____ _____ _____ our health.

28. <u>一般說來</u>，人們對自己的看法對他們生活上各方面都有深刻的影響。(83)

_____ _____, the way people think about themselves has a profound effect on all areas of their lives.

29. <u>儘管</u>眾人反對，他們仍繼續做下去。(88)

_____ _____ _____ _____ public opposition, they went ahead.

30. Jack 看起來不像運動員，但<u>事實上</u>，他擅長運動，特別是棒球。(91)

Jack doesn't look athletic, but he is, _____ _____, excellent at sports, especially baseball.

31. Carnegie 認識 Hunter <u>本人</u>。(83)

Carnegie knew Hunter _____ _____.

32. 自然界的聲音和景象，有助於控制病人<u>在經歷</u>令人不舒服的療程時所產生的痛苦。

The sounds and sights of nature can help control pain when patients _____ _____ unpleasant procedures.

33. <u>此外</u>，電視及平面媒體的酒類廣告都呈現吸引年輕人的劇情。(84)

_____ _____, advertisements for liquor, on TV and in print, show situations that are attractive to the young.

III. 克漏字選擇

A Friend in Need

I like to help people, and it makes me feel good to be a friend to someone. But once, I found myself with a "friend" with whom I had nothing __34__. She was __35__ hard times in her life and always wanted advice __36__ her complaints. She often seemed shy around me __37__, but she called me on the phone to tell me all of her problems. At first it felt good to be needed. __38__ the fact that she never seemed to show any interest in me personally, I always listened and tried to help her. After a while, she was calling two or three times a day. One day, I was really __39__ and she was __40__ me up with another long phone conversation. I guess my impatience must have shown through because she began __41__ me for not listening and hung up on me! This incident had a big effect __42__ me. I still love to help people, but I learned that if someone in my life is only taking and never giving, I need to find a better friend.

( ) 34. (A) in detail   (B) in vain   (C) in turn   (D) in common

( ) 35. (A) going through   (B) going on   (C) giving off   (D) giving up

( ) 36. (A) in reply with   (B) in addition to   (C) in response to   (D) in case of

( ) 37. (A) in part   (B) in general   (C) in person   (D) in fact

( ) 38. (A) In spite of   (B) In terms of   (C) In front of   (D) In keeping with

( ) 39. (A) in a haste   (B) in a hurry   (C) in rush   (D) in effect

(   ) 40. (A) handing   (B) picking   (C) giving   (D) holding

(   ) 41. (A) getting rid of   (B) giving in   (C) yelling at   (D) smiling at

(   ) 42. (A) in   (B) on   (C) at   (D) with

Unit 25

❶ **in that** 因為

John Glenn is admirable in that he has been to the moon more than once.

John Glenn 令人欽佩,是因為他登陸月球不只一次。

 because

❷ **in the beginning** 一開始

Nasreddin gave Ali an extra small pot in the beginning because he wanted to trick Ali.

Nasreddin 一開始多給 Ali 一個小鍋子,是因為他想要欺騙 Ali。

 at first、originally

❸ **in the distance** 遠處;遙遠的

In the distance a huge temple sits on the hilltop.

遠方有座大廟聳立於山頂。

 at a distance　稍微遠離

The building looks more splendid *at a distance*.

這棟大樓離開一點看更堂皇。

❹ **in the event of** (A) 可能出現的情況;(B) 萬一、以防

A. This exit is to be used only in the event of fire.

這個出口只能在火災時使用。

B. In the event of rain, we'd better take an umbrella.

為防下雨,我們最好帶把傘。

 萬一: in case of

❺ **in the middle of** (A) 在…的中間;(B) 在…的進行當中

A. The man stood still in the middle of the stream.

那人動也不動地站在溪流中央。

B. The speaker burst out laughing in the middle of the speech.

在演講進行中,演講者突然笑了出來。

 在…的中間: in the midst of

❻ **in this way** 以此方式;這麼一來

In this way, intimacy enabled us to thrive and grow.

以這種方式,親密使我們得以成長。

❼ **in turn** (A) 輪流;(B) 替換、下次

A. Each of us in turn introduced ourselves in the first class.

第一堂課,我們輪流自我介紹。

B. When you play a trick on others, they might play a trick on in turn.

你對別人惡作劇,下次他們就有可能會對你惡作劇。

❽ in vain 徒勞無功；白費力氣

The doctor tried to save her life but in vain.

醫生想救她的命，但徒勞無功。

 同　義　to no avail、to no purpose

All the doctor's efforts were *to no avail* and the patient died.

醫生竭力搶救還是無效，病人死了。

❾ insist on/upon **(A)** 堅持、主張；**(B)** 強調

A. The union insisted on working 40 hours per week.

工會堅持一星期工作四十個小時。

B. He insisted on the importance of a good relationship among family members.

他強調家人之間良好關係的重要性。

 用　法　insist on/upon + N/V-ing

❿ instead of **(A)** 而不是；**(B)** 代替；**(C)** 非但不…反而

A. You should take some exercise to lose weight, instead of taking the medicine.

你想減肥，應該去做點運動，而不是吃減肥藥。

B. I'll go jogging instead of bike-riding this morning.

我今天早上要以慢跑來代替騎腳踏車。

C. Instead of comforting me, he threatened to leave me.
= Rather than comfort me, he threatened to leave me.

他非但沒有安慰我，反而威脅要離開我。

 同　義　非但不…反而：rather than

 用　法　instead of 當「非但不…反而…」解釋時，常置於句首，後置動名詞做受詞。

⓫ interact with 與…互動；回應

To improve their relationship, they have to find a good way to interact with each other.

為了改善他們之間的關係，他們必須找個互動的好方法。

⓬ keep up **(A)** 繼續下去；**(B)** 維持；支持

A. I used to go jogging in the morning, but I haven't kept it up.

我以前早上習慣晨跑，但未能持續下去。

B. They tried to keep up the reputation of their company after the scandal burst out.

在醜聞爆發後，他們設法維護公司的名譽。

⓭ lead to **(A)** 導致、造成；**(B)** 通往

A. Lilly's negative attitude led to her failure.

Lilly 的負面態度導致她的失敗。

B. All roads lead to Rome.

（諺）條條道路通羅馬。

 用　法　lead to + N/V-ing

⓮ leave out　　(A) 遺漏、不理會；(B) 除去

A. He didn't realize the main idea of the article because he left out one paragraph.

因為遺漏了一段，所以他不了解文章的主旨。

B. Please leave Tom and Jack out of the list.

請別把 Tom 和 Jack 列入名單中。

⓯ let off　　寬恕；允許離去；施放（煙火）

If you make the same mistake again, no one would let you off.

要是你再犯一次相同的錯誤，沒人會願意原諒你。

The police let off the speeding driver because he was rushing his sick daughter to the hospital.

警察允許這位超速的駕駛離去，因為他急著載他生病的女兒去醫院。

⓰ look after　　(A) 照顧、注意；(B) 目送

A. When I was sick, my mother and father looked after me in turn.

當我生病時，我父母親輪流照顧我。

No one could take care of the poor old man.

沒有人可以照顧這可憐的老人。

B. The soldiers stood in line looking after the General.

士兵站成一列目送將軍。

🅰同義　　照顧：take care of、care for

⓱ look for　　(A) 尋找；(B) 期待

A. The accounting department is looking for a suitable person to fill in the new vacancy.

會計部門正在尋找填補這個新職缺的適當人選。

B. We are looking for your improvement in academy.

我們期待你在學術上的進步。

⓲ look up　　(A) 查閱；(B) 抬頭往上看；(C) 拜訪

A. If you don't understand the word, look it up in the dictionary.

如果你不懂這個字，那就查字典。

B. Look up and see the stars. How wonderful they are!

抬頭看星星，它們真是奇妙啊！

C. Whenever you come here, just look me up.

無論何時，只要你來，就順道光臨。

觸類旁通　　look it up in the dictionary
　　= consult the dictionary
　　= refer to the dictionary　　查字典

⓳ make a difference to 　使…不同；使…有重大改變

It makes a difference to our appearance, too, when we relax our facial muscles!

當我們放鬆臉部的肌肉時，亦使我們的外表不同。

 辨　析　這個片語所「造成的不同與改變」，都是「變得比較好」。

 觸類旁通　make no difference　沒有區別

⓴ make a fortune 　賺大錢

Jack and his company have made a fortune from their service.

Jack 和他的公司因其所提供的服務而賺大錢。

㉑ make...possible 　使…成為可能

Printing is important because it has made reading books possible.

印刷術很重要，因為它使得紙本閱讀變為可能。

㉒ make progress 　**(A)** 進步、進展；**(B)** 前進

A. Doctors have made a lot of progress in fighting AIDS.

醫生們在對抗愛滋病上有長足的進步。

B. The protesting group made slow progress toward the presidential square.

抗議團體緩緩前進總統府廣場。

㉓ make sure 　**(A)** 確信、查明；**(B)** 確保

A. This evidence might be the key to this case, but we need to make sure of it first.

這個證據或許是本案關鍵，但我們必須先進行查證。

B. I made sure that I had a ticket before going to the concert.

我在去音樂會之前先確保有票。

 用　法　1. make sure that + 子句
　　　　　2. make sure of + N

㉔ make up 　**(A)** 杜撰、捏造；**(B)** 制定；**(C)** 化妝；**(D)** 解決、和好

A. Terry is making up an excuse for his being late again.

Terry 又在為他的遲到編藉口了。

B. We have made up several rules for the game.

我們為比賽制定了數則規定。

C. All the actors made up their faces as heavily as they used to.

所有演員像以前一樣化濃妝。

D. The two brothers made up their quarrel eventually.

兩兄弟終於停止爭吵，重修舊好了。

 同　義　杜撰：invent

❷⑤ mess up　弄髒；弄糟

After you have messed up something, you should learn to clean it up.

在你弄亂了某些東西後，你應該學習收拾乾淨。

Unit 26 Exercise

Unit 26

I. 片語選填

make progress	insist on	in the middle of	make possible	look for
in the distance	lead to	in the event of	make up	instead of

1. Sara enjoys amusing her friends by _____ stories. (90)

2. With her teachers' and parents' encouragement, Jane regained her confidence and has _____ great _____ . (91)

3. The expansion of this empire _____ wars with its neighboring countries.

4. _____ treating the homeless man as a shame of her society, Mrs. Wang provided him with food and water. (91)

5. Like most immigrants, he was _____ a better life. (85)

6. A flexible person usually can get along well with other people, because he does not _____ his own opinion. (86)

7. Her students occasionally have to dash off from their schools _____ an exam. (90)

8. _____ rain, the ceremony will be held indoors. (91)

9. The researchers also displayed on walls large pictures of a forest with a river running through it and mountains _____ . (90)

10. Science _____ the use of new materials and new methods of producing objects. (92)

II. 引導翻譯

11. 你把客廳裡的東西都弄亂了，等媽媽回家後，你就必須面對後果。(88)

   You _____ _____ everything in the living room. When Mom comes home, you'll have to face the music.

12. 在每個安樂椅前有個與頭齊高，用電線接至地面中央錄音機的麥克風。(89)

   In front of each easy chair there was a microphone at head height, with wires leading to a tape recorder _____ _____ _____ _____ the floor.

13. 只要一抬頭，就會有一些東西掉進你的眼睛裡。(88)

   You could hardly even _____ _____ without getting something in your eye.

14. 萬一有緊急事件，撥 119。(88)

   In _____ _____ _____ an emergency, dial 119.

Unit 26

M

15. 科技的改變必然會<u>導致</u>人際關係的改變。(89)

Technological changes will inevitably _____ _____ a change in human relationships.

16. 沒有任何一件事是<u>虛構</u>的。某人的傳記是非小說類文學；你的自傳也是。(91)

Nothing is _____ _____ . Someone's biography is nonfiction; so is your autobiography.

17. 傳統的郵件彼此之間無法<u>互動</u>，但是電子郵件在回信中是可以包含原信件的部分內容。(88)

Traditional letters cannot _____ _____ each other, but with e-mail it is possible to include parts of the original letter in the reply.

18. 依我看他是被<u>從輕發落</u>了。(87)

In my opinion, he was _____ _____ lightly.

19. Willing <u>不但沒有</u>受到處罰，紐約市還把他視為能嘗試不可能的事，並面對挑戰的英雄。

(I) _____ _____ punishing Willing, the city treated him as a hero who attempted the impossible and met the challenge.

20. 參與並不需要花捐贈者的錢，但卻對別人的生活能<u>造成</u>如此重大的<u>改變</u>。(86)

Participation costs the donor nothing and can _____ such a _____ _____ others.

21. <u>這麼一來</u>，電子郵件違反了書信的規範，例如標準拼音和文法。(88)

_____ _____ _____ , e-mail departs from the norm of written letters, such as standard spellings and grammar.

22. 泛美航空 103 班機及印度航空 182 班機類似，<u>因為</u>它們都是遭恐怖攻擊而失事。(92)

Pam Am Flight 103 and Air India Flight 182 were similar (i)_____ _____ they were brought down by terrorists attacks.

23. <u>冷落</u>他們會不會不禮貌？(88)

Is it rude to _____ them _____ ?

24. 雖然科學家還不能解釋這驚人的器官的所有秘密，但<u>已有所進展</u>。(85)

Although scientists have not been able to solve all the mysteries of this amazing organ, they have _____ some _____ .

25. 在夢中，戲院接待室的服務人員在大廳擋下我，<u>且堅持</u>要我留下我的腳。(90)

In the dream the cloakroom attendant at a theater stopped me in the lobby and _____ _____ my leaving my legs behind.

26. 研究科學的醫生們設法觀察疾病，<u>尋求</u>合理的模式，然後找出人體是如何運作的。(92)

Scientific doctors try to observe sicknesses, _____ _____ logical patterns, and then find out how the human body works.

27. 在醫院裡你得到良好的<u>照顧</u>嗎？(85)

Are you well _____ _____ in hospital?

28. 我被要求正式地在航海桌上繪製航程圖，即使我們的目標是一個在遠處海上我可以清楚看到的小島。(87)

I was required to formally plot our course, using the tide table, even though our goal was an island I could see quite clearly across the water _____ _____ _____.

29. 他試圖說服她去參加演說比賽但徒勞無功。(86)

He tried _____ _____ to persuade her to take part in the speech contest.

30. 藉寫小說而致富後，他在巴黎市郊建了一處邸宅，招待一些挨餓的藝術家、朋友、甚至陌生人。(90)

After _____ a _____ by writing novels, he built a mansion outside Paris and kept it open to starving artists, friends, and even strangers.

31. 我打開錄音機，每一個人很嚴肅地輪流以最好的口音從一數到二十。(89)

I turned on the tape-recorder and each _____ _____ solemnly counted from one to twenty in their best accent.

32. 他們給予每一個家庭一隻牛，也提供有關繁殖的課程，以確保這些動物能夠繼續繁殖下去。(90)

They give a cow to a family and also offer breeding lessons to _____ _____ that the animal multiplies.

33. 如果你想比國內其他泳者游得快一些，就必須堅持下去。(90)

You will have to (k)_____ it _____ if you want to swim faster than other swimmers in our country.

34. 一開始，每一個收到動物的人將也要捐出其中一隻的幼子給貧困的鄰人。(90)

_____ _____ _____, each person who receives an animal will also give one of its young to a needy neighbor.

❶ more than 多於；超過

There is more than pride involved in both cities' claim to be the coldest.

兩個城鎮都宣稱是最冷的地方，其中包含的不只是為了驕傲。

 超過：over

❷ no doubt 無疑地

No doubt his travel experience contributed to his capacity to write.

毫無疑問地，他的旅遊經驗有助於他的寫作。

He is no doubt a nice man.

他無疑是個好人。

 undoubtedly、doubtlessly、without (a) doubt

❸ no longer 不再；再也不

Many Americans are no longer excited about space achievements.

許多美國人對於太空成就不再感到興奮。

Larry no longer lives here; he has moved to San Francisco.

Larry 不再住在這裡了；他已經搬到舊金山了。

 not...any longer、not...any more

❹ not only...but (also) 不僅…而且…

Not only did he like this car, but he also bought it.

他不僅喜歡這車，而且也買下它。

 not merely...but...as well

We *not merely* speak the same language, *but* share a large number of social customs *as well*.

我們不僅語言相同，很多社會習慣也一樣。

 not only 及 but also 之後所接的內容和結構上必須對等，如兩個名詞或兩個子句。 其中 also 可以省略，若 not only 放在句首，則形成倒裝句。

❺ off and on 斷斷續續

Paid a daily rate that ranges from $160 to $300, Neumann works off and on.

Neumann 每天工資從一百六十到三百美元不等，她的工作是時有時無的。

 on and off

If you study English *on and off*, you'll get nowhere.

如果你斷斷續續地學英文，是學不出什麼名堂的。

❻ on (the) average 平均而言

In 1930s people laughed on average for 19 minutes each day.

一九三○年代，人們平均一天笑十九分鐘。

❼ on/in behalf (of) 代表…；為了…的利益

On behalf of everyone here, may I wish you a happy marriage.

我謹代表大家祝你婚姻幸福。

 同義　on/in one's behalf

Please speak *in my behalf*.

請為我說好話。

❽ (all) on one's own 靠自己；獨自

You've grown up. You have to live on your own.

你已經長大了。你得獨立自主生活。

He runs the business on his own.

他獨自撐起整個事業。

 同義　獨自：(all) alone

 觸類旁通　of one's own　自己的

Each one of the students has a bike *of his or her own*.

每一個學生都有自己的腳踏車。

❾ on purpose 故意地

The writer capitalized the word "FREEDOM" on purpose to catch readers' attention.

作者故意將「自由」這個字大寫好引起讀者的注意。

 同義　deliberately、intentionally

 觸類旁通　by accident

= by chance　意外地

The gun went off *by accident*.

槍枝意外走火。

❿ on the basis of 根據；以…為基礎

We can infer their relations on the basis of the clues.

根據線索，我們能推測他們的關係。

 同義　according to、based on

Based on the DNA report, they are sure to be father and son.

根據 DNA 報告，他們確定是父子。

Unit 27

⓫ on the other hand 另一方面

Nonfiction, on the other hand, is all about true things.

另一方面，非小說類文藝作品則全都是關於真實事件。

 on (the) one hand 一方面

I don't like its color *on the one hand*, and the budget is not enough on the other hand.

一方面，我不喜歡它的顏色，另一方面，我的預算不足。

⓬ once and for all 斷然地；最終地

Let's talk about it once and for all.

我們只談一次，下不為例。

⓭ participate in 參加

They participate in voluntary work enthusiastically and spontaneously.

他們熱忱，且自動自發地參與志工工作。

 take part in

He refused to *take part in* any call-in program on TV.

他拒絕參加任何電視叩應節目。

⓮ pay attention to 注意

A good student always pays attention to the teacher's lecture.

好學生總會很注意老師的授課。

 take notice of、attend to

⓯ pick on 挑毛病；挑剔

He likes to pick on others, so no one likes to be around him.

他喜歡挑剔別人，所以沒有人喜歡跟他在一起。

 find fault with

Some people *find fault with* others when actually they should blame themselves.

有些人實際上犯了錯不怪自己，卻去挑別人的毛病。

⓰ pick up **(A)** 注意到；**(B)** 撿起；**(C)** 自然學習；**(D)** 搭載

A. Suddenly, my dog picked up a stranger coming close to the house and barked loudly.

突然，我的狗注意到一個陌生人靠近房子，就開始大吼。

B. Please pick up the pen for me.

請幫我把筆撿起來。

C. I picked up some French when I did business in Paris.

當我在巴黎做生意時，學了些法文。

D. Father will pick me up after school this Friday.

週五放學後，爸爸會開車接我。

⓱ play a (practical) joke on　對…開玩笑；對…惡作劇

Some naughty boys like to play practical jokes on girls.

有些頑皮的男生喜歡對女生惡作劇。

 同義　play a trick on

⓲ play a (minor) role/part in　在…方面扮演（次要的）角色

Decomposers play a role in the recycling of nature.

分解者在大自然的循環方面，扮演著一個角色。

Hard work plays an important part in achieving success.

努力在獲得成功上扮演一個重要的角色。

 用法　play a role in + N/Ving，role 和 part 之前多會加 big, major, important 等形容詞。

⓳ prepare for　準備

We should always prepare for the worst.

我們應當隨時未雨綢繆。

 觸類旁通　be prepared to + V　樂意做

I *am* quite *prepared to* be your assistant.
我相當樂意擔任你的助手。

⓴ protect...from...　保護…以免於…

Sunglasses can protect your eyes from being damaged by the bright sunlight.

太陽眼鏡能保護你的眼睛免受強烈陽光的傷害。

 同義　keep...from...

The Great Wall *kept* people *from* being attacked by the enemy from the north.
萬里長城保護人們免受來自北方敵人的攻擊。

 用法　protect + N + from + N/V-ing

 觸類旁通　protect...against + N　保護…免於…

To *protect* eyes *against* the sun, you'd better wear dark glasses.
你最好帶墨鏡，以免陽光傷害眼睛。

㉑ provide A with B　提供 B 給 A

Nature provides them with the means of survival.

大自然為他們提供求生的方法。

 同義　supply A with B.

The charity *supplies* those in need *with* food.
慈善機構提供窮人食物。

 用法　provide sb with sth

 provide for 為…準備；供給…

Everyone should *provide for* his future all the time.

每個人應該隨時為將來做準備。

❷ put out **(A)** 熄滅；**(B)** 伸出；**(C)** 激怒；**(D)** 出發

A. For the sake of safety, put out the campfire before leaving.

為了安全起見，離開前先把營火熄滅。

B. The doctor asked me to put out my tongue.

醫生要我伸出舌頭。

C. I was put out by his rude behavior.

我對他的粗魯行為感到生氣。

D. The fishing boat put out to sea at dawn.

漁船黎明時出海。

 熄滅：extinguish

❷ put up with 忍受；容忍

We have to put up with different opinions from others.

我們必須容忍他人不同的意見。

 endure、bear

❷ range from...to... 範圍從…到…

The price of this famous tenor's concert ranges from NT$400 to NT$1,500.

這位知名男高音的音樂會票價從台幣 400 元到 1500 元。

❷ rather than 而非

Rather than feeling nervous, she was actually excited and confident about performing in public.

她非但不緊張，反而對在大眾面前表演感到興奮及有信心。

 instead of

 rather than 若連接兩個主詞時，動詞以第一個主詞做變化。

I. 片語選填

protect from	on average	not only...but also	rather than
prepare for	more than	participate in	
put out	pay attention to	play an important part in	

1. The design of a building is a creative _____ a mathematical process.

2. I'm too busy _____ myself _____ the college entrance examination. (90)

3. He (p)_____ three revolutions and fought with people when he was insulted. (90)

4. There is _____ pride involved in both cities' claim to be the coldest.

5. Any IMO contest brings _____ young mathematicians together _____ their instructors. (91)

6. Fraser claims that it is colder _____ than the Minnesota town. (85)

7. To listen effectively, we have to _____ facial expressions, body movement, as well as to the quality of the other person's voice. (84)

8. The addition of an animal to a small agricultural family _____ providing valuable milk or meat. (90)

9. What suggestion is given in this passage to _____ bats _____ dying out? (85)

10. Fires in Indonesia were eventually _____ by human effort. (87)

II. 引導翻譯

11. 那邊的動物與世界其他地區的動物不再有接觸。(92)
The animals there _____ _____ had contact with animals from other parts of the world.

12. 你認為 Teresa 是故意問那個問題的嗎? (86, 90)
Do you think Teresa asked that question _____ _____ ?

13. 第二，藉由參加 IMO，世界各國的年輕數學高手可以培養友善的關係。(91)
Secondly, it is by _____ _____ any IMO contest that young mathematicians of all countries can foster friendly relations.

14. 廚師將洋芋切得比以前薄，為那位抱怨的客人而準備。(90)
The cook sliced some potatoes thinner than before and _____ them _____ the complaining guest.

15. 毫無疑問的，喜歡挑毛病的人不易相處。(89)
A person who likes to _____ _____ others is definitely not easy to get along with.

16. Grants Pass 也有許多餐飲地點，從低卡路里的點心店到美麗的餐廳都有。(84)
Grants Pass has a lot of places to eat, _____ _____ a low-calorie dessert place _____ lovely restaurants.

17. 火勢延燒到雨林中乾的煤層時，會繼原來的大火後斷斷續續延燒好幾個月或好幾年。
When fire gets into the rainforests' layer of dry peat, it can burn slowly _____ _____ _____ for months or years after the original fire.

18. 注意到青少年在電腦遊戲方面的興趣，Hilfiger 贊助任天堂的競賽，並將任天堂的總站架設在他的店裡。(92)

_____ _____ on teens' interest in computer games, Hilfiger sponsored a Nintendo competition and installed Nintendo terminals in his stores.

19. 根據這封信，Sally 和 Tom 之間最可能的關係是姐弟。(85)

_____ _____ _____ of the letter, the most likely relationship between Sally and Tom is sister and brother.

20. 其中一項要求是確定她的護照自抵達日起有效期限長過六個月。(85)

One of the requirements is to make sure her passport is valid for _____ _____ six months on the date of arrival.

21. 雖然蜂鳥平均翼長幾乎不到 4 英吋，但它能快速劃過空中，達到時速 60 英哩。(84)

Although a hummingbird's wingspread is barely four inches long _____ _____ _____, it can rush through the air as swiftly as six miles an hour.

22. 王太太並未視這無家可歸的男人為社會的恥辱，反而還供應他食物和水。(91)

Instead of treating the homeless man as a shame of the society, Mrs. Wang _____ him _____ food and water.

23. 頭腦的左右兩半球，在學習和溝通上扮演非常重要的角色。(85)

The left and right hemispheres _____ extremely _____ _____ _____ learning and communicating.

24. 我代表本團謝謝你的殷勤款待。(89)

I'd like to thank you for your hospitality _____ _____ _____ our group.

25. 另一方面，小孩較常看到事物有趣的一面，因此可能一天笑 400 次以上。(87)

Children, _____ _____ _____ _____, can see the funny side of things more often and may laugh up to 400 times a day.

26. 此外，好的傾聽者會傾向於接受或容忍，而非判斷與批評。(88)

In addition, good listeners are inclined to accept or tolerate _____ _____ to judge and criticize.

27. 無疑地，那位候選人很受歡迎，因為他已在選舉中贏得壓倒性的勝利。(89)

There was _____ _____ that the candidate was popular, because he had won a landslide victory in the election.

28. 為何我們要忍受 Sue 的自私行為？我們得教她關心別人。(92)

Why do we have to _____ _____ _____ Sue's selfish behavior? We have to teach her to care for others.

29. 現今超大型汽車的設計不僅要為高速公路上與日俱增的死亡人數負大部分的責任，也要為快速消耗石油資源負起責任。(84)

The present design of the oversized automobile is largely responsible _____ _____ for increasing death toll on the freeway _____ _____ for the rapid depletion of petroleum resources.

30. 我最後說一次：你不可以再做這種愚蠢的事。(85)

I tell you _____ and _____ _____ that you must not do such a stupid thing again.

31. 多數的人進我的車會脫帽，而有時候我必須告知乘客熄滅他們的香煙。(92)

Most men took off their hats in my car, and sometimes I have to tell passengers to _____ _____ their cigarettes.

32. Michael Jackson 帶他的孩子到動物園去，每個孩子都帶著鮮豔的奇怪面紗，目的是避免他們被綁架。(92)

Michael Jackson took his children covered in strange, bright-colored veils to the zoo "to _____ them _____ kidnappers."

33. 可是書本告訴我生存之道，處世之道和人事的應對方法，及靠我一個人是永遠想不到的問題。(87)

But books show me ways of being, ways of doing, ways of dealing with people and situations and problems that I could never have thought up _____ _____ _____.

34. Adam 對 Nelson 惡作劇。(88)

Adam _____ a _____ _____ _____ Nelson.

III. 克漏字選擇

The Fate of Pompeii

"You could hear the shrieks of women, the crying of children and the shouts of men"
Pliny the Younger, Letter 6.20

Founded around 600 BC, Pompeii became a Roman colony in 80 BC. Trade and tourism grew as many wealthy Romans established their home in the city. Pompeii was very ___35___ the volcano Vesuvius, but people were neither afraid nor worried. The Romans, who were always trying to interpret the gods' will ___36___ prevent disasters, were not ___37___ what was about to happen. Despite clear warning signs before the eruption, like a terrible earthquake in AD 63, the inhabitants were caught by surprise. In AD 79, Vesuvius erupted, projecting wet ashes and toxic gas. The eruption lasted one day, changing the course of the local river and raising the sea beach. Some historians say that ___38___ 10,000 people died. After the tragedy, Pompeii was ___39___ a charming and peaceful city, but a tomb for thousands of people. The experience was scary and the Romans ___40___ rebuild the town. But even buried, Pompeii could not ___41___ greed: thieves have managed to steal most of the valuable objects that remained on the site. Pompeii was only rediscovered in 1748, 17 centuries after its destruction. Many buildings, temples and wall paintings, preserved by the ashes, have been found, offering us a rare opportunity to understand Roman everyday life in a provincial city, 2,000 years ago. Pompeii is ___42___ a rare chance for historians to understand Roman society and culture, but also an exceptional spot, attracting millions of tourists who ___43___ by this extraordinary city.

(　　) 35. (A) besides   (B) able to   (C) close to   (D) due to

(　　) 36. (A) for the purpose of   (B) in order to

       (C) with an eye to   (D) with a view to

(　　) 37. (A) prepared for   (B) provided for   (C) proper for   (D) prevented from

(　　) 38. (A) other than   (B) more than   (C) over than   (D) more or less

(　　) 39. (A) not more   (B) at all   (C) no longer   (D) all in all

(　　) 40. (A) were about to   (B) were capable of   (C) were bound to   (D) were unable to

(　　) 41. (A) be ran away from   (B) be put up with

       (C) be appealed to   (D) be prevented from

(　　) 42. (A) nothing more than   (B) not only

       (C) not at all   (D) if only

(　　) 43. (A) are fascinated   (B) are attracted   (C) are surprised   (D) are nervous

Unit 27

Unit 28

❶ refer to   **(A)** 提及；**(B)** 參考；**(C)** 歸因於；**(D)** 派人向另一方查詢

A. Some words come into the language because they sound like what they refer to.

有些字的形成，是因為它們聽起來像它們所指的意思。

B. You can refer to the instructions of the machine while using it.

使用這部機器時，你可以參考它的使用手冊。

C. He referred his success to luck.

他將成功歸因於幸運。

D. For further information about this new TV, I was referred to the agency.

我被派去問代理商，以獲得關於這台新電視更進一步的消息。

    refer + (N) + to + N

❷ relate...to...   使…有關聯

The report tries to relate the rise in crime to an increase in unemployment.

這份報告試圖說明犯罪增加與失業增加的關聯性。

    relate + N + to + N；be related to + N

Are you *related to* Michael?

你和 Michael 有親戚關係嗎？

R

❸ rely on/upon   依靠；信賴

Many families must rely on double incomes or more to make both ends meet.

許多家庭必需依靠兩份或兩份以上的收入才能收支平衡。

    count on、depend on

❹ result in   造成；導致；結果；終於

The fire last night resulted in the death of five people.

昨晚一場火災造成五人死亡。

Hard work resulted in his getting a scholarship from Princeton.

由於努力用功，他終於得到普林斯頓大學的獎學金。

    造成：lead to、bring about、give rise to、cause

   result in + N/V-ing

1. 請比較下列同義的片語：
   a. come out   結果變成

    How did the game *come out*?

    比賽結果如何？

b. end in　最後是…

Her dream *ended in* smoke.

她的夢到頭來一場空。

2. result from　因…而引起

The accident *resulted from* his carelessness.

車禍是因他的疏忽而引起。

❺ **search for**　尋找；探尋

He is searching for a temporary lodging in the city.

他正在城裡尋找臨時住宿的地方。

 look for、seek (for)

Most of the graduates are *seeking for* employment but in vain.

多數的畢業生在找工作，但卻徒勞無功。

❻ **set up**　(A) 設立；(B) 創立（新紀錄）

A. To strengthen our customer service, we'll set up a service center at the entrance.

為加強對客戶的服務，我們將在入口處設立服務中心。

B. She set up a new record in the 200-meter sprint in last Olympic Games.

她在上屆奧運會上創下二百公尺短跑的新紀錄。

❼ **show off**　(A) 炫耀；(B) 把…襯托得更好

A. He showed off his brand-new cell phone to us.

他向我們炫耀他的新手機。

B. The setting sun showed off the church splendidly.

夕陽把教堂襯托得更美。

❽ **so far**　到目前為止

How many countries have you visited so far?

到目前為止，你走訪幾個國家？

 to date、up to the present time、as yet

As yet I haven't received his invitation card.

到目前為止，我尚未收到他的邀請函。

 1. 上面各個片語都經常與現在完成式連用。

2. as yet 多用於否定句，表「到目前為止尚未」。

❾ **so that**　因此

Turn down the radio so that I can sleep.

把收音機音量關小點，這樣我才睡得著。

 so that 引導表目的或願望的從屬子句，經常與 may 或 can 連用，亦可省略 that 只用 so。

❿ stand by　**(A)** 袖手旁觀；**(B)** 支持；**(C)** 待命

A. Don't just stand by; go and give him a hand.　別只是袖手旁觀，去幫他一把。

B. Whatever happens, I will stand by you.　不論發生什麼事，我都支持你。
　= No matter what happens, I will back you up.

C. We all stand by here and wait for further instructions.　我們都在此待命，等候進一步的指示。

 同 義　支持：support、back up

⓫ stop...from　阻止

The snow stopped us from going out.　這場雪使我們不能外出。

 同 義　prevent...from、keep...from

用 法　stop + N + from + N/Ving

⓬ succeed in　成功；順利

The teacher finally succeeded in dissuading the student from playing hooky again.　老師最後終於說服那名學生不要再逃學了。

用 法　succeed in + N/V-ing

⓭ take action　採取行動

If I had known the fact, I would have taken action right away.　如果我知道事實，我早就立刻採取行動。

⓮ take in　**(A)** 佔有、獲得；**(B)** 欺騙；**(C)** 瞭解；**(D)** 包含

A. Five soldiers were taken in as prisoners in the battle.　此次戰役共有五名軍人受俘。

B. Don't be taken in by his flattery.　別被他的諂媚所欺騙。

C. It took me a long time to take in what they were saying.　我花很長的時間才理解他們所說的話。

D. The guest list has taken in every one of you.　客人名單已包括你們每一個人。

 同 義　欺騙：deceive
　　瞭解：understand

⓯ take notice of　注意

He took no notice of the warning sign and then fell down.　他沒注意到警告標語，就摔倒了。

take note of、take heed of、pay attention to、pay heed to、attend to、
be attentive to

Jennifer *paid* no *heed to* my warning.

= Jennifer *took* no *heed of* my warning.

Jennifer 沒有注意到我的警告。

 take notice of + N/wh-cl

❶ take (a few days) off　休（幾天）假

He plans to take a few days off in September.　他計劃在九月份休假幾天。

❶ take off　(A) 從…移開；(B) 脫下；(C)（飛機）起飛

A. Whenever I see her, I can't take my eyes off her.　每當我看到她，我的目光就無法自她身上移開。

B. Take off your hat before entering the room.　脫下帽子再進入房間。

C. The plane took off at five and then landed safely in Tokyo.　飛機五點起飛，然後在東京安全降落。

❶ take one's time　某人從容進行

Take your time over dinner; we still have plenty of time.　晚餐慢慢吃，我們還有很多時間。

❶ take over　接管

Who will take over my duties while I am on vacation?　我渡假時，誰接管我的職務？

❷ take part in　參與

While in college, Peter took part in many extracurricular activities.　大學時，Peter 參加了許多的課外活動。

 participate in、join in

I *joined in* the school chorus two years ago.

我兩年前參加學校的合唱團。

❷ take place　(A) 發生；(B) 舉行

A. Major changes in economy and education are taking place in society.　經濟及教育上的重大改變，仍在社會中進行。

B. The meeting took place as scheduled.　這個會議如期舉行。

 發生：happen、come off、come about、occur

舉行：occur、be held

The explosion *occurred* at midnight.

爆炸發生於午夜。

㉒ take sth for granted   視…為理所當然

Children often take their parents' kindness for granted.

小孩常常視父母的恩惠為理所當然。

 用法　take + N + for granted

take it for granted that + cl

I *took it for granted that* you would help me.

我認為你一定會幫我。

㉓ tend to   **(A)** 留意；**(B)** 有…的傾向、易於

A. Before the train approaches, tend to standing clear from the edge of the platform.

列車進站前，注意不要靠近月台邊。

Tend to your own business.

少管別人的閒事。

B. About marriage, he tends to follow his parents' ideas.

關於婚姻，他傾向於聽從父母的意見。

 同義　注意：pay attention to、take notice of、take note of

易於：be apt to、be inclined to、be prone to、be liable to

One *is liable to* shout when he gets excited.

一個人興奮時容易大叫。

 用法　注意：tend to + N

易於、有助於：tend to + V

㉔ the other day   前幾天

I ran into an old friend downtown the other day.

我幾天前在城裡巧遇一位老友。

 同義　a couple of days ago

㉕ think up   想出

I have to think up another activity if I stop watching TV at night.

如果我每晚不再看電視，我就得想出其他的活動填補時間。

㉖ throughout the world   遍及全世界

English is spoken almost throughout the world.

幾乎全世界都在說英文。

 同義　all over the world、the world over

Unit 28

T

I. 片語選填

stand by	refer to	so far	stop from	rely on
tend to	show off	so that	take over	search for

1. Good listeners _____ listen more and to be more sensitive to what is going on around them than other people. (88)

2. Today, TV, movies, and books have _____ the activity of storytelling that people used to be familiar with. (87)

3. People who are determined cannot be easily _____ doing what they want to do. (85)

4. You can't just _____ and let him treat his dog like that.

5. Only a few people worked with the whales _____ they would not become accustomed to human beings. (84)

6. Yet the types of robots introduced to the market _____ have been more for entertainment than for practical uses. (90)

7. Robert likes to _____, which is the reason why nobody likes to be with him.

8. To _____ clues is a way to deal with dead mail. (89)

9. During this period they must _____ their noisy sound to scare away such predators as sharks. (90)

10. Some words come into the language because they sound like what they _____ . (89)

II. 引導翻譯

11. 原本廚師計劃要使吃晚餐的客人無從抱怨的計劃無法實現。(90)

    The cook's plan to _____ the dinner guest _____ complaining did not turn out as he had planned.

12. 我知道。我會慢慢地來。(88)

    I know. I'll _____ my _____ .

13. 科學家們數十年來一直在想像著一種未來：那時候，機器人可以接手日常瑣碎的家務而讓我們有更多的休閒時間。(90)

    Scientists have imagined for decades about a future when robots will _____ _____ daily household chores and give us more leisure time.

Unit 28

14. 那輛車子開得很快，衝過了公路分隔欄，引起衝撞，造成五人死亡。(84)

The car was moving so fast that it went through the highway-driving fence, _____ _____ a collision in which five people died.

15. Jane 最好的特質之一就是：她總是採取必要的行動而不是等待別人發號施令。(91)

One of Jane's finest qualities is that she always _____ the necessary _____ and does not wait for orders.

16. 多數人不注意醫生的忠告。(86)

Most people don't _____ _____ of the doctor's advice.

17. 他們已設立「聽力診所」及課程以找出那兒出了毛病。(86)

They have _____ _____ "listening clinics" and courses to find out what is wrong.

18. 語言的學習同時發生在左腦及右腦。(85)

Language learning _____ both in right and left hemispheres.

19. 到目前為止，他的手及身體仍是正常的顏色，但在他臉的兩側，很明顯的，上至顴骨是藍色的。(84)

_____ _____, his hands and body were still their normal color, but on both sides of his face, it was distinctly blue up to the cheekbones.

20. 沒人知道真實情況如何，但我們確實知道的是：她參與了 19 世紀最偉大的冒險之一。

No one will ever know for sure, but what we do know is that she _____ _____ _____ one of the greatest adventures in the 19th century.

21. 在急難中，他們勇於伸出援手，而其他的人卻只是袖手旁觀。(83)

They are brave enough to help in an emergency while others may _____ _____.

22. 但是書告訴我生存之道，處世之道和人事的應對方法，及靠我一個人是永遠想不到的問題。(87)

But books show me ways of being, ways of doing, ways of dealing with people and situations and problems that I could never have_____ _____ on my own.

23. 太多的美國人視太空計劃的成就為理所當然。(88)

Too many Americans _____ the achievements of the space program for _____.

24. 前幾天我們在太平洋百貨公司看到 Roger 帶著一個甜美的女孩。(85)

We saw Roger with a sweet girl in SOGO _____ _____ _____.

25. 當他們去打獵時，他們武器的威力並不足以殺死大型的獵物，因此他們必須依賴機智甚於武器。(84)

When they went hunting, their weapons were not powerful enough to kill big game, so they had to _____ more _____ their wit than weapons.

26. 請設法休假幾天與我們聚聚。(85)

Please try to _____ a few _____ _____ and come join us.

27. 丈夫永遠無法成功地欺騙妻子。(85)

A husband can never ＿＿＿＿＿＿ ＿＿＿＿＿＿ cheating his wife.

28. 上述文章提到的是入侵電腦密碼的「hacking」。(84)

The preceding passage ＿＿＿＿＿＿ ＿＿＿＿＿＿ the word "hacking" in the context of breaking into computer codes.

29. 猩猩專家繼續收到嬰兒猩猩，牠們的母親在果園或田裡找食物時已被殺害。(87)

Orangutan experts continue to receive orangutan infants whose mothers have been killed while (s)＿＿＿＿＿＿ ＿＿＿＿＿＿ food in plantations and fields.

30. 無主信件也會被列入電腦檔案中以便人們來電查詢是否有遺失信件在那裡。(89)

Dead mail will also be listed on a computer ＿＿＿＿＿＿ ＿＿＿＿＿＿ people can call in and check to see if a missing item is there.

31. 然而 IMO 的最終目標就是創造機會讓世界各地的數學進度及教學實踐上的資訊得以交流。(91)

However, the IMO has its final aim to create opportunities for the exchange of information on math schedules and practice (t)＿＿＿＿＿＿ ＿＿＿＿＿＿ ＿＿＿＿＿＿.

32. 聖母大教堂從裡面照亮出來，顯現出它的彩繪玻璃。(87)

Notre Dame Cathedral would be lit from the inside to ＿＿＿＿＿＿ ＿＿＿＿＿＿ its stained glass windows.

Unit 29

❶ **to and fro** 來回地；往返地

The man walked to and fro in front of his girlfriend's apartment.

那名男子在女友的公寓前走來走去。

1. here and there　到處

2. up and down　又上又下；到處

3. back and forth　來回地

❷ **together with** 與…一起；以及

He sent a red dress together with a card to the young lady.

他將一件紅色洋裝及一張卡片送給那位年輕女士。

along with

Rosa went *along with* her boyfriend to the gallery.

Rosa 和他的男朋友一起到畫廊去。

together with, along with, as well as 在連接兩個主詞時, 記得動詞以前面的主詞來做判斷, 因為三個片語都是強調前者。

❸ **too...to...** 太…而不能…

What he said is too good to be true.

他說的話言過其實。

too + adj/adv + to + V

❹ **treat A as B** 看待 A 為 B

We treated the national baseball team as the hero after they won the Asian Baseball Championship.

國家棒球代表隊贏得<u>亞洲</u>錦標賽後, 我們都視他們為英雄。

❺ **turn down** (A) 拒絕；(B) 把…關小；(C) 向下折

A. He turned down my offer, which made me angry.

他拒絕我所開出來的條件, 這令我非常的生氣。

B. Turn the radio down; the baby is sleeping.

把收音機關小聲! 嬰兒在睡覺。

C. The collar turns down; I like it.

領子下翻; 我喜歡。

拒絕：reject

❻ turn in 交出

You should turn in your report on time.　　　　　你應該如期交出你的報告。

 hand in

❼ turn out **(A)** 結果變成…；**(B)** 把…趕出去；**(C)** 關掉；**(D)** 生產

A. The rumor turned out to be false.　　　　　　這謠言最後證明是假的。

B. Turn him out! I don't want to see him again.　　趕他出去，我不想再見到他。

C. Remember to turn out the light before you leave.　記得離開前要關上燈。

D. That factory turns out mineral water.　　　　　那家工廠生產礦泉水。

 生產：produce

❽ turn to **(A)** 轉變成；**(B)** 依靠；**(C)** 求助於、查閱；**(D)** 著手進行

A. When water freezes, it turns to ice.　　　　　水結凍就變成冰。

B. I have no friends to turn to here.　　　　　　在這裡我沒有朋友可以依靠。

C. I took up the invitation card and turned to the list of guests.　我拿起邀請卡，查看客人名單。

D. After the discussion, he turned to the task at hand.　討論之後，他就進行手邊工作。

❾ up to **(A)** 達到、到…為止；**(B)** 能做…、勝任…

A. The restaurant is open up to midnight.　　　　那家餐廳營業到午夜。

B. After his illness, he quit the job because he was no longer up to it.　生病後他已無法勝任，所以辭去工作。

 當「勝任、能做」解時，用於否定句或疑問句。

❿ wait for 等待

Time and tide wait for no man.　　　　　　　　（諺）歲月不待人。

Henry decided to wait for Amy to discuss this agenda.　Henry 決定等 Amy 一起討論這項議題。

 wait for + N + to V

⓫ wake up **(A)** 叫醒某人；**(B)** 醒來；**(C)** 察覺

A. Don't wake him up! He's too tired.　　　　　　別叫醒他！他太累了。

B. Anyway, it was not until 10 o'clock the next morning that I finally woke up.　反正，我一直到第二天早上十點才終於醒來。

C. We wish you would wake up to the current situation.　我們真希望你對現狀有所覺醒。

⓬ with/in regard to　關於

With regard to your recent suggestions, I have decided to adopt them completely.

關於你最近的建議，我已經決定完全採用。

 同義　　regarding

 用法　　with regard to + N

 觸類旁通　without regard to
= regardless of　不管；無關
The flu spread and killed *without regard to* borders.
此流行性感冒感冒不分國界地散播並且奪走人命。

⓭ without (a) doubt　無疑地

Tom is without a doubt the most outstanding student in my class.

無疑的，Tom 是我班上最傑出的學生。

 同義　　undoubtedly

⓮ work on　從事

I am working on my new book.

我正在寫我的新書。

I. 片語選填

turn in	too...to...	wake up	turn to	up to
turn down	turn out			

1. You should not, however, _____ the person you're calling. (86)

2. A single colony of Arizona bats observed by scientists eat _____ 35,000 pounds of insects every night. (85)

3. When they discovered no one had a solution to this deadly disease, people _____ prevention. (88)

4. History has had many surprises for us. How events will _____ are often not predictable. (87)

5. Didn't you _____ your final paper on Friday? (89)

6. My initial offer was _____ politely. (85)

7. Robot Redford's speech was _____ difficult _____ understand. (87)

8. 我怕那將是個漫長的等待，我要去做我的歷史報告了！(89)

   I'm afraid it's going to be a long wait! I'm going to _____ _____ my history paper.

9. 直到約二十五億年前，世界上只有一塊超級巨大的陸地，叫 Pangaea。(92)

   _____ _____ about 250 million years ago the world had just one huge super-continent called Pangaea.

10. Willing 非但沒有被處罰，此市還把他視為嘗試不可能，面對挑戰的英雄。(83)

    Instead of punishing Willing, the city _____ him _____ a hero who attempted the impossible and met the challenge.

11. 據說有一次這位劇作家送 Churchill 他劇作之一的兩張首映票並附上一張卡片，上面寫著：帶個朋友來（如果你有的話）。(89)

    It is said that the playwriter once sent Churchill two tickets for the opening night of one of his plays, (t)_____ _____ a card, which said, "Bring a friend (if you have one)."

12. 但是有時候人們太匆忙，所以他們不能等到郵件的到來。(86)

    But sometimes people are in such a hurry that they cannot _____ _____ the mail to come.

13. 關於購物，知道店舖何時營業是很重要的，否則你可能會看到所有的店都關著而失望。

    _____ _____ _____ shopping, it is important that you know when shops are open, or you may be disappointed at seeing all the shops closed.

14. 然後老闆笑著指出，相同的提議在幾分鐘前才被提出且遭到否決。(86)

    The boss then laughingly pointed out that the same proposal had been made and _____ _____ some minutes before.

15. 無疑地，凡是借出錢的人應該把它要回來。

    It is (w)_____ _____ that those who lent the money should take it back.

16. 他們認為這三隻鯨魚太小了，如果回到海上，靠自己將無法生存。(84)

    The three whales were believed to be _____ young _____ survive on their own if returned to sea.

17. 老師會要求你準時交出功課來。(87)

    The teacher will want you to _____ your assignments _____ on time.

18. 焦急的父親在門廊處走來走去，等女兒回來。(89)

    The anxious father was walking _____ _____ _____ in the porch, waiting for his daughter back.

19. 百分之十四的受訪者說他們通常求助於書本而非上網找資料。(92)

    14 percent of the respondents said they often _____ _____ books for information instead of going online.

Martin Luther King

Martin Luther King, Jr. was born in Atlanta in 1929. He went to Boston University and earned a doctoral degree in 1955. During the 50', black Americans were not treated __20__ equals by the white. Like Nelson Mandela in South Africa, King protested against a racist government that denied black people all their basic civil rights, __21__ the right to vote. In 1959, King went to India and was highly influenced by Gandhi's philosophy of nonviolence. In 1963, his speech __22__ the Lincoln Memorial in Washington, "I have a dream," is without __23__ his best and most famous. It made him a worldwide celebrity and can be considered a __24__ call, not only for black people, __25__ for many white men who decided thereafter to join the movement. King won the Peace Nobel Prize in 1964. __26__ his role as an activist fighting for justice and peace, he began to express doubts about the American war in Vietnam. In 1968, James Earl Ray, who was __27__ King in Memphis, shot him dead. Thereafter Ray confessed the crime and went to prison. To honor his memory, a national holiday was claimed. Since 1993, it is celebrated on January 18.

(　　) 20. (A) to   (B) by   (C) as   (D) on

(　　) 21. (A) such as   (B) let alone   (C) as such   (D) let go of

(　　) 22. (A) in case of   (B) by way of   (C) in spite of   (D) in front of

(　　) 23. (A) any hesitation   (B) any delay   (C) a doubt   (D) a word

(　　) 24. (A) give-up   (B) take-up   (C) pick-up   (D) wake-up

(　　) 25. (A) as well as   (B) together with   (C) but also   (D) and neither

(　　) 26. (A) According to   (B) In response to   (C) With a view to   (D) With regard to

(　　) 27. (A) competing for   (B) waiting for   (C) looking for   (D) leaving for

英語 *Make Me High* 系列

108課綱、各類英檢考試適用

最新版

Key Idioms & Phrases 800

解析本

關鍵片語 *800*

郭慧敏／編著

三民書局

SECTION ONE

Unit 1

1. A flock of　一群候鳥昨天飛到我們島上。
2. a large sum of　我對約翰如何得到那麼大筆的錢感到好奇。be curious about 對…感到好奇
3. a series of　事實上，我的生活可稱得上是一連串的「起起落落」所組成的。describe A as B 稱 A 為 B；consist of 由…所組成
4. can't afford to　爸媽負擔不起為我請個家教。tutor (n.) 家教
5. Above all　尤其記得交申請表。hand in 繳交；(an) application form 申請表
6. As many as　為數多達六十隻的領航鯨游上岸。ashore (adv.) 岸邊
7. at most　我最多借你 500 圓。
8. shortage of　那位病人臉上的青紫是因為血液中缺氧所致。oxygen (n.) 氧氣
9. arm yourself with　生活在高度競爭的社會中，無疑地你必須盡可能具備許多知識。competitive (adj.) 競爭的；definitely (adv.) 無疑地、肯定地，as much...as possible 盡可能多的…
10. a bit　controversy (n.) 爭議；commencement (n.) 大學畢業典禮
11. a great deal　communicate with 與…溝通
12. herd of　buffalo (n.) 美國野牛；steep (adj.) 陡峻的；at the bottom of 在…的底部
13. large quantity　take sth with sb 隨身攜帶；canvas (n.) 帆布
14. strong sense, duty　task (n.) 工作
15. solution, problem
16. acquaint, with　do one's best 盡全力
17. aim at　measure (n.) 措施；evil spirits 惡靈；barrier (n.) 障礙
18. walks, life
19. so on　do operations 做手術；when it comes to 一提到；well-informed (adj.) 完全清楚的
20. Apart　kind of 稍微、有一點；selfish (adj.) 自私的；charming (adj.) 迷人的
21. the clock　repair (vt.) 修理；power (n.) 電力
22. As long as　get rid of 擺脫、丟棄；no longer 不再
23. scheduled　relieve oneself 指大小便；mission (n.) 任務
24. at all　agree with sb 同意某人
25. birth　cultivate (vt.) 栽培；keep on and on 持續地
26. great many　steel (n.) 鋼；construction (n.) 建造；story (n.) 樓層
27. A　28. C　29. D　30. D　31. B　32. B　33. A　34. D　35. B

Unit 2

1. back and forth　那位父親在客廳裡走來走去，似乎很擔心。
2. are attributable　那些沒有必要的死亡，部分原因是這名女子選擇了一輛大車。in part 一部份；automobile (n.) 汽車
3. are capable of　這些清潔用具雖看來沒有太大的革命性突破，但你將驚奇於他們所能做的事情。revolutionary (adj.) 具革命性的
4. am curious about　我對 John 如何得到那麼大筆金錢感到好奇。
5. be deficient in　如果你的飲食不多樣化，勢必會營養不良。lack (vt.) 缺乏；variety (n.) 多樣化；nutrition (n.) 營養
6. envious of
7. one time　belong to 屬於；VIP = very important person 重要人物

8. the beginning of　　stage (n.) 階段；advice (n.) 忠告

9. the bottom of　　drive (vt.) 驅趕；cliff (n.) 懸崖

10. the first moment　　grab sb by the arm 抓住某人的手臂；pickpocket (n.) 扒手

11. at will　　rapidly (adv.) 快速地

12. attend to　　had better + V 最好；emergency (n.) 緊急事件

13. from　　indoors (adv.) 室內

14. back out　　be forced to + V 被迫；sequel (n.) 續集

15. about to

16. all for

17. associated with　　closely (adv.) 密切地、接近地

18. attached　　even though 即使；tease (vt.) 嘲笑；awkward (adj.) 愚蠢的；invention (n.) 發明；give in 屈服；peer pressure 同儕壓力

19. compared to　　temple (n.) 寺廟

20. concerned about　　industry (n.) 企業；leading (adj.) 主要的

21. connected to　　browse (vt.) 瀏覽；download (vt.) 下載；software (n.) 軟體

22. decorated with　　pillar (n.) 樑柱；roof-line (n.) 屋簷；dragon (n.) 龍

23. disappointed at　　with regard to 關於

24. confronted　　do one's best 盡力；at the same time 同時；partial (adj.) 部分的

Unit 3

1. is famous for　　這座博物館以其現代繪畫收藏品而聞名。collection (n.) 收藏品

2. be faced with　　每當我張開眼睛都必須要面對各種不同的問題。a variety of 各式各樣的

3. are grateful for　　我們感激他慷慨大力贊助我們教育基金會。generosity (n.) 慷慨、大方；contribution (n.) 貢獻；foundation (n.) 基金

4. be harmful to　　但是新的研究發現來自香煙的煙對非吸煙者有害。

5. are interested in　　多數年輕人對流行音樂感到有興趣。pop music = popular music 流行音樂

6. was known as　　甚至在 Albert 王子去世之前，Victoria 就是眾所週知非常認真的女性。

7. was late for　　因為下大雨所以他開會遲到。as a result of 因為、由於

8. is limited to　　有些人認為抽煙的傷害只限於抽煙者。damage (n.) 傷害、損害

9. are made from　　在這種印刷方法中，每個鉛字都是由個別的金屬片製成的。individual (adj.) 個別的；separate (adj.) 分開的；metal (n.) 金屬

10. be equal to　　我可能無法勝任此任務，但我會盡力去做。as...as one can 某人盡可能…

11. equipped with　　powerful (adj.) 強而有力的

12. excused from

13. exposed to　　The more...the better... 愈多…則…愈好；environment (n.) 環境

14. fascinated by/with　　comic (adj.) 漫畫的；heroic (adj.) 英雄的

15. full of　　think of A as B 視 A 為 B；traditional (adj.) 傳統的

16. was gone

17. good at　　trick (n.) 戲法；particularly (adv.) 特別地；magician (n.) 魔術師

18. inclined to　　in addition 此外；tolerate (vt.) 容忍；rather than 而不是；criticize (vt.) 批評

19. inferior　　household (adj.) 家庭的；chore (n.) 瑣事；conventional (adj.) 傳統的；appliances (n.) 電器用品；neither...nor... 既不…也不；efficient (adj.) 有效率的

20. intimate with　　sexuality (n.) 性關係

21. involved with　　hobby (n.) 嗜好；currently (adv.) 目前

22. known　　instrument (n.) 樂器

23. likely　　regularly (adv.) 定期地、規則地

24. linked　　personal (adj.) 個人的；celebration (n.) 慶祝會

25. made　　novel (n.) 小說
26. nervous about　　technophobe (n.) 憎恨科技者（字尾有 -phobe 則表憎惡…者）
27. D　28. B　29. A　30. C　31. A　32. D　33. B　34. C　35. A　36. C　37. A

Unit 4

1. of great importance　　我發現立即處理 SARS 疾病非常重要。cope with 處理；in no time 立即、馬上
2. is pleased with　　每一位參加畢業典禮的人都對這項安排而感到滿意。commencement (n.) 大學畢業典禮；arrangement (n.) 安排
3. serious about　　我對結婚並不是很認真。
4. be topped with　　這座塔將以每個七百平方公尺的五朵花瓣的花為頂。petal (n.) 花瓣；square meters 平方公尺
5. is unique to　　流淚的能力是人類獨有的。shed tears 流淚
6. beat around the bush　　他沒有直接問她；相反地，他只是旁敲側擊。directly (adv.) 直接地；on the contrary 相反地
7. become suspicious of　　如果你送他們貴重的禮物，他們可能會懷疑你的意圖。intention (n.) 意圖
8. belongs to　　它屬於誰或它為何被遺留在那裡沒有人知道。
9. broke with　　那對夫妻分手沒有惡言相向。couple (n.) 夫妻；rude (adj.) 粗魯的
10. break my neck　　我會竭盡心力為我們的權益而奮鬥。fight for 為…而戰；right (n.) 權利
11. obliged to
12. open to　　make a fortune 賺得一筆財富；mansion (n.) 大樓房；starving (adj.) 飢餓的
13. is senior　　凡表數量上的差距，介詞用 by
14. sent, jail
15. shaped like　　jackknife (n.) 蝴蝶刀
16. stereotyped as　　wicked (adj.) 邪惡的
17. struck by　　gifted (adj.) 天才的；conductor (n.) 指揮家；disease (n.) 疾病；virtually (adv.) 事實上、差不多
18. sure of
19. torn into shreds　　rear (adj.) 後面的
20. been up
21. worth　　admirable (adj.) 令人欽佩的；find out 找出
22. accustomed to
23. all over again
24. Believe it or not　　snack (n.) 點心；potato chip 洋芋片
25. deal
26. blend　　lizard (n.) 蜥蜴
27. broke up　　as soon as 一…就…
28. broke up　　continent (n.) 大陸塊、洲
29. believed in
30. suitable for　　overseas study 出國讀書

Unit 5

1. brought about　　是因為他的疏忽才導致悲劇性的意外。carelessness (n.) 不小心、疏忽；tragic (adj.) 悲劇的
2. brought in　　那公司新產品的銷售勢不可擋，到目前為止它已經賺進兩百萬元。overwhelmingly (adv.) 壓倒性地；so far 到目前為止
3. browse through　　對比較喜歡待在城市的觀光客來說，他們可以瀏覽許多有趣的商店。prefer to + V 比較喜歡；tourist (n.) 觀光客
4. burst into tears　　Kevin 突然當場哭了，因為老師當著全班同學面前處罰他。on the spot 當場、現場；in front of 在…之前
5. by contrast　　你善良而真誠，但相比之下她更好。sincere (adj.) 真誠的；superior (adj.) 更優秀

6. by post　磁碟片通常是用郵寄寄到磁片醫生處。

7. call for　我們應該離開了；請索取帳單。bill (n.) 帳單

8. catches on　這風格在台灣很流行，但是在美國從未流行過。

9. catch up with　你先走，幾分鐘之後我會趕上你。

10. called off　由於下大雨，球賽取消了。

11. breathing in　risk + N/V-ing 冒風險；lung cancer 肺癌

12. brought down　suitcase (n.) 手提箱、公事包

13. brought around　turn off 關掉

14. bring, with

15. bring, end　conversation (n.) 對話

16. accident　drop (vi.) 掉下

17. by, by

18. no means

19. by the name　hear about 聽說；drown (vi.) 溺水

20. by then

21. call back　instead (adv.) 反之；mutually (adv.) 雙方地；convenient (adj.) 方便的

22. calls, question　suitability (n.) 合適；post (n.) 職務

23. call, up　arrive at (place) 到達；destination (n.) 目的地

24. carry on　discussion (n.) 討論；a coffee break 喝咖啡休息一會

25. caught, eye　poster (n.) 海報

26. catch my breath　enforced (adj.) 被迫的；absence from work 不上班

27. changing, better　appear (vi.) 顯得

28. A　29. C　30. C　31. B　32. A　33. A　34. C　35. D　36. B

Unit 6

1. changed, into　Belle 是將他變成紳士的那個人。

2. a cloud on the horizon　他贏得樂透，可是我擔心會有不祥的陰影，他的兒子們可能會向他要錢。lottery (n.) 樂透彩券

3. came around　他恢復知覺時發現自己躺在地板上。find O + V-ing，此時 V-ing 做受詞補語。lie「躺」的三態：lie, lay, lain, lying

4. came down with　王氏夫婦非常擔心他們的女嬰，因為她再度感染流行性感冒。the flu 是指 influenza（流行性感冒），冠詞一定用 the，不可用 a，但可用 have a cold 表達感冒。

5. come over　你第一次來台灣是什麼時候？

6. come up to　他的新作不及以往的水平高。latest (adj.) 最近的、最新的；standard (n.) 標準

7. consists in　偉大的智慧在於不對人性苛求。wisdom (n.) 智慧；demand (vt.) 要求

8. contributes to　毫無疑問地他傾聽的能力促成他寫作的能力。no doubt = undoubtedly 無疑地；capacity (n.) 能力

9. cutting in　你那樣超車會造成追撞。crash (n.) 撞車事故

10. cut off　他由於沒付電話費所以被停話了。pay the bill 付帳；bill (n.) 帳單

　　have + O + p.p.，表示受詞的被動，此時的 have 為使役動詞，作「把…」解。若用 have + O + V-ing，則表受詞的主動，作「叫…」解。

11. charged, with　violation of law 違法；permit (n.) 許可證

12. chat with　receive a phone call 接電話；neglect (vt.) 忽略

13. cheer, up

14. clean, up　mess up 弄亂

15. come across　sb + spend (time/money) + V-ing... 花時間或金錢做某事，其中 spend 後所接的介詞 in 被省略，所以在句構上用的是動名詞。from sale to sale 表一個接一個的拍賣會，注意重複兩個單數名詞，且不加冠詞 a 或 the。

16. come back, life

17. came, being　　as to 關於

18. Come on in

19. came

20. Compared to　　painkiller (n.) 止痛藥；be likely to 可能

21. congratulations on　　first of all 首先

22. costs, nothing　　donor (n.) 捐助者；make a difference to sb 對某人造成差異

23. count on

24. coupled with　　drought (n.) 旱災

25. Cross, out

26. competed for　　title (n.) 頭銜、書名

27. came by　　be curious about 對…好奇

Unit 7

1. decided on　　多次逛過寵物店之後，我們決定買一隻大麥町，取名為 Derek。

2. differ from　　為什麼你的意見常與我的相左？How come = Why，但是注意其後接直述句，而非疑問句的形式。故原句 = Why do your opinions often differ from mine?

3. do without　　他沒有錢買車子，所以只好將就了。

4. enough to　　遇到緊急事件時，別人可能只是袖手旁觀，而他們卻有足夠的勇氣去幫忙。emergency (n.) 緊急事故；stand by 袖手旁觀

5. escaped from　　這篇文章是關於一個越獄者的故事。

6. except for　　很多人的早餐除了一杯咖啡之外什麼都不吃。not...at all 一點也不

7. face up to　　成年人必須學會勇敢承擔起自己的責任。a grown-up = an adult 成年人；responsibility (n.) 責任

8. fail to　　這就是為什麼女人可以看到許多男人不能注意到的事物。

9. fall into　　多數人分在其中一種類型。

10. even so　　外頭正下著大雨，但即使如此，我仍必須離開。

11. depends on　　orphanage (n.) 孤兒院；infant (n.) 嬰兒

12. derived, from　　mainly (adv.) 主要地；popularity (n.) 受歡迎

13. devote, to　　devote to + N/V-ing，注意 to 之後要接名詞或動名詞。

14. differ from time to time　　注意用單數名詞，且不加冠詞。

15. research on　　effect (n.) 影響；liver (n.) 肝臟

16. do's and don'ts　　lab 是 laboratory 的縮寫字。in advance 預先、事先

17. mention it

18. dressed in

19. ever since　　all over the world 遍及全世界

20. Every now and then

21. excuse for

22. exposure to　　die of 因（飢餓或疾病）而死亡；starvation (n.) 飢餓

23. failed in　　scheme (n.) 計劃、方案

24. fell apart　　hastily (adv.) 倉促地

25. fell down　　twist (vt.) 扭動；ankle (n.) 腳踝

26. fell in love with

27. D　　28. A　　29. C　　30. C　　31. D　　32. B　　33. D　　34. A

Unit 8

1. fallen off　　近年來新屋需求量大幅度地下降。demand (n.) 需求；sharply (adv.) 尖銳地、鮮明地

2. fight for　　在民主社會裡人人都可以為自我人權奮鬥。democratic (adj.) 民主的

3. food for thought　該名演講人的演說內容相當有激勵的作用，提供我們不少思考的資料。lecture (n.) 演說；stimulating (adj.) 激勵的、刺激的

4. fools around　他整日遊手好閒無所是事。all day long 一整天

5. frighten away　龍蝦發出聲音是為了嚇走牠的敵人。lobster (n.) 龍蝦；in order to 為了；enemy (n.) 敵人

6. from time to time　這些想法也因時因地而有所不同。

7. gazing at　她坐著呆望著大海，想著她遠方的父母。think of 想到；in the distance 在遠方

8. get in touch with　在台灣，跟人們聯絡比較方便的方法是打電話。

9. get on　對不起，請問下一班到台中的火車在哪搭？

10. giving a talk　我雖然趕早起床，但這場會議排定的演說，我還是遲到了。

11. feed on　evolve (vi.) 進化；remarkable (adj.) 顯著地；communicate with 與…溝通；warn off 警告遠離；predator (n.) 掠食者

12. feel good about themselves　praise (n.) 讚美；encouragement (n.) 鼓勵

13. for days　on and off = off and on 斷斷續續地

14. for pleasure　be equipped with 配備有；powerful (adj.) 強而有力的；weapon (n.) 武器

15. for the last time

16. for the purpose　scenery (n.) 風景；treatment (n.) 治療；shift (vt.) 轉移

17. from head to toe　be dressed in 穿…

18. from top to bottom　committee (n.) 委員會；reform (vi.) 改造、改革；need + V-ing = need to be + p.p. 表被動，作「需要被…」解。

19. Generally speaking　apply for 申請；visa (n.) 簽證；embassy (n.) 大使館；consulate (n.) 領事館

20. get drunk　be dedicated to = be devoted to + N/V-ing 投注於；proposition (n.) 主張、看法

21. got into difficulty　on account of 因為；budget (n.) 預算

22. get into trouble　voyage (n.) 航行

23. get married　forbid-forbade-forbidden 禁止

24. got out

25. gets, nowhere

26. getting to　encounter (vt.) 遭遇到

27. get well, get sick

28. giving birth to　visualization (n.) 視覺想像；technique (n.) 技術；distract (vt.) 使分心

Unit 9

1. gives rise to　John 魯莽的行為造成他父母無窮的麻煩。reckless (adj.) 魯莽的；endless (adj.) 無窮盡的

2. give-and-take　在廣播及電視的扣應節目中，主持人與觀眾之間要相互讓步。host (n.) 節目主持人、主人；audience (n.) 觀眾、聽眾

3. go around　要辭職，做這樣的事情不是最好的方法。

4. went back on　他違背諾言拋棄家庭。desert (vt.) 拋棄

5. go on with　所有這些家庭，在他們鍾愛的人去世後都學會繼續過他們的生活。

6. hand in　我將無法及時交作業。be able to 有能力、能夠

7. hang on to　鼓起勇氣，堅持目標，直到達成為止。take heart 有勇氣決心；goal (n.) 目標；as long as 只要

8. happened to　小說可能和現實情形如此地類似，就像今天早上才發生在你身上的事一樣。close to 接近；as real as 和…一樣真實

9. had a lot to do with　我們相信他與那宗搶案很有關係。robbery (n.) 搶劫

10. greed for　他對權力的貪心引導他走入悲劇中。tragedy (n.) 悲劇

11. gives, feedback　fan (n.) 歌迷、影迷；lower (vt.) 降低

12. give out　oxygen (n.) 氧氣；supply (vt.) 供應

13. give you, lift

14. go after

15. went bankrupt　invest (vt.) 投資
16. gone crazy
17. go Dutch
18. go for a walk　take long steps 跨大步；keep pace with 並駕齊驅
19. went into, rage　compose (vt.) 作曲；refuse (vt., vi.) 拒絕；eventually (adv.) 終究；ignore (vt.) 忽視；challenge (n.) 挑戰
20. went off　bullet (n.) 子彈
21. graduated from
22. grind to, halt　starve (vi.) 挨餓
23. have trouble　vacuum (n.) 真空；tend to 有…的傾向、易於
24. grow into　embryo (n.) 胚胎；require = need (vt.) 需要
25. hang on　manufacturer (n.) 製造商；financial (adj.) 財政的；crisis (n.) 危機；economy (n.) 經濟
26. hang out　pub 指的是 public house，表「小酒館」。
27. had, greater chance of　rescue (vi.) 拯救；survival (n.) 存活
28. having, passion for　care nothing about sth 對某事一點都不關心；tank (n.) 坦克
29. have, inclination for
30. B　31. D　32. B　33. C　34. A　35. D　36. A　37. C　38. B

Unit 10

1. heard of　我說我以前從沒聽說過戲院有這一條規定。
2. here and there　在迪士尼樂園到處可見觀光客。
3. Hold your horses　不要倉促行事，別太快做出決定。rush into 匆忙進入；decision (n.) 決定
4. In a word　總而言之，成功前要吃苦。take pains 吃苦
5. in action　觀看袋鼠活動的最佳時機是晚間和清晨。
6. in advance　人們有可能事先知道地震何時會發生。earthquake (n.) 地震；strike (vi.) 侵襲
7. In comparison with　與孿生姊妹相比，Sue 更顯樂觀。optimistic (adj.) 樂觀的
8. in conflict with　建築與社會彼此相衝突。architecture (n.) 建築（學）
9. in danger　蝙蝠因農夫用來對抗害蟲的某些化學藥品而身陷危險之中。chemical (n.) 農藥、化學藥品；destructive (adj.) 有破壞性的；insect (n.) 昆蟲
10. in a good humor　Mary 心情很好，因為今天是她的生日。
11. heard about　by the name of = called = named 名叫…的
12. help me with　go abroad 出國
13. Hold on
14. hold on to　tolerate (vt.) 容忍
15. hold her ground　put forward 提出；objection (n.) 反對
16. hold out against　mentally (adv.) 心理上；pressure (n.) 壓力
17. How come
18. How on earth
19. in a minute
20. in abundance　mechanical (adj.) 機器的；peeler (n.) 削皮機；potato chips 洋芋片
21. In accordance with　cancel (vt.) 取消；ceremony (n.) 典禮
22. in addition to　emotional (adj.) 情緒上的；benefit (n.) 益處、好處；biological (adj.) 生物的；function (n.) 功能；as well = too 也
23. in ancient times　flourish (vi.) 興盛；development (n.) 發展；scientific (adj.) 科學的
24. in and out
25. in appearance　characteristic (n.) 特徵；identical (adj.) 完全相同的
26. in connection with　marketing (n.) 行銷；strategy (n.) 策略

27. In contrast to　shelter (n.) 庇護所；far from 一點也不；airtight (adj.) 密封的
28. in, control　situation (n.) 情境、情況
29. in defeat

Unit 11

1. in due time　你可以在適當的時候提出你的提案。put forward 提出；proposal (n.) 提案
2. in earnest　他認真地告訴我他會盡全力來幫助我。
3. in exchange for　他提供警方一項新證據以交換暫時的自由。temporary (adj.) 暫時的；freedom (n.) 自由
4. in love　Victoria 與 Albert 深深相愛，他們的婚姻很幸福。deeply (adv.) 深深地；extremely (adv.) 極端地；非常地
5. in need of　連續工作之後，我需要休假。successive (adj.) 連續的
6. in other words　健康勝於財富；換言之，前者比後者重要。the former 前者；the latter 後者
7. in possession of　他被發現持有非法武器。illegal (adj.) 非法的
8. in proportion to　一個人的成功與其努力成正比是眾所週知的事實。
9. in return for　他同意提供對抗敵人的證據以換取受保護的保證。guarantee (n.) 保證；protection (n.) 保護
10. in the extreme　那個百萬富翁非常慷慨。millionaire (n.) 百萬富翁；generous (adj.) 慷慨大方的
11. in, detail　fierce (adj.) 凶惡的；guardian (n.) 守護、看護人；realistic (adj.) 生動的
12. in excess of　profit (n.) 利潤；percent (n.) 百分之…
13. in jail/in prison　court (n.) 法庭；sentence (vt.) 判刑
14. In modern times　avoid + N/Ving，avoid 為及物動詞，其後接動名詞或名詞為其受詞。spread（三態同形）(vt.) 傳播
15. in need
16. in number　at will 任意地
17. in her care　per (prep.) 每一
18. in, tone　initial (adj.) 最初的；turn down 拒絕
19. in place　security (n.) 安全；measure (n.) 措施
20. in praise of
21. in prison/in jail　fall in love with sb 愛上某人
22. in progress
23. in question　apply to + (school) 申請學校；admission (n.) 許可
24. the hope　package (n.) 包裹
25. in the dark　attendance (n.) 出席人數
26. A　27. D　28. C　29. B　30. A　31. D　32. A

Unit 12

1. In the light of　依照最近的情況，這個會議最好能延期。recent (adj.) 最近的、近來的；postpone (vi.) 延期
2. in the past　它是過去生活的重要線索。clue to + N 某事的線索。
3. intends to　而 iRobot 打算明年上市一款價格如筆記型電腦一樣的家庭保全機器人。Notebook (n.) 筆記型電腦
4. joined in　她開始跳舞，而我們也跟著一起跳。
5. keep my temper　我發覺他當眾侮辱我時，我很難忍住自己的脾氣。insult (vt.) 侮辱
6. kill time　有些人以為當這個真實的世界需要花心思去留意時，閱讀故事是一種打發時間的方法。
7. knock out　新的電腦病毒能把你的整個系統徹底毀掉。virus (n.) 病毒
8. keep pace with　當他們散步時，Johnny 必須跨大步才能追上爸爸。go for a walk = take a walk 散步
9. instead of　respondent (n.) 回答者；turn to sth 向…求助；go online 上網
10. the meantime　specific (adj.) 特別的；特定的
11. in the name of　exchange (vt.) 交換
12. in the vicinity　originate (vi.) 起源

13. in those days　　waterfall (n.) 瀑布

14. in trouble

15. investing, in　　electronic (adj.) 電子的；industry (n.) 工業

16. It seems

17. just as　　make money 賺錢

18. keep, from　　break in 闖入

19. keeps, off

20. keeping, out　　apparently (adv.) 明顯地；burglar (n.) 盜賊

21. kept, waiting

22. keeping up　　have difficulty (in) + V-ing，其中介詞 in 經常省略，表「做某事有困難」。the rest 剩下的；其餘的

23. keep track of　　keep records 保存紀錄

24. knocked down

25. know of

Unit 13

1. lasted for　　Alexander Dumas（大仲馬）的小說流傳至今還不到百年。less than 少於；不到

2. less than　　洋芋片在美國風行不到 100 年。

3. let go of　　小孩直到睡著才鬆開我的手。fall asleep 睡著，三態：fall, fell, fallen

4. looked over　　這份報告我過目了一下，但沒有詳細地研究。in detail 詳細的

5. make both ends meet　　為了使我們家能收支平衡，把生活費減到最少是重要的。minimize (vt.) 使最少化；living expense 生活費用

6. made your point　　你想說的我已懂了，沒有必要再說下去。go on 繼續

7. made it up with　　該是跟你的對手和解的時候了。rival (n.) 對手

　　　　It is (high/about) time that S + 過去式動詞… 表示與現在事實相反的語氣，所以一定要用過去式動詞。

8. make room for　　往前一點，讓點位置給你弟弟。

9. look down upon　　勿輕視那些比你差的人。be inferior to = be worse than 比…差

10. laid out　　alarm (vt.) 使恐懼；studio (n.) 錄音室、播音室

11. lead/live, life　　colorful (adj.) 多采多姿的

12. lets in

13. look back, look back　　medieval (adj.) 中世紀的

14. looking forward to

15. looking into　　unemployment (n.) 失業

16. lost, temper　　at first 起初；gentle (adj.) 溫柔的

17. made, of himself　　on the list 在名單上

18. make, profit　　publisher (n.) 出版商

19. made, speech

20. make arrangements　　annual (adj.) 一年一度的

21. make friends with　　sincerity (n.) 誠意

22. make fun of

23. made into

24. make it

25. making, resolutions　　carry out 實現

26. make up　　regular (adj.) 規則的、經常的

27. A　28. C　29. D　30. B　31. A　32. D　33. C

Unit 14

1. make good use of　暑假期間設法善用時間。
2. mind your tongue　和上司說話時要有禮貌並注意言辭。polite (adj.) 禮貌的
3. more or less　每個人多多少少都有自己的弱點。weakness (n.) 弱點
4. Next to　僅次於知識，我們必須保留且絕不失去的是對生活的品味。knowledge (n.) 知識；retain (vt.) 保留
5. not to mention　我非常怕老鼠，更遑論蜘蛛和蛇。be afraid of 害怕
6. nothing but　那位雇主十分苛求，他只期待他的員工表現完美。demanding (adj.) 苛求的；perfection (n.) 完美；employee (n.) 員工
7. on a charge of　就在這一刻警察再度出現，以蓄意破壞的罪名逮捕他。arrest (vt.) 逮捕；vandalism (n.) 對公物的蓄意破壞
8. on board　在所有三個案例中，恐怖份子都未登機。case (n.) 案子；terrorist (n.) 恐怖份子
9. merged into　otherwise (adv.) 用其他的方法
10. mistake, for
11. more than once　tell a lie 說謊
12. most important, all　mathematically (adv.) 數學上；gifted (adj.) 有天份的
13. much, his surprise　harass (vt.) 騷擾；verbally (adv.) 口語上；overwhelmed (adj.) 使不知所措的
14. next to
15. No big deal　president (n.) 總裁
16. no less, than　religion (n.) 宗教；literature (n.) 文學；philosophy (n.) 哲學
17. no more than　be prepared to 準備；glance at 匆匆一看
18. No way
19. none of your business　hold one's tongue 謹言
20. doesn't, any longer　item (n.) 物品
21. but rather　communication (n.) 溝通；predator (n.) 掠奪的人
22. not, until　movable (adj.) 可移動的
23. numbered in　population (n.)（某區某）動物（或植物）的總數；人口
24. on and on　cultivate (vt.) 培養；taste (n.) 品味；at birth 出生時
25. on duty　complain of/about 抱怨；duration (n.) 持續的時間
26. p's and q's

Unit 15

1. On the contrary　自尊心低的人害羞；相反地，自尊心高的的人傾向樂觀。self-esteem (n.) 自尊
2. on the outside　這些馬鈴薯被切成厚片，炸到呈金褐色、外皮酥脆為止。crisp (adj.) 脆脆的
3. on the spot　Kevin 當場放聲大哭，因為老師在全班同學面前處罰他。burst into tears 放聲大哭
4. at a time　最初的印刷術是用手在木塊上一次刻一個鉛字。block (n.) 塊狀物；by hand 手工的
5. originated in　人類可能起源於海洋。may have + p.p. 表示「可能已經…」。
6. out of his mind　他必定是瘋了才會做出如此瘋狂的事。
7. out of the question　在台灣滑雪多半是不可能的，因為這裡很少下雪。
8. passed out　當 Jones 太太被告之她的丈夫過世時，她失去知覺。
9. paid off　他過去三年所有的努力都成功了，因為他以最優異的成績畢業。top honors 最優異的成績
10. On, way to
11. on the move　migrating (adj.) 遷徙的
12. skate, thin ice
13. on the verge of　breakdown (n.) 崩潰；be unable to 不能；pressure (n.) 壓力；daily life 日常生活
14. on time
15. once more

16. One day

17. open up　　listen to 傾聽；communicate with 與…溝通

18. out of

19. out of stock　　peel (vt.) 削（皮）；time-consuming (adj.) 耗時的；chore (n.) 雜事

20. out of style　　normally (adv.) 正常地、一般地

21. over, over again　　feature (vt.) 以…為特色；alcohol (n.) 酒精

22. owes, to　　in particular 尤其是、特別是

23. part of

24. passing on

25. pay for it　　nourish (vt.) 培育；滋潤；imagination (n.) 想像力

26. pay, visit

27. C　28. A　29. C　30. D　31. B　32. A　33. D　34. C　35. B

Unit 16

1. pie in the sky　　我無法同意你的想法，因為太不可能了。agree to sth 與 agree with sb 均表同意。

2. plenty of　　此外，身為早起的鳥，你擁有很多時間去運動或從事許多工作。

3. prior to　　早在假期前所有準備都該完成。preparation (n.) 準備 complete (vt.) 完成

4. pulled down　　這些由於地震而受到嚴重損害的舊房舍將很快地被拆除重建。severe (adj.) 嚴重的；嚴厲的

5. put off　　戶外音樂會因為下雨而延期。

6. put to death　　國王下令處死奴隸。order 為使役動詞，故其後 that 子句中的動詞要用原形。即：S + order that S + 原形動詞 emperor (n.) 國王；帝王

7. regardless of　　職缺開放給任何人，不論年紀性別。position (n.) 職位

8. reflect on　　而且如果你能反省所犯過的過錯，就可避免一再犯相同的錯誤。

9. referred to as　　我們被分開送去被視為雄偉壯觀的巡航，上面裝載了足夠一星期食用的食物。grandly (adv.) 壯觀地；cruise (n.) 航行

10. pick you up

11. piled up　　auction (n.) 拍賣

12. play with

13. pointed out

14. popping up　　master (vt.) 精通；be familiar with 熟悉

15. prefer　　browse through 瀏覽

16. present them with　　introduce (vt.) 介紹

17. provides, for　　livestock (n.)[U] 家畜

18. pulled out　　crawl (vi.) 爬；push forward 向前推

19. put, into practice

20. put, away

21. put on　　in no time = immediately 立即

22. put, in jail　　charge sb with sth 以某事起訴某人

23. put, into operation　　feasible (adj.) 可行的

24. raining down　　estimated (adj.) 估算的；confetti (n.) 五彩碎紙 ticker-tape (n.) 彩色紙帶；route (n.) 路線；路程

25. recognize, as

26. recover from　　folk (n.) 人；depressed (adj.) 沮喪的

27. regard, as　　criticism (n.) 批評；rejection (n.) 拒絕

Unit 17

1. relieve himself　　他的飛行應該只持續 15 分鐘，所以不提供他在太空船的密封艙裡解手。be supposed to 應該；provision (n.) 供應；capsule (n.) 膠囊；太空船的密閉艙

2. ride out　如果你能安然度過這次危機，你就成功在望。crisis (n.) 危機

3. ran into　她的文章刊載在報上之後遭受到嚴厲的批評。

4. save his skin　他為了免遭傷害而沒有對警察說實話。tell the truth 說實話

5. slipped my mind　我真的很抱歉忘了你的生日。我完全忘了這個日子。

6. serve as　為了作為關懷環境的象徵，這座新塔以木頭建造。symbol (n.) 象徵、符號；environmental (adj.) 環境的；concern (n.) 關心

7. see through　一個女人可以在先生知道之前就看穿他的秘密。

8. set out　他們出發去尋找芥末的種子。mustard (n.) 芥末；seed (n.) 種子

9. shed tears　動物也經驗到恐懼、快樂、寂寞等情緒，但他們不流淚。pleasure (n.) 快樂；loneliness (n.) 寂寞

10. reminds, of

11. right away

12. ran down　in a...manner 以⋯的態度；careless (adj.) 粗心的

13. ran off　bring up = raise 養育

14. ran out of　abandon (vt.) 放棄

15. ran over

16. rushed into

17. save, from　by the name of 名叫⋯

18. see, as　organism (n.) 有機體

19. sold out

20. separated from

21. set aside

22. set free

23. set off

24. shaking hands with　homosexual (n.) 同性戀者

25. slow, down　lane (n.) 車道；facilitate (vt.) 有助於；flow (n.) 流量

26. B　27. D　28. A　29. C　30. A　31. D　32. B　33. A　34. B

Unit 18

1. So much for　電影的討論就到此為止；咱們回去工作吧。

2. sooner or later　他的老闆勢必遲早會發現實情。be bound to 勢必會；find out 發現

3. speak up　練習時要試著在全班面前大聲說出來。do drill 練習

4. split off　計劃的這一部份已經從主要團隊中分裂出來。

5. stand up for　民主社會裡，每個人都可以捍衛自己的人權。human rights 人權

6. stayed away from　我和 Mary 吵架，所以她遠離我。quarrel (n.) 爭吵；吵架

7. strike a balance　一個國家要在經濟發展與環保之間取得平衡是很難的。economic (adj.) 經濟的

8. sum up　在你的最後一段總結你的論點。paragraph (n.) 段落；argument (n.) 論點

9. take delight in　賣書的人很喜歡四周有書。

10. Take heart　鼓起勇氣，堅持目標，直到達成為止。hang on to 堅持

11. smile at

12. so, that　result in 造成；collision (n.) 碰撞

13. spoke out　shout at 對⋯吼叫

14. speed up　recovery (n.) 恢復、復原；rate (n.) 速率

15. stands for

16. stand, feet

17. starts, off　sufficient (adj.) 充足的；provide sb with sth 提供某人某物

18. started out　fade away 枯萎

19. started up　rumor (n.) 謠言

20. stay up

21. stems from　　prophet (n.) 先知

22. such as　　promotion (n.) 升遷；anniversary (n.) 週年；be linked with 與…關係密切

23. such, that　　courage (n.) 勇氣；dare (vi.) 敢

24. sued, for　　discrimination (n.) 歧視；contract (n.) 合約；renew (vi.) 更新

25. take along　　suitable (adj.) 合適的

26. taken care of　　be protective of = protect 保護；make sure 確信；all the time 隨時

27. taken apart　　rearrange (vt.) 重新安排

28. take exercise

Unit 19

1. take responsibility　　在現代，我們也必須負起責任避免傳播疾病。

2. took to　　退休之後，王先生喜歡溜冰，這是他一向喜愛卻沒有時間做的事。

3. take turns　　他們輪流照顧生病的母親。

4. the minute　　他一打開門，空箱子和許多其他東西都掉了下來、散落一地。empty (adj.) 空的；all over 遍及

5. through and through　　這些火持續燃燒直到大雨將煤層完完全全的溼透為止（才停）。rainfall (n.) 降雨；soak (vt.) 浸泡、溼透；peat (n.) 泥煤

6. throw off　　我盡一切所能使牠的方向感錯亂。sense of direction 方向感

7. touch on　　如果你不小心觸及這個話題，他們會感到相當不自在或懊惱。uneasy (adj.) 不自在的

8. translated into　　大仲馬的小說已經被翻譯成超過一百種語言。

9. take, out

10. take/took, pride in

11. take, place　　acknowledge (vt.) 承認；system (n.) 系統

12. take up　　do one's best 盡全力；carry out 實現

13. takes/took, with　　goods (n.) 貨物；including 包括；quantity (n.) 數量；canvas (n.) 帆布

14. that is　　dreaded (adj.) 令人恐懼的；event (n.) 事件；occur (vi.) 發生；bully (vt.) 欺凌；dream of 夢到

15. the rest　　mourn (vt.) 哀悼

16. the same, as　　internal (adj.) 內部的；structure (n.) 結構；surface (n.) 表面

17. these days　　hear from 收到某人的訊息

18. think of, as

19. throw, away　　deal with 處理

20. threw, into

21. together with

22. good advantage　　hummingbird (n.) 蜂鳥；unique (adj.) 獨特的

23. to and from　　thunderstorm (n.) 雷電交加的暴風雨

24. transform, into　　celebration (n.) 慶祝會；capital (n.) 首都

25. try, on

26. C　27. B　28. A　29. C　30. B　31. C　32. D　33. C　34. A

Unit 20

1. turned off　　當會議結束時，我關上錄音機並一一送上飲料。

2. turn over a new leaf　　雖然 Soapy 決定要重新做人，但他又入獄了。S + be put in jail 某人被送進監牢

3. up and down　　當房東開門時，他上下打量我後才問我是誰。landlord (n.) 房東；地主

4. ward off　　已採行更嚴苛的措施來避免抽煙所帶來的潛在危險。strict (adj.) 嚴格的；potential (adj.) 潛在的；

5. with all their hearts　　他們全心全意地愛護他。

6. work with　　他們將必須學習與機器人及科技一起工作來解決社會的問題。

7. used up　　她兩星期內就花光父母給的所有的錢。

8. turned, deaf ear   face the music 面對現實；constructive (adj.) 有建設性的

9. turned on   solemnly (adv.) 嚴肅地；count (vt.) 計數；accent (n.) 腔調

10. turned her back

11. under great pressure   gain (vt.) 獲得；market share 市場佔有率

12. under the care

13. wandered about

14. warn off   feed on 以…為食；吃

15. warned, of

16. watch your back

17. What a pity/shame

18. What if

19. when it comes to   operation (n.) 手術；well-informed (adj.) 見多識廣的

20. wipe out   windshield (n.) 擋風玻璃

21. With the help   doggie (n.) 小狗；beat (vt.) 擊敗 (beat, beat, beaten)

22. worked for   invent (vt.) 發明、創造

23. worry about   concentrate on 專心；bring out the best in sb 使某人發揮到極致

SECTION TWO

Unit 21

1. at all costs   作者建議我們無論如何都要避免失敗。recommend (vt.) 建議，其後接 that 子句，助動詞 should 可以省略，故其 that 子句中常見原形動詞。

2. as well   喝酒也是這個國家慶典的部份之一。part of 一部份

3. As soon as   當這對夫妻明白他們不再彼此相愛時，他們就分手了。break up 分手；決裂

4. As a result   因此，寫電子郵件的人享有極大的自由，可以在任何時間與世界上任何地方的任何人聯絡。a great deal of + 不可數名詞：大量的；communicate with 與…溝通

5. appeals to   出名的想法吸引了很多人。

6. ahead of   高中畢業意味著在你眼前將有的一個新的人生階段。

7. add, to   也是因為 Robert Houdin，許多魔術師才能在名字上加上博士的頭銜。

8. a good number of   那座湖每季生產大量的鱸魚。bass (n.) 鱸魚（單複數同形）

9. a variety of   無主信件處理中心的員工有各種方法去處理所有無主的郵件。

10. adjust to   在薩沃國家公園裡，Zoe 已被教導去適應野外生活。

11. apply for   一般而言，所有到台灣的外國人必須透過中華民國大使館或領事館申請入境簽證。generally speaking 大體上；embassy (n.) 大使館；consulate (n.) 領事館

12. as a result of   這 60 隻領航鯨游上岸是因為一種目前科學家還不明白的行為。be unknown to sb 不為…所知

13. as much, as possible   生活在高度競爭的社會中，無疑地你必須盡可能具備許多知識。arm oneself with sth 武裝；具備

14. as to   還有兩種關於這個成語如何產生的解釋。

15. At best   這些電池不好。充其量它們只能維持兩個月。battery (n.) 電池

16. all the time   她一直不停的說話。她很愛說話。talkative (adj.) 愛說話的

17. as though/if   greet (vt.) 打招呼

18. all the time   be protective of 保護；make sure 確信

19. appeal to   drug abuse 濫用藥物

20. variety of   balanced (adj.) 均衡的；adequate (adj.) 適當的；cereal (n.) 穀類

21. as, result

22. as soon as   brighten (vt.) 使明亮；照亮

23. according to

24. as to   prove (vi.) 證明；productive (adj.) 有生產力的
25. at best   appear (vi.) 顯得
26. at any cost   architect (n.) 建築師
27. adjust to   survive (vi.) 生還、生存；flourish (vi.) 興盛、繁榮
28. all over
29. add   reveal (vt.) 透露
30. As, result   mammal (n.) 哺乳動物
31. amounts to   quarter (n.) 四分之一
32. After all   relative (n.) 親戚
33. as far as
34. achieve their goals   tend to + V 易於、傾向於…；tactful (adj.) 圓融的；indirect (adj.) 間接的；strategy (n.) 策略
35. agree with
36. ahead, their
37. number of   browse through 瀏覽、逛一逛
38. as thin as possible   slice (vt.) 將…切成薄片
39. A   40. D   41. C   42. B   43. C   44. D   45. A   46. C   47. B

Unit 22

1. by hand   最初的印刷是用手在木塊上一次刻一個鉛字。one at a time 一次一個
2. broken down   我的電腦壞了，不知有何毛病。No idea = I have no idea 不知道
3. because of   因為交通阻塞，所以他未能準時參加會議。
4. are sensitive to   許多女人比男人更具觀察力，因為她們對細微事物敏感。observant (adj.) 具有觀察力的
5. is related to   你大部分的成功，無論在工作或社交生活上，都和你如何傾聽的有關。
6. were made of   石器時代的獵人只有一些由石頭和木頭製造而成的簡陋武器。crude (adj.) 簡陋的、粗魯的
7. are familiar with   也許我們多數人對該諺語很熟悉：「笑，則世界跟著你笑；哭泣，則你獨自哭泣。」weep (vi.) 哭泣
8. been accused of   攻擊人類並帶有傳染病的罪名，長久以來一直加諸在蝙蝠身上。infectious (adj.) 傳染的
9. Based on   根據本文，台灣的寺廟有部分設計是為了防止惡靈和壞人進入。prevent from 阻止；bad spirits 壞精靈、鬼魅
10. at least   百分之四十五的學童每個月至少閱讀五本書。
11. is concerned with   一棟建築物的設計是一種創造的過程，而非數理的過程，但不像其他藝術型式，它與積極追求解決的方法有關。positive (adj.) 積極的
12. are, crazy about   這些產品只吸引那些對機器人已有狂熱的消費者。
13. be proud of   我們應該以這項結果為榮。
14. are similar to   根據研究，睡眠中的人的腦波和行走中的人的腦波相類似。brain (n.) 腦部、大腦；wave (n.) 波、浪
15. begun with   大家都相信魔術是始於西元前一千七百年的埃及人。Egyptian (n.) 埃及人
16. Breaking into   闖入銀行、大型公司、甚至政府部門的電腦密碼是天才青少年最新的遊戲。
17. at least
18. were, related to   comment (n.) 評論；loosely (adv.) 鬆散地
19. were, aware of   startled (adj.) 震驚的；similarity (n.) 相似之處
20. At times
21. similar to   lobster (n.) 龍蝦；violinist (n.) 小提琴手；bow (n.) 弓；string (n.) 弦
22. be, concerned   fail to + V 不能；patient (n.) 病人
23. Because   strength (n.) 力氣；steel (n.) 鋼；material (n.) 材料
24. is covered with
25. are proud of

26. Accused of　　neglect (vt.) 忽略；institute (vt.) 擬定、制定

27. all means

28. break down　　range (n.) 範圍；bacteria (n.) 細菌，是 bacterium 的複數；fungi (n.) 蕈類，是 fungus 的複數

29. be, sensitive　　go on = happen 發生

30. brings out　　concentrate (vi.) 專心

31. be familiar with　　master (vt.) 精通；pop up 跳出、迸出

32. be, responsible　　oversized (adj.) 超大的；automobile (n.) 汽車

33. are crazy

34. related

35. brought up

36. broke down　　drift (vi.) 漂流

37. breaking in　　architectural (adj.) 建築的

38. made of　　millennium (n.) 千禧年

39. begins with　　addressee (n.) 收信人

40. by, large　　species (n.) 品種（單複數同形）

Unit 23

1. disposed of　　一旦使用過，袋子會被封口並儲存到飛回地球之後再行處理。seal (vt.) 封口；store (vt.) 儲存

2. described as　　由於 catadupa 聽起來像 cats and dogs，所以下大雨就被描述成 "falling cats and dogs"。

3. deals with　　左半球處理規章、資訊的分類和短期的記憶。hemisphere (n.) 半球

4. complaining about　　無論它是多麼困難及無趣，都不要浪費時間去抱怨。

5. come up with　　這個問題我思考了很長一段時間之後，仍然無法想出解決方法。

6. close to　　小說可能和現實情形如此地接近，以致於就像今天早上才發生在你身上的事一樣的真實。fiction (n.) 虛構故事

7. carried out　　這個村莊裡的人已經實行許多個福利計劃。welfare (n.) 福利

8. call on　　兒童保護團體要求德國警方對這位流行樂傳奇人物採取行動。take action 採取行動；legend (n.) 傳奇（人物）

9. By the way　　我七點會去接你。順便提一下，你的貴客還和你在一塊嗎?

10. consisted of　　部分課程包括了在限定時間內綁緊數條繩結。knot (n.) （繩）結；time limit 時間限制

11. die out　　若過程中沒有二氧化碳的釋放，所有植物的生命會消失殆盡。carbon dioxide 二氧化碳

12. considered to be　　movable (adj.) 可移動的

13. came up with　　lengthy (adj.) 冗長的；resolve (vt.) 解決；crisis (n.) 危機

14. consist of　　external (adj.) 外在的；interior (adj.) 內在的；resident (n.) 居民

15. by means of

16. check out　　regularly (adv.) 定期地

17. deal/cope with　　on the verge of 瀕臨；breakdown (n.) 崩潰；pressure (n.) 壓力

18. came to　　request (n.) 要求；fulfill (vt.) 滿足、實現

19. carrying out　　procedure (n.) 程序；tube (n.) 試管；insert (vt.) 插入

20. dispose

21. by the way　　informal (adj.) 非正式的

22. died of　　heart attack 心臟病

23. care for　　put up with 容忍；selfish (adj.) 自私的

24. coping/dealing with　　meditation (n.) 冥想；anxiety (n.) 焦慮；stress (n.) 壓力

25. came off

26. caters to

27. call upon

28. concentrate on

29. communicate with   underwater (adj.) 水中的；evolve (vi.) 演化
30. close to
31. complaining, about   duration (n.) 持續期間
32. come about
33. came up
34. dealing/coping with   think up 想起
35. describes, as   extension (n.) 延伸；workload (n.) 工作量
36. die out   trade winds 信風
37. B   38. B   39. C   40. A   41. D   42. A   43. B   44. C   45. C

Unit 24

1. getting rid of   只要語言不死，它的細胞就會繼續改變，形成新字並淘汰掉那些不再使用的字。cell (n.) 細胞
2. For example   舉例來說，在美國，幾乎每個場合都準時是很重要的。occasion (n.) 場合
3. due to   由於一場有六人受傷的車禍意外，所以主街的交通受阻數小時之久。obstruct (vt.) 阻塞、妨礙；injure (vi.) 受傷
4. Do your best   盡力就好，當你自認你的創作夠好可以送給別人時，就送吧！
5. Even though   即使她的朋友嘲笑她裝在電車上的怪異發明，Mary 並未屈服於同儕的壓力。tease (vt.) 嘲笑；awkward (adj.) 怪異的、古怪的；invention (n.) 發明；attach to 黏在…；peer pressure 同儕壓力
6. figure out   直到老師做給他看，Sam 才了解如何印出文件。document (n.) 文件
7. For one thing   美國這個國家鼓勵年輕人喝酒。一則，他們的社會使喝酒成為所有慶祝活動的一部份，另一則是，演員總是在電影中喝酒。
8. get over   Peter 突然死亡對 Jane 是一大打擊，她花很長一段時間才從憂傷中恢復過來。blow (n.) 重擊、打擊；grief (n.) 憂傷
9. focus on   所有的思緒必須集中於當時所發生的事，然後身心就會合而為一。
10. ended up in   雖然獲得眾人的支持，他的計劃仍以失敗收場。failure (n.) 失敗
11. one thing   cave (n.) 洞穴；abandoned (adj.) 被棄置的；mine (n.) 礦坑
12. For example   self-esteem (n.) 自尊；confidence (n.) 信心
13. even if/though   appreciate (vt.) 感激
14. get along well   flexible (adj.) 有彈性的；insist on 堅持；opinion (n.) 意見
15. get, over with   assignment (n.) 指定作業
16. filled out/in   questionnaire (n.) 問卷；properly (adv.) 適當地；respondent (n.) 回應者
17. give in
18. found out   explorer (n.) 探險者
19. First of all
20. do, sleeping   laboratory (n.) 實驗室；researcher (n.) 研究人員；wake sb up 喚醒某人；turn out 結果變成
21. for good   kangaroo (n.) 袋鼠
22. due to
23. for the first time
24. even though/if   formally (adv.) 正式地；plot (vt.) 畫（航海圖）；course (n.) 路線；tide (n.) 潮汐；in the distance 在遠處
25. face the music   mess up 弄得亂七八糟
26. focus on
27. do one's best   reward (vt.) 報酬；partial (adj.) 部分的；confront with 遭遇
28. figured out   phenomenon (n.) 現象
29. give away

Unit 25

1. in response to 是為了因應這樣的情況而使木匠商店開張。
2. in order to 她丟掉所不需的物品是<u>為了</u>能較輕便的旅行嗎?
3. in such a hurry 但是人們有時很匆<u>忙</u>，所以不能等到信件來。
4. have nothing in common Jane 和 Sue 是雙胞胎，但她們似乎一點也<u>沒有共通點</u>。
5. going on 那位經理了解<u>正在發生</u>的狀況，就要求 Soapy 跟他進入廚房。
6. has a profound effect on 人們對自己的看法對他們生活上各方面都有<u>深刻的影響</u>。
7. in part 這些不必要的死亡，<u>部分原因</u>是因為這名女子選擇了一輛大車。
8. in person 為了最後這件工作，由於一些安全因素，Jack 必須<u>親自</u>到 Thatcher 夫人的辦公室!
9. in terms of 「女性的直覺」這個用語<u>以</u>具體例子<u>的方式</u>來解釋比較好。
10. have no idea 參加這場集會的名人大概<u>不知道</u>他們的音樂專輯 CD 價值多少。
11. terms of physics (n.) 物理
12. have no idea
13. Hang up
14. in front of practically (adv.) 實際地
15. in case
16. gives off radio (n.) 無線電；signal (n.) 信號
17. in response to organize (vt.) 組織、舉行
18. in part, in part delightful (adj.) 令人愉快的；nonsense (n.) 胡說八道，無理
19. in a hurry briefly (adv.) 簡短地
20. give up alcohol (n.) 酒精
21. in order to
22. held up
23. In contrast long-term (adj.) 長期的
24. have, in common
25. in keeping with
26. having, confidence limitation (n.) 極限；worship (n.) 崇拜；groundwork (n.) 基礎工作
27. have, serious effect on
28. In general profound (adj.) 深刻的、深遠的
29. In spite of opposition (n.) 反對
30. in fact be excellent at 精通於
31. in person
32. go through
33. In addition advertisement (n.) 廣告；liquor (n.) 烈酒；attractive (adj.) 有吸引力的
34. D 35. A 36. C 37. C 38. A 39. B 40. D 41. C 42. B

Unit 26

1. making up Sarah 喜歡編故事來娛樂她的朋友。amuse (vt.) 使娛樂
2. made, progress 得到老師和雙親的鼓勵，Jane 重拾信心並有極大的<u>進</u>步。encouragement (n.) 鼓勵；regain (vt.) 重新獲得
3. led to 這個帝國的擴張導致與鄰國的戰爭。expansion (n.) 擴大；empire (n.) 帝國；neighboring (adj.) 鄰近的
4. Instead of 王太太<u>並沒</u>有視這個無家可歸的男人為社會的恥辱，反而還供應他食物和水。treat (vt.) 對待
5. looking for 像多數的移民一樣，他在<u>追尋</u>更好的生活。immigrant (n.) 移民
6. insist on 一個懂變通的人常能和別人好好相處，因為他不會<u>堅持己見</u>。
7. in the middle of 她的學生偶爾必須在考試<u>中途</u>匆忙離校。occasionally (adv.) 偶而；dash off 衝出去
8. In the event of 萬一下雨，典禮將在室內舉行。ceremony (n.) 典禮

9. in the distance　　研究人員也在牆上展示河流穿過森林以及有遠山的大幅畫作。display (vt.) 展示

10. makes possible　　科學使得運用新材料及新方法生產東西變為可能。

11. messed up

12. in the middle of　　microphone (n.) 麥克風；height (n.) 高度

13. look up

14. the event of

15. lead to　　inevitably (adv.) 不可避免地

16. made up　　biography (n.) 傳記；autobiography (n.) 自傳

17. interact with　　original (adj.) 原來的

18. let off　　in one's opinion 依某人之見

19. Instead of　　punish (vt.) 處罰

20. make, difference to　　participation (n.) 參與；donor (n.) 捐贈者

21. In this way

22. in that

23. leave, out

24. made, progress　　mystery (n.) 神秘；amazing (adj.) 令人驚訝的；organ (n.) 器官

25. insisted on　　cloakroom (n.) 接待室；attendant (n.) 招待人員；lobby (n.) 大廳

26. look for　　logical (adj.) 合邏輯的；pattern (n.) 模式、形式

27. looked after

28. in the distance

29. in vain　　persuade (vt.) 說服；a speech contest 演講比賽

30. making, fortune　　mansion (n.) 大廈；starving (adj.) 飢餓的

31. in turn　　solemnly (adv.) 嚴肅地、隆重地；accent (n.) 腔調

32. make sure　　breeding (adj.) 飼養的；multiply (vt.) 繁殖

33. keep, up

34. In the beginning　　needy (adj.) 貧窮的

Unit 27

1. rather than　　一棟建築物的設計是一種創造的過程，而非數理的過程。

2. preparing, for　　我太忙碌為了要準備大學入學考試。

3. participated in　　他參與了三次革命，當受到屈辱時，他會起而與人爭鬥。

4. more than　　兩個城鎮都宣稱是最冷的地方，其中包含的不只是為了驕傲。involve in 參與；claim (vt.) 宣稱

5. not only, but also　　任何一項 IMO 舉辦的競賽，不僅使年輕的數學好手齊聚一堂，也集合了他們的老師。
instructor (n.) 指導老師

6. on average　　Fraser 鎮宣稱其平均溫度比這個明尼蘇達州的城鎮還要冷。

7. pay attention to　　為了聽得有效率，我們必須注意臉部的表情、肢體的動作和他人聲音的特質。

8. plays an important part in　　對一個小的農業家庭來說，增添一隻動物，在提供珍貴的牛奶及肉類方面扮演著十分重要的角色。agricultural (adj.) 農業的

9. protect, from　　文章中提供哪些建議以保護蝙蝠免於絕種？

10. put out　　因人們的努力，印尼的大火終於被撲滅了。

11. no longer　　contact (n.) 接觸

12. on purpose

13. participating in　　foster (vt.) 培養、鼓勵

14. prepared, for

15. pick on

16. ranging from, to　　calorie (n.) 卡路里；dessert (n.) 甜點；lovely (adj.) 美麗動人的

17. off and on　　peat (n.) 泥煤

18. Picking up　　sponsor (vt.) 贊助；install (vt.) 安裝；terminal (n.) 總站；終站

19. On the basis

20. more than

21. on the average　　wingspread (n.) 翼幅；barely 幾乎沒有；swiftly (adv.) 快速地

22. provided, with

23. play, important roles in

24. on behalf of　　hospitality (n.) 好客、殷勤款待

25. on the other hand　　up to 高達

26. rather than　　be inclined to 易於；judge (vt.) 判斷

27. no doubt　　landslide (n.)（競選中）一方選票佔壓倒性多數

28. put up with

29. not only, but also　　depletion (n.) 消耗；petroleum (n.) 石油；resource (n.) 資源

30. once, for all

31. put out

32. protect, from　　kidnapper (n.) 綁架人

33. on my own

34. played, practical joke on

35. C　　36. B　　37. A　　38. B　　39. C　　40. D　　41. D　　42. B　　43. A

Unit 28

1. tend to　　好的聆聽者傾向於聽得多，且對週遭發生的事物比其他人更敏銳。

2. taken over　　今日，電視、電影以及書籍已經接管了說故事這項曾經是人們熟悉的活動。storytelling (n.) 說故事

3. stopped from　　堅決的人不會輕易被阻止想做的事。determined (adj.) 意志堅定的

4. stand by　　你不可以就袖手旁觀，任由他那樣對待他的狗。

5. so that　　只有少數人照料這些鯨魚，如此他們才不會太習慣與人類相處。human beings 人類

6. so far　　然而，介紹到市場上的機器人，到目前為止，其娛樂性高於實用性。entertainment (n.) 娛樂

7. show off　　Robert 很愛現，那就是為什麼沒人喜歡和他在一起的原因。

8. search for　　尋找線索是處理無主郵件的一種方法。clue (n.) 線索

9. rely on　　這段期間，他們得依賴自己發出的吵雜聲來嚇走像鯊魚之類的掠食者。scare away 嚇走；predator (n.) 掠食者；shark (n.) 鯊魚

10. refer to　　有些字的形成是因為它們聽起來像他們所指的意思。

11. stop, from

12. take, time

13. take over　　decade (n.) 十年；leisure (adj.) 空閒的

14. resulting in　　collision (n.) 衝撞

15. takes, action　　wait for 等待

16. take notice

17. set up

18. takes place

19. So far　　normal (adj.) 正常的；distinctly (adv.) 明顯地；cheekbone 顴骨

20. took part in　　for sure 確定

21. stand by　　brave (adj.) 勇敢的

22. thought up

23. take, granted

24. the other day

25. rely, upon　　go hunting 去打獵；powerful (adj.) 強而有力的；game (n.) 獵物

26. take, days off

27. succeed in
28. refers to　　preceding (adj.) 前面的；context (n.) 上下文
29. searching for　　orangutan (n.) 黑猩猩；infant (n.) 嬰兒
30. so that
31. throughout the world　　opportunity (n.) 機會；schedule (n.) 行程、進度
32. show off

Unit 29

1. wake up　　然而，你不應該吵醒你正要打電話找的人。
2. up to　　科學家觀察的一群亞利桑那蝙蝠每晚就可吃掉高達三萬五千磅的昆蟲。single (adj.) 單一的；colony (n.) 殖民地、一群；observe (vt.) 觀察
3. turned to　　當人們知道大家對這種致命疾病束手無策時，他們轉而採取預防之道。discover (vt.) 發現；deadly (adj.) 致命的；prevention (n.) 預防
4. turn out　　歷史已給了我們許多驚訝之事：事件的結果如何，常是不可預測的。predictable (adj.) 可預測的
5. turn in　　你不是星期五就交了期末報告嗎?
6. turned down　　我最初的建議被禮貌地拒絕了。politely (adv.) 禮貌地
7. too, to　　機器人 Redford 的演說太難了而無法了解。
8. work on
9. Up to　　huge (adj.) 巨大的；continent (n.) 大陸
10. treated, as　　attempt (vt.) 試圖
11. together with　　playwriter (n.) 戲劇作家；opening (n.) 開幕
12. wait for
13. With regard to
14. turned down　　laughingly (adv.) 大笑；point out 指出
15. without doubt
16. too, to
17. turn, in
18. to and fro　　anxious (adj.) 焦慮的
19. turned to
20. C　　21. A　　22. D　　23. C　　24. D　　25. C　　26. D　　27. B

核心英文字彙力
2001～4500

丁雍嫻　邢雯桂
盧思嘉　應惠蕙　編著

◆ **最新字表！**

依據大學入學考試中心公布之「高中英文參考詞彙表 (111 學年度起適用)」
編寫，一起迎戰 108 新課綱。

◆ **符合學測範圍！**

收錄 Level 3~5 學測必備單字，規劃 100 回。聚焦關鍵核心字彙、備戰學測。
Level 3：40 回
Level 4：40 回
Level 5-1(精選 Level 5 高頻單字)：20 回

◆ **素養例句！**

精心撰寫各式情境例句，符合 108 新課綱素養精神。除了可以利用例句學習
單字用法、加深單字記憶，更能熟悉學測常見情境、為大考做好準備。

◆ **補充詳盡！**

常用搭配詞、介系詞、同反義字及片語等各項補充豐富，一起舉一反三、輕
鬆延伸學習範圍。

基礎英文法養成篇

英文學很久，文法還是囧？

本書助你釐清「觀念」、抓對「重點」、舉一反三「練習」，

不用砍掉重練，也能無縫接軌、輕鬆養成英文法！

陳曉菁　編著

特色一：　條列章節重點
　　　　　每章節精選普高技高必備文法重點，編排環環相扣、循序漸進。

特色二：　學習重點圖像化與表格化
　　　　　將觀念與例句以圖表統整，視覺化學習組織概念，輕鬆駕馭文法重點。

特色三：　想像力學文法很不一樣
　　　　　將時態比喻為「河流」，假設語氣比喻為「時光機」，顛覆枯燥文法印象。

特色四：　全面補給一次到位
　　　　　「文法小精靈」適時補充說明，「文法傳送門」提供相關文法知識章節，
　　　　　觸類旁通學習更全面。

特色五：　即時練習Level up!
　　　　　依據文法重點設計多元題型，透過練習釐清觀念，融會貫通熟練文法。